MAGICIANS
IMPOSSIBLE

MAGICIANS
IMPOSSIBLE

·····················

BRAD ABRAHAM

Thomas Dunne Books
St. Martin's Press ≈ New York

THOMAS DUNNE BOOKS.
An imprint of St. Martin's Press.

MAGICIANS IMPOSSIBLE. Copyright © 2017 by Brad Abraham. All rights reserved.
Printed in the United States of America. For information, address
St. Martin's Press, 175 Fifth Avenue, New York, N.Y. 10010.

Based on a concept by Brad Abraham and Michael Neff.

www.thomasdunnebooks.com
www.stmartins.com

The Library of Congress Cataloging-in-Publication Data is available upon request.

ISBN 978-1-250-08352-4 (hardcover)
ISBN 978-1-250-08353-1 (ebook)

Our books may be purchased in bulk for promotional, educational, or business use.
Please contact your local bookseller or the Macmillan Corporate and Premium
Sales Department at 1-800-221-7945, extension 5442, or by email at
MacmillanSpecialMarkets@macmillan.com.

First Edition: Sepetember 2017

10 9 8 7 6 5 4 3 2 1

Dedicated to my son,
born midway through the writing of this book, who
has brought magic into our lives
ever since.

THE BROKER LOOKED LIKE A pinched dick in gunmetal Armani and Damon disliked him the moment the man's hired guns shoved him into a chair and tore the black bag off his face. But it wasn't Bennett Fraim's alopecia that gave him that phallic appearance; it was the bulging frontal vein bisecting his forehead. Damon idly wondered how much that vein would gush when it finally popped as he took a head count of the room. Eight matching guns in eight matching black suits to protect one man? It reeked of overkill, but if Damon King had learned anything in a career of people jamming guns in his ribs, snapping hoods over his face, and ushering him into the trunks of waiting sedans, it was that *overkill* wasn't a dirty word. Overkill *worked,* and overkill was clearly Bennett Fraim's modus operandi.

Fraim folded his dainty hands and set them atop the penthouse suite's rectangular dining table.

"Some refreshment, Mr. King?" Fraim asked, after a measured moment.

"Glenfiddich if you have it," Damon said.

The cold steel of the handcuffs bit into his wrists as he settled into his chair as comfortably as he could manage.

"I do not," said Fraim. "I could have a bottle brought up, but I doubt it will arrive in time. You have such precious little of it."

He shifted his gaze to one of the gunmen, a burly-looking Midwestern farm boy who looked like the veteran of several Middle Eastern wars, or at least a few college football seasons.

"Was he armed?" Fraim asked.

"Only with this." The gunman reached inside his suit jacket pocket and removed a small cellophane-wrapped object that crackled as he set it down on the tabletop. Fraim leaned forward and Damon detected momentary confusion in his bespectacled eyes.

It was a deck of playing cards.

Fraim planted a finger on the deck, pulled it to his side, and examined it with confusion.

"Is this a joke?"

"From where I'm sitting it looks like a deck of cards," Damon said.

"And from where I sit, you still seem confident you will walk out of this meeting alive."

Damon shrugged. "Night's still young."

"Your bravado in the face of certain death would be admirable were it not so foolish, Mr. King. It's a wonder you've lasted this long, but then I only know the basics of your CV. Damon King, age fifty-five last month? Congratulations on reaching the milestone many in your profession do not. The thing about fifty-five is that it is one of the great last milestones. They come less frequently after that, but with greater speed."

"Retirement and death." Damon nodded. "Preferably in that order."

"*Do* men in your profession retire?"

"Not by choice."

"Does that frighten you? The idea that this will be your last night on earth?"

"Happens to everyone," Damon said. "After all, you turned fifty-six last year."

Damon didn't expect Fraim to answer, which he didn't. What he *did* expect was Fraim's heart rate to elevate, which it did, on cue.

"We're running short on time so I'll skip the finer points of *your* CV," Damon continued. "Born in Montreal, putting to bed the myth that Canadians are nice people."

"You Americans . . . you always mistake 'polite' for 'nice.' "

"Raised abroad, which explains the accent; not quite Canadian, not European either, though there *is* a dash of pretension in your word choices. You're a broker—a finder and seller of secrets, the rarest kind. Artwork thought long lost, precious heirlooms once held under lock and key; I heard you once sold a lamp with a *unique* lampshade from a private collection once belonging to Mengele to an Internet billionaire with political ambitions?"

"*That* is a despicable rumor; it belonged to Eichmann."

"Human trafficking is your bread and butter," Damon continued. "Eastern European girls mostly, though you dabble in American ones from time to time. They're highly sought, aren't they? Corn-fed teenagers who disappear on school trips to Cancun? But your real pleasure—what gets you all *tingly* below the belt—is finding those things people thought were long lost. They say you have such an uncanny knack for that it's almost *magical*."

"You know my work," Fraim said. "And you are correct; I am

a man who loves secrets. Especially the ones people thought they had kept well hidden. Secrets like the Invisible Hand."

Fraim paused, as though waiting for Damon to register alarm at the reveal.

He did not.

"I must be honest, I know little about your organization," Fraim continued, "but so few do, and believe me, I *have* inquired. The Invisible Hand is a name whispered on the lips of dying men. You are bedtime stories spies tell other spies to frighten each other; a vast organization so secretive, not even *they* know whom you serve. That's why when a contact informed me the elusive Damon King had been spotted in New York I simply had to meet him face-to-face."

"And here we are," said Damon.

"Indeed. But again I am *surprised* how easily a man of your skill could be apprehended."

The knock at the penthouse suite's closed double doors sounded though the room. The guns looked to the door with suspicion; Fraim, with confusion.

The knock repeated, more insistent this time.

"Yes?" Fraim said, with impatience.

On the other side of the doors, a woman's tentative voice sounded. "Room service."

"I didn't order room service!" Fraim said.

"I did," said Damon.

Fraim's pulse quickened again, and a solitary bead of sweat pulsed out at the base of his smooth temple and rolled down the side of his face. He studied Damon, silent for a moment, and then motioned to one of the guns, who slung his weapon and opened the door.

A young woman with fine Persian features sculpted in olive

skin stood outside holding a bottle of whisky. She was dressed in a neatly pressed hotel uniform: white shirt, dark gray vest, black skirt, and black stockings. Her skirt rode a little higher than regulation, exposing just a hint of lace below her hemline that exposed a touch more when she walked. She knew her audience: lonely traveling businessmen, husbands far from home. Flash them a little bit of heaven and earn at least 20 percent, 25 if he was *really* lonely. But clearly she wasn't expecting *this* audience because she nearly dropped the bottle when she saw Fraim, the eight guns, and Damon, with astonishment.

She was carrying a bottle of Glenfiddich.

"On the table," Fraim said.

The girl skittered over and set the bottle down with a trembling hand, avoiding eye contact with everyone as if *that* would somehow save her. She moved to leave but when she passed the burly ex-footballer and/or ex-soldier, he grasped her arm and pulled her close. She yelped in surprise.

"That will do, Mr. Gant," Fraim said. "Hold her there. We're almost done."

Damon nodded to the Glenfiddich. "Here's the deal. We open this Scotch, you sign a generous tip and send her on her way, and we get down business."

"Actually I cannot let her leave at all," said Fraim.

The girl whimpered. The fear was radiating off her.

"Give it a rest, Bennett," Damon said. "You're not here to kill me or her."

"Then why am I here?"

"To sell me the item in the Samsonite case sitting by your right foot."

Fraim's eyes widened to the point it appeared they were bulging out of his skull.

"From where I sit, it would seem I am the one holding the cards, literally and figuratively. What can you possibly offer me?"

Damon leaned forward and set the stainless-steel handcuffs, which had bound his wrists a moment before, on the table with a *clink* of metal on glass.

"How about a magic trick?"

All through the room safeties clicked off in a clattering wave, and fingers settled on triggers. The girl teetered. Gant pulled her back out of the line of imminent fire.

"Enough!" Fraim shouted.

He glared at Damon. He wanted to order his men to fire. Damon could sense it, that thirst to unleash death. That desire to win. But stronger was the desire to know just *what* game Damon was playing at.

"Is that a yes?" he asked.

Fraim considered the offer for a moment, and then nudged the deck across the table. Damon took it, peeled off and discarded the cellophane, bent the cards, and began to shuffle. His movement was fluid, like water pouring into a glass.

"Here's the deal," Damon said. "Pick a card, any card. I guess correct, you let the girl go, and we finish our business."

"You sound quite confident, considering the situation."

"The situation is that you have nothing to lose while I have *everything* to lose."

Damon slid the deck across the table, fanned the cards face-down, and leaned back.

Fraim stared at the cards.

He stared at Damon.

He stared at the cards some more.

"Come on, Bennett. Like you said, you're the man holding all the cards."

Fraim glared at Damon, like he was considering giving the order to fire after all. Instead, he reached a hand out, planted a finger on one card, and slid it out of the deck and across the table to himself and lifted it up so only he could see it.

"Got it?" Damon asked. "Then slide it back into the deck—"

"I know how it works!"

Fraim jammed the card back into the deck, gathered it up, and shuffled, awkwardly and angrily. The broker's hard exterior had cracked, finally, and Damon allowed a smile to crease his lips.

Definitely not a poker player.

Fraim set the deck down and slid it back over, but Damon didn't move to take it.

"Now you promise you'll keep your word?" he asked.

"I promise nothing, Mr. King. And I'm waiting to be astounded."

"You will be. Now, are you watching closely?"

Fraim leaned in. Everyone leaned in. Only the girl remained still. Her eyes were on Damon and Damon alone. Not with fear, but with anticipation.

"Abracadabra," Damon said.

He made a fist and brought it down.

The deck leapt into the air and burst like an artillery strike. All fifty-two cards sprayed the room like shrapnel, severing arteries, piercing eye sockets, and slashing throats. Blood misted the air red to mingle with the gurgling screams of dying men. Down they went; all of them, toppling and bleeding out as silent as a smile. There were a few final spasms, then the smell of bladders and bowels emptying their contents, and it was done. The top of the Glenfiddich bottle was sheared off clean, and fine single malt pulsed arterial from that, its tart smell mingling with the stench of death. By the time the cards had pulled free of walls, furniture, and flesh and shuffled themselves back into a perfectly formed deck, it was over.

All but one card—that remained buried in Bennett Fraim's forehead midway up and two-thirds deep, bisecting that bulging vein, which released its contents to run down his face. The amused expression never left that face as the head wearing it lolled back on its neck.

Damon pushed his chair back and stood.

"I don't think you'll be getting that tip," he said.

The girl stepped forward and looked to Gant, who was still standing, and still alive. He'd opened his mouth, likely to ask what the hell was going on, but nothing came out. The girl's uniform dissolved in the blink of an eye. One second she was room service, the next she was Lower East Side punkette, her uniform replaced by cargo pants, sneakers, a denim jacket, a Ramones T beneath that, and hair like a well-styled rat's nest.

"You could have given me a heads-up," Allegra Sand sniffed. "You almost winged me."

"A good magician never reveals his secrets," Damon said, gathering up his deck. "I've told you that I don't know *how* many times."

Allegra set her green-gold eyes on Gant, and Gant's right arm—the one with the Glock half-removed from his shoulder holster—moved slow and awkward, raising the gun to his head and pressing the barrel to his temple.

"Sorry, but there will be no encore," she said.

Gant squeezed the trigger. Blood and brain sprayed the air and the body dropped.

"Grab the case, leave the whisky," said Damon.

Allegra crossed to Fraim, limp and lifeless in his chair, blank eyes fixed on the ceiling. She crouched down, grabbed the Samsonite case from beside him, and stood, and as her eyes grazed the card buried in Fraim's forehead she gasped. That, and the look on her face, was more than enough to bring Damon over. He gripped the card and pulled. It popped free with a wet slurp.

It was the Queen of Hearts. The Red Queen.

"Coincidence?" she asked.

"In this business?"

He was about to drop the card on the table when something cold and dead clasped itself around his wrist: a hand, attached to an arm, belonging to the late Bennett Fraim.

The dead man's head lolled forward and his eyes glared through a glistening red mask.

"But we haven't begun *our* negotiations, Damon," it croaked.

The room was getting colder but that wasn't why gooseflesh had broken out on Damon's arms. He knew who was pulling the dead man's strings. The windows were icing over in intricate patterns, lattices of white slowly but inexorably blocking off the world outside. As the frost misted the walls and glass he saw symbols emerge—arcane and ancient runes—like a message written in steam on a bathroom mirror. A message written before Bennett Fraim had picked up his key for this suite.

Binding spells, closing the entrances and exits. There was no way out. They were trapped.

They'd *been* trapped from the very start.

Damon stared into Fraim's dead eyes. "What do you want?"

"I want you, Damon," the dead man said. "I want what you stole from me."

Damon could sense it. He could sense *her*. Even without hearing her voice in his head he knew.

There was nowhere to run.

Allegra was on the edge of panic. "What is it?"

"Binding spells. We can't unlock the doors; we can't shift through them—"

"But who could—"

The question died on her tongue.

She *knew* who it was.

A hollow, wet laugh echoed up the dead man's throat like some shambling thing crawling up the damp insides of a spoiled well.

"It was a good trick, darling," it croaked. "But now it's my turn."

A gunshot shattered the silence and hot jacketed steel tore the air between Damon's and Allegra's faces, but they knew it was coming the split second before firing pin hammered steel. Both of them were seasoned Mages—they *knew* when violence was about to strike before it happened. First, that electricity in the air, that coppery taste on the tongue preceding. Then the mechanical click of pin meeting primer. Then the sniff of cordite and the heat of the explosion hurling death. Gant was back on his feet, the fist-sized hole in his cranium dripping pulp and bone fragments down his black jacket. He raised the Glock as something sliced the air past his wrist. The gun and the hand clutching it fell. Blood pulsed slowly from the stump remaining, and the card that had severed bones, muscles, and tendons embedded in the wall opposite.

Allegra heard the rapid-fire shuffle of cards and saw Damon fire them from one hand into the other with a blur.

"On your six!" he shouted.

She pivoted. All through the room the dead men were shuddering and lurching upright, shirts red, guns raised; dull eyes and brains that had only just embraced the void were pulled screaming back into warmth and the light. She dropped the Samsonite case, outstretched her hands, and *pushed* against the three who'd drawn down. The first lurched back into the fireplace mantelpiece, shearing the top of his head off on the hard edge. She broke the legs of a second, sending him crumbling, and twisted the neck of a third 180 degrees around, letting him contemplate the art deco wall hanging behind him before he, too, fell.

Hot steel blasted past Damon. Two more were on their feet; one with a Joker Damon had failed to retrieve before still lodged in his carotid. Damon flicked his wrist and tore the card out. Syrupy blood pulsed, but the man remained standing, his gun still trained. Damon yanked the Joker back into his deck, planted his index finger on top of it, and with a blur of movement fired the deck through the room, a deadly flurry of sharp edges howling, slicing, dicing, tearing, rending. Ears were severed, eyes punctured, hands amputated, necks guillotined. Bullets sprayed wild. Damon sidestepped some and redirected others to strike walls and windows, trying to find some spot the binding enchantments had missed.

Allegra gripped, twisted, and turned a shooter, discharging his weapon into another's face and sending those once more lifeless remains toppling. She yanked the shooter off his feet and hurtled him through the air, sending him crashing into a window, spiderwebbing the ice and cracking the glass beneath it.

Damon noted the impact. The glass had cracked. It had spiderwebbed.

There *was* a way out.

Above the din something switched from semi to full automatic. A shooter was raising an MP5, and before Damon could deflect, the man fired. The gunfire was deafening. Bullets streaked at Damon, who disappeared and appeared behind the shooter with a thunderclap of smoke. He gripped the man's skull and twisted, and he kept twisting, pulling the man's head around to face him, until the head lolled loose over its right shoulder.

It all happened in fifteen seconds. Time enough for Allegra to mark Gant, still standing, staring numb at his severed wrist. In him she saw every man who'd fired a gun at her, had thrown stones at her; had cursed her as a heretic. In him she saw her home, her brothers, her cousins, and her father.

And she knew how to deal with men like her father.

She held out her hand, flattened her palm and outstretched fingers. The gunman's arms went rigid and his body lifted off the ground. Bones cracked, sinew tore, and she kept stretching him until there was a wet tearing sound and the joints separated, the body was quartered, and everything fell to the floor in a heap of stinking meat and blood and shit.

"Allegra . . ." Damon turned to her with worry.

Adrenaline raged through her like liquid fire. Flame shot from her fingertips, licked the carpeting and the curtains, and ignited them.

"Allegra!"

Flame raced along the wall, setting art pieces ablaze. The walls blackened and blistered—

"*ALLEGRA!*"

She blinked her eyes rapidly, like she'd just woken from a dream.

Damon gazed at her with concern, like he was wondering if she was a threat as well.

"I think you got him," he said.

She looked over the ruin: fabrics burning; bodies piled on ground glistening with blood.

"I'm sorry I—I lost control," she said.

"Forget it. You need to focus." He swept the room with his hand. A sharp, short wind blasted across the wall, extinguishing the flames. He picked up the Samsonite case and straightened his tie.

"She's not trying to kill us, just delay us."

Something crackled, like massive slabs of ice rubbing together. Allegra looked to the closed and locked penthouse doors. A handprint had appeared in its center, and darkness metastasized from its fingertips. The wood turned black, sickly, like a body ravaged by disease, and a stench of decay filled the room, mingling with the stench of death.

Damon tossed the Samsonite case to Allegra, planted his feet, and raised his hands, palms up. The entire room shuddered and everything not nailed down—chairs, the table, potted plants, and the bodies of the dead men—lifted off the floor. His hands trembled and his brow beaded perspiration as he lifted and pushed everything he could at that door. With a calamitous crash it all struck en masse, slamming and piling up and widening the barrier between them and her. He turned to the piano, focused on it and gripped it, and after a brief pause to catch his breath, pulled it across the floor with a scrape of wood, and flung it at the barrier, where it crashed with a loud and final booming musical chord. Damon exhaled, and he tugged at the cuffs of his shirtsleeves, straightening them.

"We still need a way out," Allegra said.

"That's his job." Damon pointed to Bennett Fraim's body, still sitting in its seat.

Then *that* body shuddered, and rose.

The body shattered the weakened glass of the suite's main window, pitched through, and plummeted to the fortieth-floor landing twelve stories below. Allegra exited with the case through the opening, and Damon followed. They worked their way around the side of the penthouse suite and looked down the dizzying drop to Park Avenue far below. Safety—or at least the illusion of it—was still an impossible distance away.

But there was no safety. Not with *her* nearly there. Their ease of exit told Damon that the binding spell hadn't been applied to that window by choice. She *knew* where this was all going to end and only wanted to guide them to it for the grand finale.

Cold autumn air pulled him back. He looked across the rooftop toward the Plaza Hotel, along Central Park South to the twin monoliths of the Time Warner Center at Columbus Circle, silhouetted against the ever-present glow of Manhattan. *That* was safe distance enough.

You can't run, Damon.

Her voice was in his mind, burning itself into every cell, every synapse of his being.

There's nowhere to run where I won't find you.

She was right. There was nowhere to run. Not for both of them.

He motioned for the Samsonite case, and Allegra held it out. He pressed a hand to its surface, felt around for the combination lock's dials, and turned them swiftly. There was a click, and then another, then a third, and the case opened. It was packed with a layer of foam, with a perfectly cut space in the middle holding a small silver thumb drive. He took it out, closed the case, set it down, and pressed the thumb drive into Allegra's palm.

"This thing better be worth all the goddamn trouble it's brought us," he said.

"What are you doing?" Allegra asked.

"*I'm* not doing anything." He pointed west. "Time Warner Center. That's your objective. You know the drill. Aim for the Plaza then leapfrog to Columbus Circle from there—"

"I'm not leaving you!"

"You have to!" he said. "You have to get to the Citadel and tell them! If she knows about the flash drive she knows about the Sphere! She knows about that, we just lost the advantage. I'll delay her as long as I can and I'll be right behind you!"

She stared at him numb, but not on the verge of tears. She was too cool a professional for that.

"You *promise*?" she asked.

"Have I ever lied to you?"

"*Constantly,*" she said.

She clutched the flash drive tight, turned, and set her gaze on the summit of the Plaza Hotel a block up and two avenues over. There was a loud thunderclap and burst of cloud and she was gone. A moment later, a lighter blast sounded and Damon saw a small puff of smoke alight atop the Plaza's roof. Another sounded along Central Park South, heading toward Columbus Circle. The rest were lost to the dull roar of the city.

Then the air grew cold and he knew his time was up.

As Damon reached the roof, his blood ran cold, but it wasn't the air that caused it; it was the *presence* awaiting him. A dark shape buffeted by the wind, sending her coils of red hair undulating of their own volition, the orb of her face pale above her crimson cloak and black clothing.

"Magnificent, isn't it?" she asked. "I remember my first trip to New York. I only had a day so I did all the sights I could: the Met, a carriage ride through the park, dinner at Smith & Wollensky, Times Square, and the Empire State Building. The city was a different beast then. It was dirty, and dangerous, and perfect." She gazed wistfully past him to the Empire State Building fifteen blocks south. "But up there, it didn't matter. Up there, it felt like I could leap from the observation deck and land anywhere in the world I wanted if I only wished for it hard enough."

"I know," he said. "I was there, remember?"

She moved from out of the shadows she'd cloaked herself in and drifted closer. She was as beautiful and terrible as he remembered, and not even death had diminished her power; if anything it had enhanced it. Her dark eyes gleamed. Her mouth was a thin slash of crimson against a face that seemed translucent. She wouldn't let an inconvenience like death stop her anyway. Not her.

He nodded to the Samsonite case, an afterthought resting on the ground between them. "It's there for the taking. The case, I mean; the item it carried is long gone."

"I didn't come for Allegra Sand, or the item she carries. I came for what you took from me."

"You won't find that either," he said.

She crossed the roof in a short intake of breath, past his defenses before he had a chance to raise them. Not that it would have mattered; this was his last mission and they both knew it.

"But I will, Damon. There's no place you could hide him that I wouldn't find in time."

"I know," he said.

He just hoped the person she spoke of would be ready when she did.

He stepped backward until he felt his heels crest the edge of the roof. Only empty space separated him from the street fifty-two floors below. His pulse pounded. Blood roared in his ears. Once he would have summoned the courage to flash that grin that had made her weak when they were both young. But "once" was a long time ago. That person was gone. The one who stood in her place was an entirely different creature. The Medusa coils of her hair whipped into a ravenous frenzy by the winds that had risen to a gale.

"Any last words?" the Red Queen asked.

"Just one," he said. "Abracadabra."

Then he stepped off the roof and was falling.

••••••••••••••••••••••

PART ONE

PEOPLE WHO DIED

ONE

....

TO JASON BISHOP, THE FACT that Murder Hill was still standing was something of a relief; it meant the world hadn't completely changed. The industrial ruin towered above the river at that last bend between Garrison and Cold Spring like always, a rusted sentinel that rivaled nearby Storm King Mountain in legend, if not in stature. A graffiti-festooned beacon that challenged the young and dumb to climb its summit, to pilot their skateboards, stolen shopping carts, or Rollerblades down the steep cement chute to the swift and bracing waters flowing past. Some tried, most failed, and the sensible chickened out at the last second. To Jason, it was the rusted signpost welcoming him back to the home he swore he'd never return to, but no matter how far he roamed, Cold Spring always found a way to drag him back. Jason had been one of those rare few who'd challenged Murder Hill and lived to tell the tale, but that was a story for another day. Today, he was returning home to bury his father.

"Cold Spring," the bored-sounding PA announced. "Next stop, Cold Spring."

Jason's mouth tasted like old coffee. He'd tried to wash the taste away with periodic nips from the flask he'd stowed inside his jacket pocket, but the buzz just made him more tired than he already was. The puzzle book he'd brought with him to pass time on the train sat forgotten on the seat beside him. He hadn't slept since he was handed the news about his father. There was no need to ID the remains, thankfully; it didn't take much imagination to know what a fifty-floor plunge off a high-rise did to the human body. He gazed out the passenger window as it filled with crimson. The October sun had bathed the entire valley molten and soon those leaves would fall, like Dan Bishop fell.

But Dan Bishop didn't fall. Dan Bishop jumped.

A suicide, they said. Leapt from the roof of the Four Seasons in Midtown, they also said. Dan Bishop had swan-dived onto East 57th between Madison and Park, 140 blocks south of The Locksmith, where Jason had been working that very night. What Dan had been doing at the Four Seasons was a mystery, as was his father's request his funeral be held in Cold Spring. Dan had barely spent more than a few hours there at any given time, usually to check in on Jason, occasionally to drop off a birthday or Christmas present, and most often to make excuses as to why he couldn't stay longer. By the time Jason was fifteen, Dan was pretty much just the name endorsing the checks that arrived in his absence.

But why Cold Spring?

Did he think the familiar environs would somehow make Jason feel better that Dan *hadn't* bothered to say goodbye before his big plunge? That was an answer only Dan could furnish.

Jason tugged at the collar of the dress shirt, chafing uncomfortably against his neck, and loosened his necktie. To look at him, you'd think he'd finally gotten a respectable job in a bank, not one slinging drinks in Inwood. He hadn't worn his suit since Owen's funeral the year before; now it would help usher Dan out of his life for good. His mind drifted to the flask in his breast pocket. He wanted another belt but decided to hold off. He didn't want to lapse into bad habits again. He'd partly landed the job at The Locksmith because he didn't drink, and he didn't want to jeopardize that job. He had enough drama in his life, the primary cause of which was sitting across from him.

Winnie looked resplendent, the Holly Golightly look she'd perfected fitting her like a second skin. In her black dress and matching purse and shoes, her dark complexion seemed Nordic by comparison. Her iPhone rested against her thigh and while she tried to make it look like she hadn't been checking messages the entire trip, he knew she *had* been since they boarded the Metro-North. To her credit Winifred Hobbes had stepped up after the news had come with barely a thought, like she'd in been training for just this moment since they'd met. It was Winnie who made the arrangements, not Jason. It was Winnie who told him to call Rich and tell him he'd be taking a few days off, and he had. It was Winnie who'd consented to the bout of sympathy sex Jason had thought would make him feel better, but had just made everything worse.

Winnie had handled everything pertaining to Dan's funeral, like she *enjoyed* the distraction. Like she was glad to avoid a conversation long overdue, one he had tried to start several times in the preceding days that she'd dismissed. When they'd first met, they seemed to be looking for the same thing. But now it was like she'd found what she wanted and was growing tired of waiting for him to decide if it was what he wanted, too.

But there'd be time for *that* talk on the return trip.

"This is taking forever," he sighed. "We should have rented a car."

"*I* suggested a car. *You* wanted to take the train. 'For old time's sake,' you said, remember?"

"I should have listened to you," he said.

She shrugged.

And that was that, the most words they'd exchanged sequentially since Grand Central.

She was right though; he *had* wanted to take the train. Growing up, the train to New York had meant freedom—a steel link to the world beyond. Now it was whisking him back in time; up the Hudson and past Murder Hill to Cold Spring. Those bends in the track were as familiar as they ever were, but everything had changed. He was just a tourist now, there to watch the autumn leaves change color and fall.

They cabbed it from the Metro-North to the funeral home; the same where he'd said goodbye to Aunt Cathryn six years before, the same where he'd said goodbye to Owen just last year. It was less than five minutes from the station, but then again everything in Cold Spring was less than five minutes from everything else. Main Street hadn't changed much; it was still lined with souvenir shops and cafés and restaurants all poised to lure in tourists from the city. You couldn't make it from the Metro-North station to anywhere without running that gauntlet. The town was a place for visitors now, not its residents; or maybe it always had been that way and Jason just hadn't noticed. But like everything he'd seen since news of Dan's drop, it was like he was looking at the world through eyes that were no longer his own.

The funeral director who greeted them wasn't much older

than Jason (who wondered if they *hadn't* gone to high school to-gether), and had that blandly sympathetic face that seemed to be standard issue among all funeral directors, along with the dark, conservative suits. He offered his condolences, and on learning Jason was the son of the deceased, actually seemed like he meant it. He handed over a program. It read:

A Celebration of Daniel Patrick Bishop
Father of Jason

There was his date of birth and death below that, along with a photo of Dan albeit one ten or so years out of date. His hair was just beginning to turn gray in that one. By the time they'd last done a face-to-face, the gray had marched well into the black. The grin was the same shit-eating one he'd always worn, painfully earnest, and all an act. Jason could see a lot of his face in Dan's: the cool blue eyes, the eyebrows that arched angular when he smiled. A nose not too big, a mouth not too wide: painfully av-erage and perfectly forgettable. He opened the program. The inside cover, which normally would contain a biography, was blank. No *Cherished husband* or *Beloved brother* or *Son of*.

There was just *Father of Jason,* full stop.

"Amazing Grace" was piped through the sound system, which just galled Jason even more; he hated "Amazing Grace." As they entered, Jason received his first surprise of the day: people had come. A good baker's dozen all seated down at the front of the room, near the podium where a small stand of flowers stood ringing a table on which a simple pewter urn rested.

So Dan had friends after all.

But as Jason approached, he saw these mourners were dressed near identically to the funeral director. They were employees, obviously drafted to make Daniel Bishop's next of kin *not* take offence at the slight turnout for the dearly departed. That was on Dan's head, not his.

He'd made his urn and was lying in it—but two weren't there to pick up a paycheck: an elderly man in a wheelchair, and his nurse sitting in the pew beside him. Jason recognized both. He handed his program to Winnie, told her he'd be back in a minute, and moved down to the front of the chapel to the man in the wheelchair. He knelt beside him and looked into his dull eyes.

"Hey there, Attila." Jason grinned. "We need to stop meeting like this."

Aaron Baile; Uncle Aaron—and once upon a time behind his back, "Uncle Attila"—stared uncomprehending at the boy he had raised from before Jason could remember. But Aaron's memories were gone, torn away by Alzheimer's and discarded at the roadside. A man whose deep voice and ferocious temper had terrified young Jason when he knew he'd pushed his uncle too far—a frequent act when Jason entered his teens. The man who had taken Jason fishing and canoeing, who taught him to ride a bike and how to drive a car, who'd *always* been there to talk no matter the hour, was now just a shadow of a memory. For the first time since the news of Dan's suicide landed with a wet thud, Jason felt tears brew. Thank whatever god was above that Alzheimer's had taken Aaron before cancer took his beloved Cathryn.

"How is he doing, Rita?" Jason asked.

Rita, the wide-faced, sad-eyed nurse from the rest home, smiled.

"He has his good days and his bad days," she said. "Today's somewhere in between. I'm so sorry for your loss, Jason. Truly I am."

Aaron just stared, seemingly unsure whether to smile or cry, unaware he was sitting in the very same place he'd said goodbye to the wife of forty years he didn't remember six years before. Jason patted Aaron's arm, nodded to Rita, and made his way back to his and Winnie's spot when someone entered his vision and he almost lost it there in the middle of the chapel.

"Jason . . . I'm so sorry," Carla said.

He'd been prepared for the funeral. He'd been prepared for the emotions he *knew* would drain him. Hell, he'd even been prepared for Uncle Attila. But he hadn't been prepared for Carla Rickert, née Petrozzi, not her without Owen. Carla Petrozzi, whose high-school affections Jason and Owen had once gone to war over, and whose hand and heart Owen had captured in the end. How different might all their lives have been if Jason had emerged victorious? Would it be Jason moldering in a burial plot a short drive—five minutes, naturally—away? But there she stood, the squirming two-year-old in her arms looking more like the father he'd never know than he had the year before when they'd laid Owen to rest. She'd aged five years since he'd last stood there, only then *he* was telling *her* how sorry he was. The last year had clearly been rough on Carla Rickert.

"Carla . . . hi . . ." He leaned in and kissed her on the cheek. "It's so good to see you."

"How are you managing?" she asked. "I know you and your father weren't . . ."

"We weren't." He nodded. "And I'm fine. I'm managing, I mean. *Are you?*"

Carla smiled sadly.

"We're managing. It's not easy; I don't think it ever will be. But, we're managing."

Jason nodded, he hoped, knowingly. He didn't know what

else to do and had even less idea what to say to her. The silver lining to the cloud that had been his best friend's death was that it had been sudden. Owen had gone into the kitchen of their small house in Cold Spring—Owen, unlike Jason, *hadn't* left—to fetch Noah's bottle. A heavy crash had sounded through the house, and by the time Carla raced in with Noah, Owen was lying on the linoleum, a bottle of formula spilling its contents beside him, dead before he could feel the warm liquid touch his skin. Owen Rickert, dead of a cerebral hemorrhage at thirty-one, leaving a wife to mourn him, and a child who'd never know his father. *That* had been Owen's greatest fear when he told Jason about his impending fatherhood. That nightmare had come true, for all who loved him. The turnout for Owen's funeral was massive, standing room only in the same chapel that was cavernous by comparison now.

"I can't stay," Carla said. "I just wanted to offer my condolences. . . ."

"It's all right, thanks—"

"I have to get Noah to the sitter's; I have to get to work—"

"*Carla.*" He gave her shoulder a reassuring squeeze that lingered probably a little too long for both of them. "It's *great* to see you. I'm sorry I haven't been around. I know I promised I'd check in but things have been crazy . . ."

Carla smiled, but sadness remained buried behind it.

"Owen's parents help out when they can but they're getting on."

"How *are* your folks?"

"They moved, to Greensboro—we're joining them at the end of the month."

"*You're leaving Cold Spring?*" Jason couldn't hide his surprise.

"There's nothing for us here now," Carla said. "I can't afford to keep the house and it's a buyer's market and . . . I have to think of what's best for Noah."

But Owen, he'll be all alone up in the cemetery. What about him?

Noah was still studying him intently, like he thought he should know Jason from somewhere but didn't know how or why. The boy stared at him, then his mouth widened into a wide, happy grin that was too familiar. Jason had seen it before, many times, many years ago.

Jesus, he looks so much like his father.

"I won't keep you." His voice struggled to stay even. "If you need any help, you know, packing . . ."

"We'll be fine, Jason." She gave his hand a squeeze. "Just take care of *yourself,* okay?"

She kissed his cheek. There was a moment—a very brief one—where her eyes met his and in them he saw *every* possible future they might have had. Then she hefted Noah and wiped her eyes clean. She wanted to get out of there just as badly as he did. He watched her carry Noah back up the chapel to the entrance, and as she passed, Winnie gave her a barely perceptible side-eye.

"We're ready to begin, Mr. Bishop," the funeral director said. He was standing at the chapel entrance, where Carla and Noah had departed, gazing calm but impatient.

"Is there a restroom?" Jason asked.

By the time he made it to the god-awful peaches and cream–colored restroom the tears were almost flowing. He gripped the cool porcelain of the sink and staunched them. But the sad display wasn't for Dan or Owen or even for himself; it was for Noah. He was going to have a hell of a time no matter how loving his mother or grandparents were. There would always be that hole in his life, like the one Jason had from the mother *he'd* never known, like a piece of himself had been ripped out and cast away never to be found. He just hoped Noah got it together in time; *he* hadn't, and the tired face staring back from the mirror was evidence enough of that fact.

Jason Bishop. Age thirty. Bartender. *That* would be his epitaph if he died today, and his funeral would draw an even sadder crowd than Dan's.

He fumbled for his flask, uncapped it, and sucked it dry. The whisky burned down his throat and settled like a ball of fire in his stomach. He ran the tap and filled the flask with water to rinse it out. He looked to the mirror, and stiffened sharply.

There was someone standing in the bathroom mirror behind him. Someone who hadn't been there an eyeblink before. Like he'd materialized out of thin air. That was impossible; there'd be no missing this guy. He was dark-skinned and built like a line-backer, his salt-and-pepper hair shorn close to a slightly bullet-shaped skull. A finely manicured mustache and goatee framed his wide mouth, and he towered a good foot over Jason.

He was holding something in his hand: a deck of cards.

"Do you like magic?" the man asked. His voice was British, deep, and smooth as silk.

Jason turned the water off.

"Not particularly," he said. "And certainly not right now."

"Another time perhaps," the man said.

Jason capped his flask and turned to face the man directly—

But there was nobody there.

The man had vanished. Like he hadn't been there at all.

Like he'd been a ghost.

Someone walked over Jason's grave and he stifled a shudder as something crackled underfoot. He looked down and saw it there, sticking out from under his polished black oxford.

It was a playing card. The King of Hearts.

TWO

....

"**WELL? ARE WE GOING TO** do this here or wait until we get home?"

Jason looked up from the engrossing game of sudoku he'd been lost in to take in the Hudson, and Winnie staring at him. The sun had slipped below the Palisades and they were almost back to New York, though not as quickly as either had hoped. There'd been the service, which was surprisingly long considering how little there was to say about the late Daniel Patrick Bishop. There was the reception, where Aaron had gummed down a couple egg-salad sandwiches before Rita took him back to the home. Then they'd gone to see the estate lawyer, also in Cold Spring. Of Dan's estate, most had been eaten away by debt. He may have been a businessman but he wasn't *much* of one; in fact, every last detail of Dan's life had balanced out to zero, including the costs of the funeral. It was like he'd planned the whole thing.

Jason had hoped to take a spin past the old house at the end of Cedar Street, but Winnie had been agitating the gravel and he didn't want to push things further than they'd already been pushed.

There was also the matter of Dan's earthly remains.

Jason had been presented with the simple pewter urn after the service. Dan's final wish had been surprisingly specific considering the ambiguity of his life: that his ashes be scattered on the Hudson, in view of Storm King Mountain, at night. That explained the location of the service, obviously, but not the when or why. The mystery remained as Jason glanced to the urn sitting next to him. By the time everything was finished, the train home was calling. Just popping the cap and dumping the ashes into the river on the way to the station seemed an insult; despite their relationship Jason felt he owed his father more than just a quick dip in the Hudson. It had to *mean* something, didn't it?

And there was, of course, the matter of the man in the bathroom mirror. The man who was there, then not. Jason wondered if he hadn't imagined the whole thing; he could at the very least blame the alcohol for that. The playing card he thought he'd seen under his shoe had likewise vanished in the blink of his own eye; there one second, gone the—

"*Jason.*"

Winnie had clearly waited long enough. Jason leaned back in his seat and wished he had a blindfold and cigarette handy. He felt like he would need both before this was all done.

"Go ahead," he sighed. He closed his puzzle book and set it aside.

"When we started dating, you told me your parents were dead, like mine. So when the police arrived to tell me your father just jumped off a hotel roof, I said to myself, 'They must mean a *different* Jason Bishop, because the Jason I know—the one I've been *dating* for over a year and *living* with almost as long—told me *his* parents were dead.'"

"Well they *are* now," he said.

"You're deflecting."

He sighed again. "Like I told you on date number one, my mom died a couple days after I was born. All I have to remember her was an old Polaroid taken in the hospital that's long lost. Aaron and Cathryn fed and clothed me, they put a roof over my head, they made sure I went to school and got good grades and generally kept out of trouble, the things *actual* parents do. If anybody in the world could lay claim to being my parents it was *them,* not Dan. He didn't want to be a father when I was a child who *needed* him, and even less when I was an adult who *didn't.*"

"That hasn't prevented you from turning *into* him though, has it?"

Jason almost laughed. *"Excuse me?"*

"Your dad was a businessman? Always traveling, no time for family or friends." Her gaze narrowed down to a point she drove into his chest with her next words. "How many friends *do* you have? People you can hang out with, grab a beer with? You know, *friends*?"

Jason didn't answer. Not because he was running through the lengthy list of friends catalogued in his memory, but because there *was* no list. There was Owen, but Owen was gone. The rest—the regulars who frequented the bar, the staff ten years younger than him—they weren't his friends, they were supporting players in The Jason Bishop Story.

"You're a great bartender," she continued. "People love you as long as the drinks flow. You're a friendly ear and quick with the wit, but once the bill is paid and they're off, you forget they exist. Like you're an actor playing a role and once the job is done you move on to the next one."

"They're *customers,* Win! My interest in them begins the moment they walk through the door, and ends the second they walk back out it. They don't want me to be their friend; they want a bartender. *That's* the job. And as for friends, they come and they go. The ones you think will be there forever never are—"

And some die at thirty with a baby bottle in their hand.

"But I don't see how my lack of them makes me *anything* like Dan."

"How many of *his* friends showed up at his funeral? We made an announcement in the *Times.* I figured *someone* would send condolences or flowers."

"There were flowers—"

"*I sent those!*"

"Riverdale," the PA crackled. "This stop, Riverdale."

After the train resumed its journey, neither spoke for several minutes. Jason stared out the window at the river, at cars waiting at the rail crossings, their headlights blasting their train compartment as it passed. He should have left it at that blissful silence, but as was his way, he had to go and open his big stupid mouth again.

"Well, you got me," he said. "I *am* my father's son."

"This isn't just about him, Jason," Winnie sighed. "Before I got back from Europe, I did some thinking. All the way to Barcelona, all the way back—"

He braced himself. He knew what was coming. It was written all over her face.

"Where are we going, Jason? You. Me. *Us.*"

There it was.

Us. The future. Our future.

"You've spent your entire life running away from him and who he was, but you've been running *to* him all along," she said. "You can screw around all through your twenties if that's your prerogative, but by thirty, if you're not on your way to *somewhere,* the problem is *you.* What are *you* doing now at thirty that you weren't at twenty? That you *won't* be doing at forty? Still tending bar?"

"Please, I'll *own* the bar long before that—"

"I'm not talking about a stupid *bar,* Jason."

"Spuyten Duyvil. This stop, Spuyten Duyvil," the PA crackled.

"You can be so much more than this," she said. "You're a lot smarter than a bartender has any need to be. You can fly if you just let go of the things holding you down."

"What are you talking about?"

"I'm talking about you being the man Jason Bishop could be if he wasn't so *scared* of the future that he won't let go of the past."

His grip tightened on the armrest. He didn't answer her, even as her eyes stayed on him, daring him to answer. He didn't answer her as the train slowed and stopped at Spuyten Duyvil, or as the doors hissed open and passengers exited. He didn't answer as he watched fog rise from the narrows where Spuyten Duyvil Creek met the Hudson, or when he glimpsed the George Washington Bridge gleaming metallic to the south, a silent sentinel welcoming them back to Manhattan. But when they reached the next stop—Marble Hill—he gave Winnie his answer; by the time the doors had slid shut and the train pulled away, he had gathered up Dan's urn and stepped off the train, leaving Winifred Hobbes to stare at him through the window as it ushered her away from the station and away from him.

. . .

He vaulted the steps from the station two at a time, and walked the trash-strewn street leading to Broadway. When he reached the 225th Street subway station, he considered hopping the 1 back home but he kept walking, oxfords pounding the pavement, urn tucked under his arm. He walked with a purpose: to put as much space between him and Cold Spring as possible.

Winnie was right, but that didn't make her words sting less. He *was* stuck in the past; he had been ever since Owen's death. He'd thought he'd get over it, that he'd grieve and move on, but he hadn't. Owen had done everything right: married, a child, a career, a house, a future . . . and he dropped dead in his kitchen in a puddle of baby formula. Jason had done everything wrong: dropped out of college, drifted aimless (but never far from New York or Cold Spring), and the few relationships he'd been in that lasted more than a couple months hadn't lasted much beyond that. Winnie had been the record breaker at a year and a month, but that looked to have flung itself off a high-rise, too. He tightened his grip on the urn and kept walking, past the bodegas and pizzerias and shuttered-for-the-night storefronts along Broadway until he arrived, not at their home, but at his other one: The Locksmith, just below Dyckman. It was closed—Monday was their traditional "dark" day—but Jason unlocked the door anyway and entered.

The Locksmith was a uniquely New York mess: an Irish pub in a Dominican neighborhood owned by a Jew. He'd stumbled upon it after he and Winnie had visited the Cloisters that spring. After viewing the Unicorn Tapestries and strolling through Fort Tryon Park, they'd made their way down to Dyckman and there it was, nestled in the shadows of the park like it had been waiting for him his entire life. To Jason, the moment he first stepped through The Locksmith's door and gazed on the dark wood and polished brass it felt like he had come home. To be fair *every* bar felt like home; he'd been haunting them since before he could legally drink, and could tell on sight which ones were keepers. A good bar let you do your business however you wanted. It didn't force sports or karaoke or bottle service on you; it let you imbibe however you wanted. Whether it was good conversation you were seeking or the opposite, both were always on tap. The Locksmith was a bar like that, and Jason had asked the owner, Richard Edelstein, for a job on the spot. After an impromptu audition where Rich made Jason mix pretty much every drink known to man (and Jason mixed a few Rich hadn't even known existed), he was hired. The long subway ride home had been awkward; that Winnie regretted ever suggesting Sunday at the Cloisters, she didn't need to say. It had been as clear as if she'd carved it into the bar's long polished oak counter, using words echoed in their fight not thirty minutes before.

Jason locked the door behind him but didn't turn the lights on; he knew the bar's layout like it was etched in braille. He walked over to the counter, slipped behind it, and set the urn on the shelf of bottles on the back bar. Dan always liked a good bar—the last time they'd stood face-to-face had been in one—so he could wait here until Jason found time for a return trip to Cold Spring to fulfill that cryptic final wish. His eyes lingered over the bottles of whisky, and his salivary gland kicked into overdrive. He pulled his flask from his pocket, popped the cap, dumped the water out . . . and set it empty on the counter. He'd had enough for one day. What he *needed* was to stretch out on the sofa in the staff lounge and have some alone time—

The bar's lights clicked on by themselves, one by one, a rolling chain of them illuminating the bar and spotlighting a man sitting at the far end.

"We agreed on another time," he said. "Does this meet the criteria?"

It was the man from the funeral home, the man who was there in the mirror, then gone.

"You needed time to grieve, and against my better judgment I granted it to you," he continued. "But we're on a timeline, and the here and now is as good a place and time as any."

The man gathered up the deck of cards he'd lain down on the bar top and pushed back the stool he'd been sitting on.

Jason stared, numb, and getting angry. "How the hell did you get inside my bar?"

"I opened a door," the man said.

"Then you have five seconds to open it again and walk back out, whoever you are."

"My name is Carter Block, and I see a bottle of Glenfiddich on the shelf next to your father's ashes. It was his drink of choice. Pour us a double."

Jason didn't need to glance to the shelf to know there was a bottle of Glenfiddich there but there was no goddamn way he was pouring this guy a double of anything.

"You have questions," continued Carter.

"You're goddamn right I do!"

"And I will answer them." Carter pressed a hand on the counter and then lifted it. There was a crisp folded fifty beneath. *"After* my drink."

Jason stared at the fifty and at Carter with equal disgust. But he was so goddamn tired he was prepared to do just about anything to get him to leave. He grabbed the Glenfiddich off the shelf and a tumbler from beneath it. He uncapped it and the whisky's intense aroma filled the air as he set the glass down and poured Carter his double.

"First, I wanted to offer my condolences," said Carter as he tugged the glass over with a well-manicured fingertip. "Your father's death must have been as unwelcome news to you as it was to me."

"You knew my father?"

"There is nobody on this earth I was closer to."

"Funny, he never mentioned *you*."

Carter stared at Jason, not hurt, but disappointed. Jason felt a glimmer of regret for his words but he wasn't about to offer an apology for them either. This asshole *did* break and enter after all.

"I'm not surprised," said Carter. "He was an enigma. He let me know just enough to feel comfortable, but kept much of who he was hidden from view."

"That sounds like him all right."

"Your father was a man who knew how to keep secrets; it was one of his greatest strengths. To wit, until this day I didn't even know you existed."

"That's a shocker, given he never wanted to be a father. He didn't need to tell me that either." Jason nodded to the Glenfiddich, still untouched before Carter. "So, we've talked, I poured. Now it's your turn."

Carter scooped up the card deck, and shuffled it.

"Before I go, indulge me."

"I don't like card games."

"This isn't a card game." Carter finished shuffling and set the deck down. "This is a magic trick."

"I don't like magic tricks either."

"*Pick* a card, and I'll tell you a story about your dad. A story I know he *didn't* tell you."

"I've heard enough of Dan Bishop's tall tales to fill *his* lifetime and they were all bullshit—"

"Such as how Daniel Bishop *wasn't* his real name?"

Jason had taken the fifty from the bar, but it was now clenched in his hand, crackling softly.

"Say that again . . . ?" he whispered.

Carter nodded at the cards. "I'm waiting."

Jason pocketed the fifty, and tapped a card with his finger.

Carter nodded. "Now, slide it out and look at it, but don't let me—"

"I *know* how it works."

Jason slid the card out and peeled it back far enough to glimpse the King of Hearts.

The same card as before. The one from the bathroom.

"Now slide it back into the deck."

Jason slid the card back in.

Carter gathered and shuffled the deck quickly, the cards flowing like water. He set them down.

"Now tap the top card."

Jason sighed, tapped the top card with his finger—

White flame erupted from the deck and Jason yanked his hand back with a startled cry. It burned bright and cold, then turned blue and spiraled upward, a small tornado swirling with menace. A roar like an approaching express train filled Jason's ears. The blue-and-white column of fire blasted to the ceiling like a geyser, struck it, and billowed across it. Fire surged across it to the walls, raced down them to the floor, and spread. The Locksmith should have been an inferno but there was no heat, no wind, and no smell of charring wood and burning carpeting. The conflagration barreled toward Jason and Carter Block, who remained calm the entire time. Then the flames retreated with a loud hiss, like air being sucked between teeth. They raced back across the unmarked floor, up the untouched walls, across the unscathed ceiling, and plunged back down in that single column to the deck with a roar that seemed to shake the foundations of the building.

Then it was gone, and a slow smile spread across Carter Block's face.

"*Now* do I have your attention?" he asked.

THREE

....

JASON HARD-SWALLOWED BLOCK'S GLENFIDDICH. It seared his throat but didn't do a thing to blot out any of what just happened. He set the glass down, grasped the counter with both hands, and tightened his grip until he thought the wood might break off entirely. Was he dreaming? Had he suffered some kind of psychotic break?

What the hell just happened?

Carter uncapped the Glenfiddich bottle and refilled the glass.

"Like I said, I needed your full attention. May I assume I have it now?"

Jason swallowed the refill and nodded reluctantly.

"I'm sorry it took Damon's passing for us to meet; had our paths crossed sooner, he might still be alive. . . ."

"*Damon?*" Jason scowled. "My father's name wasn't Damon, it was—"

"Daniel Patrick Bishop was an alias, the name he gave to your guardians. The name he gave to you. But he wasn't Dan Bishop and he wasn't a businessman; he was Damon King, a *Diabolist,* a *Mage* in the service of the Invisible Hand."

Jason almost laughed. "Say that again?"

"Which part?" Carter asked.

"*All of it.* Start with the Invisible—"

"The Invisible Hand is a secret society, comprised of individuals of great ability, skilled in the arts of espionage and wielding magic—real magic—as a weapon. Through deception we wage war, and with magic, we hope to win it."

Carter capped the bottle and set it aside despite Jason so desperately wanting more. Maybe he capped it because he *knew* Jason wanted it.

"Tell me, Jason. In your life, have you ever experienced *anything* out of the ordinary? Something you couldn't explain, no matter how minor it seemed at the time? An uncanny sense of foreboding? The sensation you were being watched by unseen eyes? Déjà vu?"

"Oh come on, *everybody's* experienced déjà vu!"

"*Think,* Jason. There must be something."

Jason thought hard. There *was* something there, a glimmer buried in the deep recesses of his brain. Something that *could* have been what Carter described. But Jason couldn't unearth it.

"It's all right if you can't remember," Carter said. "The Citadel can dredge those memories to the surface."

"You realize how crazy this all sounds?" Jason asked.

"As it happens, I do. I realize this is a great deal for someone to process all at once. Were we not so pressed, I'd have found a more moderate way to convince you. Ordinarily we identify candidates at a much younger age; their abilities manifest around puberty. Those we find are brought to the Citadel and trained, eased from their world into ours. A child, shown they *are,* in fact, that special person they always thought they were? It's a dream come true. But for someone of your advanced age—"

"I'm thirty," Jason protested. "I wouldn't call that *advanced*."

"You've had a lifetime of believing you know how the world works. I'm here to tell you otherwise."

Carter must have seen the confusion on Jason's face.

"You think I'm crazy. That's understandable. Were our positions reversed I wouldn't believe what I'm saying either. But you *saw* what happened with the deck of cards. You saw the flames, you feared for your life. The fact I'm still speaking and you're still listening—"

Jason raised a hand for silence. To his relief Carter granted it.

"Okay, do me a favor and put yourself on my side of the bar. You get the news about your father's death. You make the arrangements, you go home to say goodbye. You have a fight with your girlfriend, who says a lot of the same things *you're* saying, then you step into *your* bar with *your* father's ashes tucked under your arm . . . and a guy *literally* appears out of thin air to tell you everything you believed about your dad was bullshit and he was, in fact, some kind of magician spy. No sane person would believe any of it!"

"The human mind clings to the rational the way a drowning man clings to a life preserver long after his ship has sunk. Letting go of the rational is the first test a Mage faces; it's how we transcend the boundaries of this world. It's how we're able to control it. You should consider this your test, for your own sake."

Jason's brow furrowed. The air seemed to drop a few degrees around him. "What do you mean *my sake*?"

"Because your father didn't kill himself," Carter said. "He was murdered."

Murdered. The word seemed to hang in the air between them.

"Your father was the most powerful Mage I've ever known. But we aren't the only Mages plying our trade, and he wasn't immortal. Damon was attempting to acquire something of great value, a clue that will lead us to something that could shift the balance in an ages-old conflict and bring us what we've long sought: victory. He managed to secure it, but lost his life in the attempt. There was someone else there. There was a battle and your father was killed."

"You were there?"

"I was not, unfortunately. Had I been, the outcome might have been much different and Damon might still be alive."

"So who killed him?"

Carter glanced at the clock above the bar. "I cast a concealment spell over this tavern when I arrived. We're hidden, but not for long, not with them hunting you."

"*Them?*"

"They're called the Golden Dawn," Carter answered. "They are magic users, but not us. We are born with these abilities; they are Alchemists, but the more common terms would be *sorcerers,* or *witches,* or *warlocks*. Individuals who acquired their abilities through the study of the dark arts. Through books and spells, bindings and enchantments, through pacts with the primordial forces that would tear this world apart if we didn't stand in their way. *They* killed your father, and now they want you."

Pinpricks of ice trod slow up Jason's spine. He tried not to show it but couldn't stifle the shudder that ran through him. That sensation of someone walking over his grave again, the second time in one day. Had to be a coincidence. Had to be.

"But *why* me? I'm not anybody. I'm not special or—"

"Jason, *you're a Mage,*" Carter said.

Now Jason knew Carter was full of shit. He was almost relieved, too.

"A Mage . . ." Jason snorted with as much disgust as he could manage. "Sure, Carter, sure. Like I've ever done anything like . . . well, like what you just did."

"That's because you never learned how," Carter said. "I've recruited dozens like you. The ones who didn't believe me didn't believe in themselves. They clung to that life preserver because what I was telling them was so impossible that the calm, ordered side of their brains wouldn't accept it despite all evidence to the contrary. But I *am* telling you the truth."

"How do you know?" Jason asked slowly. "How do you know I'm what you say I am?"

"Because all your life you've felt like you were meant for *more* than this. You've known this, because you *are* meant for more. This other life—the life of a Mage—has been calling to you but you wouldn't listen to it. It was the same for me, and it was the same for your father. He saved my life on countless occasions and to the end of my days I'll suffer with the knowledge that I couldn't save him. But I can *still* save you. During your father's final mission, your existence became known to the Golden Dawn and they will come for you. Your only chance at survival is with us now."

Jason looked to the capped Glenfiddich. He *really* wanted that drink.

No, he wanted to wake up in his bed and realize that *everything* from the moment he was told Dan—not Damon, *Dan*—was dead, had been a dream.

Carter scooped up the cards and pocketed them.

"You think this is a dream but it isn't. Everything I've told you is a fact. You can accept it or not but that changes nothing.

Your friends, your loved ones, they're in danger by association. Your uncle, your girlfriend? Damon thought he could protect your mother, too, but he failed, and they killed her for it."

"*Murdered?*" Jason gaped. "That's bullshit; Dan told me she died, not long after giving birth to me!"

"He told you what you needed to hear. He couldn't let you share her fate, so he hid you away, abandoning you because he had no choice. Now a decision stands before you, the most important you will ever make. By denying your lineage, you've put the ones you love in great jeopardy. I came here to tell you who your father was and to offer you a choice. I also knew you wouldn't be easily convinced. Perhaps you *are* too old to change your ways. I can offer you the way forward, Jason, but I can't force you to take it. *That* must be your decision. But do know this: you can't outrun the past, and you can't outrun what's coming. You have to confront it, or you'll always be running."

Carter pushed his stool back with a scrape of wood and crossed to the front door. He paused, his head canted, like he was running a scenario through it. Finally he turned, reached into his jacket pocket, and pulled a card from it.

"If you change your mind, here's my card. But as of this moment my debt to your father is paid in full. He was a great man, Jason; do think kindly of him."

The card left Carter's hand and glided across the room to the countertop where it landed faceup.

It was the King of Hearts, the same card as before.

And the astonishing lack of surprise at that reveal was equally matched a moment later when Jason looked up to see that Carter Block had vanished again, as silently and as suddenly as he'd first appeared.

. . .

Jason was lucky he'd met Winnie when he did; there was no way he'd have been able to afford the condo on Fulton Street on a bartender's salary. How she afforded it on *her* salary was a mystery, but so was her interest in him. Deep down, a part of him wondered what she saw in him at all, though he'd never quite found the courage to ask. Like he feared her answer. Like willful ignorance was preferable to any truth. By the time the elevator reached the seventeenth floor, he had almost convinced himself he'd dreamt the entire encounter with Carter Block. The whisky *was* the likely culprit for everything that had happened after leaving Winnie. For all he knew, he'd hit the sauce the moment he crossed The Locksmith's threshold, taken that nap, and imagined the rest. He'd nodded off on the subway ride home as well, nearly confirming the entire trip to The Locksmith had been that: a dream. Carter Block and his tale *were* a figment of alcohol-fueled grief; it was the only sane explanation.

And still, doubt lingered; some tiny grain of it buried deep inside that wished it all *had* been true. But as he reached his door and fumbled his keys out of his pocket with a loud jangle, reality came crashing back in like a wave to wash that grain away.

He entered and closed the door quietly behind him. He kept the lights off and stepped softly down the hallway toward the closed bedroom door at the end. But when he reached the living room, he decided not to push his luck; the sofa was comfortable enough, and morning would hopefully be more hospitable to assessing the state of his and Winnie's union than the middle of the night. He entered the living room, kicked off his shoes, and glanced out the big bay window looking north from Fulton, up

Manhattan's glittering nightscape to the distant Chrysler Building, gleaming like a beacon. Ten blocks north of that was the
patch of pavement where Dan had landed.

Not landed, *died*.

He'd gotten used to Dan never being there, but the fact his
father wouldn't be back, that he'd never see that cocksure grin
crease his father's face . . . for the first time since the news broke,
he realized how *alone* he really was. Every tie he had to the person
he was, from Uncle Aaron to Owen to Aunt Cathryn and now Dan,
was gone. Even Carla was leaving Cold Spring. He felt the weight
of thirty years pressing down on him. Once, a long time ago, he'd
looked to the future with hope and dreams. Now he was looking
in the rearview, wishing he'd done *everything* different.

"You're drunk," Winnie said.

She was standing in the living-room entrance clad in a white
housecoat that, along with the blank expression on her face,
made her look like an apparition.

"I had a couple," he said.

"More than a couple; I can smell it from here."

"Look, Win, it's late, I'll sleep on the sofa tonight—"

"Don't bother. I'm up anyway."

She entered the living room, clicked on the end-table light,
and sat on the sofa.

"I was worried something had happened to you," she said.

He sat beside her. His hand brushed hers, tentative, and to
his surprise she took it.

"Look, I'm sorry about before," he said. "I shouldn't have just
bolted—"

"No, I'm the one who should apologize. Your dad just died. I
was pushing you when I should have stepped back and let you
mourn."

"Win, you were right; I *have* been running in place. Owen last year, my dad now; the signs have been there the whole time."

"It's understandable, Jason. I should let you have more time to think things over."

"I've had enough time. I . . ."

He trailed off. He'd worked overtime between The Locksmith and home to convince himself it had all been his imagination when a thought strayed into his vision. He reached his hand into his jacket pocket, and felt around—

His fingertips brushed against something thin and flat. He dug deeper and pulled it out.

It was the King of Hearts. The card Carter Block had left at the bar.

Winnie stared at the card, and at Jason. His grip on her hand tightened.

"Jason, *what is it?*"

He told her everything.

He talked and she listened without interruption. He'd actually wanted to drag it out because he feared what she *would* say when he was finished: that he *had* cracked, that he *needed* to see a doctor. But she just listened. When his story, which sounded even *more* unbelievable spoken aloud, ended, the silence that followed was near total.

Finally, she did speak.

"You need help," she said.

"I was afraid you'd say that."

She wrapped her arms around him and pulled him toward her.

"You need help," she said again.

"Tell me about it—"

She squeezed him tight. "You need help."

And she kept squeezing, tighter and tighter, her shoulder thrusting into his windpipe.

He gasped.

"Winnie—I can't breathe—"

He pushed against her but her grip was iron, squeezing him tighter and tighter to the point he feared his bones would shatter. Her voice was a harsh whisper in his ear. . . .

But it wasn't Winifred Hobbes's voice that spoke.

"You need help. But it won't come in time."

She grasped him around the throat and tightened her grip. He gulped air as his esophagus was forced shut and she stood, lifting him off the sofa. He struggled against Winnie, but her grip was a vice. His feet left the floor, there was a brief pause, and then he was airborne, soaring and crashing into the entertainment unit. The flat-screen shattered beneath his weight, the shelf above broke loose, and its contents—the clock, the cable box, a heavy glass paperweight—came crashing down. Pain tore through him. His head throbbed, his ears rang, and his eyes struggled to focus on Winnie as she flicked her wrist and the coffee table leapt through the air like a discarded newspaper caught in a gust. It slammed into the bay window, radiating fissures across it, and fell to the floor with a mighty crash. Wind screeched through the cracks in the glass, and the hard moonlight that fell through it bathed Winnie's face, making her cruel smile a jagged nightmare.

"You should have listened to Carter Block," she said.

FOUR

....

THE SCREECH OF WIND LIFTED the King of Hearts off the floor and yanked it across the room to slap against the window's face. Fissures radiated further across the glass and filtered moonlight over Winnie's face, bisecting it, like reality had just split itself seventeen floors above Fulton.

"You have *no* idea what a relief this is, Jason," she said. "After your pops Jackson Pollocked himself all across Madison, I thought, *Jesus I'm going to have to be the shoulder to cry on. I'm going to have to comfort him, soothe him; I'll probably even have to fuck him.* And I did all of that, because that was the job."

She raised her hands. His necktie pulled taut and tightened and lifted him.

"But that job is finished. I'm tendering my resignation."

Jason tried to speak but the tie was tightening around his neck, closing it up.

"Winnie," he choked. "Please, don't—"

"Winnie?" Her grin was like a shark's. "You've got the wrong girl."

His tie yanked even tighter. He gripped it, trying to ease the pressure on his neck as his feet left the floor. He was choking, struggling. Dark spots blossomed in his vision. Then she pushed him and he was soaring again. His legs caught the back of the sofa, he toppled over it, and his face struck the hardwood floor. Starbursts obliterated the darkness. Pain followed.

"Help!" he rasped. "Somebody, please!

Winnie's gaze was as cold as her voice.

"Nobody's coming to help, Jason, and why would they? What have you done in thirty wasted years to make anyone care to help you?"

She flicked her wrist. The sofa upended and collapsed into the end table, sending the lamp crashing and the bulb bursting. She stepped through the shadows and as she did seemed to sink into them, disappearing from view before reappearing.

"Winnie, why—what are you—" he gasped.

"What, this? *This* is a celebration. I'm finally rid of this wretched charade, and rid of *you*."

She lunged at him. He thrust his hand at her reflexively, the final desperate act of a dying man.

Something struck her with the force of a speeding truck. She lurched backward, bare feet sliding across the floor. The momentum carried her into the bookshelves and she slammed into them with enough force to collapse the entire thing and send books crashing to the floor around her. The heavy *Treasures of the Louvre* coffee-table book he'd bought her on their one-month anniversary hit the floor with a gunshot thud.

His palm stung, like he'd struck her from across the room.
Did he do that?!

Winnie struggled to free herself from the tangle of shattered wood and heavy books. As she did, her face seemed to melt; her nose decayed down to the hollow, like some ravenous thing had bitten it off. Her eyes sunk into her skull, like cornered animals waiting to strike. Then those disfigured features vanished, and once again it was Winnie's face focusing its wrath on him.

"So, you *are* a Mage . . ." she said. "Too bad that won't save you."

She rose up out of the wreckage and Jason rose along with her. He struggled; he kicked, flailed, he pushed at her again with one hand, then both, but nothing happened. She pushed and he flew back, striking the bay window, that invisible force pressing him up against it. Fissures spiderwebbed across the glass. It was breaking away beneath him, like a frozen pond giving way.

"Send Damon my best when you see him," Winnie said.

Then she pushed a final time.

The window shattered, he pitched back through it, and everything slowed to a crawl. He saw the King of Hearts flit past. He heard the wind shriek. He felt the cold air embrace him. For a moment he hung in space long enough to see Winifred Hobbes smile.

Then he was falling.

He tumbled, the ground swinging in and out of view as he plummeted to the pavement far below and getting closer with each second. He couldn't cry, couldn't scream; he could only hear the roar of wind, feel the air press against his face, taste the blood and fear in his mouth. Time elongated, enough for him to regret a life wasted. Time enough to witness all those years of lost chances flash past, a lifetime of kicking the can further down the road instead of picking it up and running with it. Time he'd been handed and wasted at every turn. But what really latched onto his brain and rode it all the way down to his death was the knowledge that Carter Block *had* told him the truth. Magic *was* real, but no magic would save him now—

A bomb blast crashed through the air, and something was falling beside him.

Not something, *someone*.

A boy, clad in striped track pants and white sneakers, his light jacket billowing about him as they fell. He grasped Jason in a bear hug and pulled him close.

" 'Ang on, bruv', I gotcha!" he shouted.

Thunder and lightning crashed simultaneously and the taste of ozone mingled with blood settled on his tongue. A second later he landed hard on unyielding ground and the boy landed hard atop him. Jason's skull struck hard and pain tore through him.

The boy crouched over him, his eyes boring holes into Jason's.

"Anythin' broke?" he asked.

Jason struggled for air but his lungs wouldn't fill. The boy swatted him across the face. Jason took in a deep shuddering breath.

"You'll be all right," the boy said. "Don't go nowhere; this won't take long."

He clambered off Jason and raced to the edge of the building they had somehow landed on, and leapt off it. There was another thunderclap and an eruption of smoke, and he was gone.

Jason slowly sat up even though his aching body screeched in protest. He could smell fresh sawdust in the air and saw builder's plastic, tools, a band saw, and heavy-looking sacks of cement scattered across the site. He knew where he was: the roof of the condo being constructed half a block down Fulton from his and Winnie's building—

Winnie!

He looked to the seventeenth floor and the jagged hole that had been their bay window. Winnie stood there, her nightgown billowing. But she wasn't looking at him; she was looking at another building a block and a half north, one of those old art deco ones littering the city that Jason had never paid much mind to before.

But gazing at it now, it would be burned into his memory until the day he died.

When he was seven, Aunt Cathryn had put on her old VHS copy of *Fantasia,* her favorite film. He'd enjoyed the movie and the music, but the segment that stuck with him wasn't, ironically, "The Sorcerer's Apprentice," but its penultimate section, "Night on Bald Mountain," which had given him nightmares for weeks, and he never quite looked at Storm King Mountain the same way again. Bald Mountain's colossal demonic figure conjuring creatures from the depths of Hell through billowing smoke and shoots of flame had been seared into his memory. Gazing at that building now, he could almost hear the Mussorgsky amidst the flashes of light and fire rending the sky around its terraced summit. Sonic blasts heralded the arrival of three dark shapes alighting atop the roof, hurling flames that gleamed against the night sky like rockets. His rescuer exploded into the fray, leaping in and out of view in blasts of smoke and crashing noise that clattered like gunfire across the cityscape. Jason staggered to his feet and over to the northern edge of the roof to get a closer look, supporting his battered body against the freshly lain parapet. He looked about for someone—anyone—who could see what he was seeing, but he was the only spectator; the only audience to witness what was unfolding.

The boy was in the thick of the battle and another figure had his back, blocking offensive bursts of fire, countering the attack with ones of their own as the attackers converged. The boy raised his hands, and high above the battleground, pieces of masonry ripped free from the adjacent high-rise and plummeted. As they fell, he pushed and the projectiles rocketed at the attackers. One was struck, staggered back, and toppled over, plunging like Jason had. Midway down, the attacker disappeared in an explosion of noise that shattered the windows he plunged past, and reappeared back on the building's summit, back in the fray.

The ground Jason was on shook. The building beneath him trembled like a fault line had opened across Lower Manhattan and was pulling it apart along Fulton. The parapet buckled and gave and he staggered backward as bricks toppled off the edge. The building lurched violently and when he looked up he saw why.

Winnie had thrust her hands out and was twisting them, and the building was twisting with her. A fissure tore across the roof, splitting it off of the main structure. Jason lost his footing and tumbled to the edge and, with the parapet gone, nothing could stop him from going over.

Then he was falling again.

This time he *did* cry out, hoping someone—the boy, his accomplice, anyone—heard him.

And as the ground raced up he felt someone grab him, felt the air explode around him—

The hard aluminum made an echoing boom beneath him as he struck it, and the sound echoed through the tight confines of what appeared to be the hold of a panel van. Sudden sharp pain broke his reverie and his eyes settled on the one who'd saved him: a twenty-something girl in ripped denim jeans and jacket and a Ramones shirt beneath that. Her hair was a rat's nest, framing dark Middle Eastern features and the most remarkable green-gold eyes he'd ever seen.

"Are you all right?" she asked. "Is anything broken? *Are you hurt?*"

There was an earsplitting thunderclap and someone appeared behind the wheel of the driver's seat. The key in the ignition turned by itself. The engine roared to life.

"Yeah, 'e's not much for the gab," the boy said. He threw the van into gear and stomped the gas. Everything lurched, but the girl didn't budge as the van pulled away, rubber screeching.

"Who are you people?!" Jason asked, once his pulse had settled to a machine-gun rattle.

"My name is Allegra Sand," the girl said. "The kid who just saved your life is Teo Stone."

She reached into her pocket and pulled out a card.

The King of Hearts.

"We got your call," she said. "And you *better* have been worth all this trouble."

FIVE

THERE WAS DARKNESS AND SILENCE, like he was deep, deep under water but could still breathe. He had no sense of up or down. He was drowning, like he had the day he nearly lost his life on Murder Hill. He struggled to shatter the surface he sensed was just out of reach, and felt resistance with every spasmodic movement of his limbs. He kicked, flailed, his lungs screaming for air, and just when he thought it was the end, his face broke the surface.

He lurched upright.

He was in bed. A bed as familiar as every creak of spring beneath him. He shifted his weight, sat up, and took in a sight that snatched his breath away.

It was his bed from Cold Spring, in his childhood bedroom.

And it was impossible.

Aaron and Cathryn's powder-blue Colonial Revival at the end of Cedar Street had been sold after she died, the proceeds from which were currently paying for Aaron's long-term care. But this was the house he'd grown up in. His desk still sat by the open window, lace curtains billowing gently in a fragrant summer breeze, even though when he was last conscious it was early October. Through the window he glimpsed Storm King Mountain rising above the landscape. Everything was as he remembered: his dresser, his shelves laden with the books that he'd read and cherished. His CD rack stood in the corner, along with the portable stereo he'd lost track of. The music and movie posters that adorned every available space of wall and angled ceiling were tacked up where they should have been. It was the room in every way except one: a small, faded photograph in a frame on his nightstand that held a photograph of a smiling, sad-eyed woman in a hospital bed clutching a newborn to her breast. His mother, dead almost as long as he'd been alive. But the photo wasn't there where it should have been, which only raised the question that followed even quicker.

Where the hell was he?

The last he remembered he was lying on the floor of the van Teo Stone was speeding through Manhattan. The exhaustion of the previous days had wiped him out and the adrenaline from being thrown from two consecutive buildings had drained him. Allegra Sand had been explaining something to him but he'd passed out before she got three words in.

He pulled the bedspread back, swung his feet out, planted them on the floor, and stood. He was wearing blue cotton pajama bottoms and a light white T-shirt. He had no memory of dressing or undressing himself, but he saw neatly folded clothing—blue jeans, a gray T-shirt—and black Converse sneakers sitting atop the dresser. He found socks and underwear in the drawers and, after dressing, looked to the mirror on the back of the bedroom door, half expecting to see his sixteen- or seventeen-year-old self stare back. But it was his thirty-year-old face that met his gaze.

He entered the living room with its light-blue painted walls and classical furnishings. Everything was as he remembered, as if this place's architect had dug those memories out of his brain and added a fresh coat of paint. Everything in the living room was imprinted with memory, and he sensed that no matter which room he stepped into, everything would be as he remembered. Even as he negotiated the upstairs hallway and stairs, every creak of hardwood was accurate. There was even the patched and painted-over hole he'd punched in the wall when he was fifteen and learned Dan had canceled *another* birthday appearance.

It was home.

As he neared the kitchen adjacent to the living room, the smell of coffee reached him and he slowed his pace. Would Aunt Cathryn be there, bright-eyed and chipper? Would Uncle Aaron be reading his newspaper and muttering about fascism coming to America again? Jason's pulse quickened. If this *was* Heaven, he'd take it, and ask for seconds.

But it was Carter Block who sat at the kitchen table, dressed the same as he had been the day of the funeral. One of Cathryn's brown coffee mugs sat across from Carter, steam rising aromatically.

Jason took a seat and pulled the mug close. The coffee was black.

"Cream's in the fridge. Sugar's in the bowl," Carter said.

"I know," Jason said. "You guys clearly did your research." He gestured to the décor.

"You're mistaken, Jason; we did not create this place—you did."

"*Sure* I did." Jason nodded. "I was holding out on you, Carter; I'm actually a very powerful wizard. Slinging drinks was my cover the whole time. Seriously, pull the other one while you're at it."

"This kitchen, indeed this house, is all your doing, Jason. Your subconscious mind told the Citadel what you most desired to see when you awoke, and it provided it for you down to every last detail, no matter how minute it may have seemed."

"This is the Citadel?" Jason looked around the kitchen again, and shook his head. "But it's *too* perfect; I mean . . . it's nailed details I forgot years ago. Hell, I haven't *been* inside this house in six years. It hasn't been home even longer than that."

"You may have forgotten the less salient points, but a part of you imprinted yourself on it and it on you. You never *really* forget the most important places and moments in your life no matter how much you sometimes wish to forget. But the memory remains, if you dig deep enough for it."

Jason's head was spinning, at Carter's words, at the kitchen—at all of it. He drank the coffee black and washed the remaining cobwebs of sleep, and his own doubt, down as he swallowed.

"Okay, I believe you," Jason said, setting the mug down. "If that's what it takes for you to explain everything that's happened over the last day and *then* some, you have it."

"I should hope so after the events of last night," Carter said. "I took the precaution of having you followed home. I suspected the Golden Dawn knew of your existence, and I was right."

Winnie, Jason remembered. She attacked him. She tried to kill him.

But was that person *really* Winnie?

Carter seemed to sense Jason's thoughts, because it was his turn to look uncomfortable. This was the part of their conversation he hoped not to have but Jason gave him an easy out.

"She's dead, isn't she?" Jason asked.

"I honestly don't know," Carter said. "It could have happened after you and she parted ways on the train. It could have happened before. What, exactly, transpired between you two, from the funeral to the attack?"

Jason gave Carter the quick rundown on everything, from his return home on the subway and his encounter with Winnie, to the moment she hurled him through their living-room window. Carter seemed skeptical, like he was almost *too* eager to pen Winifred Hobbes's obit. But Carter was also a Mage. And if anyone could accept the impossible . . .

"Assuming everything you believed about her was true, it's possible, even likely, that somewhere between the train and your home, she was murdered . . ." Carter conceded. "But eliminating Winifred Hobbes would raise too many questions. One corpse—a suicide, despondent over the death of his father—would be a tragedy. A suicide *and* a murder, while all-too-common, raises many more questions, and the Golden Dawn, like the Invisible Hand, prefers to remain hidden."

"If she's alive, then we have to find her!" Jason pushed the chair back and stood. "She said she had a sister somewhere in Texas. We never met, but if she has the address back at the condo—"

Carter raised his hand. "I'll look into it, Jason. You must—"

"We're only a couple hours from home!"

"*No,*" Carter said. "You must remain here, where it's safe."

"Where, in *Cold Spring*?"

"Come now, Jason, you're still clinging to that life preserver."

A smile crept slowly across Carter's face. "Or do you *honestly* believe you're in Cold Spring?"

"I know you've had your share of jolts over the past few days," said Carter as he led Jason toward the front door. "But this next one may be a touch disconcerting."

Carter stepped aside; it was Jason's move now. He gripped the brass knob, cool to the touch and as familiar as it was countless times before. He turned the knob, there was a click, and the door opened. As he gazed through the opening, the fact that he didn't consider running back upstairs to his room, crawling back into bed, and pulling the covers over his head counted as some kind of progress. He took a breath, exhaled, and stepped through.

The summer after they graduated from high school, Jason, Owen, Carla, and Carla's friend Ally took a trip to New York. They roamed the streets, got tossed out of Don Hill's, and ended the day at the Empire State Building. As they stood there, gazing out over the glittering expanse, they all felt the endless possibilities before them in that magnificent landscape. The cavern Jason was standing in now could have easily held that expanse with room to spare. It was so large he couldn't see where it began or ended. Despite no visible light source it was bathed in cool amber-tinged moonlight that seemed to come from all around them. The chamber stretched off before him but it was far from empty; there were rows upon rows of shelves facing them. Twenty, fifty, a hundred rows—and in all likelihood more—filled his panoramic view and continued off into darkness and up to a shadowy ceiling. They looked like bookshelves, stacked on top of each other and climbing to disappear from view through sheer distance from the ground. But as Jason stepped forward and squinted, he saw they weren't books at all; they were doors. Doors of all kinds, from the old and weathered to the new and ornate, to the graffiti covered, and the utilitarian. Wrought-iron spiral staircases lined the ends of each stack, allowing access to the second, third, fourth, and higher levels. He could see *everything* with a clarity that didn't seem possible, like his brain had switched from analog to hi-def. Like he was utilizing senses *he* never knew he even possessed. Like he'd been blind from birth and only now learned how to open eyes that were functional all along.

"What is this . . . ?"

He turned to Carter, and gaped. Behind them was a cavern of equal size, with an equal number of rows and shelves and doors. One of those doors sat on the floor behind them and still hung open. Through it, he could see the front hall, the living room, and the stairs of the house in Cold Spring. Then the door swung shut, there was a click, and then the entire door rose off the ground and soared up into the heights of the cavern to disappear from view. High above he could see other doors uncouple and drift silent to unidentified locations, while others returned home.

"This is the Athenaeum, the gateway into and out of the Citadel," Carter said with a smile. "And yes, after all these years it *still* takes my breath away. I grew up in libraries; to me, every book on every shelf was a portal to another world. The shelves of the Athenaeum, however, do not hold books; they hold doors, and each door is a portal to a different place on this earth."

Carter led Jason down a central aisle, the door-laden shelves rising twenty-five, fifty, a hundred floors above, and the stacks climbing into the sky and giving the appearance they were walking down a long, deep trough. Jason gaped at the shelves and the doors upon them as they passed; he couldn't even begin to fathom how many doors the Athenaeum held. In close among them, the sense of vertigo was intense. Every time Jason looked up to see those stacks rise to a vanishing point far above, he felt dizzy. Occasionally doors would uncouple, float free of their shelves, and rise into the sky. Occasionally others returned to their holding place, settling into their brackets with a clatter.

"The Athenaeum began with a single doorway," Carter explained. "It was designed to carry a person from one point on the map to a point far distant and back again. From that one door, others were made. One became two, two became four, and from there it grew exponentially. The Citadel doesn't occupy one space; it's not a mansion or a castle or a bunker deep underground; it occupies the space *between* spaces. What you are looking at is a network of *Soft Places* spanning the globe; locales where the veil between the mortal and magical worlds are at their thinnest. Once they were plentiful; now what you see is but a fraction of what remains. The Citadel harnesses those Soft Places; summon the proper door leading to the proper location and step through, and you'll find yourself back amongst mundanes anyplace in the world with a corresponding portal to pass through."

Jason frowned. "Back up a bit. *Mundanes?*"

"Our term for people possessing no magical ability whatsoever."

"Isn't calling them mundane a little insulting?"

"More insulting than *inferior*?"

"Touché."

Carter stopped, and before Jason could ask why, a heavy-looking oak door uncoupled from a stack above and lowered itself gently to the stone floor. It was carved with ornate markings, some ancient language Jason didn't recognize.

"The language is long dead, but it means 'By Subterfuge We

Wage War,'" said Carter. "And the moment you step through that door, you're committed to our cause."

"No turning back, huh?"

"You're a quick study. That's good, because in this game, the rules are complex, the outcomes murky, and the stakes life-and-death."

"And if I don't go through?" Jason nodded to the door.

"Then I'm sure you'll be quite comfortable in that house in Cold Spring. You can spend your days there in the embrace of comfort, of familiarity."

"But it wouldn't be real." Jason sighed. "It would be just an illusion."

"That doorway leads to your house, your *real* house," Carter said. "You could live there, in the space between spaces, but it would be an empty existence. Like living in a museum. It wouldn't *be* home. But for some the illusion is more appealing than the reality."

"Not for me," Jason said with finality. "And not anymore."

He gripped the handle, there was a loud clank of metal, and he opened it.

The room they stepped into was little more than a bunker big enough to hold maybe five people comfortably, and constructed with cold concrete blocks. There was no furniture, just hard buzzing halogens in the ceiling and a row of angled windows along the wall before them. After the colossal spectacle of the Athenaeum, it seemed almost ordinary. Jason approached the windows and Carter followed silently, not explaining, not preparing him for what he was about to see. He didn't need to either, for as Jason reached the windows and gazed through them, no words could suffice.

Below them lay an immense arena, but calling it immense sold it short. On first glance he thought you could fit the old and new Yankee stadiums into it, and still have room for Storm King Mountain in the cheap seats. As Jason focused on one corner of the arena, the view seemed to get closer even though the room didn't move; like everywhere he focused the viewing window magnified to see every last detail. To call the effect disorienting was as great a disservice as calling the arena immense.

On the ground, a large racing track surrounded a patch of green Astroturf that was covered with obstacles set up its length and around it. But the track seemed to undulate, looping in and around itself like the coils of a snake, and Jason felt dizzy just trying to figure out where it began and where it ended. Heavy-looking crates rested on the field and more floated in the air, stretching all the way up to the ceiling hundreds of feet above. There were people visible, too, all dressed in red-and-black training uniforms. He saw a girl leap gracefully onto the stack of crates and vanish in a puff of smoke. She reappeared midway up, balanced on one of the floating crates. She disappeared again, then reappeared again balanced on the edge of the highest one. She held there for a moment, peered over the edge, like a child contemplating the distance from the high board at the local pool. Then she stepped off, plummeting like a rock. Jason sucked air as she fell. Midway down, she disappeared in a thunderclap of smoke, and reappeared back on the ground, light as a feather.

Another girl who couldn't be more than twelve levitated cinder blocks with trembling hands, slowly but deliberately constructing a wall with them. Every time it threatened to topple, the girl paused, and focused, and the wall straightened. At the far end of the field Jason saw two figures hurl columns of flame from burning pots beside them at each other, molding them into serpentine shapes that spat at each other in the air between. Another boy assumed command of a pile of scrap metal, raising and twisting and bending the individual pieces into a colossal hand. The hand clenched into a fist and, after a moment's hesitation, the boy sent the fist hurtling into the girl's carefully constructed wall, shattering it and sending debris falling. The girl deflected the pieces and directed them back into the boy's hand, smashing it apart.

He saw two others manipulate human figures clad in suits of armor. A suited warrior swung its mace; there was a loud echoing clash of metal on metal, and his opponent crumbled, empty pieces clattering across the pitch. Closer to Jason's and Carter's vantage, a group of six sat, legs tucked under them in a Lotus position, floating several feet above the ground. They shifted their faces and bodies, each shifting into the Mage floating opposite, and vice versa, the metamorphosis rippling through the circle like a churning ocean wave. Others moved through an obstacle course, passing through walls, disappearing and reappearing, fading from view then tightening into sharp relief. And as Jason widened his perspective, he could see that the training room's walls and ceiling each held their own moving dioramas. Earthly physics didn't hold power here, like an M. C. Escher landscape of walls and ceilings and stairs snaking about in a configuration defying all laws of gravity.

"Jason Bishop . . . meet the Invisible Hand," said Carter.

Jason took it all in. With wonder. With apprehension. With an electricity he'd never felt before.

If *this* was his destiny . . . he was ready to face it.

SIX

········•·•·•·•·•·•·•·•···

THE SMOOTH, CONCAVE WALLS OF the concrete tunnel snaked through the earth like they'd been carved by some prehistoric serpent. Lights were embedded in the high ceiling, and the floor was covered in a mesh grating that clattered beneath them as they walked. Carter called it the Ingress, a back-door passageway linking the Citadel's many chambers. There was a low mechanical buzz in the air, and as they trod its winding confines they passed closed doors embedded in the tunnel on either side. None of these doors had any latches or handles or knobs that Jason could see, but he knew any one of them could whisk them anywhere in the world they wanted.

"There was no small amount of books in your bedroom in Cold Spring," Carter said. "Am I correct in assuming you were an avid reader?"

"Still am," Jason said. "It's a long subway ride from Fulton to Dyckman."

"Did your readings ever include any folklore or mythology?"

As they walked, a smile crossed Jason's face as a warm memory intruded on him. When he was ten or eleven, Cathryn and Aaron got him a set of books for Christmas they'd found in a second-hand store. Aaron told Jason they'd once been advertised on television by some old horror actor, but they were far from a quick cash grab; the books were quite exquisite—handsomely bound, beautifully illustrated. He couldn't recall how many times he'd read them but he remembered every last one of them. Tales of giants and ogres, of magical lands and great adventures, and of witches and wizards; he told as much to Carter as they wound their way through miles of conduit.

"Then you'll know who Merlin was," said Carter.

"*Everybody* knows who Merlin was," Jason replied. "He's kind of ubiquitous, isn't he?"

"Did you know he once existed?"

"I didn't, actually."

"He was actually a lesser Mage of his day," said Carter. "Yet the stories you have read—folklore—are the remnants of a world much different from the one we inhabit now; stories about Merlin, and Gwydion in Wales, of Väinämöinen in Lapland, of Baba Yaga in Russia, the Medea of Greek mythology, and legendary schools of witchcraft and wizardry. All real. All true."

"Schools of witchcraft and wizardry? Sounds charming." Jason grinned.

But Carter didn't smile. In fact, Carter was deadly serious.

"They are far from that," he said. "Such institutions exact a profound toll, and demand a heavy price. We know one once lay in the rugged Apennines of central Italy, another in the Black Forest of Germany, another deep in the Louisiana bayous. They're all gone now. The most infamous however was—and possibly still is—somewhere in Spain. Outside Toledo or Salamanca, we can't be sure—a place where students studied forbidden tomes for five years, never venturing outside, never communicating with one another or the outside world, and never meeting their instructors. They delved deep into these mysteries and enchantments, and gave themselves utterly to their study, etching spells and bindings into their own flesh. At the end of those five years they were released back into the world . . . all but one. They didn't know they had been chosen; they only found out when the way out slammed shut before them and they finally gazed upon the face of the school's master. They belonged to him now, and were never seen again."

Jason's skin pinpricked gooseflesh. He didn't want to press Carter for more and Carter didn't offer. Instead, he stopped beside one of those closed doors lining the tunnel.

"Inside the Citadel, you are safe," he said. "The Golden Dawn won't find you; entry is granted only to a true Mage. But out in the mundane world . . ."

Carter pressed his hand to the door. There was a click and clatter of gears turning and bolts being drawn back, and the door opened. Harsh daylight spilled in, buffeted by a wave of heat and humidity. Carter stepped through and, after steeling himself for what lay beyond, Jason followed.

Jason had endured a dozen summers in New York and after the second of them decided that anybody who said they love summer clearly never spent it there. But he had *never* experienced heat like this; the sudden jolt from what felt like a cool sixty-eight degrees into the dense humidity and scorching sun made it feel like they'd stepped into an oven instead of a marketplace. The market itself was crowded and noisy, a cacophony of shouts and laughter and hard sales. He tasted grit and dust on his tongue, and the odor of piss and shit was seasoned with periodic wafts of curry and cardamom from the spice merchants. The lot housing the market was crammed with stalls hawking everything from food and clothing to cassettes and CDs and pirated DVDs. Sun blasted the parched ground and Jason had to strain his eyes against its brilliance. His T-shirt was stuck to his sweating back after the first minute, but beside him, Carter looked unruffled in his dark suit.

"Mumbai," said Carter. "I know you were going to ask but we haven't much time for question and answer; they'll be here soon. The Golden Dawn keys to a Mage's presence the moment we enter the mundane world, but it takes time to filter background noise out. Alone, on an isolated street or a place where you think you're well hidden is actually more dangerous than a good crowd. With a crowd, you can blend in, you can cast an enchantment on yourself to appear as another. But in the end they always find you."

Carter gestured with a nod. Jason followed, and at first glance didn't see them; the market was busy. Judging by the heat of the sun it was midafternoon and things were heating up from there. Then he saw her by one of the vendors, an old woman with a face like a raisin had broken off from whatever argument-slash-negotiation she'd been embroiled in, and stared at Carter and Jason. The stainless-steel bowl of curry powder she'd been measuring out fell to the ground with a noisy clatter, and its contents stained her blue and gold–patterned sari. She turned, and took a shuddering step forward. Then another. And another. Her eyes were empty, her movements disjointed, like her limbs were no longer hers to control.

"Do you see?" Carter asked.

The woman's jaw hung slack. Drool stained her neck and sari and mingled with curry powder, sending brown rivulets streaming down her front.

"I've seen enough," Jason answered.

Carter motioned Jason to follow. They crossed the marketplace to a rusted metal door along its periphery, a utility or storage door by the look of it. It was crisscrossed with chains and locked up, but when Carter pressed a hand to it, the chains fell to the ground with a clatter. The door swung open and cool air spilled out as Carter passed through. Jason followed, but not before glancing back to the woman. Her lifeless eyes were still fixed on him. She was still approaching.

Jason didn't need an invitation; he stepped through the doorway, felt a pop in his ears as the pressure changed, and when his eyes adjusted to the darker light, choked back a startled cry.

He was in a grand hall facing an imposing wooden ship that towered four, maybe five stories above them. It was a colossal galleon and it had been coated with some sort of varnish. It sat in the center of the chamber, and was framed at its stern by two observation levels. The ship's prow jutted majestically high above Jason's head and its masts soared even higher. He stepped to the railing ringing it and looked down to its hull another story below, lined by display cases containing artifacts, iron and wooden tools, broken clay pots, and farther back, what looked like human remains preserved and protected under glass. Tourists milled about on every level, taking photos, and gazing at the vessel's decayed majesty.

"Welcome to Stockholm, Sweden," Carter said. "This is the *Vasa*, built in 1626, the greatest ship of her day, and sunk on her maiden voyage. She was lost for three centuries, then found by chance and salvaged largely intact in 1961. The *Vasa* survived centuries underwater precisely because of where she sank: at the very spot raw sewage emptied into Stockholm harbor. That sewage killed the wood-eating bacteria that would have destroyed her in a matter of decades. Had she sunk farther out or farther in, she wouldn't be here today. Amazing, isn't she?"

"If you say so." Jason nodded, impatient. "But if there's a point to all this running around I'm dying for you to make it."

"The point, Jason, is that the *Vasa* survived precisely because of the location of her sinking. You survived because of where you grew up—in Cold Spring. To live thirty years with neither the Invisible Hand nor the Golden Dawn being aware of your existence? That is a circumstance even rarer than the collection of ones that preserved this ship. Someone should have found you and the fact we did not tells me *someone* or *something* else is at work here. It is *impossible* for a Mage to remain so hidden for so long in the mundane world; or have you forgotten what you just saw?"

Jason shook his head. Hell no; he wasn't likely to forget that, *ever*.

"That woman in Mumbai," he said. "She was Golden Dawn?"

"She was an old woman, no more, no less. But in the hands of our enemy she is a weapon, like any mundane. They used her to observe us, to see through her eyes."

"They can do that?"

"As can we. It's a valuable skill, and a rare one. There are five levels of magic: Adept, Archmage, Enchanter, War Seer, and Diabolist. Each has its own skill set; from sleight of hand and levitation to the ability to control inanimate objects and people. Attend any magic show and you'll see those illusions and more performed, but they're just that—a performance. Yet every magic trick of the stage is based on one that can be performed by—"

"Carter . . ." Jason nodded to a small tour group who had entered the museum. Most were engaged by the guide, but two, and then a third had turned to stare slack-jawed at him. One took a shuddering step forward, then the other, and the one after that.

"I see them, and they see you," said Carter. "Roughly six thousand miles separate Mumbai from Stockholm. It took them less than three minutes to reacquire us . . . to find our scent. That's how fast they move. They have agents deployed in every city, all set to one purpose: to find us, and to stop us. But let's not give them an invitation to do that. Shall we?"

He led Jason to a closed fire exit. Jason expected the alarm to sound as Carter pressed a hand to the door, but it opened without incident. As Carter disappeared through, and before Jason followed, he looked back into the Vasa Museum.

The entire tour group, and their guide, was staring blank-eyed at him.

They were standing in the atrium of what appeared to be a very large and modern hotel. At least two dozen floors rose above and encircled a common area the size of a football field. A large skylight spanned the opening in the ceiling high above and it all reminded Jason of the Guggenheim in New York; there were no elevators or stairs linking the floors together—just a ramp that started on the ground that slowly corkscrewed its way up. The only other notable feature of the atrium was a large fountain on the main floor where plumes of water propelled themselves through the air, formed heaving shapes in midair, then splashed back down. As he and Carter approached, the waters formed a single swirling column three people wide, and split off into two of equal size that circled each other like serpents waiting for the other to strike.

"You want to know *who* they are, don't you?" Carter asked, finally.

"You can throw in 'what,' 'where,' 'why,' and 'when' while you're at it," Jason said.

"The Golden Dawn is chaos to our order, the darkness to our light," a woman said from behind them. It was Allegra Sand, leaning casually against one of the atrium's support columns where she hadn't been a second before. Her eyes blazed gold and green fire as she smiled. "In layman's terms, they're very bad people who do very bad things."

"You've met Allegra Sand," said Carter. "She's one of our finest Diabolists."

"*One* of?" Allegra looked both amused and offended.

"She'll answer your questions and see you to your room."

Allegra arched a perplexed eyebrow. "Will I now?"

"Why else would you be here?"

"Actually, I came to speak to you."

"I'm here now," Carter said. He gazed at her, expectant.

Allegra didn't speak, and right away Jason knew why.

She wants to speak to him about me.

"It can wait," she said.

"It will have to," Carter said. He turned to Jason and studied him long enough for it to be uncomfortable, like there was something else he wanted to say. But in the end he made it brief.

"Training commences tomorrow. I've brought you this far; the rest is up to you. Good luck."

"Thanks, Carter, for everything."

Jason offered his hand, but Carter was already walking away. He passed behind the column Allegra was leaning against and didn't reappear on the other side.

Allegra remained there, hands tucked into the pockets of her denim jacket. She studied Jason from that vantage for a moment, and then she approached him. As she neared, the waters, which had lunged at each other a moment before, splashed back into each other and formed a swirling pillar, spitting, tearing apart, and reforming to repeat the process. As she drew near, Jason's gaze was drawn to a fishhook-shaped scar on her forehead above her left eye. She must have seen him looking because she stopped with a frown and he suddenly felt self-conscious.

"So . . . you want to know their story?" Allegra asked.

"If I'm supposed to dedicate my life to fighting them, it might be a good idea."

"You know, I asked the very same thing when I was brought here and do you know what they told me? They told me the Golden Dawn was *the enemy* and that's all I needed to know. . . ."

She must have seen the disappointment on his face because hers softened a little.

"But I can tell you what I was told by the Mage who found me and brought me here."

She sat at the fountain's edge and Jason joined her there. The pillar of water towered over them, but its movements settled, like it was waiting to hear Allegra tell her story, too.

And after a moment, she did.

"Once, long ago, there was a farmer. He was a modest man who owned a modest farm on a modest patch of land. He was an un-remarkable man, as was his wife and his young sons, but it was a good life in a time of great uncertainty. His crops grew tall; his livestock grew fat and were butchered at market for a comfortable sum. He should have been happy to live out his days there, to watch his sons grow up, and to grow old with his wife. But his mind wondered at the lands beyond the borders of his. There was a wider world out there, and he wanted more than to just be a simple farmer and a modest man.

"One day while leading a milk cow to market, he passed a fellow traveler on the road. This was a woman, old and stooped, but possessed of a great nobility. He'd heard of this woman and had heard the stories about her, that she was, in fact, a very powerful sorceress. That she had unearthly gifts that she had yet to share the secrets of. They passed each other silently, but when he got to the village, he began to ask the others about her. They confirmed she was not a woman to be trifled with; they feared her, for they, too, had heard stories, of arcane rituals and dark visitors to her humble home in the forest bordering the farmlands. But one of the villagers told the farmer that she was a devoted player of the game of chess, and in her heart longed for companionship beyond the cats and rats she kept as her pets. And as this modest, unremarkable man made his way home, he pondered this new turn. By the time he returned home, he'd hatched his plan.

"The next day the farmer sat in his workshop, and made a chessboard from an old tabletop. He carved, by hand, a complete set of chess pieces, painted them, and varnished them. Then, the day after, when this work was done and his other chores had been handed off to his wife and sons, the farmer took his chessboard and pieces and left the farm. He found a spot by the roadside beneath a gnarled oak, set the board down, set the pieces, and waited. He waited all day but the old woman did not come. He returned the next day, having again tasked his wife and sons to their work, set the board beneath the gnarled oak, and waited, and again, the woman did not come. On the third day, he again sat at the roadside beneath the gnarled oak, and waited, and was about to pack up his board when he heard footsteps approach. A figure crested the road like it had appeared there by magic. It was the old woman. He hailed her, and gestured to the chessboard and asked if she would like to play a game. The woman eyed the board—she was a lonely old woman, and hadn't much opportunity to play—and approached it.

" 'What shall we play for?' she asked.

" 'Knowledge,' the farmer told her. He was an unremarkable man but he wanted to be exceptional. He wanted to learn what she knew. He wanted to learn her ways. If he won, she would take him as her apprentice and teach him every mystery of the universe.

" 'And if you lose?' she asked.

" 'I am a fine chess player,' he told her. 'I will not lose.'

"So, the old woman took a seat across from the farmer, and made her first move. By the time the game ended, the farmer had lost, and lost handily. The woman gathered herself up and returned to the road and continued on her way and that should have ended it. But the farmer returned the next day, set his board, and waited. Again the woman came, again he issued his challenge, again, she took it, and again, he lost. Still, he returned, every day, to set his board and wait, to challenge her, to play her, and to lose. Days became weeks, weeks became months, months became years. Over time, the farmer's sons grew to manhood and left, his fields went sour, his neglected livestock died, and his wife, who had thought her husband was happy with his place in life and with her by his side, died brokenhearted when she realized it was someone else he loved.

"A decade passed, then another. The farmer grew old and stooped, his eyes weakened, and his joints ached. The oak that had shaded them had rotted and collapsed and died, and even though the old woman had remained the same age throughout all of this, she beat him again.

"Finally, after losing yet again this now very old man knocked the board aside and scattered its pieces over the ground.

" 'Enough!' he croaked. 'I have wasted my life in this wretched pursuit, I have lost everything, and for what? For what?!' He stared at his gnarled, aged hands . . . and saw with surprise that they were a younger man's hands once again. He felt his face; what had been wrinkled and sallow had tightened and was smooth. He found he could stand without the pain that had taken root in his joints. The gnarled oak tree was once again alive and well. There had been no game, no *games*. The decades that had passed for the farmer had passed in the real world in only minutes, on that very first day he had issued his challenge to the old woman.

" 'Now you know why I will not play you,' she said. 'Now you know that some secrets are not meant to be told. *Now you know where you belong.*' Then the old woman resumed her path down the road, and the farmer never saw her again.

"It should have ended then and there. The farmer should have learned his lesson. He should have returned to his farm and his old life. He should have tended his crops, and his livestock, and he should have been thankful for every aspect of his mundane existence.

"But he was not thankful; he was angry. And again, he hatched a plan. After returning to the market, he wandered past the stalls until he found one he sought; a merchant of books and parchments, a dealer of arcane amulets and protective charms, a seller of secrets. In all his previous journeys to the market, the farmer had given this stall a wide berth; there was something about its contents that had unsettled him. But on this day, he approached it, and he bargained, and after all the coin the farmer possessed was pressed into the merchant's palm, the farmer was provided with the dusty tome he sought.

"Several nights later, he returned to that place on the road with one of his goats, and walked until he reached a crossroads. He slit the animal's throat there, spilling its blood over the road and marking a place. He cut the animal open and, with its still-steaming entrails, made a circle, and inside that circle he made a symbol. He entered the circle, and waited . . . and at midnight, someone much more powerful than that old woman, and much more obliging to the farmer's request, granted his wish."

The atrium had grown uncomfortably silent. The waters behind them had stilled, like they, too, were absorbing the story Allegra just told.

"Does that answer your question?" she asked.

No, it only raises like a hundred more, Jason thought.

The threads of everything Carter had told him—about story-book characters who were very real, about schools of dark arts—had been pulled taut, but it only left more dangling. When Carter left, Jason thought he was ready for the challenge. Now he was as uncertain as he'd been about anything in his life, but it was too late to back out now.

Allegra stood and offered her hand. "I'll show you to your room."

He took her hand in his—there was a loud noise and everything went white. When his eyes readjusted, they were facing a door with *3019* on its face. Thirty stories above the atrium floor and at least thirty more between that floor and the glass ceiling high above.

"Goddammit, you could have warned me you were going to do that!"

"And spoil the surprise?"

"Am I going to be able to do that, too?"

"That is entirely up to you." She nodded to the closed door. "Fridge is stocked, cupboards are full. Get some food, get some rest. You'll need both . . . because tomorrow things get interesting."

She turned to leave. No "goodbye," no "good luck," no "welcome to the team," just someone very glad to be rid of him. He got that a lot in the mundane world. It was almost reassuring that in the Citadel, it was pretty much the same.

"Wait," he said. "When you see Carter, can you tell him something for me?"

Allegra turned back, folded her hands in front of her, and waited expectantly.

"Tell him that all my life I've had this . . . I don't know . . . *feeling* that I was meant for more. I used to think it was just that 'everybody is special' bullshit they feed you in school. I never believed it; life has a tendency to knock those delusions out of you. But was it the truth? Am I meant for something more?"

The color seemed to drain from Allegra's face. He knew that look, and he knew that feeling.

That *someone walked over my grave* one.

"We're told not to speak of it," Allegra said, "but there's a prophecy, a very ancient one, alleging that in a time of great upheaval, a savior would rise; a Chosen One to restore Balance and lead us to a victory over the Golden Dawn."

"Chosen One?" he asked. "Could I . . ."

Allegra threw her head back and laughed. The laughter echoed through the cavernous space, and it seemed to Jason he could hear other voices join the chorus. He didn't need to look in a mirror to know his face had turned a deep red. Allegra wiped her eyes and fixed them back on his.

"First lesson, genius? Prophesies are bullshit; especially Great White Savior ones. Everybody comes to this place thinking they're the next Mozart so you can imagine the disappointed look on their faces when they learn they're a Salieri at best. You're not a special snowflake; you're a recruit in a war, and while Carter may believe you have some ability I need more proof than his convictions. So whatever delusions you have, best drown them in the tub . . . *after* a shower because you stink like a third-world marketplace."

Thunder split the air and a burst of smoke clouded it. When both cleared, she was gone.

The room was nothing much to look at; it was cozy and functional, if a little impersonal. There was a bathroom; a kitchen with microwave, oven, and refrigerator; a sitting area with sofa and table and no TV. Adjacent to that was a bedroom holding a comfortable-looking king-sized bed. The fridge was stocked with food, the cupboards with dishes, and the drawers with utensils. He grabbed an apple from a fruit basket sitting on the counter, crossed over to the living room, and drew the curtains back. As he gazed out, he almost dropped the apple midbite.

There was nothing outside except a wintery blue ocean churning whitecaps beneath a chalkboard gray sky. It looked cold, like the ocean must have looked when glimpsed out an airplane window somewhere between New York and London. There was no sign of land anywhere, and the angle from his window down was so steep and so sheer he couldn't tell whether this building stood on solid ground or floated above the angry surf. A momentary vision of those dark waters rising into a tsunami to slam into his suite overcame him and he yanked the curtains shut reflexively. He closed his eyes, breathing in slowly, until warmth closed back around him.

He tossed his apple into the trash and entered the bedroom where he collapsed onto the bed. He felt electric there, lying in the dark. From burnout bartender to grieving son to potential Mage, it had been a hell of a run of days for Jason Bishop, which is why, despite already sleeping part of the day away in his old room in Cold Spring, he was again fast asleep, and the memory of that life he'd once lived was as distant as a barely remembered dream.

INTERLUDE

•••••••••••••••••••••••

JASON BISHOP'S FIRST THOUGHT, as he stared down the rusted and rickety concrete chute descending down to the Hudson, was how different the world looked from atop Murder Hill. The river was eight stories down and eighty feet away from Murder Hill's summit but it might as well have been ten times that along either track. Murky eddies churned the cool green-and-blue waters, but the rusting industrial hulk blazed heat in the summer sun and Jason could feel its heat radiate through the soles of his Chuck Taylors. His second thought was less idealistic.

What the hell am I doing?

This had been Owen's stupid idea, *his* and Jamie Hurtubese's, whom Jason didn't even *like.* But Jamie was Owen's friend, visiting from Brewer, wherever the hell *that* was, and Jason was stuck with this poseur all day as they'd skated up Main and back down it the better part of the afternoon. The Fourth of July celebrations were just getting started: cotton candy, hot dogs, ice cream, bands, music, a parade that afternoon and fireworks that night.

God, it was so *boring*.

The day had dawned hot and gotten hotter, and after having rolled past the cemetery to Foundry Brook and back, they found themselves right where they had started: the park at the river's edge just past the Hudson House Inn and the ice cream parlor, jutting out into the water like the stiff middle finger that summed up the trio's feelings about the town nicely. Some rug rats were scampering around the old Revolutionary War cannon, their parents doing their best to ignore them from the shade of the gazebo, until one kid inevitably fell and skinned a knee and then the entire place filled with shrieks and screams. Marching-band music from West Point just south of them was echoing across the waters, and that was when Jamie asked if they were just going to skate around town all day or were they going to have *fun*.

You don't like it, you can leave, dipshit, Jason had thought but hadn't spoken. In fact, he hadn't spoken much since they left Owen's. He sat there and stared at the river flowing past Cold Spring, past West Point, all the way down to New York City and the ocean beyond. Jason watched, and wished *he* could be washed out to sea, all because of Dan.

Dan, not *dad.*

Dads spent time with their kids; they didn't promise to visit, to take you to see the new *Star Wars* in Peekskill, to hit up Rye Playland and maybe even the Big Apple on your birthday. Yeah, it was his birthday yesterday; Jason Bishop, age twelve, born on the third of July. He'd hoped this year would be different, but it wasn't, and the only surprise was that Jason had thought it would be different. Things never changed, not in Cold Spring. Not for Jason.

At first Jason thought Dan had been joking. It was the long weekend and nobody *worked* on a long weekend, but apparently

Dan did. That had been his excuse to Jason over the phone; an "opportunity" up in Canada where they didn't celebrate the Fourth of July. Jason had listened, and nodded, and muttered it was all right, that they'd catch up when Dan got back, but by the time Dan apologized again because now he *really* had to go (because he *always* had to go somewhere), Jason could barely hold back his tears.

Aunt Cathryn knew what Dan had said without hearing a word; she watched as Jason tried to replace the yellowing kitchen telephone receiver in its jack as it had slipped from his trembling hand and fell to bang against the wall and bob up and down on its cord like a yo-yo. Jason had fled the kitchen before she could reach him, scooping up his board and racing outside. He'd rolled all the way down Cedar Street, past Uncle Aaron, who stopped washing his car to call after him, down to where Cedar crossed Main before he'd stopped, hunched over, and let the tears flow. By the time he was done he vowed he wouldn't waste tears on Daniel Bishop ever again.

When Owen found out about Dan's change of plans (again), he'd tried to make light of it, telling Jason the new *Star Wars* was kind of lame anyway and he wasn't missing much. But the movie wasn't the point; it was spending time with the father who never seemed to have time for Jason at all.

"C'mon, guys, we've got do *something*," Jamie whined.

"You want to do something, suggest something!" Owen said. "Otherwise you're just whining and wasting everybody's time."

Owen was looking tired of Jamie, too. Or maybe that was just his irritation at Carla Petrozzi ignoring him when they'd skated past her and her friends Libby and LeeAnn earlier. Jason allowed himself a smile at that for no reason other than that he liked the idea of Carla having zero interest in Owen. The guy had a major boner for her and Jason did, too, but Owen was his friend and there was no way Jason had a chance with her anyway. Owen was everything girls liked: handsome, outgoing, self-assured. Jason was everything girls didn't: plain, shy, and awkward. Aunt Cathryn had an affectionate tendency to call them Jim and Will, after the boys from her favorite book, *Something Wicked This Way Comes*. Jim Nightshade was dark and dangerous; Will Halloway was the "good kid," the straight and narrow one. She'd meant it as a compliment but to Jason it was an insult. Girls liked dark and dangerous, not "good" and, frankly, "boring." They liked *excitement,* something in short supply this July day.

Owen suddenly got to his feet, his board in hand, eyes gleaming mischievously as he swept sandy hair from his narrow, freckled face.

"I know what we can do." He grinned.

And now, perched atop Murder Hill, they were *doing* it.

Or more appropriately, they were *waiting* for someone else to do it.

The "it" was what had earned Murder Hill its legendary status in the scattering of towns up the Hudson. Back in the early decades of the twentieth century, McMurphy & Hiltz had been a major player in the exponential skyward growth of Manhattan, and their factory was the center of their empire, where rock was ground into powder, packed in burlap, and sent down a long steel chute to barges waiting to ferry it south. They claimed half of Manhattan was built with M & H concrete, and for a time it had been. Then it became cheaper to buy concrete from Asia and ship it across the Pacific than it was to ship it from Cold Spring, and by the early seventies McMurphy was dead, Hiltz was dead, and company had joined them. The factory had been shuttered but lingered on the river's bank like a bad memory for another decade. The other buildings had been razed, but by the early eighties, only the chute that had carried concrete to the waiting barges remained: a graffiti- and bird shit–crusted ruin that eventually drew would-be daredevils to it like flies to a turd.

Nobody knew who had been the first, but legend had it that sometime in the 1980s someone had lugged a stolen shopping cart up the unstable, rusting service stairs adjacent to the chute and set it upright at the top. Then they had climbed in and, protected by only a football helmet and some shin pads, propelled the cart and themselves eight stories and eighty feet down the rusting ramp, then catapulted off the end of the oversize slide to splash down into the swift Hudson waters. The fact this person—whoever they were—had apparently lived to tell this tale, meant the floodgates had opened and for the two decades following, "Murder Hill" had drawn the young and the foolish forth to test their nerve with bikes, shopping carts, roller skates, Rollerblades . . . and skateboards.

Jason felt like he needed tetanus shot just from gazing down the incline. It was battered and rusting and there was a dark patch midway down that was either a *darker* shade of rust or a gaping hole. What had seemed like a good idea on the ground seemed like a terrible one the higher they'd climbed. They all knew it, too, but were all too chickenshit to say it out loud. They could easily slip away, head back to town, and never speak of their failed attempt to conquer Murder Hill, and nobody would know . . . except them.

The ramp shuddered as Jamie joined them, sweat pouring off him like he'd left the tap running.

"I don't—think—this is—a good—idea—you guys," he said between gulps of air.

"It looks a lot higher than it is," said Owen.

"Really? It—looks—pretty—high!"

"That's an illusion. Besides, you said you wanted to do something exciting."

"Yeah, but . . ."

"Yeah, but *what*?

"It—looks dangerous."

Owen slapped his forehead with the palm of his hand.

"That's why they call it Murder Hill! Dangerous is the whole flippin' *point*!"

The boiling wind eased and for a moment all was silent, save for the creak of rusting iron.

"Well? Who's first?" Owen asked finally.

Jamie didn't answer. Jason didn't answer. Jason had barely spoken at all, except for saying "duck" *after* Jamie had banged his oversize melon on the edge of the NO TRESPASSING sign above the opening in the chain-link fence that cordoned off Murder Hill. That had earned a laugh from Owen and more whining from Jamie, and Jamie kept on whining.

"This was your idea!" he said.

"Yeah, and you *wanted* excitement. You want a push, just ask."

"Don't push me!" Jamie squealed and gripped the railing of the chute with his chubby hand.

"Relax, Porkins, I'm not gonna push you, Jee-zus!"

Owen shot a "can you believe this guy" look at Jason, but the vein in Owen's neck was throbbing hard. *He* wasn't going to go. Jamie sure as shit wasn't either.

If Dan had kept his promise Jason would be at the movies. He wouldn't be on top of Murder Hill, setting his Tony Hawk skateboard down, planting his sneaker on it, and steadying himself with his other foot. Gazing down the chute, he quietly gave himself even odds he'd make it to the bottom in one piece. When he factored in the likelihood he'd scratch, spill, and slice his guts open along the serrated edge of the chute, those odds dropped like his stomach. This was insane. This was doomed to failure. But that didn't stop him from rearing back, holding there, and kicking off.

He was rolling. The entire ramp shuddered as Jason crested the top, and that shudder became a screech of plastic wheels against century-old iron as he pitched down the steep incline.

Then he was dropping.

The skateboard tugged violently to the left. He angled his body, and directed his weight back into the board. It yanked to his right, to his left again, straightened, and steadied. Everything blurred as the vibrations from the metal and from the board intensified. His vertebrae banged against each other, his leg muscles tensed and tightened and tried to keep balance, but when he glanced the rust spot, his stomach clenched. It wasn't rust at all; it was a hole, gaping wide to swallow him in one piece. Rust had torn fissures into the metal, like the talons of some great beast had scraped the chute's skin. There wasn't much space between it and the right edge—two feet at most. He could angle toward that but risked broadsiding the jagged edge. If he did that, it would tear him open and the worst thing about that was it *wouldn't* kill him, not quickly enough, anyway.

As he closed the gap the choice before him opened wide: scratch now, fall back, and tear the shit out of his clothes, his skin, possibly break a limb and be hospital-bound.

He chose the second option: pray to whatever god was above and promise that he'd give anything—*anything*—to survive this. But he didn't just want to survive; he wanted to succeed.

He wanted to clear the hole, to rocket down the chute, splash safe into the river, and surface to immortality. To never be forgotten.

The Boy Who Broke Murder Hill.

The vibrations that had threatened to knock his teeth loose . . . faded. He felt himself steady, like a massive hand had grabbed him and lifted him just slightly off the chute, and glancing down it looked like his board's wheels *had* left the metal entirely. There was just the roar of wind and the thud of his racing heartbeat.

He was doing it!

He reached the hole, he bounced wheels and rose above and cleared it, landing almost unnaturally gently on the far side. He imagined he heard a triumphant whoop from further behind and up from the chute—Owen and Jamie cheering him on. Or maybe it was that voice in his head telling him he'd done it. That he was going to do it. The screech of metal against plastic broke his reverie and he rocketed down to the end of the chute.

He hit the lip of the chute and soared. The skateboard fell away beneath him. He took a breath as he hit the water. The impact struck him senseless and stars exploded in his vision, the cold seizing him as he plunged down and deep, flailing madly as the shock of the bracing water gave way to sudden panic. The swift current had him and was pulling him under and away from shore, dragging him into darkness. His skateboard tumbled past him, disappearing into the murk. He had no sense of up or down; his cargo shorts and T-shirt weighed him down, as did his sneakers. He struggled, his lungs straining, precious air escaping from his mouth. He let a burst go and watched it bubble up to the surface—

Follow the bubbles! FOLLOW THEM UP!

He kicked hard and swept his hands through the water but the current was too strong. He was being pulled from shore, pulled from safety. He was going to drown. He struggled against it but it was inevitable. His arms and legs were heavy, their weight pulling him down into the depths. One final burst of air from his lungs and that would be it.

His struggles slowed, and in the silence that followed, he heard a voice whisper—

Relax, Jason, you got this.

The water seemed to calm around him. The current weakened, and it was like he was in a swimming pool, not a powerful river. He felt himself rise, and darkness gave way to day. He saw the surface above glisten, and saw it fall to meet him. His face broke the surface. He swallowed crisp, clean air and coughed water in a rattling paroxysm. Whatever had carried him up from the depths held him steady as the swift current eddied around him. His heart pounded; his adrenaline peaked, crested, and subsided. He kicked toward the riverbank and gripped its edge, his fingers digging into the earth that broke away in wet, dirty clumps as he grasped at it.

Something grabbed his wrist. Owen's frantic face filled his vision.

"I gotcha!"

He dragged Jason up onto the riverbank and they both collapsed; Jason from his journey, Owen from his frenetic clamber down Murder Hill's rickety stairs and across its clearing to where he'd thought his friend had just signed his own death certificate. Jamie was still on those stairs, gingerly working his way down, his and Owen's skateboards clutched under a chubby arm. Jason's board was long gone, at the bottom of the river, or swept away with the current, but he didn't care. After Murder Hill, the thrill of skateboarding would *never* be the same.

"You crazy son of a bitch!" Owen slapped Jason's back. "*Never* do that to me again!"

"Next time I'll give you a warning." Jason grinned.

"Next time?! You pull that shit again the fall won't kill you—I will!" Owen laughed.

Thudding footsteps preceded Jamie's arrival. He dropped his and Owen's boards beside them.

"Jesus—Jason—are—you—you—"

"He's fine, Jamie! I mean—you *are*, right?"

Jason nodded slowly. He *was* all right. He was alive, and he'd broken the back of Murder Hill. His story was now as much a part of it as its legend was a part of Cold Spring.

Owen laughed, with relief as much as joy. He stood and offered Jason his hand. Jason took it and he was yanked up to his feet.

"We better book." Owen scooped up his board. "Too bad you lost your board. I saw it go in with you. . . ."

Jamie pointed to something on the grass. "No, it's right there."

"Bullshit, I saw it go in . . ." Jason began, but the words died in his throat.

Sure enough, his skateboard was lying on the grass at the edge of the river, glistening wet in the warm sunshine. It had gone in—Jason had seen it plummet away into the depths—but somehow it was back on dry land, and somehow, so was he.

••••••••••••••••••••••

PART TWO

DANDY IN THE UNDERWORLD

SEVEN

JASON CURSED UNDER HIS BREATH and then cursed at the top
of it for the benefit of anyone who missed it the first time; it was
his first day of Magic Spy School . . . and he overslept. He showered quickly and found a black-and-red training outfit like the
ones the other Mages had worn hanging in the closet. He donned
it quickly and found a snug pair of sneakers on the closet floor
that fit perfectly. He laced them, entered the kitchen, and grabbed
a banana from the fruit bowl.

As he swallowed the banana down, his thoughts turned back
to his dream of Murder Hill. That day had been run through his
memory so many times it had been polished to a gleam, but this
time, it had been different. This dream had played out *every*
detail with precision—like he'd been watching a movie of his own
life—right to the point he entered the water. For years after, all
he could remember was blacking out and waking on the riverbank, Owen and Jamie crouched wide-eyed over him, his skateboard beside him, his clothing sopping wet. But the memory of

being grabbed by some unseen power and being guided to safety was new. If it *had* played out like that—if he *had* wielded some sort of magic at age twelve—why *hadn't* he remembered?

He shook the memory off. There'd be time to ponder that later. He tossed the banana peel into the trash and double-timed it to the main door of his suite. He threw it open and stepped outside into what should have been the atrium . . . so when he found himself standing inside a candlelit gray stone chapel it took several moments for him to realize he'd made one hell of a wrong turn.

The chapel was medieval, like something from a monastery. Cold stone walls led down a short distance to a curved stone archway framing an altar and reliquary cross perched atop. Two sturdy iron candelabras framed that, each carrying a full complement of nine lit candles that cast flickering light and undulating shadow throughout the chapel, from the curved and domed apse, past the narrow stained-glass windows of the transept and the cold stone walls of the nave. Two sets of a dozen wooden chairs lined the center aisle before the altar. Between the chairs and Jason were two carved figures set on either side of the nave, resting on display stands and encased in Plexiglas.

Plexiglas?

He strained his eyes against the diffused candlelight. A velvet rope was drawn across the front of the chapel, cordoning the altar off. The carved figures in the first case were the Virgin Mary and her child, and the second was of some crowned king. He was in a museum, not a chapel, and when he realized *which* museum he couldn't believe it.

He was in the Cloisters; the Met's medieval art collection nestled within a reconstructed medieval abbey in Fort Tryon Park, and a short hike from The Locksmith. He was back in New

York, back in the mundane world. The how of it wasn't at issue; the where and why of it, however, was the greater concern. Carter's words of warning were as raw as his throat had been in the aftermath of Winnie's attack; if he was *outside* the Citadel's protective barrier, he was exposed to the Golden Dawn. He needed to find his way back inside before they found him; and if the jump from Mumbai to Stockholm had proven anything, it was that they *would* find him, and quickly.

He turned to head back to the double doors he'd entered through, but they had vanished, as though they'd never even been there. The doors to the chapel—outsized, ornate carved wooden ones—were replaced by a solid brick wall. Only the high arched and carved lintel remained above where the doors should have been. The side entrance that led into the rest of the museum was similarly blocked off, the doorway likewise bricked up. He was trapped like a bug in a box, and whoever had done the entrapment knew he was there the moment it sprung around him.

A human shape flitted briefly through the room, its shadow looming large amidst the other shadows cast by the candelabras. It wasn't his shadow; he hadn't moved.

Someone else was there.

He pondered his options and chose the only one available; he moved deeper into the chapel. As he got closer to the altar, he spied a heavy-looking wood door along the wall to his left. A way out of the chapel, and possibly a way back to the Citadel. He was almost to it when a pale, clenched fist materialized out of the air before him and hurtled itself into his jaw. Sharp sudden pain exploded through him and Jason reeled, stumbling and almost falling.

By the time he recovered, the fist had disappeared.

"Yer late."

It was a boy's voice, high and nasal with a Scottish burr. It seemed to come from everywhere.

Something struck the back of Jason's head. He staggered, lost balance, almost fell, then something hooked his ankle and yanked and the floor raced up to meet him. He hit *hard*.

"Rule number one: me time is precious so don't fuckin' waste it."

A teenage boy appeared out of thin air, seated atop the altar and grinning. The messy thatch of red hair atop his head was buzzed skater style and hanging casual above bright, playful eyes. He wore baggy cargo pants and sneakers, a red checkered flannel shirt was knotted around his waist, and a Dundee United T-shirt rounded out the ensemble.

He reminded Jason of himself at that age. Jason disliked him immediately.

He stood and brushed himself, attempting to salvage as much of his pride as he could gather.

"And you are . . . ?" he asked.

"The one who drew the short straw and has to train yer sorry arse."

"You? Jesus, you're just a kid!"

"Perceptive of yeh. Do any other tricks?"

"And what the hell happened to the training room?"

Derisive laughter echoed through the chapel.

"The Spire's for closers. *It's for Mages,* and y'aren't one of us."

"I'm *not* a Mage? But I thought . . . ?"

The kid sighed. "She warned me about you."

"She?"

"Your fairy godmother, you daft tit! *Allegra!* She said be

ready for a lot of doaty questions and, well, ye've delivered *them* in spades."

"But—"

"But nothing! Enough lip flap, enough questions, try an' keep up."

The kid snapped his fingers, and the candelabra to his left extinguished in a wave. By the time the candles had blown out, the kid had disappeared, too, but his voice still rang through the chapel.

"So, level one. Adept level. Now, you're probably asking yourself, 'Self, what's an Adept?' And I'm glad you did, because Adepts are highly fuckin' skilled . . . at doing this!"

A chair leapt and careened through the air. Jason dodged as it sailed past, struck the stone column behind him, and shattered to the floor.

"An' this . . ."

Two more chairs lifted into the air. Jason grasped a third and brandished it defensively as they hurtled at him. He swung at the first and shattered it and his chair simultaneously, the impact shuddering through him like Murder Hill had as he raced down its incline. The second chair broadsided him. He teetered backward, feet slipping out from under him, and falling—

Hands grasped him and held him at a forty-five degree angle off the floor.

"An' let's not forget this . . ." the kid whispered in his ear.

The kid released him and he fell to the ground. He hit hard and his nose stung—not hard enough to break, but hard enough to stoke anger into a raging fire. By the time he scrambled back to his feet, the kid was back on top of the altar, grinning, like he'd never left it.

"Adepts are your entry-level Mage. We're talkin' simple sleight of hand: makin' things disappear, making 'em reappear. We'll pick your pocket 'fore you put your wallet inside it; we're *that* good. We're also good at unlockin' things: windows, doors, vaults, ways in and out. It's all misdirection; I focus my thoughts on you, I push distraction at you. I make you think you're hearin' me in one place . . ." The kid's voice seemed to come from behind Jason, then above him, then below. ". . . when I'm someplace else. I make you think you're seein' somethin' when nothin's there. I'm not disappearing or reappearing; I'm making the mark—tha's you, dunderhead—jump at the shadows while I'm strolling out the main door."

The kid snapped a finger. Three candles on the second candelabra hissed out, leaving six remaining.

"Now, rule number two?"

He snapped his fingers again and three more went dark.

"I don't go easy on new recruits."

He snapped a third time. Two more candles sputtered out.

"Now, let's see what yer made of."

He snapped his finger a final time, and this time the kid, not the last candle, extinguished.

Jason stared at the space where the kid had been a moment before, but only found shadows. He looked to the left side of the chapel. The doorway that had been hidden when he entered before was there now. It was tantalizingly close . . .

. . . but so was the kid. He didn't need to see him to know it either.

He glanced at the remaining candle, flickering dimly. He wondered why it hadn't been extinguished as well. Then he realized . . .

Because he needs it to see me.

A thought nestled in his brain. It took root there, and grew, and finally hatched into a plan.

"First, can I ask you something?"

There was no answer.

"Come on, *one* question?"

From somewhere in the chapel, the kid sighed.

"Get on with it."

"Blind man's bluff: ever play it?"

"Aye . . ."

"Well, my friend Owen and I used to play a version of it back when we were kids."

As he backed toward the remaining candelabra, he pinched his left eye shut.

"Our version was called Guns in the Dark. We played it in the basement of my house, and at his house. Mine was better though because there was only one window and—"

"Walk down memory lane on yer own time, aye?"

That's it, get impatient . . .

"We each had a cap gun, and a penlight. The rest of the lights were off. Now the thing about our basement was with the lights off, it was *dark*. I'm talking black as pitch, even at midday, even in the middle of summer—"

"S'all fascinating, man, but I wish ye'd get to the fuckin' point already."

"The point is the only way to see each other, to mark him and make that kill shot, was to use the penlight. But we also knew the second we did that, we revealed *our* location and became a target. But if neither of us turned the light on we were safe."

"Yeah? And . . . ?"

Jason hooked his foot around the base of the candelabra and yanked. It toppled and struck the floor with a loud echoing clang of metal on stone. The last candle broke off, rolled, and extinguished, plunging the chapel into total darkness. By the time the clatter of the falling candelabra had echoed away, Jason was standing immobile, waiting to see if the kid could see him.

Waiting for him to make the first move.

And, after what must have been several minutes, the kid finally did.

"Well tha' was some sneaky shite, wasn't it? Yeh a lot smarter than ye look."

Jason hoped the kid couldn't see him or the slow smile that spread across his face. He didn't have the kid on the ropes yet but he'd evened the score. He stood as motionless he could. He breathed slowly, relaxed, and let his racing pulse settle. When it had, he opened his left eye and shut his right. It was a trick Uncle Aaron had told him to use on late-night trips to the bathroom: close an eye in the darkness and keep it closed when turning the light on. When your business was done and the light was back off, open the one you'd closed, close the one you'd opened, and your vision would be clear, if not as day, then enough to see.

The total darkness had brightened just enough to see the altar, the chairs—shattered and sitting—and the door. He didn't know if the kid's parents had taught him the same trick. The kid didn't speak, and if he was moving, Jason couldn't see him. So the kid *was* clever, or had at least assessed the situation and determined silence in this case was golden. Jason set his gaze on the door. It was a dark shape against slightly lighter shadows. It was so close, but he made no move toward it. He held still, slowed his breath, and concentrated like the kid had told him.

I'm moving toward the door.

You can see me moving toward it.

I think I've outfoxed you but you know better, don't you?

I'm just a mundane but you're a Mage and you see me and you're going to stop me.

The chapel was getting brighter. The moon in the sky above was cresting past one of the stained-glass windows. Jason was going to be exposed regardless of what he did if he didn't—

Movement. There was a glimmer of it, something moving slowly and silently as a whisper that passed through shadows that seemed to grow darker and stronger with each thud of Jason's heart.

It's him. The kid. He's on the move.

He felt the lengthening shadows cast by the moon brush against him like they were tangible . . . because they *were* tangible. He shifted slightly and sidestepped into them, then he was sinking into them and they were wrapping themselves around him. They were cold but comfortable, enveloping him like he was lying in a bathtub and allowing himself to be submerged beneath the surface. The shadows smelled familiar: dusky, rich, like an old campfire long burned out that still held some memory of flame. All around him had gone dark, until it was as if he was staring through a tunnel with a dim light at the end.

Something passed through that light.

It was the kid. He was staring directly at Jason.

"Shit," Jason *almost* said.

I'm not here, he thought.

The kid furrowed his brow.

The door.

The kid sniffed the air.

I'm at the door.

The kid stepped back.

Jason pushed his last thought at the kid with everything he had.

THE DOOR IS OPENING, I'M OPENING THE DOOR!

The kid sidestepped Jason and swung his fist at the door. It connected with a loud echoing bang so hard even Jason felt it.

"FUUUUCK!" The kid clutched his hand and winced in pain. "FUCK! FUCK! *FUUUUCK!*"

"You say *fuck* a lot, you know that?" Jason asked.

"Fuck you!" the kid said.

Jason stepped forward and felt the shadows slip off him like he'd shed a wet and heavy raincoat.

"You also talk too much; anybody ever tell you that?"

"Yeh, they tell me that a lot actually."

Jason offered his hand. "Jason Bishop."

"Kelvin Ash, at yer service. Unnerstand if I don't feel like shaking hands."

"Anything broken?" Jason asked.

Kelvin stood and shrugged. "Just me pride."

Kelvin rifled through his pockets with his good hand and pulled out a thin, slightly bent joint. He straightened it, recovered a candle, and as he lifted it, it ignited. He lit the joint, inhaled, and crossed to the still-standing candelabra and lit another candle. Flame cascaded from that one to the next one, then the next, and soon the entire candelabra was blazing warmth and casting shadows.

Kelvin sat at the foot of the altar, took a hit from his joint, and exhaled pungent smoke.

"Now then, we have ourselves a bit of a conundrum," he said. "See, I figured this to take all day, singular, if not days, plural, to figure you out. By my count, we've been here a half hour, tops . . ."

Jason realized what Kelvin was circling without saying.

"I'm a Mage?"

"Ahh, yer something, but *what* that is, is the mystery. You misdirected me, which was impressive, but it still coulda been a fluke. . . ."

Kelvin scooped an extinguished candle off the floor with his good hand, and tossed it to Jason, who caught it.

"Let's see yeh make it disappear," Kelvin said.

Jason stared incredulously at the candle. "And . . . *how* does one do that?"

"Same as moving unseen in the shadows, same as making me think I saw you goin' for the door. Yeh convinced me you were invisible by convincing yourself you *were*; now yeh need to convince me the object in your hand *isn't* in your hand. To do tha', you have to convince yourself. Do tha', an' yeh can convince anyone."

Jason clenched the candle in his hand and closed his fingers around it. He pictured it fading from view; he pictured his hand empty. He could feel its weight, its texture, and forced both from his mind. He could feel the candle melting out of sight, and could feel his hand lighten. But when he looked down, he saw with disappointment that the candle was still there.

Kelvin grinned. "Not as easy as it seems, is it?"

"Seems pretty damn impossible from where I'm standing."

Kelvin snorted. "Tha' fuckin' word. *Impossible?* Tha's what's holdin' yeh back. *Nothing's impossible* for a Mage . . . so prove it."

Jason's grip tightened on the candle. He felt his fingers soften the wax. He pictured it fading from view, and pictured his hand empty. He felt its weight, its texture, and forced them from his mind until he felt the candle disappear.

He looked down at his hand. The candle was still there.

"Dammit!" he shouted.

An angry voice in his brain told him to throw it, to throw it hard, to throw it in anger—

He did. It arced through the chapel, arced down onto the altar . . . and vanished between the air and the hard surface.

Kelvin coughed smoke and Jason staggered back, his eyes wide.

"Did I . . . just do that?" Jason asked.

"I sure as shite didn't!"

"Well, where the hell is it?"

Kelvin jabbed the joint toward Jason's hand.

He looked down. The candle was still there.

"Impossible, me arse." Kelvin grinned.

Jason held the candle aloft, let it fall flat atop his palm, and concentrated. He pictured it melting away in his hand, fading from existence. And through his hooded eyelids he watched, not with amazement, but with satisfaction when it did just that.

"Show-off," said Kelvin.

The candle reappeared. Jason blew its flame out, and tossed it to join the pile of debris on the chapel floor.

"Is there a spell that cleans this up so we don't have to?" he asked.

"Nah, it'll right itself. Shite we do in the outside world don't stick. Things revert back the way they should, like we was never there. It's why out here in the mundane, magic is still just a fairy tale."

Jason almost said *impossible*. He settled on "bullshit" instead.

"Couple weeks ago we had an epic throw down with some Golden Dawn at some gallery in Florence," Kelvin said. "There was a clash; priceless shite was *fucked* beyond repair in full view of hundreds of mundanes. You know Michelangelo's David? We decapitated *and* castrated the sad bastard when the Golden Dawn animated him—"

"Animated him?" Jason gaped.

"Aye, they can do tha'. Now we got Invisible Hand, we got Golden Dawn, and we got mundanes milling about with smartphones an' camcorders, so it was all over the news, yeah?"

Jason shook his head. If what Kelvin was saying was true, it would have made international news. The Internet alone would have had hundreds of videos uploaded within minutes.

"Go on and call it bullshit then," Kelvin continued.

"What about the bodies . . . ?" Jason asked, with no small amount of trepidation.

"Bodies?" Kelvin frowned.

"Well, you just said priceless shit got 'fucked.' You can't look me in the eye and tell me nobody was hurt."

Kelvin looked Jason in the eye, and sighed softly.

"I'll level with ye'. In this work, people die. Us . . . them, an' sometimes mundanes. There's a strict no-kill policy towards mundanes tha' both sides try an' honor, but sometimes shite just happens. Balance clears the slate an' removes all traces of magic, aye . . . but the only thing it doesn't change is death. *That's* permanent."

There was a creak of metal and a clatter of stone. Jason looked to the chapel and gaped in amazement. Everything was back the way it had been when he entered, the damage undone.

"Aye, like tha'." Kelvin grinned. "All the shite that gets obliterated resets like someone flicked a switch and the mundanes who see it forget it just as quick. Those pictures and video they record? Wiped. The ones who manage to upload somethin' magical to the Web? Hash. But there's still a tiny part of their mind that tells them something happened; they just can't remember what."

"Déjà vu . . ." said Jason. "Carter explained it to me. But that still doesn't explain how I was able to do what I just did. Before today I never . . ."

He was wrong. Before today he *had* performed magic.

Eighteen years before. At Murder Hill.

But he kept that to himself. He didn't want Kelvin or anyone to know about that.

Not yet anyway.

"There's a simple explanation for tha'," said Kelvin. "The Citadel, it's like a magic greenhouse, only instead of growing plants, it nurtures Mages. Mages feed off one another; my magic boosts yours, and vice versa. So yeh got the gift . . . but it won't come near as easy in the mundane world with distractions aplenty and with the Golden Dawn breathin' up yer arsehole."

"Then why was I able to push someone away, just by thinking it?"

Kelvin waved smoke away. "You *pushed*? Out in the mundane, you pushed?"

"Just the once." He gave Kelvin a brief recap of his battle with Winnie, and as he did Kelvin's eyes grew wider and wider.

"Jason, that's *Archmage* shite! And you did that without knowing you had any ability at all? *Nobody does that!*"

"I did," Jason said.

Kelvin stubbed the joint out in his palm.

"All right, far as I can tell, you've graduated. There's just one more thing standin' in your way."

He gestured to the entranceway behind Jason. He turned, and saw the heavy double doors had reappeared. They were closed, and waiting for him to open them.

Jason stared at them, and felt his body tense.

Here goes nothing. . . .

He approached the doors and reached for the handle but as his hand brushed the molded iron it sunk into the wood, slipping beneath the surface with a gentle ripple, and was gone.

" 'Course it wasn't gonna be tha' easy," Kelvin said. "But an Adept can unlock a door just by feelin' his way inside, by lettin' himself go in. A lock is just steel an' gears an' tailpieces an' cylinders . . . an' no lock worth its weight can stop a Mage."

Jason pressed his hand to the door where the handle was and where the locking mechanisms should still be. He held it there, and let his mind drift, like he'd sunk into the shadows earlier. He could feel something heavy and iron beneath the surface: gears and cylinders and tailpieces. He could see them, between the grains of wood, waiting for him to reach in and manipulate them. To turn the large gear, which would turn the tailpiece, which would turn the smaller gear, which would turn the cylinder and—

There was a heavy click, and the door swung open into darkness.

Kelvin applauded with a grin. Jason opened his mouth to speak, and Kelvin rolled his eyes.

"Any questions you have, someone else'll hafta answer them."

"It wasn't a question, Kelvin. It was a thank-you."

"Call me Kel," he said. Then he retreated into the shadows and was gone.

EIGHT

....

THE NEXT MORNING JASON ROSE from the deepest, most dreamless slumber of his life. There was no replay of Murder Hill, no replay of another revelatory sequence from Jason Bishop: The Early Years. His body should have ached; he should have been famished from the previous day's exertions, but there was an energy coursing through him like nothing he'd ever experienced. That energy felt supercharged, and if he raised his hands before him and stretched his fingers wide, he imagined he'd see bursts of power arc between them like on a Tesla coil.

It was no fluke. It was no accident. Carter was right.

Jason *was* a Mage. But was he just an Adept or was he something more?

That was what he was about to find out.

He'd showered, dressed, ate, and when he opened and stepped through his front door this time, he found himself striding out into an exceptionally spacious library. Iron chandeliers hung suspended from its high vaulted ceiling and the yellow light they cast gave everything an unearthly glow. Stained-glass windows lined either side on the upper levels, and the air was filled with the musty, aging-paper aroma that occurred when cracking the spine of an old hardcover. Jason used to find that smell reassuring; now, it was just unnerving.

And, of course, there were books; thousands of them on rows of shelves that filled the main floor. The second floor ringed the main on a sturdy-looking apron supported by thick and ornately carved wooden columns rising from the ground, and he could see the edges of bookshelves and rows on the floor above. It was impressive, even in comparison to the grandeur of the Athenaeum, and under normal circumstances he would have loved to peruse the shelves, uncover some dusty tome, and plunge into another world. Instead, he walked, slowly, through the space. At the far end of the main floor, a set of double doors stood, and between them and Jason was a scattering of long tables and chairs eight deep. The checkout desk sat empty in the center of the library, vacant, like the rest of it. The only sign of movement was from the dust motes swirling in the shafts of early-morning light cascading through its high soaring windows.

His gaze settled on a printed sign by the desk: IL SILENZIO NELLA BIBLIOTECA, SI PREGA.

Italy; he was somewhere in Italy. That was obvious, and the fact he'd arrived there just by opening a door didn't faze him at all; he was getting surprisingly used to the unexpected. In this new world that must have counted as *some* kind of progress. He took a moment to orient himself, and continued. His sneakers padded soft on coarse gray carpet and he listened for any corresponding footsteps but there weren't any. Yet *something* twisted in his gut, that uneasy sensation of being watched. Obviously he *wasn't* alone; this all would have been a colossal waste of time and effort if there *wasn't* a Mage there, silently studying him like he was a rat in a maze. He walked casually past the first table and from there turned toward the shelves beneath the apron, and the shadows they cast. As he stepped into them he concentrated like he had before, and felt their comforting darkness slip over him. He sunk deep into them, until everything darkened and he was staring through that elongated, shadowy tunnel again. He waited there, focusing on the sound of his slow steady breath and pulse—

Something flitted past his vision: a blur of darkness, there one moment, gone the next. He held his breath and his place, but after one torturous moment became several more, and the passage of time became indiscernible, he slowly moved himself closer to the surface to steal a glance—

Something heavy struck his forehead hard. Throbbing pain blasted through him and he staggered out of the shadows; his foot caught on something and he nearly tripped over it.

It was a book. As he stared at it, he sensed more movement and looked up in time to see another book fling itself at him. He dodged, but it clipped his ear and stung like a son of a bitch. Another hurtled past his face, then another, and another . . . and then an entire row of books launched at him. They struck his arms and legs and chest, and one cracked his kneecap with a sharp jolt. He cried out and toppled. The books swarmed and swirled into a singular mass that reared back and dropped like the hammer of god.

He raised a hand defensively . . . and the books held in midair. But it took another moment to realize he wasn't the one who'd stopped them; it was the girl who'd stepped out of the shadows of the opposite row of shelves, where she'd been the entire time.

"Y'all finished playing hide-and-seek?" she asked.

She was short, barely five feet tall, and looked to be in her early twenties. Her dark eyes were nestled beneath a darker pageboy-style haircut framing a heart-shaped, vaguely Asian face. The floating books parted as she approached and spoke with a voice that dripped Mason–Dixon honey.

"I'm Abigail Cord. And if you're done lyin' down we can get started already . . ."

He stood and brushed himself off.

"How'd you do that? Hide in the shadows? I thought only Adepts—"

The girl's gaze narrowed, like she was the magnifying glass and he was the anthill.

"Levels accumulate, hon. An Archmage has the skills of an Adept, an Enchanter has the ones of an Archmage, and a War Seer has the skills of every level before that, and *please* tell me y'understand a lick of what I'm saying?"

"No, I get it. Like belts in karate."

She applauded, slow and sarcastic. "Congratulations; it can be taught."

"Ain't you a peach," he said.

"Sweet talk will get you nowhere fast, hon. Now hush up, because I'm not repeatin' myself. An Archmage can do everything an Adept can—unlock doors, pick locks, hide in the shadows—but unlike an Adept, an Archmage can levitate objects and wield them in defense and offense. If it's not nailed down, you better believe it's a weapon." There was a flutter of pages caught in a breeze. The books hovered up off the floor and hung in the air like they were floating underwater. "Has what I said penetrated your skull deep enough to make sense?"

He nodded.

"Good. Then we'll start with a simple game of catch; you *do* know how to play catch?"

"No, but I saw someone do it on TV once." He smirked.

"Concentrate," she sighed.

Abigail released one of the books still floating in the air above them. It fell to the floor with a heavy thump and a burst of billowing dust. She released another. It struck the table with a loud thud. Another dropped, and another, then they all fell en masse. Abigail glared at Jason like he'd just dropped his pants and taken a dump on the library floor.

"You're not even *trying*!" she sighed.

"You haven't even shown me how!"

She grabbed the book off the table and threw it at him. He caught it in his hand reflexively.

"Not with your hands!"

"I keep telling you *I don't know how*!"

"You didn't know how to hide in the shadows before yesterday either." She gestured to the book he was holding. "Look at that one closely. What do you see?"

He looked at the cover; it was a lurid-looking Italian thriller called *Inferno per Collazone*. The yellow-and-black face depicted a barely clad woman cowering in the shadows from the blade of a black-gloved man in the foreground. Jason felt a twinge of revulsion just looking at it.

"A book is just molecules," she said. "Molecules comprising paper and card stock and ink and laminate. You have to dig deeper, like you did with the shadows. You controlled them; you can control this, too."

He turned the book over in his hands. He opened it and skimmed the pages. He closed it, noted its weight, and ran a hand over its cover, studying its every bend and contour. The spine was cracked, the cover was creased, white lines bisecting the vivid artwork. The paper was aged in that familiar, comforting way all old books were, the corners bent and swollen by decades of finger oils.

"Do you have it?" Abigail asked.

"Yeah, I think so." He nodded.

The book was pulled from his hand and launched itself across to a shelf a dozen feet away, slipping into a space between two others.

Abigail crossed her arms and waited.

"Prove it," she said.

He set his gaze to the shelf where the book had nestled. He could barely make out the cracked yellow-and-black spine; it was only twelve feet away but it might as well have been a mile. He focused everything he had on the book. He recalled the feel of its surface, of its every bend and contour, its cracked spine, the creases in its cover, and its aged and swollen paper. He remembered its aroma and a memory flashed past of every old bookstore he'd visited. Of tightly contained words at the turn of a page. Of endless possibilities hiding beneath a multitude of covers.

The sensation faded. He was falling backward, like he'd been suspended between the waking and sleeping worlds and the rope holding him in place frayed and broke. Only he wasn't falling, he was rising, grasping onto but losing his hold on the dream where he was a Mage.

He sighed, angry.

"Damn! I almost had it!"

He looked to Abigail, expecting to meet her disappointed face.

But she wasn't disappointed. Her eyes, which had been unimpressed the moment she'd set them on Jason Bishop, were wide with surprise.

Something was in his hand: a book, its creased spine not quite obliterating the title—*Inferno per Collazone*—in garish yellow on black.

"Even a blind hog finds an acorn now and then," she said. "Now, put it back."

He could barely hold the book; he could already feel it slipping through his fingers. He was exhausted, but in the mundane world there'd be no time to catch his breath. In the mundane world it would be life and death. He held the book flat on his palm and stared at it. It throbbed, slowly and rhythmically . . . and he realized that was because *his* pulse was thundering its signal to ripple through the book. It vibrated in synch with his heartbeat and after a moment more, it shuddered awkwardly, like a baby learning to crawl, and floated off his palm. It rose before his stunned gaze, and held there, and with his thoughts marshaled, he gently pushed at it. The book drifted back across the floor toward the shelf.

"Holy . . ." he whispered.

The book lurched and toppled to the floor with a muffled smack of paper against carpet.

"Shit," he finished.

"*Concentrate!*" Abigail snapped.

He focused on the book. He felt his mind close around it. He pictured it rising . . . and it did, lifting off the floor and up toward the shelf. It closed the distance silently, and when it was even with its place on the shelf, he pushed softly. The book brushed the ledge and almost fell, but he held on, lifted it higher, and pushed again. The book slipped into place with a whisper.

His arms fell to his sides and his legs felt ready to collapse. The book had weighed barely a pound, but lifting it and pushing it with his mind, it felt like it had weighed a hundred times that. He needed to sit. He needed to *sleep*.

"Another," Abigail said.

"Give . . . me a minute," he huffed.

"You don't have a minute!" she shouted.

The other books on the floor leapt into the air and hurtled at him. He raised his hands defensively and beat them aside before they could reach him. They fell, bouncing off tabletops, skidding across the floor, old and heavy tomes splitting spines and spilling pages everywhere.

All in a matter of seconds. All without touching them.

"Well, doesn't that beat all?" Abigail finally said.

He stared at his hands. They'd ceased their tremors. He clenched them into fists and lowered them to his sides.

"I don't get it," he said.

"What's not to get?"

He stared at her like *she* was the slow one, not him.

"How can I be so good at this when a week ago I didn't know any of it was possible?"

Abigail gazed at him with something bordering on understanding.

"Because before now you never tried. I was the same way once. Alone, afraid, unable to understand why I was different. Why I could do the *things* I did. That feeling, like there's something more? Like you're meant for more? You know what that's like, don't you?"

"I do." He nodded. "Then again, we *all* want to be Mozart, don't we?"

"I was lucky," she said. "Carter found me when I needed a friend more than anything. He showed me I wasn't the abomination my parents said I was. He showed me I *wasn't* broken. Do you know what the very worst thing in the world is, Jason? It's having a family that doesn't love you for who you are. It's believing the people who tell you you're broken and can never be fixed."

There was so much pain in her eyes he found it difficult to meet that gaze. He dropped *his* gaze to the floor and at the books lying scattered around them.

He focused, he sucked in his breath, and he slowly raised his hands.

The books lifted soundless and floated silent. He outstretched his fingers and pushed with his hands and his mind and with whatever magic had taken root in them. The books flowed through the library to their respective shelves and slid into place.

"Well, shut my mouth . . ." Abigail said.

More books pitched off the shelves. They tumbled through dull shafts of daylight, tore through the dust, and swooped back down as more pulled from both floors of the library to join the ones in the middle. They swirled slowly, pulling tighter together into the shape of a funnel cloud.

"Now, now; don't bite off more than you can chew, hon," Abigail said.

Jason stared at her with confusion.

"I'm not doing it . . ." he said. As he spoke, his breath fogged the air, which had just turned ice-cold. His skin pricked into gooseflesh, and he shivered under the sudden onset of winter.

And the look of horror on Abigail's face turned his blood colder than the library had become.

NINE

....

THE LIBRARY FILLED WITH THE sound of thousands of birds
beating their wings as the howling gale fanned the countless
pages of unknown volumes. Jason's eyes darted about in confusion and in fear, and Abigail stood rooted to the floor, staring
helpless as books tore from their shelves and hurtled past them
to join the funnel cloud gathering strength in the center, swirling and heaving like something out of a nightmare.

"What is it?" he shouted over the fluttering clamor.

Abigail didn't answer; she just stared. As Jason looked past
her, the funnel cloud altered shape, shearing off at its top and
splitting into fingers, then into an immense hand spanning the
expanse above. The fingers tightened into a fist.

It held there for a terrifying moment . . .

Then it came down.

Survival instinct tore through the animal part of Jason's brain.
He grabbed Abigail, pulled her down, and rolled them both
beneath the nearest heavy table. The hand hammered down atop

it like the fist of an angry god. The table shuddered, the floor quaked, and above the din there was a heavy crash, followed by another, and Jason realized two or more bookshelves had toppled with the impact. The hand reared back and came down harder this time. The table splintered over them, and Jason peered through the newly opened fracture to see the fist rear back to strike again. As it came down he raised his hand instinctively like he had when Winnie attacked him—

And he *PUSHED*.

The table catapulted up off the ground and slammed through the fist like a battering ram. The table continued through the air, soaring, arcing, and dropping onto the information desk with a crash barely audible amidst the howl of wind. The desk disintegrated in a maelstrom of paper and wood, brochures and pamphlets scattering to the storm. The impact rippled through the hand, which collapsed in a shower of books that rained down atop Jason and Abigail. Torn pages fluttered like bloated snowflakes and through them Jason glimpsed a human shape standing at the now open main doors at the far end of the library. He could only catch snatches of it between falling papers, but as he stared he felt the temperature plunge, and heard a woman's voice whisper close, like her lips were mere inches from his ear.

You can't run, Jason.

Her voice was unforgiving, like nails dragged across a chalkboard, like a dentist's drill grinding enamel in a mad race for his nerve endings. Through the now resuming swirl of books he saw her: a figure with pale, lifeless skin and crimson hair buffeted by an arctic wind that rose in ferocity.

There's nowhere you can go I won't find you.

A hand clasped his arm. Abigail dug her fingers in.

"We have to get out of here!" she shouted. "Stay in the shadows, stay hidden, move for the rear doors! *You can do this!*"

She jabbed a finger at a door in the rear of the library and he marked it, but when he looked back to Abigail she was gone. He glimpsed movement in the shadows of the shelves and the apron; she was slipping through the dark places to the rear of the library.

The fist had reformed and rose above Jason for another strike. Jason rolled back to the next table and rolled underneath it, and held fast as the hand came down. Just before it hit, he rolled out from under the table as the hand met it, shattering the table with blunt force and sending wooden shrapnel cascading through the library. Jason felt Abigail's hands grasp him and pull him, and he slid back across the floor until he hit a support column. He scrambled around it, dove for a pocket of shadow behind a shelf in the far corner of the main space, stood, and let the shadows swallow him.

The wind turned arctic and howled like a ravenous, living thing. Pages tore loose from scattered books, were whipped into a frenzy, and fluttered through the library like murderous crows on the hunt, and a horrible ripping noise blotted out everything but the woman's voice in his head.

You belong with us, Jason. . . .

Something heavy slammed into the shelf. It buckled and lurched and knocked books loose and he was pushed out of the shadows and into the light. He didn't need to look back to know the hand was pushing against the shelf because a second later he heard the crash, and books skidded across the floor past him. He ran; he ducked into another pool of darkness, and sunk briefly into it but more books struck him and sent him scrambling.

The rear door swung into his view and he saw Abigail dart out of shadow and throw herself into it, knocking it open and tumbling inside. Jason summoned what strength he had left and ran into the open, toward the door already swinging shut. As he reached it he glanced back to see the woman standing amidst the wreckage of the table he and Abigail had taken momentary refuge under. The books and table fragments were circling her, and her eyes blazed ice from within.

You belong with me.

She raised her hands. The books and wood and debris and detritus scattered over the library floor leapt up and gathered and collected into a spiraling cloud, then charged at him like a rattlesnake. Its head split into fingers again, but this time they weren't going to smash into him. They were going to grasp him. Capture him. Pull him away from safe harbor toward their owner.

Toward *her.*

Abigail grabbed the back of his shirt and yanked him backward. He slammed into the door, toppled through, and landed on the smooth floor and steel grating of the Ingress. The heavy steel door clanged shut just as the battering ram of books met it with a violent crash.

Abigail stood rigid, her arms outstretched, her palms flat, focusing her strength on the door pounding under the force of the attack. Jason scrambled to his feet and did the same, thrusting his hands out like Abigail's, feeling impact tremors tear through him, but focusing every thought on keeping that door closed. It bent inward as the assault intensified, the steel buckling like an anvil was striking it repeatedly from the other side.

The sound of thunder crashed so loudly and so violently Jason feared the door *had* broken, but it was a lean and athletic

South Asian man who'd appeared beside him amidst swirling smoke, arms outstretched and pushing. More thunder tore the air, and they were joined by three more Mages of varying age and ethnicity. The door flattened with a screech of rending metal. Then, there was another sonic blast and Carter Block strode forward, determination etched on his face.

"Hold the line!" he shouted.

Carter thrust his hand out to join the others. Jason could still feel the hammer of the door rolling up his forearm.

She was going to break through!

"Allegra, wherever you are—" Carter shouted.

The blast that split the air of corridor drowned out Carter's cries and disgorged Allegra, striding through the blast of smoke like an avenging angel, her right hand clenched into a fist that burned with the ferocity of the midday sun. She threw that fist into the metal door and there was a sound like two freight trains colliding. The door collapsed under the impact, splitting, and shattering, and then splintering like it was just a thin sheet of ice covering a window, heavy metal cascading to the floor with a cacophonous din that made Jason think of a car crash. The silence that fell was almost as deafening as the assault had been. But the assault had ended. They were safe.

Allegra massaged her knuckles gingerly and looked to Abigail.

"What the hell happened out there?" she asked.

Abigail stared at where the door had been moments before. She didn't speak.

"Abigail?" Carter asked.

No answer. Abigail remained silent, rigid with fear.

"Abigail, I won't ask again. . . ."

"Give her a moment!" Jason snapped.

Carter turned his gaze to Jason and stared at him, like he was willing Jason to look away.

But Jason held his ground. He wouldn't give Carter the satisfaction.

"What happened?" Carter asked, quietly this time.

"We were attacked by a woman," Jason said.

"A woman?" Carter stiffened. "Describe her."

"I only got a brief look. . . ."

"Describe her!"

"Pale skin, red hair . . ."

Allegra gazed at Jason with something he never imagined he'd see on her face.

Fear.

The woman—whoever she was—knew his name. She knew *who* he was.

But who the hell was she?

The question remained unanswered as Jason entered the atrium. Carter had dispersed Allegra and the other Mages to sound out the Ingress, to check for weak spots and close them off if need be. The Citadel was in lockdown. Carter told Jason the day had been long, that he should go back to his quarters and rest. Jason was about to insist he wasn't moving a goddamn muscle until Carter answered him, but something in the Carter's eyes told him now wasn't the time. Jason had taken the hint and made his way through the Ingress, until he realized he didn't know which door led to the atrium. In the end he chose a random door, opened it slowly and found with mild surprise that it was the right one after all.

Of course it was the right one, he'd thought. *The Citadel knows. It always knows.*

The fountain waters roiled as he approached, rising into a single column and breaking off again into two separate ones that swirled and circled each other like warring serpents.

"We call her the Red Queen."

Jason looked away to see Carter approach. The waters slunk low now, and swirled around in their tank, surging in two rings, each running counterclockwise to each other.

"She's the leader of the Golden Dawn, and she's very dangerous. She has but a singular purpose in mind: to finish what she started when she murdered your father."

For a time neither of them spoke. Like one was willing the other to break the silence. There was just the gentle ripple and splash of the fountain's waters.

Finally, Carter did. "You needn't worry yourself about it right now, Jason."

"Easy for you to say! She wasn't *after* you!"

"It's complicated . . ." Carter began.

"Really? Because it seems straightforward: she killed my father, and now she wants me!"

"It's complicated because of *who* she is. I told you that the Golden Dawn aren't born Mages. They're conjurers who learned their craft through years of study and—"

"Yeah, I know, Allegra told me the story about the chess players. *What's the complication?*"

Carter was holding something back. Circling some truth he didn't want Jason to learn, which only pissed him off more. Carter must have sensed it, too.

"The complication comes from *who* she is. She's one of us, or more appropriately, was. She's a genuine, born-and-bred Mage of the Invisible Hand, who once went by the name of Sofia Aguirre."

"*Formerly* Invisible Hand? How the hell does that work?"

"Come now, Jason, you *can't* be this naïve. You've heard of double agents? That's Sofia, a traitor, who threw in her lot with the Golden Dawn and all they hope to achieve. She long aspired to lead the Invisible Hand. When our previous leader died, she lobbied for the job and lobbied hard. She thought it was hers; she thought she had support. But in the end I was chosen, by a vote of its standing members. It was a close vote and it came down to a tiebreaker—a single vote. You needn't guess whose vote because you already know the answer."

Jason tightened his hands and dug fingernails into his palms. He was trying not to lose it but even as his nails broke skin he felt ready to explode.

"That's why she killed Damon? *Revenge* for not picking her?"

"She killed Damon because he had something she wanted.

"But why would she join *them*?"

"There's a natural order to the universe. Light and dark, good and evil, order and chaos. We stand on the side of the former, the Golden Dawn with the latter. Their goal is to sow chaos on the universe, creation—all of it. The Red Queen . . . was trying to regain entry to the Citadel; it's what she wants more than anything. That, and the item your father died to protect, the Sphere of Destiny."

"*Sphere of Destiny?*" Jason's eyes went wide.

"An object of great power, believed capable of shattering the balance between order and chaos, between the Invisible Hand and the Golden Dawn, and turning the tide of all creation in favor of whoever possesses it. I've been seeking the veracity of its whereabouts for the last week."

Jason's jaw dropped. "*You don't know where it is?*"

"We don't even know if it's *real*. There are clues to its existence, but they all dead-end—"

"*You have clues?*" Jason snorted. "Wow, for a moment I was *worried*!"

"You need to concentrate on your training, Jason. Leave the Sphere to us—"

"Damon died to keep it from her. I'd say I've earned the right."

The look on Carter's face told him the opposite.

"I explained that the Citadel is drawn together through Soft Places, where the veil between the mundane and magical worlds is at its thinnest. Our one advantage over the Golden Dawn is that we can access these places and harness their power. Entry to the Citadel is barred to any non-Mage, but the Red Queen has her people scattered across the globe, watching, searching for a way in. If only one gets inside, the devastation they could cause would be catastrophic. She believes the Sphere of Destiny is the key that can shatter those barriers and if she can find it she will use it. The Golden Dawn is chaos, pure and simple. We've been locked in a struggle with them ever since that farmer from that long-forgotten land challenged that old woman on that lonely road. Their chess game never ended; and the most powerful piece on a board is its queen."

"And now she's after me." Jason shook his head. "I wish I knew why. I'm not important or—"

Carter's gaze drifted back to Jason, like an idea had just presented itself to him, an idea so obvious it was as though Carter was amazed he hadn't considered it before.

"There is a way, Jason," he said. "And if there's an answer to be uncovered, I know just the person who can help."

TEN

THE FIRST THING HE NOTICED was the smell: sterile and anti-
septic, like everything had been soaked in bleach. It reminded
him of the last time he saw Aunt Cathryn, by then a withered
shell in a Poughkeepsie hospice bed waiting for death. That air
had been thick with ammonia tinged with the rot of her dying
lungs, seasoned by the burned-coffee smell emanating from the
reception desk down the hall. She'd been so heavily medicated
that last time he'd been relieved she didn't recognize him; all she
could do was take wet, shuddering swallows of breath as he held
her hand. He'd experienced his share of traumas since, but they
all paled in comparison to those choking rasps, the beep of
machinery, the hiss of morphine injected into her dying body. He
wasn't there when she died; he'd taken a drive through town to
clear his head, had parked, and hiked the span of the then newly
reopened Walkway Over the Hudson, traveling from the eastern
bank of the river to the western one and back again. By the time
he returned to Cathryn's room, she was gone.

The odor of *this* room was where the similarity ended. There was a hospital bed propped up forty-five degrees, its sheets mussed but empty. Medical equipment—BP and heart-rate monitors and morphine drips—were clustered around it, and across the suite sat a small lounge with a white sofa and glass coffee table. The floor was tiled white, the walls as alabaster as everything else. The dark clothing Jason wore stood out in stark relief, like a solitary exclamation point on a blank page. There were no windows; instead, there were two dozen flat-screen TVs embedded in the wall opposite the bed. Each was on and tuned to a different station from seemingly every corner of earth—news channels, all of them. Jason zeroed in on the US cable news program, where two talking heads were arguing about freedom and liberty and the Bible. Jason hadn't had much time for TV in the past months; work kept him busy enough and on days off the last thing he wanted to do was stare at a TV set. Watching the unfolding argument on that TV, Jason was more thankful than ever that he was in the Citadel and far from the cares of the mundane world.

"I wasn't really watching," a soft voice said. "You can change the channel if you like."

She was staring at him from her bed, even though he could swear she hadn't been there a moment before. But then he realized she *had* been there all along; she was just so pale she'd blended into the bed. She was small, and ageless. She could have been in her midteens; she could have been decades older judging by her voice and her watchful gaze. Her skin was almost translucent against the monochrome of the room, her scalp devoid of a single strand of hair. She depressed the morphine trigger in her tiny hand, the drugs flowed with a whisper, and she sat up.

"It's okay, I wasn't really watching either," he said.

She slipped her feet into a pair of white slippers that matched her pajamas.

"What are your thoughts on politics, Jason?" she asked.

"Someone much smarter than me called it 'showbiz for ugly people.' That about sums it up."

She climbed out of bed, grasped the IV stand, and wheeled it with her as she approached.

"I learned a word the other week," the girl said. "*Simplexity*."

"I don't know that one," Jason said.

The girl wheeled her IV to the sofa and sat with a weary sigh.

"*Simplexity* means an idea or concept that appears too complex to understand is actually much simpler. Take politics; the narrative, when you get down to brass tacks, is always simple, and always the same. One side believes the other wants to turn their country into a theocracy: women subjugated, homosexuality outlawed, immigrants rounded up and deported. The other side sees their traditions challenged, their right to self-defense taken from them, and are told that despite their considerable hardships they're 'privileged.' Both sides are told the other is the enemy and that it's *their* fault the world is the way it is. But they both miss the larger point: that those in power play to their fears to win their loyalty. Politics is conflict, conflict is drama, and drama is the narrative where everybody believes *they're* the hero."

Her radiant smile warmed the room.

"I'm Vasilisa Volkov; you're Jason Bishop. You have questions; I hope to answer them."

She nodded to the sofa and he sat down beside her. The wall of television sets clicked off in a rolling wave and then the room was silent, except for the beep and hum of medical equipment.

"That's a relief," he said. "Everyone else thinks I ask too many questions."

"That would be Allegra. Most Mages know only the Citadel

for most of their lives. They forget they were once Potentials, new to a world as fantastical as the fairy tales they once read."

"*Potentials?*" There was a term he hadn't heard before.

"People we believe who have magical abilities but are as yet untested. You've had a lifetime of experience in the mundane world, and you're bound to instill envy in the other Mages."

"Envy?" He laughed. "For what? Paying taxes? Getting—"

He stopped short.

How did she know . . . ?

"That it was Allegra who said you ask too many questions?" Vasilisa smiled warmly. "I've been called a Diviner, a Telepath, and a Medium . . . though most here call me an Oracle."

"An Oracle?" Jason's eyes widened. "Like, 'Give me your hand, I'll tell you your future'?

"No, those people are charlatans, their customers, fools. I'm a seer; one of an ancient order now all but extinct. As for what it is I do . . . there are many names for it but I have taken to calling it 'drifting,' because that best approximates the experience. To drift means to leave one's body and enter the consciousness of another to watch, to observe, to dig into memory. I cannot control the subject, but I can feel what they feel and know what they know; a first kiss, the birth of a child, the death of another. Like living a lifetime in moments—"

"Hold on—you sneak inside people's minds without permission? Just pop in, dig through their private memories without asking?!"

"When the need arises. Most often it's part of the mission debrief; I drift into the mind of whatever Mage has returned, I analyze what happened, I pick up on details they have missed in their report—" Discomfort crossed her face. She fell back into her seat and triggered her morphine. The machine hissed as the drugs flowed. After a moment she smiled weakly.

"As you can see, it takes a toll."

"On you, or on the person whose mind you just invaded?"

"Do you feel violated?"

"Hell yeah I do! I'm not sure how you're used to running your little mind games but out in the real world what you're doing is a massive invasion of privacy!"

She triggered her morphine again. The machine hissed again. She sighed with relief.

"Then I apologize. I promise I won't do it again."

Jason didn't believe her, but he wasn't there to argue the finer points of privacy. He was there for answers.

"So all this—this room, the drugs, your . . . condition. This is all from 'drifting'?" Jason couldn't hide his shock. "I thought it was something else, like—"

"Like your aunt's illness?" She smiled with sympathy. "It's not. The accumulation of a lifetime's experience ages you. Our energies are finite; soon this body will die . . . and I will find another."

Jason was so busy making sense of what she said, he thought he'd misheard. When he realized he hadn't, it hit with nearly the same force that colossal hand had brought down on the library table.

Jesus, how old is she?

"How old do I look?" she asked.

"Fourteen, maybe fifteen," he answered. "But I'm guessing you look young for your age?"

"I'm a lot older than my physical age, but may I ask *you* a question?

"You can ask."

"What do you remember of your mother?"

"Not much," he said.

Actually that was a lie, not because he remembered her but because he *didn't*. She was just a sad-eyed but smiling face in that faded photograph he'd lost years ago. When he closed his eyes he could see it, but over time the memory had faded even more. But as he struggled to recall more, he *did* remember something: a lullaby, the words a mystery, but the lilting melody she had sung was always with him. As a child he heard it in the wind, and in rain pattering against his bedroom window late at night, but that memory had faded as he'd aged. Still, it had imprinted itself long ago and he was only now remembering. But how was that possible?

Then, he remembered what Kel had told him. About the Citadel. About its power.

"The Citadel," he said, finally. "It's unlocking those memories, isn't it?"

"The Citadel *is* magic," said Vasilisa. "Magic capable of unlocking memories long-forgotten. You will find, the longer you're here, the more you will remember. But tell me, Jason; what was your first memory?"

That was an answer he knew right away. It had always been strange to him and to people he told that his first tangible memory came at only six months of age. He was in a swimming pool—an indoor one—in one of those floating foam chairs, being passed from smiling adult to smiling adult. He remembered their faces, the way the artificial light had gleamed across the clear, warm water, and that first whiff of chlorine. But more than that he remembered a sense of peace and happiness he'd never experienced since. He told Vasilisa this, which prompted another question.

"How do you know that memory is real?"

"There were pictures of it. My aunt had them in a photo album."

"Imagine having no photograph to reference," Vasilisa said. "Imagine centuries of memory lost. The mind is deep but it is not bottomless; when a new memory enters an old one departs. I've lost husbands, and wives, and children; entire lifetimes erased, like they never existed. I've lived and died, and lived more lives and more lifetimes than I can *ever* hope to remember. I am, for lack of a better word, immortal."

Jason stared at her, numb, but not because of what she told him—because of how easily he accepted it. In a place where nothing made sense, this made a surprising amount.

"So I take it Vasilisa isn't the name you were born with?"

"The name I was born with is a mystery even to me. Vasilisa Volkov, however, was a schoolgirl from Mariupol, Ukraine. She loved pop music and comic books; she wanted to be an artist, and she would have been a great one had she not contracted acute bacterial meningitis from a sinus infection and lapsed into a coma. I was there as her brain ceased to function, as her family gathered around her and wept. Then when Vasilisa was gone and her spirit departed, I slipped in and she was reborn—a miracle to her family, a medical mystery to her doctors. The celebration was short-lived, however; one sunny day several months later, Vasilisa Volkov, the 'Miracle of Mariupol,' left home for school but didn't arrive. That was three years ago; now her body is exhausted, which is why we need to get down to business quickly."

"I don't know where to begin," he said.

"Begin at the beginning."

The beginning? The beginning was so recent and so distant he could barely sort out the questions he *did* have. Obviously the Red Queen took precedent, but he had Vasilisa's full attention, and the face that next appeared in his mind drove him to the question he'd been avoiding.

"Winnie. My girlfriend. Is she alive?"

A glimmer of something crossed Vasilisa's face. Not reluctance: sympathy.

"Carter told me you might ask that. In advance of our meeting I searched. There *is* an answer. You will not like it."

His heart sank. He *knew* the answer, and took small comfort in the fact he'd already accepted it.

"She's dead, isn't she?"

"No, she isn't," Vasilisa said.

He gaped. "*She's alive?*"

Vasilisa rested a hand on his.

"Jason, *she never existed to begin with*. She was an illusion."

Jason stared at Vasilisa for so long he didn't realize his hands were shaking. He felt weak, then nauseous. He'd accepted Winnie being dead, and held out a sliver of hope she was still alive somewhere, but he hadn't been prepared for the possibility she was *never* Winnie. That she was—

"An illusion . . . ?"

"An Enchanter," Vasilisa said. "Someone who insinuated herself into your life from the moment you met."

"The moment we met?" Jason shook his head. No. This couldn't be true. This was impossible. "We met over a year ago. We lived together almost as long. She was real; she had to be real!"

"She was real, Jason; but she was *never* Winifred Hobbes."

"Then why did she keep up the charade? Why didn't she act? If the Red Queen wanted me dead why am I still alive?!"

" I don't know," Vasilisa said. "If she wanted you dead, you *would* be. If she wanted to use you as leverage against Damon and against us, she would have used you. No, the Golden Dawn kept you under their watchful eye and did nothing . . . which can only mean they need you for some other purpose. We *must* determine what that is. With your permission, I want to go into your mind. To drift through your subconsciousness, through memories you've long forgotten but remain, deep under the surface. Do I have it?"

He nodded, slowly.

"First, you need to lower those barriers you've erected around you."

"Barriers . . . ?"

"Walls. They were plain to see the moment you entered. You don't like people getting close to you, though you weren't always this afraid of them."

"I'm not afraid. . . ." He sighed.

"Of losing more people you care about? I think you are, and I don't need to be a mind reader to tell. You think setting a bulwark against others keeps you safe, when in reality it keeps you weak. Our strengths come from those we've let into our lives, not by pushing them away. People can tell this about you, and they stay away so *they* aren't the ones you hurt. That's why you're alone."

"Yeah, well, the ones who *do* get close have a nasty habit of dying on me."

"My point, brilliantly illustrated," she said. "If this is going to work, you must let me get closer to you than you've ever allowed anyone. You must let those defenses down."

Jason didn't like it: her request, or how succinctly she'd just nailed his ass to the wall. But he'd come this far already. And he *had* to know.

She held out her pale, ghostly hands. He slipped his fingers into her warm ones and breathed slowly. But his pulse still hammered.

"Relax, Jason. It's just like watching a movie, only the movie in question unfolds all around you," she said. "You will see and smell, and taste, and even touch those memories, though nobody in the memory will see you. But I will need you to picture a specific moment: a happy one if you must, but a sad one may be better. Those emotions remain raw despite the passage of time, like a broken bone that never set properly." She gave his hand a reassuring squeeze. "Close your eyes and let go. I'll do the rest."

He closed his eyes and forced away every stray thought. Soon, all he felt was Vasilisa's skin against his. His entire body felt warm, like he was no longer in a climate-controlled room but sitting on the porch of some house somewhere in the summer heat. The room seemed to brighten around them, grow warmer, and lighter. Vasilisa's hands slipped from his and left him in darkness and in silence. When they didn't return he began to worry. Had her pain become too much? He opened his eyes slowly, expecting to see her triggering her morphine.

But what he didn't expect was the face now staring at him with that familiar cocksure grin.

"Hey, kiddo," Damon said. "Long time no see."

ELEVEN

....

HEY, KIDDO. LONG TIME NO *see.*

The stock greeting. The wide smile. The rental car in the driveway, the hood still warm from the drive from JFK to Cold Spring. The gift-wrapped package—a book—under his arm. His father might as well have left the engine running. It was going to be a short visit. They were all short visits.

Hey, kiddo.

Jason sat on the front steps, staring at his sneakers, at his cargo shorts and legs tanned from outdoor life, at anything *but* Big Dan.

But he wasn't Big Dan, was he? He was Damon King, in the flesh.

It was July 3, 2002. Jason's fifteenth birthday. Three years ago he was The Boy Who Broke Murder Hill; now he was just Summer Stock Boy. Jason had been working at Uncle Aaron's garden-supply store that summer. Up at seven, on the lot by eight, done by five, though he was given today off because today was a Very Special Day. Life was barreling toward adulthood and there were few luxuries; even the White Stripes T-shirt he bought on St. Mark's earlier that summer and was wearing now was a rare treat.

Long time no see.

His father grinned, and the birthday boy offered a weak smile in return.

Vasilisa was right; it *was* like watching a movie from inside it. But it wasn't just watching; it was living in it with the full five senses and 360-degree experience. He could feel the warm breeze on his skin. Could smell Cathryn's prized lilacs in the front garden. Could hear the buzz of the Frasers' lawnmower three houses down. He could taste the copper electricity in the air that told him a storm was on the way. He was there while not actually *there* because this was memory and these were just ghosts. He wondered if these ghosts could see him. He took a creaking step toward the handrail lining the porch and rapped it with his fist. A hollow noise sounded but neither Damon nor Jason Bishop, age fifteen, looked up.

"They can't hear you," Vasilisa said.

He looked to her but it wasn't the Vasilisa he'd met in her chamber, the one knocking on death's door; this one was the model of health. Her eyes were bright, her blond hair lush and golden and shimmering in the sun. Her cheeks were full, her skin healthy. If fifteen-year-old Jason had seen Vasilisa Volkov standing there on his front porch he'd have fallen for her in a heartbeat.

"Just making sure," he said.

"You know this moment?" she asked.

"Just wait," he said. "July Fourth fireworks are about to pop a day early."

She watched silently, and so did he. But it was more than watching: it was reliving the moment in every detail. This was the day the thin thread connecting father to son had broken. Whatever fleeting moments of closeness they'd shared ended this day. They'd never be close after it, and the times they did see each other over the following fifteen years could be counted on one hand. This was the day all that ended. The birthday Jason would never forget. If Vasilisa had wanted an unhappy memory to open a door to the past, she'd found it, but Jason's gaze wasn't set on his younger self; it was set on Damon, truly *studying* his father for the first time in his life. Why hadn't Damon told him who he was, or what Jason had the potential to be? Why had he had abandoned his only child to live with two mundanes when he could have been raised in the Citadel? At twelve, he should have been beginning his training, not piloting a skateboard down Murder Hill. All the years Damon could have said something but he hadn't.

Why?

Because he didn't want you, Jason thought. *Because you were an obligation.*

"Happy birthday," said Damon. "Bet you thought I'd missed it."

"You missed the last one," Jason answered moodily, "and the one before that."

"Yeah, well, you know how it is. . . ."

"I know how it is."

Damon handed the red-and-black giftwrapped book to Jason, who took it gingerly.

"Go on, open it," Damon said.

Jason set it down. "We're opening presents after dinner. You *are* staying right?"

He knew Damon wouldn't be staying the moment he saw the car pull into the driveway but he asked anyway. His father was dressed for business, not pleasure, and definitely not for his son's fifteenth birthday party.

"I wish I could, pal. I really do, but I have a plane to catch."

"Where to this time?" Jason sighed.

"A long haul to Dubai."

Jason stood and handed the present back to Damon.

"Don't let me keep you."

"C'mon, kiddo, don't be like that! I'm really sorry! I was going to stay but—"

"Stop calling me kiddo!" Jason said. "I'm *fifteen*!"

"Okay, okay, what do you want me to call you?"

"What's the point? You never stay around long enough anyway."

"The point is you're my son and I love you—"

"You have a funny way of showing it!"

A hard wind tore across the yard, and Damon looked to Storm King looming distant. The sky above it had turned cobalt blue and dark clouds billowed around it. Jason remembered the storm—it had smashed through Cold Spring in moments, uprooting trees and downing power lines before it disappeared as quickly as it had come. The birthday celebrations held that evening were held by candlelight. Damon tried not to glance at his watch but it was clear he wanted to get out of there just as badly as Jason wanted him to leave.

"If you don't want to open it now that's fine," Damon said.

"I don't want to open it at all! Why do you even bother showing up if you won't stay?"

"If you think this has been easy for me . . ." Damon began.

"Don't act like you care!"

"I know you think I don't want to be around you but you're

wrong. When you're older, *when you're a father,* you'll understand that."

"The world already has enough crummy fathers," Jason said. "It doesn't need another."

Jason stood, crossed the porch, and stormed inside. The screen door banged shut, and then it was just Damon, alone with an unwanted birthday gift and two unseen watchers.

"What was the gift?" Vasilisa asked.

"A puzzle book," Jason said. "Stuff like sudoku, and anagrams, and crosswords. I don't know why, but he was on some sort of kick because he gave me one for that birthday, the one before that, and the one before that. But I guess they kind of stuck with me because I still buy—"

He felt a chill. Not from the approaching storm, but from a realization. Right now his fifteen-year-old self was stomping up to his room, but he and Vasilisa and Damon were still on the front porch. He looked to Vasilisa for some explanation but she looked as confused as he was.

"Why are we seeing this?" he asked. "I already left so how can this be part of my memory?"

"Because this isn't your memory," she whispered. *"It's Damon's."*

"But that's—"

"Impossible." Vasilisa nodded.

"Next time just send money," a woman's voice said.

Jason's heart skipped a beat. He steeled himself. He didn't need to look to the speaker to know who she was, and if seeing Damon alive again was a shock, this was a hundred times that.

It was his Aunt Cathryn, as she had been in life, not in the last days and weeks of that life. A petite blond wisp of a preacher's daughter turned California surfer turned legal guardian of one

Jason Bishop, age fifteen. Seeing her alive again was one thing, but God help him he could *smell* her, a rosewater scent he'd barely noticed when she *was* alive. He'd entered into this memory reluctantly, but now he didn't want to leave it. He wanted to reach out to her, to touch her, to tell her he was sorry he abandoned her at the very end. That he wasn't a better son to her or Aaron. But he couldn't reach out and he couldn't speak; he could only watch these ghosts face each other.

She descended the steps and snatched the gift from Damon.

"Look, I'm not happy about it but it has to be this way," he said. "Like I explained, my work—"

"The *heck* with your work! Your son should be your priority, not whatever it is you do! No, all you have to do is give him a present, tell him you're sorry, and then abandon him. Again."

Jason couldn't help but grin. Aunt Cathryn was still that preacher's daughter and talked like one; her vocabulary peppered with *heck*s and *gosh darn*s and *darn tootin'*s when her blood was up. And boy was it *up* now; if she called Damon a motherfucker, Jason wouldn't be one bit surprised.

"You don't understand . . ." Damon began.

"How many years do you think you have left before he shuts you out entirely? What place will you have in his life when you have so little time for him *now*?"

"It's not like that—"

"You know what would have been better? You not calling him or visiting him at all! You should have stepped out of his life when you brought him to us! That way we could have told him Aaron and I were his parents. That way he wouldn't have to deal with you at all!"

"This is what we agreed to!"

Cathryn took a reflexive step backward. The wind picked up

and the sun slipped behind the clouds cresting Storm King, like Damon's fury was responsible for it.

His voice remained hard ice.

"That's why the checks clear. That's why your mortgage gets paid. That's why your husband's business stays in the black. That's why Jason is safe; that's why *you're* safe. Everything you have, everything he has, is because of *me*."

"And . . . ? You want me to congratulate you, for doing what you promised?"

"I'd like a little bit of respect for it!"

"You don't receive respect for doing the right thing; you earn it."

"He's my son, not yours, Cathryn; never forget that."

If Damon expected her to be cowed by his words, well, he didn't know her.

"Jason has been more of a son to us than he will ever be to you," she said. "He's a kind and compassionate boy who will grow to be an even better man than his father could ever hope to be."

She threw the screen door open and stomped inside. The inside door slammed shut, and the screen door banged closed a moment after.

Damon remained, staring at the door and the house and, unknowingly, at Jason and Vasilisa.

"How can we be in Damon's memory?" Jason whispered.

"We aren't," Vasilisa said. "We're in mine. This memory was placed here for us to find, and it drew us both in."

"*Placed* here? But who could place Damon's memory inside . . . ?"

Jason trailed off. He knew, and Vasilisa knew because they

turned to stare at Damon simultaneously as he eyed the approaching storm, turned, and quickly walked back to the rental car.

The memory had been left there by Damon.

Damon climbed in behind the wheel and turned the key. The rumble cut the sound of wind whipping the trees overhead. He stared at the house one last time, then threw the car in reverse, backed out of the driveway onto Cedar Street, and drove off, alone.

"How far does this memory run?" Jason asked, as the car pulled out of sight.

"Only one way to find out."

Vasilisa grasped his hand, and there was a lurch of movement. They were surging down the street toward the taillights of the rental car as the sky darkened. Then they were inside the car, in the backseat, as Damon drove them out of Cold Spring. But he wasn't driving them away from the approaching storm.

He was driving them into it.

TWELVE

THEY DROVE IN SILENCE THROUGH the dead man's memory, and he drove angry. The scenery outside the window was a blur, unfocused and indistinct, like Damon's focus hadn't been on the road or the towns they passed through but in putting as much distance between Cold Spring and himself as possible. The journey up 9D to I-84, across the Newburgh–Beacon Bridge to 9W, and down that to Cornwall-on-Hudson and up Storm King Highway passed like a hazy, scare-remembered moment when in reality it must have taken almost an hour. The dark clouds above spread out from beyond the mountain summit, stretching dark fingers across the valley like they were searching for something. Damon accelerated, the rental negotiating the tight turns and blind curves of the highway without heed for his safety or that of any oncoming traffic. Jason had always felt uneasy when driving Storm King Highway. With the mountain face to one side, and the fieldstone barrier to the other, it always felt *too* narrow, too easy to lose control, like you were speeding through the cemetery gates in a mad dash for your own grave.

Damon's eyes weren't on the road, though; they were on the sky churning above, like he was anticipating danger coming from there, not from the road ahead.

Thunder rumbled with ominous portent. Charcoal clouds stained the sky.

"Why is he still driving?" he asked Vasilisa. "Why didn't he just use his magic? Disappear?"

Vasilisa stared out her window at the mountain face lurching closer, then further away.

"He's leading them away," she said. "Away from Cold Spring. Away from you."

"Leading who . . . ?"

The question died on his lips. He *knew* who. They were searching. *She* was searching.

Searching for him.

"Damon wanted us to see this," Vasilisa said. "He wanted *you* to see it—to know why he couldn't stay. They were looking for you even back then and he knew it. That's why he sent you to Cold Spring. That's why he could never stay, not because he didn't *want* to but because he *couldn't.*"

"But how is this even possible?" Jason asked. "How could he plant this memory in my mind and hide it there for fifteen years until you came along to unlock it? Hell, how did he know you and I would meet at all? If he was so determined to keep me away from the Invisible Hand—"

That was when Damon's car exploded.

There was no fire, no smell of gasoline, no burning metal or rubber or heat. There was just a violent lurch from fifty-five miles per hour to a full stop. Then the car broke apart, separating piece by piece, wheels from rotors, rotors from chassis, and nuts from screws, like the car had run through an assembly line in reverse as fast as the pause between two heartbeats. The car's frame lifted off its base; the console imploded in a spray of plastic and wires; gears and glass separated from their mounts and became shrapnel that bounced through the passenger compartment. The engine block dropped out beneath them and hit the ground with a heavy crash that gouged asphalt as it tore into the road.

Everything slowed to a crawl. Jason saw a shower of automotive parts drift past, gleaming in a lightning flash. He felt Vasilisa's hand close around his and before they were ejected he saw Damon, still at the wheel, his face etched in stone. He raised his hands, his seat belt unlatched itself, and then he was catapulting out of the wreckage, arcing through the air, and coming down hard and landing in a crouch. The car wreckage struck the road behind him and the mass of twisted metal roiled toward him trailing gasoline and oil. Damon pivoted and thrust his hands out, and the car struck the resultant invisible barrier. It catapulted back into the air and launched itself over Damon to come down on the road behind him, then skidded and slammed into the mountain face, dislodging rock from it and sending it clattering down upon the wreck. Heat from the engine block ignited the gasoline and oil spilled across the road and they erupted, burning bright against the dark sky and illuminating the figure that had appeared in the middle of the road.

He had been there the entire time, watching and waiting. He was young and fierce, like he'd been raised by a pack of feral wolves in some primeval forest. His hair looked like it had been hacked short with a dull knife, and there was a coal-black smear of war paint across his face that made his eyes gleam bright and angry. A sharp gust of wind fanned his duster coat as he rolled up his sleeves to expose tattooed writing up and down his forearms.

Damon stood and swept his jacket open. The object holstered inside it leapt into his hand.

It was a deck of cards.

Watching from the roadside, Jason felt the hairs on his neck stand rigid.

Damon held his ground. The attacker held his.

There was a crash of thunder and lightning that fell simultaneously. . . .

And then Damon snapped the deck open.

"*Et versus ad mortem!*" Duster shouted.

He swung his hands out, his tattoos glowing incandescent. There was a rending groan as a tree on the embankment above Duster was torn from its moorings and pitched toward the ground.

Damon threw the deck of cards into the air. They billowed into a cloud of fifty-two.

The tree launched up the road through the patch of burning oil and gasoline, igniting and sending the flaming trunk hurtling at Damon.

As the cards fluttered down, he pushed. They heaved down the road and into the tree, cutting through branches and limbs and scattering both along the ground. Damon pushed again and the burning debris exploded backward at Duster, igniting his coat and setting it alight. He screamed and flailed, and as he tried to pull his coat off, his connection to the trunk was cut. But the burning tree kept charging at Damon on its own momentum. There was a blast of smoke, and Damon reappeared on the opposite side of the road a second later to watch the tree plow into the fieldstone road guard and lay there, its flames illuminating a second figure descending from the sky like a spider dropping down a thread of webbing. Her eyes were black coals in a pale painted face, her head shaved except for a dyed and braided topknot. Her tattooed arms burned brighter than the flames beneath her.

"*Volat ignius mortem!*" she screamed.

The flames from the burning trunk leapt into the air and billowed toward Damon, spiraling like an out-of-control Roman candle. As they reached him, there was a flash of light and a loud bang, and he disappeared again as the fire roared past. He reappeared down the road, equidistant between the girl and Duster, but the girl must have anticipated that, because she screamed her command again, and the entire burning tree launched itself back at Damon.

He didn't blanch; he didn't blast out of the way; he planted his feet as the tree barreled at him, clasped his hands together, pointed them at the tree, and spread his arms wide. The flaming log split down the middle like it had slammed into the sharpened blade of an axe. One half smashed into the mountain face, and the rest crashed through the road guard and toppled down the mountainside, a clattering shower of stones trailing in its wake.

Damon was so focused on the girl and her assault he didn't see Duster had beaten the flames from his clothing, held out his palm, and whispered something. The cards that lay scattered across the ground leapt into a stack in his hand. He crouched, ready to launch them into Damon's back.

"Dad *look out!*" Jason shouted.

"*Supplementum perditio tua erunt!*" Duster roared.

The cards rose. And then, the cards flew.

Damon pivoted sharply, clenched his hands into fists, and pulled. The ground shook and heaved and pitched, and a jagged slab of granite the size of a bank safe peeled off the mountainside above them and plunged. Just before it hit the ground, Damon pushed, and the stone slab launched through the cards, batting them aside, and colliding with Duster like a boot heel onto a cockroach. He had just enough time to utter a cry before it drove him into the mountainside, smearing him into it with an explosion of blood and bone that left a wet red stain across its face.

The girl screamed in anguish, in unhinged fury, and her scream became another cry.

"Ut fiat ultio fulminis!"

She rose into the air, the scattering of debris from the car rising along with her. Lightning streaked the sky above, and as the girl swung her arms back to direct the automotive remains into Damon, he clenched his hand and pulled. The lightning blast redirected itself down and arced directly into the girl's center of mass. A blinding flash obliterated everything and a simultaneous thunderclap deafened the air one final time. When both faded, the girl was gone; only ash remained, falling like snow to mingle with the clatter of car parts pattering to the road.

Then there was silence. The storm, which had reared up from nowhere, had broken. The wind died, and the black clouds broke apart to drift lazily over the valley and finally fade away.

Jason exhaled with relief. It was over.

Damon opened his palm. The scattered playing cards launched into the air with a flutter and landed in his hand. He slid the deck back into his jacket pocket, straightened his tie, and strode over to the shattered road guard. He gazed down, across the valley to Cold Spring, and to the house at the end of Cedar Street. The house, the town, and the world seemed insignificant against the display Jason and Vasilisa had just witnessed. The expression on Damon's face—of relief, of sadness, of regret—spoke volumes before he finally *did* speak.

"Happy birthday, kiddo," he said.

Then there was a burst of smoke, and he was gone.

Bright light stung Jason's eyes and the smell of ammonia bathed his senses. Vasilisa's brow was damp with sweat. Her fingers fumbled for, found, and pumped the morphine trigger. The machine hissed, the drugs flowed. Her eyelids fluttered and she sank back into the sofa, breathing shallow. Jason moved to stand and find help when her hand brushed and grasped his. Her eyes opened and struggled to focus.

"Does . . . that answer . . . your question?" she asked, softly.

Given her condition, and what he'd just put her through, Jason felt ashamed to answer truthfully. But she'd know he was lying if he *didn't* answer honestly. He owed her the truth.

"It answers *a* question," he said. "He was trying to keep me safe. All those years I thought he didn't care, that I was an obligation. He was keeping me hidden, but for what I don't know. . . ."

Vasilisa stared through her morphine haze with disappointment.

"Because he loved you, Jason. More than anything."

Her words hit with blunt force. All he wanted to do was go back to his room and sleep for a year. He was drained, by the memory, by reliving a day he'd hoped never to even think about again. But the knowledge of what Damon had done, what he'd sacrificed? *That* hurt more than anything. His father *had* loved him, and Jason threw that love back in his face.

"A greater question remains," Vasilisa said. "What was *that* memory doing in *my* mind? I drifted into Damon's thoughts on many occasions. After a mission it's standard procedure to go in, and see what happened, and pick up on any details the agent may have missed. But somehow he planted that memory in my mind without my knowing. It had been locked away all this time, waiting for a key to open it. That key was you. He knew we'd meet one day, but that's—"

"Impossible," Jason said. "I've been using that word a lot lately."

Her grip tightened. "It's impossible because that skill is open only to someone with abilities like mine. Somebody who can read thoughts and see the past, and the future. Don't you see? Damon had that ability! He was an Oracle, and a very powerful one! Your abilities aren't as attuned yet, but in that memory I sensed a powerful concealment spell cast over Cold Spring. That spell protected you, keeping you hidden all those years—a spell cast by Damon. He didn't want the Golden Dawn or the Invisible Hand to know about you. The only person who could tell us why is Damon. . . ."

"And he's dead," finished Jason. "He wasn't much of one, though. If he was, maybe he could have predicted his own—"

The look on Vasilisa's face stopped him in his tracks.

He knew what she knew, and didn't need to drift into her mind to know it.

Damon *had* predicted it. He knew that fateful mission was going to be his last.

He knew he was going to die.

THIRTEEN

....

FOR A TIME, JASON WANDERED the Ingress without a destination. He *needed* to walk; he needed blood to flow through a brain swollen and bloated with sounds of the storm, and of Damon in his element, battling the Golden Dawn to protect the child he'd *never* abandoned at all. The walk helped, but it wasn't a cure-all, not with what he'd seen inside Vasilisa's mind, and not with what she told him after they'd returned to her room.

Someone had arrived as he was helping her back to her bed: a matronly woman in shadowy robes, like a priest's, with a high collar and stitching devoid of any markings or ornamentation. There was something familiar about her, too, something Jason couldn't quite place. Vasilisa must have sensed his thoughts because as she was being tended to she explained the woman was an Acolyte, a Potential who'd failed the tests but chosen to remain inside the Citadel as a servant.

The woman was a mundane; that's why she'd felt different. Even though he'd only been inside the Citadel and exposed to its magic for a couple of days, he was already beginning to tell the difference between a magical and a mundane person. But there was *still* something familiar about her that burrowed into his subconscious; or maybe it was some forgotten thing trying to crawl its way back out.

After Vasilisa had been tended to, Jason had decided to slip away without a word but she motioned him over.

"I need you to promise me something," she said when he joined her at her bedside.

"Anything."

She looked to the Acolyte. The woman finished checking the IV and departed as silently as she'd arrived. When she'd gone, Vasilisa fixed her gaze on Jason.

"Tell no one about what you saw; not Carter, not Allegra, not anybody. I was supposed to drift into your mind, but somehow *you* drifted into mine. I don't know how, but you did. And it's for your particular benefit that nobody else knows you possess that skill, until I can discover why. You *do* understand, don't you?"

He didn't, but he nodded anyway. She triggered her morphine and sank back into her bed. He stood with her for a moment, and should have left, but lingered.

"You want to know where they are." Vasilisa's eyes were closed. "Your aunt? Damon?"

He nodded. Vasilisa had lived and died and lived unknown lifetimes through untold centuries; she *had* to know what happened after the lights went out permanently.

"Are they in a better place?" Vasilisa opened her eyes. "I don't know, Jason. I don't know if there's a Heaven or a Hell; that's a mystery not even I have been able to solve."

． ． ．

Mysteries upon mysteries.

Damon's ability to plant a memory in an Oracle's mind. The identity of Winifred Hobbes. The Red Queen's plans for Jason. They were piling up on him, but they paled in comparison to the Big Mystery that had moved into center stage: *What was he?* An Adept? An Archmage? Or something more powerful? Those questions rattled through his subconscious for what must have been an hour before they and his walk left him spent. By the time he returned to the atrium and his room, the only thought on his mind was solitude and silence.

He unlocked his door and entered, and as he did he saw someone was there waiting for him.

"So, what did Vasilisa show you?" Carter asked.

Jason recalled Vasilisa's warning, but there was something *else* that told him not to trust Carter.

"She told me to keep it secret," he said. "Private stuff, you know."

"You're quite full of surprises," Carter said. "I anticipated it would take weeks for you to master the Adept level, let alone the Archmage one, and you did both in two days."

"I wouldn't say I *mastered* them. Hitting a couple line drives doesn't make me Babe Ruth."

"That's quite humble for a Mage," Carter said.

Jason stared, uneasily, at Carter. Something wasn't right.

"Something the matter?" Carter asked.

Jason kept staring. Something *was* the matter. And what was more surprising was that he realized exactly *what* that was.

"You're not Carter," he said.

Carter smiled and as he did his face rippled, like a wave had washed over it. His skin lightened; his hair lengthened and turned blond. His body lessened in heft and stature, and shifted silently into a smaller woman with light, almost elven features and eyes as warm as a polar vortex. There was something else: an old and worn scar that ran from below her right nostril through the corner of her mouth to her chin, like she'd been bitten by a ravenous dog as a child and that scar had grown with her. There was also something about her Jason didn't like; nothing he could articulate, just *something*. He'd mastered that quick read from years of bartending: who'd be pleasant, who'd be a handful, who'd be a lousy tipper. Maybe it was the way she was staring at him, like she had quietly judged everything about him and found *everything* lacking.

"How did you know I wasn't Carter?" she asked. Her voice had a cool, crisp Scandinavian lilt.

"You don't smell like him," Jason said. "He smells like aftershave."

"And what do I smell like?"

"Like winter," he said. "Let me guess; you're an Enchanter, right?"

She bowed, smartly.

"Katja Eis, at your service. They said you ask many questions."

"Did they also tell you I'm a quick study?"

She shook her head.

"Well, you can tell Carter you checked in. Thanks for the conversation."

She sighed. Clearly she was as thrilled to be there as he was to have her.

"Carter asked me to escort you," she said.

"To . . . ?

"And spoil the surprise?"

"I've had enough surprises for the last few days. Pleasant, unpleasant . . ."

"You will like this one," she said. A statement of fact, but no smile accompanied it.

"Do I have a choice?"

"You always have a choice. Stay. Follow. That's the choice."

He wanted to stay; he was exhausted, but there was something about Katja that made him want to go. Probably because he knew that would annoy her.

"Ladies first," he said.

They trod the Ingress in silence. The halogens hummed, and the mesh flooring clattered beneath them. They passed the empty spot where the door to the library had been and Jason felt a chill. The Red Queen. She was still out there, and she was still searching.

Searching for a way into the Citadel. *Searching for him.*

As they walked, he contemplated his escort. There was something off about Katja that he couldn't read but when he let her enter his peripheral and concentrated, he realized it was because he couldn't read her *at all*. She was a blank slate: cold, detached, both beside him and a thousand miles away. While he was sure she was happy to keep any tête-à-tête brief, he wanted to know: "How does it work? Enchanting?"

Katja continued in silence for several more steps before answering. "An Enchanter possesses the ability to control the will of others. To make them see what we want them to see: a friend, a confidant, a lover. We wield these enchantments to manipulate the minds of the easily led. A good Enchanter will tip the balance where a War Seer or Diabolist will not. Subterfuge is our weapon—"

She shimmered and faded. Her footsteps became heavier, her face darker, and her body taller, and it was now Carter Block walking beside Jason.

"And I am an exceptional Enchanter," "Carter" said. "Though I prefer the feminine designate."

Carter's visage shifted again, this time into "Allegra." The illusion was perfect, right down to the fishhook-shaped scar above her left eye.

"Enchanting builds on the Archmage and Adept levels. It's the same principle as levitating objects, and hiding in the shadows, only in an Enchanter's case your plaything is a living, breathing person with fears and desires. But it's not as easy as a casual glance on the street—you must *know* the person you're imitating. How they look, how they speak—the intimate details of their lives that you can build layers of deception upon, like a grain of sand becoming a pearl."

She shifted again . . . into "Jason." The ease of her transformation and its accuracy was unsettling. She'd mastered his appearance and his body language in only the minutes they'd faced each other.

"I'm impressed" was all he could stammer.

She shifted back into Katja. "Now, may I ask you a question?"

"You can ask."

"I want to know about Winifred Hobbes."

"Winnie?" Jason furrowed his brow. "Why do you want to know about *her*?"

"Carter told me you and she were together for well over a year? To maintain such an illusion for so long takes—"

"I know, I know," he sighed. "She was an exceptional Enchanter of great skill. Pardon my French, but it's still kind of a raw wound, okay?"

"It will help, to know what we're up against. . . ."

He didn't want to tell her anything, frankly, but he knew she wouldn't take no for an answer. He also knew he had to put what had happened behind him, because the small nagging thought telling him not to trust Katja was also telling him he'd have to face Winnie, whoever she was, again.

"It was a private party," he began. "Back when I was doing the bartending thing but before I started at The Locksmith—that was where I was working when Carter—"

"Did I ask about Carter?"

He side-eyed her. She stared back, expectant.

Yeah, he *really* didn't like Katja Eis.

"Anyway, Francisco—this guy I worked with at Traders, which is a bar on Wall Street—got us a one-off job pouring drinks at one of those fancy Upper East Side soirees. You know, the type where rich assholes invite other rich assholes to support their latest cause du jour? Lots of rich assholes, in other words. Oh, and rich assholes? They're really shitty tippers, if you must know."

Katja didn't answer. She just nodded and kept her pace.

"Anyway, Francisco and I spent the night switching off, one of us with a tray of Krug, the other tending bar. Back and forth, just like that. Anyway I was on tray duty, I made my rounds everywhere in this huge fifteen-room penthouse, making sure everyone and their checkbooks were well lubricated. I glanced into the library, just to make sure everyone was looked after . . . and she was just there, like she was waiting for me the whole time."

"What was she doing?" Katja asked.

"Sitting in a black wingback chair, flipping through an art book. I was going to leave her alone but then she asked me if the party sucked as much as she thought it did. Turns out she wasn't even a guest; she was there because the owners wanted to spruce the place up for their fund-raiser. The entire penthouse was full of art, you see, but it turns out every single piece was on loan. She was an art dealer, she said, working for some firm that hunts down expensive paintings for one-percenters to buy and lock away in a vault, to appreciate in value. These were rentals, you see, and it fell on her to select a range from those vaults her employers managed, to see that they were shipped to the penthouse, and set in place. When the party was over, she'd take them down, pack them up, and have them sent back to their respective vaults to resume dust-gathering. I don't know how long we talked, about art, about living in New York, but I had to get back to work. We said our goodbyes, and she gave me her card. We had our first date at the Met and it was—"

"Magic," finished Katja.

She was right; it *had* been. Those first weeks and months of their relationship had passed like one of those dreams where everything was bathed golden, like a midsummer's sun on clean water. If anything, what should have been a happy memory just made Jason sadder.

"But if she was a fake, why the enchantment?" Jason asked. "Why conjure Winnie out of thin air when they could have just sent anyone?"

Katja's hand drifted up to her cheek and gently touched the scarred, torn corner of her lip, before she lowered it. They walked in silence for nearly a minute before she finally answered.

"Because shedding one's skin is the easy part. The emotional connection, the scars, last much longer. For an Enchanter, creating an illusion is as much a survival mechanism for them as it is an act of subterfuge; it's much easier to shed *that* skin than to live in your own."

If he was hoping for any sympathy from Katja, she wasn't offering it. Instead, she stopped before a door with an ornate carved wooden face, opened it, and nodded him inside.

It was a large room the size of a spacious assembly hall. Chairs and sofas were arranged throughout, a row of glass-enclosed refrigerators containing food and drinks stood behind a long counter lining one wall, and the pleasant aroma of freshly brewed coffee lingered in the air. There even looked to be a fully stocked bar farther down. Rows of pool and game tables stretched down to the far end where a fireplace blazed soothing blue fire. Through windows lining the wall to the right sat an Olympic-sized swimming pool. Jason watched a bathing-suited woman stride out onto a diving board, dive, and jackknife into the water with barely a ripple. She broke the surface and propelled herself up into the air with lunging sweeps and strong kicks. She arced into another dive and plunged back into the water. Back in the main room, Mages lounged, read, shot pool, and ate. Jason saw Abigail seated at a table playing what looked like three simultaneous games of solitaire by maneuvering the cards with her mind. At a table across from her, two older Mages played chess, moving the pieces without touching them. He saw Kel at a pool table chalking a cue.

"What is this?" he asked. "It looks like a resort."

"That's because it is," Katja said. "Rest and relaxation are important to a Mage, especially after a mission. If all one does is train and fight, you *will* crash hard and be no use to anyone. You are welcome here; I suggest you take advantage of it."

He nodded. "So when do I begin Enchanter training?"

Katja frowned. "I'm sorry . . . ?"

"Well, I aced the Adept and Archmage levels, so I figured we were going to see if—"

"If you have the skills of an Enchanter?" Katja's gaze narrowed. "To become an Enchanter takes years of study. You cannot ace it, not in a day, or a week, or a month. You would be better use to us by whetting the abilities you *do* have, before attempting to master ones you do not!"

"I'm sorry," he said. "I didn't mean to offend you. . . ."

"Knowing when to keep your mouth shut is a valuable skill; you should try studying that."

She didn't give Jason the chance to respond. Without further word she strode away, passed back through the main door, and then she was gone.

"Don't mind her," said Kel. "She's been a wee bit touchy ever since that girl from Kansas dropped a house on her sister."

"Enchanters spend so much time pretending to be someone else they lose all sense of who they are," Abigail chimed in. "That's why there aren't a lot of them; most Mages who can enchant move on to become War Seers and Diabolists."

"I take it she's been an Enchanter for a while?" Jason asked.

"Oldest an' most experienced," said Kel. "Just back from a long con, I hear, deep-cover assignment. Long cons take a lot outta you; lesser Enchanters crack under the strain."

"The rest become like our Miss Eis," said Abigail with a grin. "They become assholes."

"Think fast!" Kel shouted.

The cue ball was soaring at Jason's head before Kel's warning had finished. He caught it reflexively without touching it and it hung there in the air between him and Kel, spinning in place.

"Been practicin', have ye?" Kel grinned.

Jason focused on the ball, on its cool, smooth surface, and pictured its weight.

Then he pushed. It arced back to the pool table, crested down, and struck the balls Kel had finished racking. They scattered, and two stripes sunk with a hollow, satisfying sound.

"I'm a hell of a pool player, too," Jason said. "Now, if you're done playing with yourself, you mind racking them back up so we can have a game?

"Smartarse," said Kel.

Jason couldn't help the grin that stretched across his face. For the first time since arriving in the Citadel, and even longer than that, he felt like he *truly* belonged.

Like he'd *finally* found his way home.

FOURTEEN

....

AFTER CONQUERING MURDER HILL, JASON Bishop, age twelve, had known there'd be a reckoning once word got out, and he was right. By the time he'd returned home, clothes still sopping from his plunge, Aunt Cathryn knew *everything*. How she knew remained a mystery, but his punishment came quickly, as if she had it planned the moment word of his exploits reached her ears. After exile to his room without dinner, and a heated downstairs discussion between husband and wife that Jason could hear through his floorboards, it was Uncle Aaron who'd roused him at dawn the next day with his orders. The firing squad had been put on standby; Jason had instead reported to duty in the backyard before the sun had brightened the sky. A wet spring had resulted in basement flooding, and Aaron had said time and again he needed to deepen a drainage trough so the water ran downhill, not down the basement stairs. That had been Jason's job: to dig. And that was his punishment.

It had taken months. Day in, day out, no time for summer, no time for friends, no time for Owen, who had begun his long courtship of Carla Petrozzi in Jason's absence. Whenever he made progress, his uncle pulled him off the job to aid with some other task: helping at the store, repainting the back deck, clearing heavy, water-damaged boxes out of the basement. Progress on the trough became measured in inches. His uncle called it "the necessary drudgery of routine" and by the time it was done mere days before school resumed, Jason had learned his lesson.

He'd hated his aunt and uncle for ruining what was already a terrible summer, but now, more than anything, he wished he could thank them, because that necessary drudgery of routine was shaping him into a skilled Archmage.

After Kel had "whooped his arse" at the pool table four games out of five, Jason slunk back to his room with his tail between his legs. But he didn't return alone; once he was inside, he took the deck of playing cards he'd borrowed from the games room and set it on the table. With the memory of how Damon wielded a similar deck of cards to lethal effect on Storm King still fresh, he did as Uncle Aaron had showed him: he dug that trough, and he dug it deep.

He'd never been much of a card player, always finding some excuse to decline invitations to post-work poker games and bridge with his aunt. So when he took the deck in hand and began to shuffle, half the cards ended up scattered across the floor and table. He recovered them and shuffled again, slowly and awkwardly, one over the other, folding them into the deck, slipping them back out. He knew how to shuffle, to weave, and to fold, but fluidity of movement was elusive, and wasn't the point; *knowing* every card in the deck was. By their touch, by the sound of them slapping against each other, by the paper cuts that stung his fingertips when he lost focus. His blood traced the edges of the deck, seeping into the cards, marking each of them and making them a part of him. He practiced until staying awake became impossible, then he slept, and when he awoke the next day he resumed that necessary drudgery.

But he wasn't completely alone; when the day's training was done, he pocketed his deck and left for the games room, where he rested and resumed his ongoing battle with Kelvin for supremacy of the pool table, and by the end of the first week he'd evened the score, winning half the games played.

For the first time in a very long time he felt he belonged. For too long he'd been looking backward at what might have been, and now he found he could look ahead to a future of endless possibilities. Even the looming sense of unease at what would happen when he was *finally* sent on his first mission filled him with anticipation, not dread. At night, he forced himself down into sleep just so he could kick-start the next day's activities that much sooner.

He swam in the pool, and he lifted weights in the adjacent gymnasium. Muscles that had gone soft from years of neglect tightened, and he painfully rediscovered others he'd forgotten. He set a schedule and stuck with it; he rose, showered, ate, did a round of push-ups and sit-ups to get his blood pumping, then he practiced. As his first week in the Citadel rolled into the second that routine never changed; in fact, it intensified, with more of it performed without use of his hands. He opened drawers without touching them, turned faucets on and off with a thought, locked his suite door behind him without a key. He even made his meals without laying physical hands on a single ingredient. His practice never ceased except in the evenings when he went to the games room to play Kel, and then he returned to his rooms to crash and resume the routine the next day and the days that followed.

Then, when he'd mastered the cards to the point he could identify each of them by touch, he sat, hands folded, and shuffled the deck. He made them split, fold, split, fan, and slide across the table, diamonds to diamonds, spades to spades, hearts to hearts, clubs to clubs, reds to blacks. Like Abigail's game, his was solitary: his deck, his mind, *his* magic. He felt his brain and body rewiring itself, jettisoning the old and embracing the new. Then, two weeks after Katja Eis brought him to the games room, he levitated an apple from the fruit bowl on the kitchen counter and lowered his gaze to the card deck on the coffee table, breathed in, breathed out, and he *pushed*.

A card leapt from the deck, sailed at the apple, and sliced through it at its radius. The card and the bottom half of the apple fell away, bouncing off the counter and onto to the tiled floor. The top half held in the air and, after a moment, lowered and gently settled on the counter. He felt his mind take the card and yank it back. It fluttered back through the air and settled atop the deck, sticky pulp coating the face of the Queen of Hearts.

The Red Queen.

Jason smiled, but there was no joy in it, and no warmth, just a promise he uttered silently.

The next card's for you. I'm going to bury it in your goddamn neck.

There was no sign of Kel when Jason arrived in the games room that evening, so he racked up the balls alone and was chalking his cue in anticipation of his arrival when Clas Guld spoke to him directly, a first for the studious Dane.

"Kelvin is on a mission," he said, not looking up from his chessboard.

He'd met the Archmage and his fellow War Seer, a Somali named Barkhad Biyaha, the previous week. They'd been playing chess then, and they played it now, Clas wrinkling his nose in distaste as Barkhad stuffed a wad of sharp-smelling khat into his mouth to join the one already there.

"How long will he be gone?" Jason asked.

"Until the mission is completed," Clas answered. He didn't look up.

Jason set the cue down. He shouldn't have been surprised. He remembered what Vasilisa had said, that the other Mages had practically grown up inside the Citadel, whereas he'd had a lifetime of experience outside it. While all of them were polite enough, he knew what they were thinking, because the Citadel had unlocked another memory he'd buried long ago.

Buck "Buick" McCain had been a summer hire at Uncle Aaron's gardening center the year Jason graduated. Buck was a long-haired, mustached guy in his late thirties who'd acid-washed himself out of high school sometime in the early eighties and drifted aimlessly through his twenties, eventually ending up in Cold Spring. Buck was there to study for his GED, to finally get that diploma he bailed on the first time, to make something of what remained of his life. Buck had made his case to Uncle Aaron, who had listened patiently, and to the surprise of Jason, who had been eavesdropping, Aaron hired Buck on.

Buck had been comically out of step with the times; the worn cutoffs and ratty Journey T shirt he wore daily marked him as an also-ran. He'd been friendly enough, telling the other summer help—college kids, or soon to be—to call him "Buick—like the T. Rex song," which made him even more of an anachronism and earned him the nickname "Buick McLame." Buick had laughed it off; he'd known it would come with the territory, but it still stung. Jason had learned this when he saw Buick at the ice cream parlor down by the Hudson House Inn on a Saturday evening a few weeks later, when Cold Spring's Oldest GED had been there with his plump wife and their frizzy-haired preschool daughter. Buick had seen Jason and Jason had seen Buick, and in that single glance the older man had pleaded, *Please, not in front of them*.

Jason hadn't joked, not then, and not after. Buck had been trying to make a life for himself and his family. He'd been making up for past mistakes, and who could laugh at that and still look at themselves in the mirror? Come September Jason had handed in his resignation and moved on to flail through and ultimately fail college. Whether Buck had stayed on after that summer Jason never knew; he never saw the guy again and never asked Aaron what had become of him. But he knew now what it must have felt to *be* him. To see people half his age and twice as skilled judge his every move.

They couldn't *wait* to see him fall flat on his face, and he didn't need to be an Oracle to—

Something exploded into the room in an eruption of thunder. The attacker was clad head to toe in black, the hood of their jacket pulled low. Something heavy and unseen crashed into Jason's chest and sent him reeling and toppling backward over the pool table and landing hard. The attacker thrust aggressive hands out, and Jason thrust back with his. The air slammed between them with a sonic boom, the attacker was knocked back, and by the time Jason was back on his feet, the attacker had recovered, raised the chairs scattered about, and let them all fly.

Jason focused on the pool table and clenched his hands around it. The table leapt off the ground and smashed through the chairs, sending everything slamming to the floor. The attacker bounded over the debris, thrust out their hands, and threw fire at Jason. He felt the flames lick his face, but there was no heat—they were an enchantment. He lifted a hand and pitched another chair at the attacker, who shattered it to jagged splinters with a clap of the hands and redirected them. Jason pivoted and sent the shrapnel spraying into the recessed lights above. There was a shatter of glass as they burst and Jason slipped into the shadows and sunk deep into them. The attacker leapt forward, disappeared, and reappeared in front of Jason, who leapt from the shadows and snatched his assailant in a chokehold and applied pressure.

He could use magic, but breaking the attacker's neck would be a lot more satisfying . . .

"All right, uncle . . . UNCLE!" the attacker shouted.

"*ENOUGH!*" a voice thundered.

Jason felt his hands yanked off the attacker, who stumbled forward, his hoodie slipping to reveal Teo Stone's contrite face, as Allegra stormed into the room, fire blazing in her eyes.

"Are you two quite finished?" she snapped.

"It's all right, marm," Teo said. "I was just makin' sure he's been practicin'."

"Christ, you could have just asked!" Jason said.

"Teo, what's the rule?" Allegra asked.

"We don't talk about Fight Club?"

"*The rule,* Teo."

Teo sighed. "No fighting in the games room. C'mon, marm, we was just 'avin' a go."

"Don't make me tell Carter."

That threat, implied or otherwise, chilled Teo. He nodded, apologetic, and looked at Jason innocently, like they hadn't just wrecked half of the games room.

"Heard you was making waves. Had to see for myself. Archmage, yeah?"

"So it seems," said Jason.

"We'll see about that. Up for a little fun?"

"If by fun you mean this . . ." Jason nodded to the wreckage surrounding them.

"I'm thinking an excursion. A field trip, yeah?"

"Everybody's on lockdown, Teo," said Allegra. "Carter's orders. With the Golden Dawn on the offensive . . ."

"Yeah, well, Carter's not 'ere, is he?"

Allegra's gaze narrowed. Teo sighed.

"All right, marm. Plenty trouble we can get up to in here."

"*No*," said Allegra. "*No* trouble. *No* messing around."

"Lemme guess: Carter's orders?"

"Mine." A cloudburst hammered the air. When it cleared, she was gone.

"Oh, she likes you, Jason," Teo said. "You're the bee's knees, as they say."

"I'd hate to see her around people she really dislikes."

"You got a lot to learn about women, doncha?"

"I'm like, ten years older than you, you know," Jason protested.

"Thanks for making my point for me."

Teo glanced up the games room and back down it, like he was making doubly sure Allegra wasn't there.

"I think she's gone," he said. "This place is a damp squib; wanna go stir up some shite?"

"What, leave the games room?"

"No . . ." Teo lowered his voice. "The Citadel."

Jason frowned. "But Allegra said we were—"

"On lockdown?" Teo grinned mischievously. "Yeah, I heard that, too."

FIFTEEN

THE AIR STUNK OF BURNED plastic, a sickly sweet scent that reminded Jason of the crackheads who darkened the doorstep of the shitty Alphabet City walk-up where he first lived in New York. The fact he'd remained there for three years was more a testament to his own entropy than any defiance, but it all came rushing back with that first familiar whiff. The stench intensified when Teo pushed a rusted service door open with a screech and they stepped from darkness into a trash-strewn concrete tunnel.

"You take me to the best places," Jason said. "Is the contact high a perk?"

"We need to keep down low, not attract attention, out here or in the Citadel," said Teo. "Carter don't know about me little back door, an' I'd like to keep it that way. See 'ere?"

He pointed to a small *T* carved into the brick beside the door.

"That's the key. Picture this mark on this door in the Citadel, and you'll find yourself here. Put the Citadel in your mind when you open this one back up and you're back there, easy peasy."

Teo led them up the tunnel to a set of crumbling concrete steps. They climbed those quickly and found themselves at the edge of a barren plot of ground flecked with dead and dying patches of grass caking the surface like clumps of psoriasis. Piss-yellow halogen blanketed the area and drew Jason's gaze to a fifteen-story slab of concrete that resembled a hunk of moldy cheese. The flickering lights of TV sets through windows were the only signs of human habitation.

"Welcome to Peckham." Teo led Jason across the diseased grass. "The 'hood, not the tower. Tower's called Elysian Fields, which were either some lofty promise or a sick joke, I dunno which."

"This is *England*?"

"This is the rough part of it; Peckham, to be precise," Teo said. "What, you pictured something else?"

"I didn't picture *this*."

"Like I said, this is a back door. If any Golden Dawn *are* sniffin' about, this is the last place they'll look. We hustle to the tube we'll be in central London in no time. I just need to check in on something first."

A pile of smashed shopping carts greeted them at the entrance to the tower. The door was ajar, the lock broken, and Teo opened it. They entered the hallway. Stale fluorescents flickered above, and that piss smell was worse than it was where they entered. They walked the cracked linoleum corridor in momentary silence.

"If we do get into trouble, how do we get out?" Jason asked.

"Cross that bridge when we come to it." Teo shrugged.

Jason's thoughts settled on the deck of cards in his jacket pocket. He'd use them if he had to, but could he use them to lethal effect? That was another test he had yet to face.

"Teo, you're a War Seer, right?" he asked, after a moment.

Teo nodded coolly. "War Seer. Assassin. Jack of All the Fucking Trades . . ."

"If you're that good why not go all the way? Why not be a Diabolist?"

Teo chewed it over as they continued down the corridor.

"Typically we send out five-Mage teams; ideally, one from each level. You want an Adept to perform the simple mechanical stuff and get you in. Your Archmage, they're your line of defense because the best of 'em 'ave ice water runnin' through their veins. Your Enchanter confounds an' confuses the opposition; they're the subterfuge. The War Seer . . . ?"

"Jack of All the Fucking Trades, right?" Jason said.

"So you 'ave been listening. As I said, when things get fucked, you want at least one of us watchin' yer backside."

"And the Diabolist?"

"Diabolist assembles the team, they call the shots, an' they're the ones who eat shite when everything goes tits up. I don't need that kind of responsibility; War Seer's where all the fun is."

They passed through a large central airshaft and as they reached the elevator doors at the opposite side, Teo grabbed Jason's wrist and winked.

"No elevators. We're takin' the express."

There was a thunderclap and a flash of light, and Jason staggered and hit a concrete abutment. He looked down the face of the building, plunging twelve stories below.

"Jesus!" he hollered. "Give me a warning next time!"

"Beats an elevator ride, don't it?" Teo said. "If you're worried about Golden Dawn twiggin' to us, don't. We're safe, from them anyways."

"You mean there's someone *else* we need to be afraid of?"

"Peckham Boys; this is their turf. Nothing two Mages can't handle, but the more we use magic out in the mundane, the sooner the real threat'll twig to us."

They continued down the corridor, which was cleaner than the lobby, but not by much. A long concrete abutment lined the way down, and the view that stretched out from there revealed a landscape dotted with even more bleak and depressing tower flats.

"So how does it work; you called it 'blinking'?" Jason asked.

"You can call it what you want: teleportation, transmission . . . I just call it 'blinking' as in 'the blink of an eye.' Like your basic Archmage stuff, only you aren't pulling things toward you or directing them away; you're focusing on a solid point on the grid, up, down, left, right—it don't matter which—and *pulling yourself* toward it. To anyone watchin' it 'appens so fast it looks like you've disappeared one place an' reappeared another. But for you it's continuous, and it needs to be continuous—you need to keep your eye on the ball. You don't, you'll wind up stuck in a wall, or impaled on something sharp and nasty and that's it for you."

"Wait, I thought you weren't disappearing. How can you get stuck in a wall?

"Because if you're good, you're moving so fast you'll pass through solid matter like it's air."

"Well, I don't know if I'm that good yet. I'm still just an Archmage."

"Well, with that attitude you always will be. Hell, I became a War Seer pretty much by accident. I was an Archmage like you on my first mission, a snatch-and-grab in Oslo during the Nobel Peace Prize ceremonies. Things went sour—not Golden Dawn—just a buncha mundanes with gats. Bullets was flying, people was shouting, an' I have to say it wasn't one of my finer moments.

I panicked, an' I ran, fast as I could, just tryin' to keep my sorry arse safe. Then this bloke just appears outta nowhere right in front of me with a shiny metal gat in 'is hand. He had me dead to rights. I saw the muzzle flash, I smelled the powder, I *knew* that bullet 'ad me name on it, I *knew* I had to get outta that bullet's way. Next thing I know I'm behind 'im. No training, no nuffin—I just blinked right past 'im. Like the ability'd been locked up in me the entire time but I hadn't figured out how to unlock it. Sometimes you need to get outta class to learn. It'll be the same for you."

"So what happened to the guy with the gun?" Jason asked.

"The gat?" Teo grinned. "I made him eat it."

When they reached the end of the corridor, Teo stopped before the last door on the floor and turned to Jason. The expression on his face was anything but jocular.

"Some ground rules; you can come in but leave the door open and keep watch, yeah? This won't take long, but every minute goes past there's a better than average chance someone we don't want to see us *will*. Got it?"

"Got it."

Teo wiped his hand over his face, and when he was done, his appearance had changed from a boy in his early twenties to a child of ten or eleven with bright, alert eyes. He even seemed to have shrunk in height, shedding a couple feet in the process. Next, Teo moved his hand over the locks bolting the door. There was a repeating clatter of metal as they retracted and slid, then it opened with a creak. Teo stepped inside, and Jason followed, propping the door open with his shoe and leaning against it.

The door opened into a living room bathed in the cathode rays of an old TV. The décor was simple; a table and mismatched chairs in a corner, a sofa opposite the set, and a scratched coffee table between them. There were shelves loaded with small porcelain figurines that seemed to be standard issue among the elderly, and there were dusty framed photos on the wall inside the entrance hall. In them, Jason saw the same young boy who was now moving through the flat. Smiling, laughing; one was a school photo of a wide-eyed, happy child.

Looks like I'm not the only one finding it difficult to let go, he thought.

Reclined on the white-and-yellow floral patterned sofa was a dark-skinned woman in her sixties; her creased skin seemingly grayer than her short-shorn hair. There was a stack of medicine bottles on the end table, a pink shawl was draped over her shoulders, and a thick gray blanket was wrapped around her lower torso. She remained dozing as Teo knelt beside her and took her withered hand in his, and when he spoke, it was to Jason.

"You know, I think you spend half your life running away from home and the rest of it trying to run back." He nodded to the woman. "So allow me to paint you a picture of one Antonio Odain. His dad disappeared 'fore he was born, his mum's heart gave out when he was five. He was raised single-handed by his Aunt Emma, and she's the reason he survived this place. She's the one kept him on the straight an' narrow. When the Peckham Boys come round she told them where to get off. 'My Antonio's off-limits,' she said, and it's a sign of 'ow respected she was that they backed off. Well, that an' the vase she stitched 'cross the face of one of 'em. You know what that's like? Having someone in your corner? Someone who'll do anything for you and expect nothing in return?"

Jason nodded. He did, once, and by the time he realized that, it was too late to say goodbye.

"When the Invisible Hand came, when they showed me the things I could do weren't because I was a freak but because I was special, it was the most incredible thing someone growing up in a place like this could ever hear. I could do *anything,* they said, but I couldn't be Antonio Odain. I had to be Teo Stone and there could be no going back. To go back would be a danger for me, and for the ones I loved. That was the price, the one we *all* pay."

Teo stroked the woman's hand gently. When he spoke again it wasn't to her, it was to himself.

"Some days I wish I'd stayed Antonio Odain, made some scratch, moved her out of here. But I made my choice and she hasta live with it now, don't she?"

The woman's eyes fluttered open and focused on the boy holding her hand. She studied him for a moment, and then slow recognition crept across her face.

"Antonio . . . is that you?"

She moved to sit up but he eased her down.

"No, you rest, Auntie; I'm 'ere."

"Where you been, Antonio? You 'aven't come round to visit in so long."

"I know, Auntie. I been busy. I been having all kinds of adventures."

"My little Lost Boy . . ." She smiled. "Like the Peter Pan stories I read to you, remember? They tell me you're dead, but I tell them Antonio still comes to see his auntie. He visits and he holds my hand and he's a good boy who didn't forget."

"Never, Auntie. I'll never forget." Teo's voice sounded raw.

"You'll stay this time?"

"I wish I could, Auntie. But I have work to do. Important work—"

She looked past Teo to Jason, and leaned forward, her eyes struggling to focus.

"Antonio, who's that by the door?"

"He's a friend, Auntie. He's all right—"

"*All* of them . . . ?"

Jason sensed them before he saw them: three figures looming in the doorway. They weren't Golden Dawn, but he could sense danger radiating off them like they were on fire. He'd been so caught up in the familial drama he'd missed their approach until it was too late.

"The fook you doin' 'ere?" a booming voice asked.

The leader stepped forward. His cheek was creased by an old scar that curled the corner of his lip into a permanent sneer. Behind him, two others filled the doorframe. One was almost as wide as he was tall. The other one was barely into his teens, his right hand shoved into his bulky olive drab army jacket pocket. Jason didn't need to see the gun to know that's what he was clutching inside it.

"No speaky English?" Scarface smiled. "I'll repeat myself. The *fook*. You *doin'*. 'Ere?"

Teo had shifted back to his present-day form, but he said nothing until he stood and turned to address the group.

"Turn round, piss off, and don't you dare darken her doorway again."

"Or . . . ?" Scarface asked.

"Or you'll regret it more than your mum regrets 'aving you."

"'Least I know who my mum is," Scarface said. "Yeah, I remember you. I remember you runnin' around the towers like some mangy dog. I remember this woman stitchin' a lager bottle 'cross my face for talkin' to you. Got the scar to prove it, don't I?"

Teo held his cool, but Jason could sense anger building, like an electrical charge.

"Turn 'round, step back, fuck off. Final warning."

"No, we got us some unfinished business, you and me," said Scarface. "Lonnie, fetch 'im 'ere."

The big one—Lonnie—cracked knuckles that sounded off like gunshots.

Teo's right hand clenched. Jason could sense the energy pulsating from it.

Oh shit, he thought.

Jason side-eyed the kid. He was slowly pulling the gun from his pocket.

"I gave you a chance . . ." Teo said.

Then he *pushed*.

Jason felt air blast past him. A hurricane-force wind ruffled his hair and jacket, but Scarface took the brunt and was thrown off his feet, careening backward into Lonnie and sending them both crashing to the ground.

The kid had his gun on Teo and by the time Jason raised *his* hand the bullet was already blasting out of its chamber. As it passed Jason he reached out and felt his thoughts brush cold jacketed steel. He *pushed* at it, and drove it off its path, sending it into the end table beside Teo's aunt, blasting the pill bottles and sending plastic spraying.

Teo pulled, and the gun yanked out of the kid's hand and sailed past Jason, disassembling into its individual components down to every last screw and bolt. The shrapnel cloud held for a moment, then redirected back into the doorframe beside the kid, shredding wood and sending splinters into the side of the kid's face. He screamed in pain and surprise and staggered backward as Scarface and Lonnie recovered from the strike. Teo disappeared in a blast of smoke, and slid out of the cloudburst between them crouched and kicked into the side of Lonnie's knee. There was a sharp snap and Lonnie dropped like a sack of hammers. Teo delivered another kick to the thug's nose, breaking cartilage and smashing Lonnie's skull down to the floor with a sharp crack. He collapsed like a garbage bag stuffed with meat, and was still.

Scarface was running but not fast enough. Teo blinked into his path, landed a blow to his face, and disappeared. Scarface swung his fists blindly. Teo reappeared to deliver another strike, then another, then another. As Jason watched, something staggered through his peripheral; the kid, clutching his face and wailing as he hit the abutment. He teetered, and Jason sucked in a horrified breath as momentum carried the kid over the balcony edge. Jason reacted instinctively, reaching for the terrified boy and grasping his sleeve just as the kid's weight pulled him over the side and yanked him off his feet.

And for the third time in as many weeks, Jason Bishop was falling off a building.

But this time it was different. *This time* he was a Mage.

And gravity didn't apply to a Mage.

Even as the wind roared in his ears and his remaining moments on earth were measured in feet, his pulse beat steady. He grasped the kid, whose screams reached an earsplitting pitch, and pulled him close. He pictured the cracked, cold twelfth floor hallway. He pictured himself and the kid landing there, hard but alive. He could do this. He *would* do this.

He felt something tug at his jacket.

They were still falling.

Another tug. Another pull.

They were still dropping.

C'mon, goddammit!

The kid was still screaming.

The ground raced to meet them—

C'MON—

There was a deafening noise and a flash of light. Pain exploded through him; the first sign he was still alive. He let the kid roll out of his arms and fall to the corridor floor, where he sighed in relief and was then still, consciousness slipping away. When the kid awoke, balance would be restored and he'd think this was all just a bad dream. He would forget all of it like Teo's aunt would; the universe would make sure of that. But Jason wouldn't forget, because *he* hadn't saved his or the kid's life; that had been Carter Block, who was standing over Jason now, smoke drifting from his immaculately tailored suit, and gazing at him with a barely suppressed fury.

SIXTEEN

CARTER HADN'T SPOKEN TO THEM after leaving Elysian Fields, hadn't spoken as they reentered the Citadel through a supply room door at the Peckham Rye railway station, and still wasn't speaking as he led them down the Ingress. Jason had almost wished Carter *would* explode in fury, because the silent treatment was much worse. Silence meant a punishment would be forthcoming and on Carter's timetable; one that threatened to fall at any moment. The fact he'd brought them back to the Citadel through a different point of entry told Jason he didn't know about Teo's secret exit. A glance from Teo was enough to tell Jason to keep that between them.

Carter opened a steel door and strode through it without ordering them to follow.

"On a scale of one to ten, how pissed is he?" Jason asked Teo.

"Carter don't do one-to-ten; he's an either-or type," Teo replied. "When he's this quiet it means one of two things: one, he's pissed at you, or two, something's happened that's so urgent he doesn't have time to be pissed at you, which just makes him *more* pissed."

"So what's through that door? The firing squad?"

"The Amphitheater."

"Sounds charming."

Teo's expression was grave. "When we're summoned to the Amphitheater, it's because we just lost an agent."

Jason looked back to the door. Carter's footsteps were echoing from somewhere inside. He wouldn't wait forever, and they'd *already* angered him.

But before Jason could enter, Teo blocked the way.

"Not a word why we was in Peckham. We was in London for kicks, we got sidetracked, and that's it, yeah?"

"That's it," Jason replied.

Teo passed through the doorway and disappeared inside. Jason took a breath and followed.

With a name like the Amphitheater, Jason expected something like an ancient Greek or Roman one with rows of carved stone seats rising up the side of a bowl-shaped depression. This was the same idea, only the rows looked to be made of metal, the stage floor a flat, polished obsidian. Two doorways flanked the stage and Carter strode to the center to address the crowd.

And there *was* a crowd; the Amphitheater was filled with Mages; at least five hundred, and possibly a thousand. Some he recognized: Abigail, Clas, and Barkhad sat in the third row, and he glimpsed Katja a few rows behind them, seated as far away from everyone else as possible. Others he recognized from the games room, but he didn't see Kel, and that, along with Teo's account of what this place was, sent a chill up his spine.

Allegra emerged from the shadows to join Carter on the stage.

He spoke to her, and for a brief moment Jason thought Carter set his gaze on him.

Teo gave Jason a nudge. "Might as well tear the bandage off, yeah?"

He took a seat in the front row and Jason joined him. Allegra and Carter finished speaking, and then she crossed the stage floor and sat to Jason's left.

He asked her to sit beside me. To keep tabs on me. Again.

Carter gazed out over the auditorium, and the dull din of chatter silenced.

Then he spoke.

"We've lost contact with our team in Scotland. They found something—some clue in a Highland cairn that sent them north, to the Orkney Islands. But it was a trap; the Golden Dawn was waiting for them. Enchantments had been placed, exit points closed off. They *knew* we were coming, and when we arrived, they sprung the trap. We're going to attempt to reestablish contact, and find a way for them to get out. As you know this is quite dangerous . . . but she *insisted*."

There was a squeak of wheels and the rattle of metal. From the darkness at the edge of the spotlight illuminating Carter, two dark-robed Acolytes rolled her out in her hospital bed. BP, heart, and EKG monitors were attached to the frame, but her IV drip was gone. The drugs would only cloud her mind and she needed to be focused, despite the pain. Jason was horrified by how much she had deteriorated, and the acoustics of the Amphitheater augmented the shallow rasp of her breath. She was drenched in perspiration, her skin waxy and lifeless, and the pale dome of her cranium flashed white in the hard light. Even her bright playful eyes were shrouded by imminent death. The fact she was still alive was either a miracle of science or sheer force of supernatural will.

An Acolyte locked her bed in place; another wheeled out a saline drip that was quickly connected to her stent. They drew a syringe, inserted it into the line, and plunged it deep. She remained slumped for a moment, then her eyes opened wide and she sat upright.

Carter rested his dark hand on her thin, pale one, and stared at her until her eyes opened.

"Vasilisa, can you see?" he asked.

Vasilisa's tiny body tensed, then shuddered, then lurched. The monitors chimed warnings. Jason was up out of his seat reflexively, but Allegra's hand grasped him and eased him down.

"She knew the risks," she said.

Vasilisa cried out. The Acolytes watched the readouts closely. The heart monitor beeped rapid-fire as she lurched upright and spoke with a frantic voice.

"We're in the Orkneys," Vasilisa said. "Skara Brae, the old Neolithic village. The ruin on the surface is *just* the surface! It goes down for fathoms, but we found it, Carter, we fuckin' found it!"

Carter leaned in close. "What did you find?"

"It was hidden," Vasilisa continued. "In an antechamber, walled off from the rest of the ruin! Nine levels down, circles, squares, hexagons—all locked, all linked, more below even that! One unlocked, another reconfigured itself. You unlock that, the one behind you slams shut. It took too long but I cracked the code! The man was a fuckin' genius but I beat him Carter, I—"

"*What did you find, Kelvin*?" Carter asked.

Kelvin. He was speaking through Vasilisa.

Oh no, thought Jason . . .

"The machine," she said. "We found the *machine*!"

Something flashed before Jason's eyes: an impression of a wooden frame suspended above a table the size of a midsized car. Gears and levers and pulleys crisscrossed a rectangular frame, and there was writing etched into the wood in a language he couldn't recognize. A bowl-shaped depression sat in the tabletop, and a corresponding one sat in the heavy wooden press hanging above it, like the machine had been built for a singular purpose. The chamber itself was circular, with small stone slits carved into the walls and ceiling and floor. Periodic flashes of lightning from outside sparked through them to illuminate the machine. Light from above. Light from below. Like the chamber was constructed to harness energies from the heavens *and* the earth, and direct them to this machine and to whatever purpose it was built for.

Jason jolted. He was back in the auditorium, back in his body, back watching Vasilisa lurch and twitch, her tiny body pummeled by unseen forces. She tensed, clutched blindly at things not there, and as she did Jason felt something pull at him again, tugging at his skin and his mind.

Something that wanted him to see what she was seeing.

"Carter, I don't think we're gettin' outta this one . . ." Vasilisa said.

Jason felt that pull again. All he had to do was let go.

Something flitted into his vision: a solitary snowflake, falling from the darkness above. It was fat and bloated, and it was joined by another, then by more, and soon snow was falling throughout the Amphitheater, coating the floor, covering Vasilisa's bed, and blanketing her in white. But by the time Jason realized he was the only one who could see it, he'd already let go.

. . .

Cold, damp snow fell over the ancient and shattered stones of the settlement, and unforgiving sea wind blasted it through the ruin, kicking up a grit that swirled through the grounds and sent cold sleet to pinprick Kelvin Ash's skin. The salty ocean rain he tasted on his tongue couldn't dampen the fear pervading everything about him. He was going to die; that was a stone-cold fucking certainty, and the fact it would happen on Scottish soil didn't reassure him. Not with the dead, and dying, strewn about the cauldron-shaped basin of Skara Brae.

Ova Skygge's broken body lay atop a heap of shattered stone, the Archmage's lifeless eyes crusted with wet snow. The War Seer Ignatius Kamen lay sprawled nearby, arms and legs broken, bones jutting through his fatigues. A vaguely recognizable human heap of meat and bone that in life had been the Enchanter Tsui Hei rested amidst a patch of ground scorched black. Alexandra Berit, the agile swimmer and their second War Seer, lay bleeding against the opposite wall, alive and breathing through sheer force of will. Only Jok Oro, Diabolist and leader of this doomed mission, stood at the ready as the storm churned overhead. But as the walls and ground shuddered, Kel realized it wasn't thunder at all.

It was her. She was coming.

The surviving Mages readied themselves, but it was all futile. They knew it, and Kel knew it, too. *They'd* set the traps and watched and waited for them to arrive. They'd planted the clue in the Highlands that led them to this ruin on the storm-lashed Orkney Islands. They waited for Kel to open the chamber door, and then they attacked.

They knew its secret. The machine *was* real.

That meant the Sphere of Destiny is too, Kel thought.

Stone and rubble lifted off the ground, held there, and then fired through the basin, hammering the walls and all in their way. Alexandra was struck across her skull by a chunk of stone, cleaving it open, and she fell, spasming as steaming blood pulsed life out of her. There wasn't time to mourn her, though, as tendrils of smoke spiraled down and took shape on the walls of the ruin, coagulating into humans. Their clothing was stitched together from scraps. Some had war paint across their eyes; others had it across their mouths and in their mouths, staining their teeth black. The tattoos on their flesh glowed in the night, and the spells they mouthed were lost amidst the cyclone howl that swept through Skara Brae and swirled inside it like a tornado wind.

Kel sank into the shadows, and took a breath. If he hid, maybe they wouldn't see. If they thought he was dead, maybe they would leave. Maybe . . .

You know who says maybe? he thought. *Dead guys. Dead guys say maybe.*

He was going to die, but he wasn't going to go cowering.

He emerged from the shadows with a smile on his lips.

"C'mon, ye Red Bitch, quit hidin' and show me what you're made of!"

The ground shuddered, there was a breach, then a crash, and Kel turned just in time to see the wall behind him crumble, an avalanche of brick and stone that slammed into his legs and crushed them and pinned him to the ground beneath their weight. He cried out in anguish as pain tore through him. Already he felt death's cold embrace struggling to grasp him and pull him under. He clung onto his fading life with desperation, despite the dying cries of his comrades echoing across the ruined ground. Death came quick for some, slow for others, but it came for them all. A final plaintive wailing cry seemed to echo for an eternity before it was cut short.

Then there was just silence.

Pour us a pint, lads and lassies; I'll be there soon, he thought.

The wind howled, and just below its banshee wail, he heard her footsteps. Through the encroaching darkness spilling into his vision he saw her approach, the cruel scar of her mouth curled into a triumphant smile.

"Any last words?" the Red Queen asked.

"Just two, ye' murderous cunt," Kel laughed. " 'Fu—"

The Red Queen grasped Kel's head in her cold hands and twisted—

Pain shot through Jason's neck and he grasped it with his hand. He looked around to see if anyone had noticed his reaction, but everyone was focused on Vasilisa, whose body had gone rigid, levitating off the bed like some unseen force had scooped it up in its hand, her back arching to the breaking point. The IV and monitor tubes pulled taut, like they were mooring lines keeping her earthbound, and threatened to rip out of her flesh. Her arms stiffened, her mouth screamed soundless—

The body dropped back down onto the bed with a heavy clatter. The IV toppled, the monitors flatlined, and before anyone watching could react, she was gone.

Silence filled the void left by her passing.

Nobody spoke.

Nobody moved.

Nobody even breathed.

Carter approached Vasilisa, reached a hand down, and gently closed her eyes. An Acolyte switched the machines off, muting the flatline screech that had invaded the stunned silence. Carter grasped the edge of Vasilisa's bed and tightened his grip on the railing. After a long moment, he let go, turned, and departed. His footsteps echoed through the cavernous space as he disappeared into the darkness, and then faded away entirely. An Acolyte pulled a sheet up and over Vasilisa's body. They soundlessly wheeled her bed and silent machines out.

Whispers echoed through the Amphitheater once they'd gone. Whispers became murmurs, murmurs became shouts, and shouts became heated arguments that cascaded down the seats to the front row and the stage like a waterfall. Jason looked to Teo. His head was buried in his hands. Allegra's face was a blank slate. The enormity of what had happened had rendered them both mute.

Vasilisa was dead. She would return, but the others wouldn't. Kelvin wouldn't. No more pool games, no more crass jokes. He'd been in Jason's life a little more than two weeks; now he was just another person who had died. But there was something tangible left of Kel, his final thought still echoing in Jason's mind, beating at his skull like the wings of a caged bird.

"The Sphere," Jason muttered. "It's real. . . ."

"Say that again," Allegra said.

He looked to Allegra. Her eyes were digging holes into his.

"The Sphere of Destiny," he said. "It's real. Kel told me."

"Kelvin said nothing about the Sphere!"

"He didn't *say* it. I was in his mind. I was there, in the ruins. I saw them die, and I saw *her*—"

Allegra's grip on his arm was like steel.

"You have a three-count to tell me how you saw that! Only an Oracle has that power. . . ."

Jason met her gaze, and he saw it: his opening. Carter had

been hiding the truth from him the moment he set foot inside the Citadel, and possibly well before that. They weren't playing straight with him; none of them were. Now, he had something *they* wanted; he had leverage, and he planned to use it. If Allegra wanted an answer, he wanted ten times that, but he'd start with the one weighing heaviest on his mind.

"I will," he said. "*After* you tell me everything you know about the Sphere of Destiny."

SEVENTEEN

·······················

THE WALLS, CEILING, AND FLOOR of the octagonal chamber reflected hundreds of copies of Jason and Allegra back at them as they entered. The ceiling vaulted above them to three times the standard, giving the sensation they were standing at the bottom of a pit. At a central dais, a charcoal-robed Acolyte entered data into a keyboard, but there was no monitor or computer Jason could see connected to it. The man didn't look up from his work or from the leather-bound book he was transcribing, sitting open on the pedestal beside him.

Allegra picked the book up off the Acolyte's workstation and handed it to Jason.

"You wanted answers," she said.

He took the book, a handcrafted leather-bound journal. The stitching on its face was simple, and it had a comfortable smell and touch. It also felt quite new, like a reproduction of a much older tome. It creaked gently as he opened it and he ran a hand over the paper inside. It wasn't the kind mass-produced from a pulp and paper mill; this was thicker and coarser, rough around the edges, as if it had been cut by hand. There was writing on the pages, too, a language he didn't recognize. He turned more pages, and found more of that strange writing, and stopped on the first page that featured a drawing. It was of a circle; the outer ring divided into forty squares, each containing a number, a letter, or some unidentifiable symbol. A seven-sided shape came next, inside the circle, and similarly marked with symbols. Inside that were two more seven-sided shapes that overlapped to form a seven-pointed star, then two more seven-sided shapes, followed by a five-pointed star, which overlapped a smaller circle comprised of seemingly random groupings of letters. The drawing gave Jason such a sense of vertigo-induced nausea that he had to look away.

"I know, right?" Allegra asked. "I managed a full minute before I had to stop."

"What is this?" he asked.

"The *Sigillum Dei Aemaeth,*" she said. "It means 'Seal of God.' Do you know the Bible?"

"I know *of* it."

"Book of Revelations?"

He nodded, slowly. "End-of-the-world stuff, right?"

"If you're Christian."

"So this is, what, some kind of doomsday prophecy?"

"So some believe. But in physical form such seals took the shape of amulets, with the function of, according to legend, giving its wearer power over beings of supernatural ability; Angels, and Demons, and even Mages. They first began to appear in the early Middle Ages, but the most powerful of them were refined into the drawing you see here, by the owner of this journal."

Jason turned more pages, past more writing, past more symbols. He stopped when he reached the first drawing of the first machine. It looked like a triangular canvas tent, with a basket holding a small human figure underneath it.

"A parachute?" he asked.

"Keep going." Allegra nodded.

He turned more pages, moving past something that looked like an airplane; another was a cross between a spinning top and a tank with cannons jutting from it. He saw boats and bridges, parachutes and trains, cars and rockets, and one that looked like the International Space Station—

He stopped on the next page and tightened his grip on the book. This was a machine that looked like a cross between an old-fashioned printing press and an iron forge.

He'd seen this one before: through Kel's eyes not thirty minutes earlier.

"This is it—the machine they found," he said. "But what is it?"

"That machine was constructed by the owner of this journal, a man named John Dee. He was a mathematician, astronomer, astrologer, and court wizard to Elizabeth I."

Jason's eyes widened. "He was a *Mage*?"

Allegra shook her head. "No, not a Mage, and not a conjurer like the Golden Dawn. He was an occultist, obsessed with magic. And he was so successful at it that the line between what is fact and fiction has been blurred. Some say he coined the word *Britannia,* and foresaw a British Empire spanning the globe. He founded the Rosicrucian order, the Protestant response to the Jesuits, and may have been instrumental in the creation of the British Secret Service. He was also said to be Shakespeare's basis for Prospero in *The Tempest,* a fact given some credence by the claim Dee conjured a storm that swamped a fleet of invading Spanish galleons in the English Channel in 1588, saving his queen and her kingdom."

Jason furrowed his brow. "He's got to have been dead for, what, four hundred years?"

"Four hundred and eight years, to be exact," Allegra answered.

Jason closed and brandished the journal for emphasis.

"No way is this book five hundred years old. The pages are still indented from the drawings, there's no aging or discoloration; hell, I have paperbacks at home that smell older than this."

"That's because it was written recently. This journal appeared in the Citadel three months ago. None of us have been able to figure out how it got here, or by whose hand."

"I thought it was impossible for a mundane to breach the Citadel."

"It is. But somehow, John Dee did."

"Come on," he sighed. "You just said the guy was long dead!"

Allegra took the journal from him, flipped through the pages, and turned the book to face him. There was a drawing of a building on it that needed no description, because he'd seen it with his own eyes countless times before. It was the Empire State Building, drawn by the hand of someone dead more than three centuries before they broke ground at 34th and Fifth.

"John Dee was a man keenly attuned to the passage of time," Allegra continued. "He obsessed over clocks and timepieces. Time was an ever-present concern, especially in his later years. This notebook is filled with drawings of buildings and machines men could only dream of in his era. He was a genius, they say, because he saw things that became commonplace centuries later. But you and I know that isn't true. They weren't dreams; somehow he was able to transcend time, to travel forward in history, to witness great events and great machines. . . ."

"He didn't imagine them." Jason realized. "He *saw* them. He saw them because he was *here*."

"Still a quick study, I see," Allegra said.

"Still, that doesn't answer my question. What is the Sphere of Destiny?"

Allegra handed the book back to the Acolyte.

"Show him the drawing."

The Acolyte set the book aside and tapped keys. The lights dimmed and panels clicked on in a wave. The walls, floor, and ceiling of the room were one big viewing screen. Images scrolled through it rapid-fire until resolving into a scan of a notebook page depicting a single, perfectly etched circle that seemed to glow with incredible power even though it was just a drawing.

Allegra stepped into Jason's view, between the screen wall and him.

"According to Dee's journals it came from a dream he had, of a great power that would shatter the barriers between the mundane and magical worlds, upsetting the balance between chaos and order; a power forged in the fires of creation itself. He believed he had stumbled upon the secrets of the universe, and set about to perfect his greatest work. Using his skills in astrology, and with the aid of his Sigillum, he sought out this power, to contain it, and to wield it."

"And did he?" Jason asked.

"Until three weeks ago, we assumed he didn't. Not until Damon unearthed what may be a clue as to its whereabouts." She turned to the Acolyte. "Bring up the paintings."

More keys clattered. The drawing of the Sphere disappeared to be replaced by another image, one Jason recognized immediately: the *Mona Lisa*. It split off to occupy a panel, and another painting appeared, again familiar: *The Raft of the Medusa*. It sectioned off to another panel, and a third—*Liberty Leading the People*—appeared. They'd been labeled with their name, the artist, and the date painted. More paintings with more info joined them, some familiar, some not, until twenty-seven covered the walls, a collage of medieval to more contemporary nineteenth-century works.

"These paintings—twenty-seven of them—were on a flash drive, secured from a broker named Bennett Fraim, by your father," Allegra said. "Do you recognize any of them?"

"Some." He nodded. "Winnie was the real expert, and even then that might've been just another illusion. I bought her an art book on our first anniversary—one of those big heavy art books they have on clearance at the bookstores? I don't think she ever opened it."

Allegra's eyes were focused on the paintings as she spoke. "Fraim, or whoever he was working for, claimed these paintings have something to do with the location of the Sphere of Destiny. We just don't know what. Until the machine was unearthed in the Orkneys by Kel and the others there was still doubt as to whether or not it was real. But the existence of the machine proves it. The Sphere is real, and now we have to find it."

Jason looked at *The Coronation of Napoleon* at his feet, and as he did there was a flash of red. A glowing symbol appeared on it: a circle beneath a five-pointed triangle, identical to the one at the center of the *Sigillum*. His eyes watered painfully and he looked over to another painting—*The Astronomer* by Vermeer. Another flash of red, another symbol—the subdivided circle from the outer edge. He looked over the room to see flashes of other symbols on all of the paintings on display, all circles and squares and triangles and stars, and all filled with the strange, coded writing of Dee's Seal of God. His eyes felt like they'd been rubbed with sandpaper and doused in vinegar. He pressed his palms against them until the pain subsided.

"Are you all right?" Allegra asked.

He shook his head. "Eyes hurt, like someone just jabbed needles into them—"

He rubbed, then opened his eyes. Allegra was staring at him with concern. As his vision cleared, his gaze settled onto the fishhook scar on her forehead above her left eye. Something shimmered there, like the symbols had shimmered.

"What are the symbols for?" he asked.

"Symbols?" Allegra frowned. "What symbols?"

"The symbols on the paintings."

"Which paintings?"

"All of them!" He pointed.

"I don't see anything."

"They're all around us!" Jason said.

Allegra looked to the Acolyte. "Did you run a scan?"

"All spectrums," the Acolyte said. "There's nothing there."

A sharp pain fired through Jason's skull. He clutched his forehead and cried out in agony.

"What is it? What's wrong?!" Allegra asked.

Anguished pain roared through him, and through it he caught a glimpse of the scar on Allegra's forehead. Something tugged at him, pulling him toward it, like it was a river's current pulling him under, beneath dark waters enveloping the room, the Citadel, and the world entire—

A rock, bloody on the ground.

Carrion birds feeding on the dead.

The smell of burning gasoline in the air.

Thick black smoke choking her.
The howl of the enraged chasing her.
Her father calling her apostate and throwing the rock.
The rock striking her above her left eye and pain shooting
through.
A snowfall of rose petals.
A storm of stones.
A child's hand slamming into the ground.
Fissures radiating.
Buildings crumbling.
The earth turning.
A city dying.
A face—looming in the darkness.
A voice—Damon's voice.
"It wasn't your fault. None of it was."
Night became day, became the surface of the sun blinding
him—

Allegra gasped. Jason broke the connection, staggering back-ward, stumbling and falling hard to the floor. The paintings surrounding them began to blacken in a wave of rolling darkness. Allegra's shocked face lurched into view. Then she was fading, and the last conscious thought Jason had was that it was he, not the room, who was falling into darkness.

It was the crash of waves that forced his eyes open. He was lying in his bed, in his bedroom, inside the Citadel. The room was dark, the curtains drawn, and the light outside dim and lifeless. He felt no pain, not from his fall, not from those symbols that had stabbed his eyes like needles. In fact, he couldn't feel a thing; not his arms, not his legs. He tried to move but could not. Tried to scream, but his mouth wouldn't open. He took a breath and found his lungs could still fill with air. He exhaled slowly and focused on his heartbeat. Then he tried to lift his arms, then his legs, but still he couldn't.

He looked to the bedroom door and focused his thoughts on it. He'd opened it without touching it dozens of times before, but even as he felt his mind slip over the handle he couldn't turn it. Something clenched painful in his stomach: fear, uncertainty, and panic.

Ice ran up his neck.

Someone else was in the room.

"The amygdalae: have you heard of them?" a voice asked.

Jason's eyes settled on a corner of the room between the window and the wall opposite his bed. A figure stood there, dark even against the surrounding shadows. A pair of eyes gleamed from within them, and teeth flashed white. "Carter."

"Of course you haven't; you can't speak at the moment and even if you could you wouldn't know because you're just a bartender, so allow me to further your education. The amygdalae are a pair of almond-sized regions deep in the brain. They are the orchestrators of fear. They read sounds and smells and taste and touch and filter them. PTSD victims suffer from faulty amygdalae; those sights and smells are triggers—fire, charred flesh, and gasoline in particular affects soldiers returning from war because war smells like gasoline. These amygdalae induce panic, induce flashbacks . . . and sometimes even paralysis. A skilled Diabolist can manipulate the amygdalae and generate panic in the body—to give someone PTSD with a mere thought. It's a difficult skill to master, even for a Mage. Naturally I devoted a significant portion of my training to it."

Carter stepped forward into the dim light, a shadow moving through shadows as he approached. He gazed upon Jason with absolutely none of the warmth he'd shown during their first meeting in The Locksmith.

"I've never been one for fieldwork, but I do know that subtle knives cut deepest and their wounds linger, like betrayal lingers. Betrayal is the very worst thing you can do to a person who trusts you. Sofia betrayed your father, me, and the Invisible Hand, and you betrayed me when you left the Citadel despite my orders not to. What were you looking for in Peckham?"

Jason felt a shift in him, like his paralyzing fear had been banished with a release of pressure.

"Tell me," said Carter. "Tell me, and this ends."

Jason opened his mouth to speak . . . and remembered Teo with his aunt, the lost boy who had returned home for a brief moment, brightening the life of the woman nearing the end of hers.

Jason didn't answer. To his surprise, Carter smiled.

"Your devotion to your friend is admirable. Had you told me, I would have let you lie here for a week. That's why, for your loyalty to Teo, I'm only leaving you here for twenty-four hours."

There was a whisper of movement and the shadows dissipated, like steam belching from an exhaust on a cold winter's day. When they faded away, Carter was gone.

Jason was alone.

And the sound of the crashing waves outside his window was his only companion.

EIGHTEEN

THE ROOM WAS QUIET, BUT for the thunder of the surf outside.

The doorknob filled his vision. He'd grasped and turned the cool metal so many times his mind slipped over it like it was a physical extension of his body. He felt it take hold. He'd opened it that way before and he would open it now. If he could do that he would break Carter's spell and his imprisonment would end.

As he felt his mind turn the knob a wave of nausea washed over him; sickly sweet bile rose up his throat. If he threw up he'd choke on it. That was the worst-case scenario; the best case was lying there with vomit on his face and in his hair and clothing for the next twenty-four hours.

He forced the bile back down his throat. Once he was sure it had settled he lay there, breathing heavily. That was the extent of what he could do.

A dull pressure was growing in his bladder. Not screaming for release yet, but it would sooner than later. He let his body settle. Let his mind drift. And as he did, the solution presented itself.

Just go to sleep, he thought. Twenty-four hours could be cut down by eight, ten if he *really* pushed. The remaining fourteen would be difficult, but they wouldn't be twenty-four. And if he pissed himself during those eight to ten, so be it. He got comfortable: no small feat given he couldn't shift his body, or lie on his right side, his default position to start sleeping.

He didn't know how long he lay there. There was no clock, no way to measure time. There was just that crash of waves far below. Slow, rhythmic, never ceasing. The light outside his window remained dull and lifeless. He felt his eyelids get heavy; he felt his mind uncouple from his body and drift into his subconscious. Felt himself falling back into the bed, sinking into a grateful slumber—

Something grasped his windpipe and squeezed, choking him, cutting off his supply of air. He bolted back awake. The amygdalae released their hold on him and he took heaving swallows of oxygen. He'd nearly choked himself to death. Carter's orchestration of fear held him in his grip. His pulse slowed and steadied. There would be no sleep for him. Not for twenty-four hours.

The waves crashed, one, followed by another five seconds later. They became his clock; 12 times a minute, 120 times every ten, 720 times an hour. After 2,160 crashes, he realized he'd have to hear those waves crash another fifteen thousand times before it was over. The waves had another undesired effect: increasing the pressure on his bladder. What he'd been able to ignore before soon screamed at him. He wondered if this was what Uncle Aaron faced every day, that there was some small part of his brain intact enough to know he was trapped inside a body that was betraying him. Jason stared up at the ceiling with resignation. He feared his amygdalae wouldn't allow him to release, like they would trigger some long-forgotten childhood fear of punishment for wetting the bed. Finally, when he couldn't resist it anymore, he let it go. Damp warmth spread across him, relief flowed, and the ammonia stink that reached his nostrils two crashes of waves later brought Elysian Fields and Peckham flooding back with them.

Then, after another 1,080 crashes of waves, the voices came.

If you'd told Carter the truth you wouldn't be here, they chattered.

And throw Teo under the bus?

You think Teo isn't being punished right now?

I made a promise.

He wouldn't do the same. He barely knows you. You barely know any of them.

I knew Kelvin.

Kelvin's dead.

Shut up.

Vasilisa's dead.

Shut up!

You don't "do" friends, Jason. Friends are complications. They betray you, they die on you . . .

Shut THE FUCK UP!

Silence. In his mind. In his room. Save for the crashing waves outside. Twelve of them.

A minute down, 8,600 to come.

Give or take.

The waves crashed in darkness. The room was dark. Night had fallen. His stomach churned angrily for food. He felt helpless—that was the worst thing about it. He was as helpless as a neglected infant crying for food and warmth and love and left instead to wail forgotten in its crib.

Jason couldn't even cry.

He could only lie there in his piss, and wait.

He was so tired. Before he had tried to force himself to sleep; now he had to force himself to stay awake. That fear remained pronounced, closing around him every time he felt exhaustion take him. Clasping his throat. Squeezing. Until he forced himself awake. If he slept, he died. If he didn't, he'd go mad.

He cursed Carter Block. He cursed the Invisible Hand. He cursed himself.

He was thirsty. He gathered reservoirs of saliva to lubricate his throat but it just made him thirstier.

Wings beat frantically at the madhouse of his skull.

He would do anything for a sip of water.

He'd kill for one. He'd burn the Citadel to the ground. He'd—

A child's hand slams the ground. Fissures radiate. Buildings crumble. The earth turns.

The memory had crashed into his mind like a rolling wave. His pulse quickened with the confusion and the realization.

That's what he remembered from the chamber of paintings.

Allegra. She'd taken his hand, and he saw inside her mind. Her memories.

Like Vasilisa had seen inside his. What was happening?

He forced his eyes shut and concentrated. Not on the door,

not on the room, but inside himself. He needed the distraction. He needed to think.

And Carter had given him the gift of time to do just that.

Damon had planted that memory inside Vasilisa's mind without her knowing it. It had lain there for unknown months or even years, waiting for the key to unlock it. He wanted them to see. He wanted them to know. Both of them.

Jason had been the key.

But how had Damon known Jason would meet her?

The answer was as obvious as it was impossible.

Damon was an Oracle. Or at least possessed enough clairvoyance to know it would happen.

Just like he had known he was going to die.

Why didn't he prevent it? If he knew that last mission was going to be his last, why did he go on it? Why hadn't he changed the outcome?

Unless dying was part of the plan.

Jason's thoughts kept him company through that long night. It took him down dozens of paths and as many dead ends before retreating back to the start. By the time the darkness slowly brightened to morning, he still circled the truth. Something that loomed in his vision so large and so close that he couldn't see its beginning or end. He needed to step back and see the entire picture but he was too—

The picture. The paintings. Something about paintings.

He pulled his thoughts back to the octagonal room. The symbols he saw that Allegra and the Acolyte hadn't. There was something about the paintings he was missing. Something so obvious but obscured by complexity. . . .

He would have laughed out loud if he could. Two new words learned in just as many weeks.

Amygdalae. Simplexity.

Carter and Vasilisa. Two teachers. Two words.

Simplexity. Something seemingly complex that was, in fact, very simple.

The paintings. He'd seen them before—most of them. But where?

He thought of Winnie. He thought of their confrontation. The bookshelf crumbling, the heavy book that slammed to the floor. The one he'd bought her on their anniversary.

Treasures of the Louvre.

The Louvre. That's where he'd seen those paintings before.

Winnie may not have looked through the book, but Jason had.

All of the paintings Allegra had shown him were part of the Louvre's permanent collection. It was obvious to him; why hadn't it been to the Citadel, with all its knowledge?

Simplexity again.

A laugh erupted deep in Jason's chest and passed his lips and echoed through the room. He flexed his fingers, planted his hands on the mattress, and slowly sat up. A smile spread slowly across his face. Before, he would have killed Carter; now he couldn't wait to tell him that he knew where the Sphere of Destiny was.

Jason sketched on the notepad the Acolyte had provided, glancing at the paintings long enough to note their names and make a quick drawing of the symbols upon them. When he'd noted all twenty-seven, he finished and handed the notepad to Carter, who studied it silently. All the anger, the rage, the hatred he'd directed at

Carter that long twenty-four hours in his bedroom had been supplanted by an excitement he'd never before felt.

He waited. Aside from him, Carter, and the Acolyte, Allegra and Katja were the only other witnesses. He assumed Allegra was ordered to join them in the chamber when Jason finally tracked Carter down. Katja's presence, however, was a mystery to everyone but Carter.

Carter turned through the pages. "This is all of them?"

"All twenty-seven." He looked to the Acolyte. "The *Sigillum*: can you put it back up?"

The Acolyte punched keys. The paintings disappeared, to be replaced by the *Sigillum Dei Aemaeth*. It floated there, on every screen, a multitude waiting for Jason, like they all were.

"I think it's a map," Jason said.

"The *Sigillum*?" Carter asked.

"The *paintings*."

Carter stared, incredulous, at him. They all did.

"Here, look." Jason took the notepad from Carter and turned pages. "You have a circle, okay? Then this seven sided-thing, whatever it is . . ."

"A heptagon," said Katja.

"A heptagon, thank you. Next you have two squares— asymmetrical ones—that overlap to form this seven-pointed star, you have two more heptagons inside *that,* and then inside that you have a pentagram with another circle underneath. Now, look at the *Sigillum*. First shape: what do you see?"

Carter studied the screen. "A circle . . ."

Jason flipped through the book until he found a circle.

"*Terrestrial Venus*. Next is the heptagon . . ."

He flipped back through the book, and stopped on the corresponding page.

"*Liberty Leading the People.*"

He flipped through more pages as he spoke.

"One asymmetrical square, that's *The Raft of the Medusa.* Another, that's *The Lacemaker,* those two overlap to become a seven-sided star, that's—"

"So you're a code breaker now?" Katja asked. "*You?* A *bartender*?"

"You spend a lot of time tending bar, on a slow night you need distractions. Sudoku, puzzles, the works. You can buy books filled with them at any bodega." He closed the notepad and pointed to the *Sigillum.* "Each painting holds a different symbol from that sketch. Put them in the correct order, they provide a path. From the outer circle, to the inner circle, and then repeating."

"But what about the letters etched on the symbols? What purpose—" Allegra began.

"The letters don't matter; the shapes matter! The shapes are the key!" Jason said.

"There's a problem." Carter gestured to the screens. "Twenty-seven is divisible by nine, three times. If each symbol is found on three paintings, they do add up, but we don't know the proper order. We start in the wrong place we could be mixing and matching for weeks. Given how close the Golden Dawn is to finding the Sphere, time is not our ally."

Allegra stepped forward, her eyes focused on the *Sigillum.*

"Bring up the paintings. All of them."

The Acolyte did as instructed. The paintings reappeared on the screens, and Allegra studied them for a moment, and then pointed to one, which depicted a young man in robes and flowing golden hair seated in profile by a window, resting a hand on a desktop globe and studying it intently.

"That one. The globe he's touching: that's a circle," Allegra said. "That's also a sphere."

Jason flipped through his notepad, and smiled.

"*The Astronomer,* by Vermeer. Just like John Dee. Add them all up, and we have a path."

"Through the paintings?" Carter asked.

Jason shook his head. "Through the Louvre. These paintings are all a part of the Louvre's permanent collection. Follow them in the right order, and they'll lead us . . ."

"To?" Allegra prodded.

Jason pointed to the screen still displaying Dee's sketch.

"The *Sigillum.* What's in the center?"

"A circle," Allegra said.

Carter stepped forward, his mouth agape.

"A sphere." He stared at Jason, stunned. "You believe the Sphere of Destiny—"

"Is somewhere in the Louvre," Jason finished.

For a long time nobody spoke. Not Carter, not Allegra, not the Acolyte. Even Katja remained silent. There was just the *Sigillum Dei Aemaeth,* the screens, and the hum of machinery.

"Just because something's part of a permanent collection doesn't mean it'll be on display," said Allegra. "One or more of these paintings could have been loaned out to another museum on another side of the globe, or gathering dust in storage. If you're wrong, this goose chase you're proposing could lead us to a dead end."

"Or worse, to the enemy," said Katja.

"And if I'm right . . . ?" Jason asked.

"If the Sphere *is* in the Louvre, who put it there?" Allegra asked.

"The same one who put the symbols into the paintings. The

same one who placed this notebook in the Citadel: John Dee. You said yourself he was a time traveler. I think he hid the Sphere in the Louvre, marked these paintings with symbols, and created the *Sigillum* so we could find it."

"So *you* could find it, through symbols only *you* can see." The doubt in Katja's voice was obvious. "What makes *you* so special?"

"I don't know," he said. "Believe me, I wish I did."

"It can't be that simple," she said.

"Not simple: *simplex*."

Carter folded his arms and stared at the paintings.

"Carter, you can't believe this. It's—" Allegra began.

"Too simple?" Carter asked. "Most magic tricks are. Sleight of hand, misdirection, making your eye focus on one thing when you should be looking at the entire picture."

"We still don't know who supplied Fraim with the flash drive," Allegra warned. "It could be the Golden Dawn trying to draw you out and eliminate you."

"Why go to all this trouble when they could have killed me at any time over the last year?" Jason asked. "Besides, the Red Queen says she wants me. Maybe we need to draw her out."

"And then you'll take care of her, will you, Archmage?" Katja asked.

"I can't hide forever, and I'm not going to. If she wants me, she'll have one hell of a fight."

Katja snorted derisively. "She'll have her fun with you, she'll draw you in, and then she'll strike. It's what she does, and we have dozens of dead Mages, including your father, to prove—"

"Katja, enough." Carter studied Jason intently. "The moment you step outside the Citadel, the Golden Dawn will know. That's the magical threat; the mundane one is the Louvre itself. The world's greatest art museum is France's national treasure. It is their home of culture; it is who they are, and they have taken steps to protect it. Security cameras, body scanners, guards in every gallery—and those are the ones you can see; the others are incognito, but they are there. All part of a private security force armed with explicit orders to shoot to kill. The Louvre is, for lack of a better word, a fortress. The most secure one in the world. Now, knowing all of this, can you look me in the eye and tell me you're certain what we seek is there?"

Jason met Carter's gaze and was surprised his didn't waver.

"As certain as I've been of anything."

Carter held Jason's gaze for a moment that became three . . . and smiled.

"Then let's go see some art."

NINETEEN

••••••••••••••••••••••

A HARSH AUTUMN WIND CUT through Jason and he drew up his jacket and tightened his scarf. Paris in late October was more like New York in late November, and he'd been in the Citadel's warm comfort for too long. The sky was chalkboard gray and there was a bone-chilling dampness to the air. But the speed at which Parisians walked, the bustle of the streets, the pods of visitors gaping at their maps and guidebooks and trying to figure out which way was which; at least he was less conspicuous than the paunchy, fanny pack– and sneaker-clad American tourists clustered nearby.

Paris. *He was in Paris.* And all he'd had to do to get there was open a door.

He crossed the street to join the team. There were five of them, one from each level of Mage, as Teo had explained during their escapades in Peckham: a wide-faced Slavic Adept named Illya Molotok; Abigail, their Archmage; Katja, their Enchanter; and Teo, their War Seer. Allegra was the team's leader and its Diabolist. They were, however, only one of three teams who had arrived in Paris; one had been dispatched to Versailles, the other to a notorious *banlieu* in the city's eastern suburbs. While a doorway could be opened directly into the Louvre, such an intrusion would likely bring the Golden Dawn down on them in less time than it would take to locate the Sphere. The other two teams were the distraction; the Louvre was the mission. Subterfuge would be their best weapon.

And there was Jason, the sixth member, and the one with the most important task: chart a path through the Louvre, and locate the Sphere. *He* was the advantage the Golden Dawn lacked; the secrets to decoding the symbols lay in his mind, and if the Golden Dawn captured him, those secrets would have to die with him.

Jason felt the weight of the card deck in his jacket pocket. He was ready.

They knew where to begin: Vermeer's *The Astronomer*. The team would get him there.

The rest was on him.

They crossed the grand Place de la Concorde to the tree-lined Jardin des Tuileries, where dead branches clawed the sky and the ground underfoot crunched with dead leaves as they walked down it. Autumn had tightened its grip on the mundane world; to Jason it seemed like only yesterday he was gazing out the window of the Metro-North at a sea of sun-kissed red and orange. It seemed like only yesterday for a lot of things.

He followed the team, taking advantage of his position to watch them all, especially Teo. A white bandage was wrapped around his forearm, and he could see a spot of red seeping through. Teo hadn't commented on it when the team had assembled, but Jason knew the bandage and the wound had been Teo's punishment for leaving the Citadel. Not even a skilled War Seer could escape Carter's wrath.

The closest to the Louvre that they could safely enter Paris had been inside a restaurant and museum called Maxim's. The museum was on the upper floors: a three-level collection of art nouveau objects housed in a turn-of-the-century apartment block. They'd entered the museum through a wardrobe door, startling a group of Spanish tourists and their guide in the process. Allegra and Katja had enchanted them into silence, and once that was done, the Mages departed. The corresponding doorway in the Citadel would be destroyed as a precaution. There was no way to the Citadel through Maxim's now, or ever; a new door would be opened when they found the Sphere.

If they found it.

As Jason gazed at the Romanesque statues lining the Jardin des Tuileries, alabaster white against the gray day, he passed a group of tourists admiring one of the sculptures. One—a teenage girl—was focused on him. He didn't look directly at her, but as he continued past, he felt her eyes following him.

The Golden Dawn *was* watching. He caught up to Allegra and fell into step beside her.

"We're being watched," he said.

"I know."

She nodded to a larger group of tourists ahead on their left, and one on the right farther up. She didn't point or comment, but each group they passed had at least one pair of eyes on him, all the way down to a large circular fountain and the ornate brick and stone archway beyond that. The Louvre and its imposing glass pyramid loomed just beyond.

"They know we're in Paris, but not why," she continued. "Right now they've probably spotted the other two teams and are splitting their resources to track all three of us. What each watcher sees is just a piece of the puzzle. As long as we move quickly, by the time they get the whole picture we'll be long gone."

"You think so?"

"That's your job." she said. "And don't think I've forgotten those answers you still owe me."

"Answers?" He frowned.

"Playing dumb is not a good look for you, Jason. I'm talking about how you read Kel's thoughts at Skara Brae, for one. How you can see these symbols no one else can, for another."

"When I know, you'll be the first I tell," he said.

"I wait, with baited breath," Allegra said.

Then she picked up her pace and left Jason in her wake.

It wasn't until he gazed upon the majesty of the Louvre that Jason realized just how much he'd become used to New York's museums. With so many packed into so small an island they tended to blend into one another. But nothing prepared him for the Louvre; it wasn't a museum—it was a palace, comprising a half-dozen different styles into its two-story structure; Gothic, Renaissance, Baroque, Neoclassical, Modernist, and some that were unknown to even Jason, who'd spent the sleepless night before studying a book on the Louvre he'd acquired in the games room. The sheer amount of space the museum occupied filled him with awe and dread; it flanked the entrance in a *U* shape, with the towering crystalline pyramid at its center granting its visitors access through stairs and an elevator leading below ground. The pyramid stood bordered by seven slightly smaller triangular shaped fountains and three smaller glass triangles arranged on the outside edge, like the design had sprung from John Dee's *Sigillum Dei Aemaeth* itself.

A line of people stretched across the approach to the pyramid, hundreds jockeying to enter the museum. As the team approached, the sun made a momentary appearance from behind a wall of slate-gray cloud, the pyramid illuminated in its beams gleaming like molten gold. The team, all of them, paused as if to admire this brief moment of beauty. Then the sun slipped back behind the clouds, and cold reality crashed back in. They had a mission, and that mission began in earnest now.

Allegra sized up the crowd, and turned to their Adept.

"Showtime, Illya" she said.

"I will need assist," he said, in broken English.

"Katja, you're on," said Allegra.

Katja sighed and nodded to Illya, who lifted his fedora off and set it on the ground. He rolled up his sleeves, shook his hands loose, clapped them together, and looked to Katja. She raised a hand and Jason caught a shimmer of luminescence, and she directed that into Illya's hands. He pulled them apart to release a white dove that took to the sky with a flap of wings. All down the line the crowd gazed at the bird as it flew high, disappearing into the blanket of low-lying autumn clouds. Children squealed, applause sounded, and a few euros fell into Illya's upturned hat as a card deck slid out of his sleeve. He caught, separated, and manipulated it, shuffling fast, firing the cards from one hand to the next and making Jason feel woefully inadequate with his own skills. The crowd soon found their attention drawn from the Louvre to the agile Adept, and when everyone was watching, Jason felt a hand grasp onto his shoulder.

"We got our entry point," said Teo. "Buckle up."

There was a flash of light, and they were below, in the lobby of the pyramid, its glass structure vaulting above them and filtering another brief burst of sunlight over the crowded floor. They'd materialized beneath the enormous spiral staircase, and moved quickly across the lobby into an immense polished-stone and marble passageway with an arched ceiling and lined with statue-festooned alcoves. At the far end of the corridor Jason glimpsed the majestic *Winged Victory of Samothrace* perched atop a staircase leading to the next floor. It was surrounded by a horde of selfie-happy tourists, and the statue was the first of what was sure to be many works of art he'd lay eyes upon before their mission was complete. The palatial Louvre was as much a work of art as the city it stood in; it was also crowded to capacity; patrons passed throughout the corridor, audio guides and phones glued to their hands. Their eyes were fixed on maps, on their WiFi connections—everywhere but on the two among many who had materialized in their midst. As far as the crowd was concerned, Teo and Jason were just two more faces among hundreds.

Three faces: Allegra emerged from an alcove to their left and fell into step with them.

"Katja will take the Richelieu Wing, Abigail will handle the Napoleon Hall, and Illya will dazzle the punters upstairs. As long as we stay scattered and keep moving the Golden Dawn won't know who to follow." Allegra nodded to Jason. "That leaves us, and you, and Mr. Johannes Vermeer."

A gaggle of squawking British tourists passed, and as they did a museum guidebook visible in an open handbag leapt out and landed in Allegra's hand. She opened the guide, scanned the pages, and held it up to Jason and Teo. A black-and-white photo of Vermeer's *The Astronomer* was visible on the page, along with a gallery indicated on the corresponding map beside it.

"Let's go see some art," she said.

. . .

The ceiling of the Richelieu Wing vaulted two, definitely three, and possibly more stories above them, and their walls held a vast array of painted treasures. Everywhere they looked there was something to take their breath away. It was also laid out in as nonlinear a fashion as could be imagined, and they'd actually walked past *The Astronomer* twice before they found it. It was small—less than twenty inches tall—and nestled in a thick wooden frame. Jason looked over the room for any sign of Katja, who was supposed to be there, but he couldn't see her. Then again, as an Enchanter, being seen would have defeated the purpose.

Allegra nodded to the painting. "All right, you're on."

Teo set his eyes on the crowd and any looming signs of trouble.

Allegra stared at Jason, expectantly.

Showtime, he thought.

He set his eyes on *The Astronomer*. He was in profile, long golden hair tucked behind his ears as he sat at a cloth-covered table, his right hand resting atop a globe and studying it intently. Warm light fell through a partially obscured window to the left of the frame, and a chart—circular, naturally—was pinned to a cabinet beside him. Books were piled atop that, and behind him were the beginnings of a painting within the larger one, but Jason couldn't make out much detail. The colors were warm woods, blue-and-gray-patterned fabrics, and soft shadows. He felt like he could slip inside and live in it forever.

He narrowed his gaze. The symbol *should* have been there, but it wasn't. What was happening?

Or more specifically, what *wasn't*?

"Anything?" Allegra asked.

Jason stepped closer. He narrowed his gaze. Where was it?

"*Anything?*" Allegra asked again.

"Not yet, but please, keep interrupting because that *really* helps."

He expected a pushback, but she backed off, leaving him with *The Astronomer*.

He stepped even closer, allowing the painting to fill his vision, so there was nothing to look at but it. He envisioned the warmth of the room, the comforting scent of old books, the feel of the smooth wooden globe under his hand. Jason could almost feel its cool, concave surface.

Something tugged at him, a gentle pull on his skin, like when he drifted into Vasilisa's mind.

He leaned in closer and took a step forward, and his foot landed on hardwood with a dull echo. The temperature of the room changed from the cool dry air of the gallery to the warmth of an artist's studio. His eyes adjusted to the dark confines of the astronomer's chamber, and his nostrils filled with the smell of wet paint.

He was inside. Inside the painting itself.

The astronomer was seated as he had been on the outside, telltale brushstrokes denoting the illusion of light and color on him. Up close those fine brushstrokes were crude and without detail, like they'd been applied with a housepainter's roller. Here his gentle, knowing face looked like something out of a Cubist nightmare. Jason looked to the rest of the room, and found it trailed off into darkness beyond the borders glimpsed from outside. He looked out the window but there was nothing outside but bright paint strokes.

Yet he could sense *something*. Something lurking unseen, tracing gentle fingers along the back of his neck. He felt them brush his skin there, and he turned around to look back to where the window into the painting and the astronomer's world—the frame—would be. He expected to see the gallery, and Teo and Allegra staring at him, like they were looking through a window. He expected to see himself staring slack-jawed into the painting. Instead, he saw a circle, glowing with unnatural reddish light that shifted colors the longer he stared at it. Red to orange to yellow to near translucent, and repeating the cycle. It was the circle from the *Sigillum Dei Aemaeth,* slowly turning clockwise and drawing him closer to it.

He stepped toward it, reached out a hand, and touched it. His hand passed through it and it dissipated, glowed and rippled, and then reformed, not into a circle but into the seven-sided heptagon. As he stared through it, he caught a glimpse of a tricolor flag rippling in the breeze, the whiff of gunpowder in his nostrils, and the shouts of *liberté* in his ears.

He sucked air with a shudder and almost fell. Allegra rushed to his side.

"Are you all right?" she asked. "We lost you there for a moment."

He looked about in confusion as noise crashed back in. He was back in the gallery. The sudden crush of sound jolted through him. Teo darted over; even Allegra looked concerned.

"Was I gone?" he asked.

"Not physically. But it was like you were far, far away from here."

"I was." He pointed to the painting. "I was inside . . ."

"Inside the painting?" Allegra grasped his hand. "What did you—"

—*Anush kneels in the market, the howl of the mob encircling her rising to a pitch. The man clutching the rock points an accusatory finger at her and lets the rock fly. It strikes her forehead. Pain screams through her tiny body and she falls to the ground. Her gaze settles on the bloodstained stone rolling across the dirt beside her. Blood runs over her eyes, submerging her vision in crimson. Through its red veil she sees others snatch rocks from the dirty ground. She sits up and holds up her hand, her fingers splayed, then she brings her hand down and fissures tear into the foundations of the earth—*

"—see?" Allegra asked.

He tensed, and yanked his hand out of hers. She reeled and stared at him.

"What is it?" she asked.

Jason shook the vision off and stared at Allegra. At the scar above her eye.

"I—I was—" he stammered.

Inside your mind. But how to explain that to her when he couldn't explain it himself?

"What did you see got you so spooked, mate?" Teo asked.

"The Sphere?" Allegra asked.

Jason considered his response and then nodded slowly.

"The second painting. I *was* right; it *is* a code! And it's going to lead us right to the Sphere!"

If Jason had presumed locating the other sigils would be as simple as finding *The Astronomer*'s, that assumption died the moment they located *Liberty Leading the People* and he stepped inside. The difference couldn't have been starker: *The Astronomer* was a quiet, meditative piece; *Liberty* was a battleground, and the air inside it was a noxious mixture of gunpowder and paint, and filled with the screams of the dead and dying under his feet. Liberty herself held the tricolor aloft heroically, and the people she led trailed in her wake with devotion, but the ground was littered with corpses, and Jason's feet slipped through them like they were globs of fresh paint, his footsteps trailing oils the color of flesh and clothes and blood. Volleys of gun- and cannon fire streaked the clouded skies above, slicing through them as easily as a painter's brush through his palette. But in the end he located the next sigil—the first of the off-centered, asymmetrical squares—in the red of Liberty's flag, and it opened a doorway into the next painting: *The Raft of the Medusa*.

The dark waters had churned slowly, and the raft he stood upon roiled with the current. Several times he was about to pitch over the side and sink beneath the angry surface, but he managed to nudge through its desperate, dying occupants to its makeshift mast and grasped onto it, staring at the windswept sail and noting both the sigil on it, and finding the way to the next painting; the vast *Tuileries Palace* by Melling, which from the inside occupied as much space as the Louvre did on the outside. It took him close to an hour of searching to locate the second asymmetrical square that led him to Provost's surrealist *Sacred Allegory*, with its Christ, Mary, and hand of God clutching a pale-blue sphere adorned with a cross, held between two single eyes staring forward from the infinite. Despite its heavy symbols and symbolism, the sigil he sought—the first hexagram—was tucked away in the woodwork of a wooden chest by Christ's left knee, and served as the gateway to another Vermeer, *The Lacemaker*, and the next symbol the girl was embroidering into her swatch of blue fabric. The next sigils—a heptagon found in Backhuysen I's *Ships at Sea off Amsterdam* and the pentagram in Bouhot's *The Attic of a Museum*—fell in rapid succession. By the time they'd completed the first third of the *Sigillum* with the discovery of the second circle in Gossaert's *Diptych of Jean Carondelet,* it felt like three hours had passed. But when Jason emerged from that painting with the location of the next sigil, Solario's *The Head of St. John the Baptist,* he discovered to his dismay that barely forty minutes had passed in the Louvre itself.

"You've got to be *kidding* me!" he exclaimed.

"I wish I was," said Allegra.

He took a seat on a bench and exhaled. He was exhausted from his travels and they were only a third of the way through. He needed food and drink . . . hell, he needed a goddamn *nap*. But as Allegra crossed her arms and narrowed her gaze he knew none were forthcoming.

"This is taking too long," she said. "It's been almost an hour."

"Yeah, for you!" he said. "Every minute out here is like three in there. . . ."

Allegra cupped a hand to her ear and listened.

"Did you hear that?" she asked.

"Hear what?" The only noise was the din of patrons tromping about the high-ceilinged gallery.

"That whooshing sound that just blasted past your ear. That was the point I'm trying to make."

Despite his weary bones, Jason stood. He was glad he stood a head taller than Allegra; it made it easier for him to be the one glaring down at her. He saw Teo across the gallery. Teo saw him, too, and must have sensed the blowup about to occur, because he was double-timing it to them.

"Say that again," Jason said.

"What's to say?" Allegra asked. "Every minute we spend here is one closer to the Golden Dawn finding out what we're seeking; only it's been nearly an hour and we're *still* looking!"

"I'm going as fast as I can! You don't like it—"

Teo slid smoothly between the two of them, all smiles.

"Children, let's not make a scene in fronta the mundanes. He's trying his best, marm."

"His best better get a *lot* better," she grumbled.

Don't push her. She's dangerous. Don't push her.

He pushed anyway.

"Anush. That's your name, right? Your *real* name?"

Allegra's stunned eyes narrowed into slits. Fire blazed incandescent in them.

"*Who told you that?!*" she whispered.

"You did," he said. "Now, are you going to do my job, *Anush,* or are you going to shut the hell up and let me do mine?"

The fire in her eyes settled. She thrust the guidebook at him, turned, and stormed off, brushing past a tour group and exiting the gallery entirely.

"You have a real way with women, doncha?" Teo said, after she'd gone.

"It's a gift," Jason said.

"Don't mind her. She don't have much love for men, or women for that matter."

"Well, she's got even less for me."

"Can you blame her?"

"Actually, I can; what did I ever do to her?"

"You remind her of Damon. He was like a dad to her, you know?"

"I'm glad he was a dad to someone . . ." Jason began.

"C'mon, mate, you're better than that. Allegra's just anxious. You're doin' a bang-up job, but she's right; we hafta hustle."

Jason nodded. "Then we'll hustle; *after* I get a coffee."

. . .

Maybe it was because he was becoming an expert in navigating the strange physics of the artificial worlds John Dee had hidden his sigils inside, maybe it was the very strong coffee he now had in his system, or maybe it was because for the first time since arriving inside the Louvre they could sense the eyes of the Golden Dawn gathering, but the next nine puzzle pieces fell into place with greater speed. *The Head of St. John the Baptist* led to Jacques Louis David's massive *Coronation of Napoleon,* and through the seven paintings following. Jason trod painted galleries and religious scenes and attics and villages and markets, but this time he was energized by the knowledge that each step was bringing them closer to the Sphere. The cycle repeated itself a third and final time, from Bazzi's *The Allegory of Love* all the way to Memmi's *Crucifixion:* the location of the last pentagram. Despite the lateness of the hour—the view outside glimpsed through the windows had grown increasingly dark—and despite Jason's fatigue at what had been, to him anyway, six hours of searching, his pulse pounded. He didn't need to look for the next symbol, because through a process of elimination there was only one painting and one sigil remaining.

The journey was nearly complete. The Sphere was nearly theirs.

There was just one more person to see.

She had a gallery of her own, and it seemed like all of Paris was there to see her. It took much longer than Jason hoped it would to reach the front; he had to maneuver past raised cameras and smartphones and tablets as the patrons took photos, more concerned with preserving their place in the moment than experiencing it. He reached the barrier separating him from the painting. It was behind glass, flanked by museum staff, and he took note of four guards in the corners of the room, and the conspicuous bulges in their breast jacket pockets. He stared at her, pushing all other noise away. The sound faded, darkness closed around them, and then it was just him and the *Mona Lisa*.

Nothing happened. No pull, no sense of slipping out of his body and into her world. He tried again, and again; nothing. There was *nothing*.

What was happening? Was he tapped out? Was he being blocked?

"What's wrong?" Teo asked.

Jason shook his head. "I don't know; it's not working."

He focused on her eyes, the most famous in the world, and felt nothing. No tug. No pull.

Where was it? Why wouldn't she let him in? What was she staring at . . . ?

He slowly turned, positioned himself in her eyeline, and followed her gaze back through the crowd, back out of the room to the corridor outside the gallery, and to the painting facing her.

"Crafty son of a . . ." He smiled.

While everyone with a camera and selfie stick seemed to be cluttering the *Mona Lisa*'s gallery, the Leonardo mounted in the corridor outside it was passed by with the scarcest notice. That was where they found *John the Baptist*—the second in their journey. But where Solario's Baptist was post-execution, his openmouthed head resting on a silver platter, this was a much younger, much more sensual John. He had almond eyes, waves of dark curls, and an alluring smirk that seemed to draw you in like *Mona Lisa*'s smile did. He was framed in darkness, his hand pointing to the sky, and as Jason leaned in closer he felt that tug and pull, and stepped over the precipice and into the painting. Everything surrounding the Baptist was without light or form; there was just John. There was no symbol anywhere, and Jason felt his pulse race. This was it; it *had* to reveal the location of the Sphere. They'd come all this way; he'd promised Carter and the others he was right. But there was nothing; no symbol, no sphere, just the smell of wine and grape, and John . . . pointing to the sky. Jason slowly looked up, above the top of the painting's frame, and beyond it to something that flashed briefly through the darkness.

It wasn't a symbol, or the Sphere. It was a hand clutching a stone.

For a moment Jason thought of Allegra and that blood-covered rock.

But this was a very different one.

The noise crashed down in a swarm of bodies and Jason staggered back into the museum. Teo was about to ask him what he saw when Jason snatched the guidebook from him and flipped through its pages quickly.

"Did you see it?" Teo's eyes were wild with anticipation.

Jason looked up from the book, met Teo's gaze . . . and smiled.

He was a giant cast in bronze: muscular, angular, with a smooth, polished, cylindrical stone clutched in his raised hand. In his other was clenched an equally giant serpent, mouth open, fangs bared, the coils of its body piled beneath it like spilled intestines. Both were set on marble, and the Cour Marly sculpture garden housed a good twenty more statues. It was four levels in descending order from the roof to the lowest point, and the gallery's windows and archways vaulted two stories above them to a majestic glass-domed ceiling spanning the entire length and breadth of the garden below. Dim daylight spilled in through the dome, and spotlights cast the mix of bronze and marble statues in hard shadows. The space was ringed by stone archways where people entered and exited, taking selfies and mimicking the dramatic poses. Two large stairways ran parallel down either side of the first floor to the levels below. There was a cross section of classical and Romanesque styles: heroic figures astride rearing horses, gods and goddesses clutching tridents. It was impressive, even to Jason and Teo, as they entered.

"*Heracles Battling Achelous.*" Teo studied the inscription on the pedestal. "I don't unnerstand."

"I didn't either, at first." Jason pointed to the hand. "What's he holding?"

"A rock," Teo said.

"Bronze statue? Bronze is hollow isn't it?"

Teo studied the statue. Jason watched his eyes and saw the moment of realization.

"It's inside the statue . . ." Teo said. "Inside the rock."

Jason pointed. "That's what I saw. No symbol, just John pointing above to that hand."

"Brilliant," Teo said. "All we hafta do is get it out of a priceless statue inna middle of the Louvre with no one noticing."

"Nobody said it was going to be easy," Jason said.

"*Nobody* was spot on," Teo said. "We need to find Allegra, 'ave her—"

A loud metallic clang sounded, and the statue shuddered. Mundane eyes looked from their cameras to Heracles and Achelous. Another clang, and the bronze stone buckled, like something was punching its way out. The hammering became more violent, steel striking an anvil. There was a rending of metal; a fissure tore the stone open and something round and wooden crowned the opening like it was giving birth. It tore free, launched past Jason and Teo, and fired across the gallery into the hand of its summoner with a loud smack of wood against flesh.

Not unlike Heracles, this man was a giant also, six-plus feet carved in Nordic muscle. Tattoos ran the length of his powerful forearms, and he contemplated his prize for a moment before looking to Jason.

"Our Queen requests your presence, Jason Bishop," the man said.

With a sigh, the mundanes who were cluttering the gallery— all of them—dropped away in a dead faint, their guidebooks and phones and cameras clattering to the floor. As they fell, smoke erupted in sharp explosions and disgorged eight conjurers, all tattooed. They'd been watching the entire time, waiting until the moment of discovery to snatch their prize.

"Mallet," said Teo. "Surprised she sent you, after the pasting we gave you in Riga."

"You want this? We want Bishop," said Mallet.

"I didn't think it was your style to bargain," Jason said.

"It isn't," Mallet said. "The Queen demands it."

Thunder tore the air, and a figure dropped from midway up the gallery, landing in a crouch and standing to fix her fiery eyes on Mallet's.

It was Allegra.

"The Queen will have to take it," she said.

Light flashed, thunder blasted; Teo blinked out and blinked back in behind Mallet, dropped, and kicked the back of the hulking man's knee. Mallet pitched back, the Sphere fell, and Teo caught it, then vanished, and reappeared above Mallet to deliver a heavy kick to his face. Mallet's face hit the marble floor with an excruciating-sounding crack that sent shattered teeth scattering across the ground.

Teo pivoted and threw the Sphere. It arced back toward Jason and Allegra. Something blinked between the Sphere and them: a woman in ripped and worn denim with shaved hair and tattoos covering her skull. She intercepted the Sphere, clutched it to her chest, and dropped to the floor in a crouch. The air split, Allegra grabbed the girl, and both disappeared in a flash and reappeared in a loud crash high above that cracked the domed ceiling. They fell, disappearing, reappearing, and falling in a clatter of thunderous blasts. They grasped the Sphere as the floor raced to meet them. There was an explosion of smoke and noise and they blinked across the gallery floor toward the lower floors like stones skipping across water.

More dark shapes appeared in the alcoves. One with sharp Asian features spotted Jason, raised his hand into a fist, and howled an enchantment. A pedestal cracked, buckled, and toppled, sending a priceless marble figure shattering to the floor. The pieces launched at Jason, who raised his hands defensively and pushed. They glanced off the barrier and deflected into the walls and floor, chipping marble and stone loose. That debris rose into the air in a jagged cloud that redirected itself back at the Asian man. He was struck and recoiled, the shrapnel tearing skin and shredding flesh, misting the air with blood.

Jason gaped. Christ, did he do that?

"Don't just stand there!" Abigail shouted from the archway to his left. "Fight!"

Illya bounded in after her, slipped into shadows behind a Golden Dawn, and bodily slammed the enemy into an archway, knocking him senseless.

Jason yanked his jacket open. The deck of cards leapt from its inside pocket into his hand.

A tattooed figure slid through his periphery. He pivoted, planted his index finger atop the deck, and flicked his wrist. Cards sliced the air and tore the Golden Dawn agent's arms, face, and bare chest. Blood sprayed and the man staggered, clutching his wounds and screaming. Another charged in right after him, mouthed a spell, and clapped his hands together. The cards bounced back, and the conjurer directed them at Jason. He dodged, felt one sing past his ear, reached out, grasped a marble column, and pulled, toppling the pedestal and its heavy marble bust onto the second agent's leg. There was a loud snap and a scream, the leg broken at a hard right. The man fell, but another took his place. Jason pulled the fallen cards back into his hand and threw the entire deck into the air. He pushed at the billowing cloud, like he'd seen Damon push on Storm King, and the cards fluttered through the garden, sending the swarming Golden Dawn scrambling for cover.

Allegra was still blinking in and out of space above the floor and at points on it, battling for possession of the Sphere in staccato bursts of sound. Then she lost her hold on the Sphere, and the girl pulled it close. Allegra grasped the girl's shoulders, blinked them both above and down to a statue of Poseidon holding his trident aloft. There was a sickening wet crunch, and the girl was impaled on its bronze blades. The Sphere dropped, hit the floor, rolled for the stairs, crested them, and bounced down, one step after the other. In the chaos of battle nobody noticed—but Jason did. He let the cards fall and he was off, scrambling for the Sphere.

He reached a hand for it. His fingers brushed its smooth face. He pulled—

It resisted.

Someone else was holding onto it. Over a dividing wall and down the next set of steps he saw Mallet, arms thrust forward, his ruined mouth spitting enchantments. Jason tightened his grip on the Sphere. His feet slid to the edge of the stairs.

There was another thunderclap, this one piercing enough to shatter the glass dome high above. Two figures blinked into view in midair, and three others followed.

Barkhad Biyaha plunged, jagged panes of glass plummeting alongside him. As he fell, he pushed and directed the shards into whatever enemies he could see. Anguished screams tore the air, and the marble floor was painted with blood as multiple targets dropped. Clas Guld followed, hurtling a ragged shard at another conjurer, slicing his carotid and sending gouts of crimson spilling across cold marble. Three other War Seers fell in behind Clas and Barkhad, landed in crouches, and leapt into the fray.

Reinforcements had arrived.

Barkhad landed across from Jason and directed fallen bits of marble at Mallet. He deflected, sending them smashing into other statuary, alcoves, and columns. Mallet's grip on the Sphere slackened. Jason pulled. The Sphere halted its descent, held, then bounced back up the stairs, two, three at a time, to him. He almost had it when something big and dark swung into his periphery.

"Jason!" Barkhad shouted—the first and last time he spoke Jason's name—and slammed him aside.

The Sphere bounced away but before Jason could react, heavy metal came down on the Somali like an anvil, smashing the War Seer's spine, bursting his torso, and spilling red everywhere. The bloody foot lifted off of Barkhad, dripping gore as it pivoted and planted back down with a metallic clang. Jason looked up the leg and naked torso to the impassive bronze face of Heracles, hand still clutching the stone the Sphere had been wrenched from.

Clas charged at Heracles, his hands tightening. The statue's right leg crumpled with a screech, and the giant toppled with a heavy crash that shook the floor and nearly sent Jason falling with it. The Sphere brushed Clas's foot and he darted for it. Jason gazed at Heracles, almost idly wondering what had happened to Achelous . . . when a slither of bronze against marble sounded and the mighty serpent rocketed from the shadowed alcoves, fangs bared.

Clas saw it and dodged as its mouth clanged shut with a heavy bronze-against-bronze sound. He kicked off the snake's head, driving its reopened mouth into the floor and burying its fangs in marble, but the serpent writhed, its coils snapping, like a bullwhip. It broadsided Clas and sent him careening into a wall. The tail struck the Sphere, sending it bouncing. Clas rebounded, and was midway through the air when something long and sharp pierced his chest, sent him reeling backward, and spiked him to the wall like an insect pinned to a specimen board. He slumped limp against the spear shaft of the trident that killed him.

The marble Poseidon lowered his throwing arm and strode forward, footsteps cracking the marble and stone floor. It stooped down to grasp at the Sphere, but its fingers were clumsy and hard. The Sphere jumped between them like a basketball bouncing around the rim of a hoop.

Jason pulled, and the Sphere leapt across the floor to him. Poseidon saw, pivoted, charged, and was on top of Jason in two lunging strides. The statue raised its hands into fists to strike.

Teo blinked into the air above Poseidon, fell onto the statue's head, grasped it, and blinked away, taking the Greek god's cranium with him. The headless torso staggered, teetered, clawed at the space where its head had been, then fell forward. Jason dove between its legs, slid, and grasped the Sphere as the statue toppled onto the still-writhing Achelous, crushing the serpent beneath its weight. Marble shattered, bronze caved in, and after a brief shudder, the titans were motionless.

Teo blinked back into view and dropped Poseidon's head with a crash.

"We got this, Jason, get it outta 'ere!" he shouted.

Boot steps clattered across the floor as more Golden Dawn streamed into the gallery. Some he recognized from the Orkneys, others were new; all were lethal. Teo blinked and attacked, his moves a blur in light and shadow. Illya dove in and out of darkness, striking, sinking back, and striking again. Abigail had torn a light fixture from its mounting and, as the bulb burst, harnessed a puff of flame, feeding it oxygen, making it rage. She sent that flame arcing through the gallery, striking Golden Dawn, igniting them, sending them flailing and screaming. Burning flesh and the stink of piss and fear pervaded the air. Jason saw Allegra weave amidst the flames, blocking attacks, redirecting them, and smiling with every crippling blow she delivered.

They had this. He had the Sphere. And he needed to get it out of there.

Jason thrust a hand out and, across the gallery, the cards fluttered back into his palm, reforming a deck. He shoved them into his pocket, clutched the Sphere tight, and was off. He ran, down the stairs, boosted himself over the wall, dropped, tucked, rolled, and recovered. He ran, fueled by instincts he'd only now been able to harness.

It was Murder Hill all over again, only this time *he* was in control.

He was going to make that jump. He was going to clear the edge of that ramp and plunge into those cleansing waters. Only this time he wasn't going to sink. *He was going to fly*.

A hulking shape entered his path. Mallet raised his beefy hands to strike, tattoos shimmering as he marshaled whatever dark powers the Golden Dawn swore allegiance to.

He collided with Mallet and felt his feet leave the ground and his body leave the gallery. There was a sudden jolt and he felt his feet plant on the smooth stone floor, and saw something at the end of the corridor that snatched air from his lungs.

It was *Winged Victory of Samothrace*.

He was near where he and Teo had entered the Louvre, and he'd done it himself.

Level Four. A War Seer. *He did it*.

A gurgle sounded above him. He looked up, and it took everything he had in him *not* to scream.

Mallet had followed but not all the way; he was embedded in the ceiling. A muscular arm reached blindly for him and Jason could hear his muffled screams. The arm flailed, spasmed, tensed, and finally hung limp, a macabre piece of art now part of the Louvre's permanent collection. Jason couldn't stifle the horrified shudder that coursed through him.

"Arrêtez!"

Metal rattled behind him as gun safeties clattered off.

"La bombe! Deposer la bombe!"

There were six of them: men in insectile body armor. Men with guns. The Louvre's private army had mobilized. Those guns were trained on him, laser lights dancing across his chest.

"It's all right, I'm an American!" Jason shouted.

"Drop the explosive!" The leader's English was heavily accented.

Explosive? Jason realized they meant the Sphere. He also knew they wouldn't repeat the order.

One of the guards shuddered violently like he was having a seizure. He raised his gun and fired a burst point-blank into the lead officer's Kevlar vest. The man lurched and fell, clutching at his wound and writhing. The others reacted too slowly as their comrade fired again, kneecapping two, shattering another's elbow, and blowing the thumb off the last.

The shooter fell unconscious to the ground with a thud of armor and gunmetal.

"You have it?" a familiar voice asked.

Katja was standing in an alcove just ahead, leaning casual against the wall, like she hadn't just crippled six people doing their jobs.

"What did you do to them?" he demanded.

"What I had to." She nodded to the Sphere. "That's it?"

He pulled the Sphere closer and in the brief pause took his first good look at it. It was the size of a grapefruit, smooth and wooden, and felt hollow. But there was a weight to it, and it felt warm to the touch. His fingers traced markings on its face, small carved symbols he could barely make out in the corridor light—

"Gawk later. Move. *Now!*"

Katja strode down the corridor and Jason followed, moving quickly past the wounded but breathing guards, and caught up to her.

"They'll live," she said, as if she'd sensed his thoughts. "We need to get to the extraction point."

"Yeah? Where's that . . ."

The question trailed off as a rumble echoed through the corridor ahead. A louder rumble sounded behind, and they turned in time to see a heavy steel door slide down and slam into place.

Katja shoved Jason, sending him careening into the side of the corridor, behind an alcove. Katja took cover behind the support column on the opposite side.

The guards didn't bother with a warning. A dozen of them opened fire from cover as the next security door slammed down behind them. Jacketed steel tore the air, hacked the walls, and pinged off the steel barrier behind Jason and Katja. They were trapped.

"Can you get out?" Katja shouted.

Jason shook his head.

"I don't know what's on the other side of that door! I could end up embedded in it!'

"We need to backtrack, find another way!" Katja shouted again. "Follow me–"

The ground shuddered again. Rhythmic beats, gaining speed, gaining strength.

But it wasn't another security door. *Something* was coming.

There was a rending of metal as the door behind Jason and Katja tore and something massive galloped through the opening. It was a statue, a horse carved out of marble and animated by its rider: Allegra. She hunched low, gripping the marble beast's mane as the guards emptied their clips into it. The equine face was hacked to pieces by bullets, but she propelled the beast at them as surely as if she was piloting a boat down the Seine. The horse stiffened and toppled and she kicked off, backflipped, and landed in a crouch. The statue smashed into the floor and sent heavy slabs of marble slamming into bodies, breaking bones, knocking them senseless, and continued, to smash a hole through the base of the security door behind them, creating a fresh opening. The entire battalion lay broken, writhing and groaning, but alive.

Jason exhaled with relief, and his breath misted in air that had suddenly gone cold. His blood chilled with near equal speed.

She was coming.

Allegra and Katja sensed it, too.

"You have your exit point!" Allegra shouted. "Get the Sphere out of here!"

"But where do I take—"

"Jason, she's coming! RUN!"

Jason ran.

He felt his speed rage uncontrolled. Unstoppable. He reached the security gate, pictured the ground outside, cool and hard, and unyielding . . . and blinked—

He was in the Louvre's main entrance, the glass pyramid vaulting above. He sighted the spiral staircase winding up to the surface, blinked again—

He was up the stairs to the ground level. He sighted the grounds outside the pyramid, and blinked again—

The area surrounding the museum entrance was filled with people running, screaming, and crying. Police directed them away from the museum as helicopters beat the air, spotlights sweeping the crowd. Jason moved, blending in, walking fast and steady. The Sphere was tucked under his arm, and he avoided eye contact, the police, and the spotlights. He kept to the shadows all the way down to the Jardin des Tuileries and didn't stop walking until he was back at the Place de la Concorde. He was out, but he'd lost sight of Allegra and Teo, Abigail and Katja, and whoever else was left.

There was no sign of any of them. *He was alone.*

But not entirely. He could feel her icy fingers radiating across the city, searching for the Sphere, and searching for him.

He had the Sphere. Now, he had to *run*.

TWENTY

························

THE CITY OF LIGHT HAD astonished him when he'd arrived hours before, but now its streets filled Jason with dread. Every turn he took, every cross street he passed, he expected someone to leap out of the shadows and attack. With the Sphere tucked under his coat that feeling was amplified tenfold. He veered north from Place de la Concorde, up Rue Royale, and deeper into the city. The Parisians he passed took no note of him; he was just another face in the crowd and was happy to keep it that way. A cold wind blew down the street and stopped him in his tracks. For a moment he thought it was her, but it was just the wind. He moved again, quicker this time, staying in the shadows, not giving her or any of them a chance to lock on to him.

But he was still being followed.

He didn't know *how* he knew, but they were a block or so behind him.

They knew who he was. They knew what he was carrying.

He knew they were hostile.

A police car tore up Rue Royale, lights flashing. Jason cocked an ear and listened, but aside from the roar of the city, the sirens and thud of helicopter blades around the Louvre had gone silent. Damaged statuary would have repaired itself, shattered glass and chipped marble reformed, and some enchantment—a fire alarm, a report of a suspicious package forcing an evacuation—set in place to cover their tracks. Of the wounded mundanes there was no easy answer. What would be the explanation for the bullet wounds and broken limbs this time? A bomb? A terror attack? An accident? It still pointed to the fact Jason had to keep moving . . . but to where? He had no money, no passport, no way out . . . and he was still being followed.

He felt the ground shudder beneath him.

The subway. Should he risk it? Underground he'd be vulnerable. No easy way in or out. But if he hopped a train, at least he'd be moving. And Allegra had said as long as they kept moving the Golden Dawn couldn't get a lock. He could stay on the train until he figured out something.

Anything.

By the time he reached the lavish gold trimmed Beaux-Arts Palais Garnier and the Opera Metro stop situated across from it, the swollen clouds above had begun to spit fat drops of rain onto the pavement. It was followed by more, as if the heavens themselves were driving him underground. They spurred him down the stairs with the crowd, and he merged with the stream of commuters and followed the current inside. Descending the steps his thoughts returned to his escape from the Louvre. He'd blinked out of the sculpture garden and out of the museum; he *was* a War Seer. But could he cast an enchantment? Levels were cumulative, each skill set blending into the next. He could hide in shadows; he could levitate and manipulate objects. Enchantment should be the same principle: instead of manipulating an object, he was manipulating a person, wearing their persona like a mask.

A row of electronic turnstiles stood ahead. Commuters waved cards and slipped tickets in; easy if you had the euros to pay for either, which he didn't. He could try blinking but that would attract too much attention with this many people around, even though balance would make them forget it minutes later. But too bold a display would alert the Golden Dawn to his whereabouts as if he'd fired off a gun in the middle of the crowd. There had to be another way . . .

Someone jostled him—

A flash—

A long day at work, a long ride home. A wife he hasn't slept beside for months.

Jason steadied himself. The man muttered what was either a curse or an apology, tapped his card to a sensor, and passed through the turnstiles.

Another bump, another flash—

She was late, the sitter wouldn't wait forever and money's been so tight . . .

Anger, panic, despair all washed over Jason as she passed.

But she had left something behind, just as the man had.

Could he do it? It would in all likelihood alert the Golden Dawn to his location . . .

But if they couldn't *see* him . . .

Jason spotted a sixty-something man, gray hair, gray skin, heavyset. His tired, beaten eyes glanced at Jason as he passed and as he did, Jason grasped the man's arm—

Recently widowed, no kids. Just the evening news, and a night of sleep in a lonely bed.

The man stared at him. Jason was still holding the man's arm. "*Excusez-moi,*" Jason muttered. He let go.

The old man muttered something and passed through the turnstile. As the man was dropping his swipe card into his pocket, Jason reached out his thoughts, felt his fingers grip the plastic, and pulled. The card leapt out of the pocket, flitted back through the turnstile, and landed in his palm. Jason looked down at his hands. They were chubby and liver-spotted, clutching the swipe card. A glance at the shiny tiled wall beside him reflected the old man's face back at him.

Like Teo said, sometimes you needed to get out of the classroom to learn.

He swiped the card and the gate slid open. He slipped through and didn't exhale until he descended the rest of the stairs and strode to the end of a tiled, advertisement-plastered platform with a high arched ceiling. There, he positioned himself so he could get a good look at the crowds on both sides.

He maintained the illusion; the older man's skin wrapped around his. He knew the magic he was using was broadcasting a signal to the Golden Dawn, but what else could he do? He was so new at this; he could only hope the Invisible Hand was locking onto the same signal, and that they'd find him before *she* did.

The wind rose and the clatter of an approaching train followed. After a moment the train blasted into the station, slowing to a stop with a screech of metal on metal. The doors parted, people scrambled off, others nudged on, and just as the doors closed, Jason slipped inside.

The train plunged down the neck of the tunnel. The car was full, every seat taken with people checking their phones, consulting tour guides, or staring into space. He felt that presence get farther and farther behind him. Whoever had been following him, he'd definitely lost them.

He glanced to a seat opposite him; a young woman held a baby girl on her lap. The baby smiled at Jason. He smiled back, which delighted the child more. Jason held onto that child's smile for everything it was worth, grasping that single moment of light in a world filling with encroaching darkness.

He thought of Carla and Noah. He wondered if they were still in Cold Spring.

He wondered—

The din ceased abruptly, like something had caught the attention of everyone on the train. Jason glanced from the baby down the car and felt ice close around him.

Everyone on the train was staring at him.

"Why do you run, Jason?" A man, his French accent pronouncing it *Zhayson*.

"Weren't you listening?" A woman; her Gaelic lilt was like a dagger to the chest.

"In the library. I said that you didn't belong with them." The old man Jason had enchanted himself into, seated midway down the car.

"You belong with us." A young woman in nurse's scrubs, phone abandoned at her feet.

"You belong with me." The woman seated across from him. The baby in her lap looked about, confused, like she had sensed something was very wrong with her mama.

"You can dispose of that shroud you are wearing," a callow youth said. "We found you, if that weren't painfully obvious."

Jason took a breath, and slipped the man's skin off like an old, weather-worn coat. They had him, and they knew it. He considered his options. They were few.

"Listen very carefully, *Zhayson*."

The train rocked as her words rippled through the car. One passenger picked up a sentence, then another, then another. The concoction of voices crashed around him.

"A train speeds north on its track at twelve point four miles per hour. This southbound train increases its speed to twenty-five miles per hour down its track."

The train's speed increased. The car shuddered.

"In two point four miles, this train will jump its track and collide with the oncoming one."

There was a screech of steel and a blast of horn and the train rocketed through the next station without stopping. Jason had a moment to glance at the confused faces of hundreds of commuters waiting on the platform as the train plunged back into the tunnel.

"Each car on this train carries eighty to a hundred people," the voices continued. "There are eight cars on this train. The other train carries the same number. It is, after all, rush hour."

The train lurched back and forth on the track.

"Now, can you tell me how many of these people will survive the crash?"

By the time the train had blasted through the next station, the baby's confused whimper had become a full-on wail. Aside from the sound of the train, it was the only noise in the car. The Sphere suddenly felt very heavy inside his coat. She had Jason right where she wanted.

"What do you want me to do?" he asked.

The train dipped down as the tunnel plunged beneath what must have been the Seine.

"I want you to get off this train at the next station."

The train climbed. Its speed began to slacken with a screech of metal to metal.

"Promise you won't hurt any of these people and I will."

"You aren't in a position to issue orders, Jason."

"*Promise,* or kill me."

There was a pause. All voices halted, all eyes remained on him.

"As you wish . . ." A solitary woman's voice spoke.

The lights of Invalides station spilled into the train as it entered, slowed, and shuddered to a stop. As Jason glanced out the window, his heart leapt into his throat.

The platform was littered with the bodies of countless commuters. They lay where they fell, briefcases, pocketbooks, phones, books, groceries all scattered about them. It reminded Jason of old TV news footage he'd seen once as a child; some poison gas attack in the Tokyo subway. People trying to get home, lying on the platform. It gave him nightmares for a week. He took a tentative sniff of the air. . . .

"They're just sleeping," the mother said. "That sleep will be permanent if you disobey."

The door unlocked and opened behind him.

He glanced at the baby, her cheeks stained with tears as she wailed.

"Don't hurt them," he said.

"I give you my word," the mother said.

Jason stepped onto the platform and stepped gingerly past the prone bodies on the floor around him. They were all breathing, their eyes fixed blankly on the ceiling.

"All right, I'm off the train," he said. "What do I do now?"

A hand grasped his ankle. He looked down into the face of a college-age woman sprawled on the platform, the contents of her purse spilled alongside her. Her eyes were open and fixed on his.

"Now, you walk," she said.

He walked.

Through howling wind. Through screaming rain. Through unearthly chill, he walked. Cars passed on the street, their wheels broadsiding puddles and sending spray over the sidewalk and him. He walked as rain thrashed his skin with a shower of needles, down Boulevard Raspail toward his still-unknown destination.

A news seller had been standing outside Invalides, a bundle of newspapers soaking into the rain-drenched ground. He'd told Jason in halting English to walk south. Jason did that, as light rain became a wind-whipped torrent. At each intersection, another somnambulist signpost told him the same—to walk south—and he did. His clothing became saturated with water and the droplets caught in his eyelashes made every car head- and tail-light streak contrails through his vision. He was soaked to the bone by the time he reached a square bisected by five streets crossing each other. Apartment blocks and shop fronts rose alongside them, blazing warm, inviting light from every window. A stone gray bunker-like building sat like a bloated tick beside a fenced and gated park in the center of the square across from him. He didn't need anyone to tell him that was his destination; he knew as soon as a passing taxi's headlights illuminated CATA-COMBES DE PARIS on the building's front.

He crossed to the entrance and ducked under a stone archway, out of the rain for the first time in what felt like hours. He clasped his trembling hands before his mouth and blew hot breath over them, rubbing them slowly. When he'd warmed himself, he found the main doors beside a shuttered ticket window. The catacombs were closed, but no door was truly closed to a Mage.

If I go down, there she'll be waiting. It's what she wants, he thought.

The card deck was in his pocket, still crusted with the viscera of the agents she'd sent. They'd tasted blood, and they'd taste hers if it was the last thing he did.

He pressed a hand to the door. Gears turned, and there was a loud, heavy click. The door swung open and a warm blast of sepulchral air met him. Lights inside the entranceway flickered on, and he stepped inside to see a spiral staircase before him, hewn into the earth and leading down into it. Then he steeled himself and began the long descent beneath the city.

The air warmed the deeper he went, the stairs taking him down so far it felt like he was journeying into the earth's core. The circular stairs made him dizzy, and just when he thought he'd never touch bottom, he did, stepping out into a wider entryway.

The chamber was carved, low-ceilinged, and supported by a wide hexagonal pillar. Recessed lights set in the corners illuminated the way forward. Jason had never been one to feel claustrophobic before, but he was feeling it now; just breathing took effort.

He pulled the Sphere from the folds of his wet coat, slid the card deck into his pants pocket, and bundled the coat back around the Sphere before resuming his path. He rounded the pillar and moved through a narrower corridor leading into the next chamber. The lights seemed to dim as he walked, burning low enough to see without seeing much of anything. It wasn't until he emerged into a larger entranceway and saw the sign mounted above that he felt a chill course through him again.

ARRÈTE! C'EST ICI L'EMPIRE DE LA MORT, it read.

Darkness gaped like an open mouth beyond, waiting to swallow him whole. He knew enough French to read the sign, but the translation did little to comfort him. He knew where he was, just as he knew what was waiting inside. Fear cloaked him, but it was fragile beside the resolve he felt building up within.

This was it. The reason he'd come all this way. The end of the road he'd trod for thirty years lay inside the catacombs, and with her. There was no running, there was no going back.

He swallowed hard, steeled himself, and, after summoning every reserve of strength he had, passed beneath that doorway and into the Empire of the Dead.

TWENTY-ONE

HE MOVED SLOWLY THROUGH A labyrinth of shadows and the dead watched. He passed down narrow, winding quarry tunnels from one chamber to the next. But the catacombs weren't entirely silent, and he wasn't entirely alone. The walls he passed were piled with waist-to chest-high stacks of bones stacked like cordwood; the tombs beneath Paris were as much a work of art as the streets above. Periodically, there were mosaics and reliquaries and monuments comprised of the remains of those dead, their skulls and bones fashioned into macabre works of art. Every so often there were simpler adornments, limestone crosses carved into the walls as a monument to those without one. His every footstep was marked by their eyeless sockets, his passage reflected in the yellowed enamel of their grinning teeth. In chamber after chamber they lay, the remains of millions who had lived and loved, who'd known fear and joy, who'd felt summer's warmth and winter's chill, and experienced first love and first heartbreak. They'd died old and young, in sickness and health, by means natural and violent. But down here they were all equals, their stories lying, like their remains, silent and forever entombed beneath the streets of Paris.

As Jason rounded yet another bend in yet *another* tunnel, he heard a sound—something scraping from deep within the catacombs. It could have been behind him or further ahead, but it was like brick against brick, like fingernails on stone, like bones loosened from their resting place. He envisioned the dead rising en masse to accompany him on his lonely trek through their empire.

It wasn't them; it was *her*. Playing with him. Playing on his fear.

He clutched the coat and the Sphere inside it closer to his chest. Despite the inner voice screaming at him to run, he continued. These grim surroundings were the perfect setting for what remained, the realization of which slowly wrapped its brittle, bony fingers around him.

The awareness that he was walking toward his death.

The knowledge should have terrified him, but he was surprised by how readily he accepted it. He'd always wondered, after Cathryn's death—and especially Owen's—how he'd react if one day he found a pea-sized lump on his testicle or discovered blood in the toilet bowl. Would he pump himself full of drugs and blast himself with radiation to halt its inevitable progress? Would he end his life before the disease ended him? Or would he fight, tooth and nail, to his dying breath?

In this dreary place, in this moment, the last was the one he embraced.

He wasn't walking out of here and he knew it. The question was whether he could take her with him. Was this how it had been for Damon? Marching head-on into the death he'd known was waiting for him with his head held high?

He passed through another limestone chamber, then stepped into the next tunnel—

He gazed down the long, dim passageway ahead. He could see femurs and tibias jutting out along either side all the way down to the larger, more brightly lit chamber beyond.

She was in there.

He knew it, and knew there was no point in hiding. He considered the Sphere, still in the folds of his coat. Too bad he wouldn't live long enough to see it opened. That would have been a sight. He pulled the card deck from his pocket and tightened his grip on it.

"Well, I'm here, like you asked," he said.

His words echoed down the tunnel. Silence followed.

Then another voice replied. A voice as cold as a winter's night.

"They trained you well," she said. "To keep your head, to keep your wits. I was worried you wouldn't be up to the task, but to come so far in so short a time? That's impressive."

"I have the Sphere," he said. "You want it, you'll have to take it from me."

"Who says I want it?"

"*Now* you're playing hard to get? This, after we just totaled half of the Louvre? You killed my friend, you killed my father, and you sent your Enchanter to kill me!"

She faded into view, like she'd pushed through a curtain hanging over the mundane reality. The serpentine coils of her hair twitched about her pale face and her thin smile. Terror seized him but he held it close—that was an emotion he could use against her.

All she had to do was push him to it.

"Oh, my child, you have so much to learn . . ." she said.

He dropped the bundle, split the deck in two, and let both halves fly. They sliced down the tunnel, glancing off ancient bones and brick, carving grooves into the walls. The Red Queen batted them aside with a sweep of her hand, scattering them over the floor. But before the last of the cards had settled, he pushed. A wind howled down the tunnel, dislodged bones from their moorings and propelled them forward like bullets through the barrel of a gun. They shattered against her defenses, sending yellowed shrapnel spraying. He focused on the debris, lifted his hands, and an angry cloud billowed. He pushed harder, sending it back down the tunnel at the bones lining it, dislodging femurs and tibias and launching them at her. She blinked away as they crashed through but he was already sending another salvo to meet her as she blinked back and deflected the bones with ease, sending them crashing into the ceiling and floor.

"You have *much* to learn," she said.

He screamed and thrust out his hands and ran, everything taken from him—Cathryn, Owen, Damon—erupting in a hot rage. Stacks of bones loosened and funneled through the tunnel at her. They propelled her backward into the wall behind her, cratering it, and sending bones cascading to the ground. She raised a defensive hand as Jason charged in, but as he felt the force of her push, he blinked past it and was across the chamber in a heartbeat, his hands clasped around her throat.

He squeezed.

No mercy.

No magic.

This was his moment to fucking kill her and he wouldn't stop until she was dead.

A wave rippled over her, and suddenly it was Damon's face gasping for breath.

"Carter—told you—I killed—your father?" "Damon" said.

Jason tightened his grip. "Damon" thrashed wildly beneath him.

Another wave washed over her and it was now Allegra's eyes staring into his.

"That—was another lie—everything he told you—a lie—" "Allegra" said.

He squeezed her neck as tight as he could, but it was like steel in his hands. When Allegra's face rippled into Kelvin's, he almost broke his grip.

"We're not—your enemy, Jason," "Kel" rasped. "I'm not—your enemy—"

He drove his knee into "Kel"'s sternum. He felt the rib cage shatter beneath it, driving shards into heart and lungs, bursting organs and spilling fluids into the chest cavity. Kel's face contorted in agony, and froze in that rictus mask as his eyes toppled back into his skull, his nose caved, his forehead cracked, the skin of his cheeks shredding like a thousand years of desert wind had mummified it. The body buckled and belched a noxious cloud of dust that, when it finally settled, revealed a pile of broken bone and shattered enamel.

Silence settled just as quickly. After the battle, after everything, the stillness of the crypt felt like a dull roar. It was over. She was gone. He fell back, numb. He did it. She was dead.

"It's Carter you should be afraid of."

The Red Queen's voice echoed all around him. He turned slowly and stared back down the passageway, where her dark shape stood, as immobile as the dead surrounding them.

"Everything he told you was a lie. The moment you entered the Citadel, you were his pawn."

His bundled coat lay at her feet. In his anger he'd dropped it and now the Sphere was just steps away from her. But she made no move for it; her gaze was focused on him.

"Do you know what an illusion requires, Jason? It requires an audience."

He stood and clenched hands into fists.

"Someone to convince that the impossible is real."

He stepped into the tunnel.

"That the people who want to do you harm want to help you."

His feet crunched on shattered bone.

"That the ones you think are your friends are anything but."

He kept his eyes on her even as panic churned in his gut.

"You were that audience, Jason, and they played you for a fool . . ."

Fury howled through the animal part of his brain and he charged at her with a scream that shook the walls and floor and rattled bones in their crypt.

She raised her hands and the bones lining the passageway erupted in a wave and slammed into his legs, slowing him, nearly knocking him off his feet. The fact he stood upright as they battered him was a miracle. But then he heard the scrape of bones against stone get louder, and turned in time to see the second wave slam into him, propelling him on its crest into the chamber. He struck the floor hard. Pain exploded through him and he tasted blood on his tongue. Then there was silence, like the pause between the intake and expulsion of breath.

Her bootheels scraped the ground as she approached.

She had him. She'd won.

He lay there, helpless, a child at her mercy. He could only wait for that final blow to come.

He realized in those final moments that he belonged among the bones of the nameless and the forgotten. His life had been wasted well before he set foot in the Citadel and no amount of magic would change that. He'd die unremembered, buried deep with no marker. Jason Bishop would disappear and in time nobody would remember he had existed at all.

"Jason . . . that's enough." Her voice was soft now, and gentle. And familiar.

He knew that voice. It had imprinted onto his DNA when she held him that one time, when she sang that lullaby, but that was impossible. He pushed up, rolled onto his back and sat, and as he gazed at her, the Medusa coils of her hair flattened. Age spots blossomed through the alabaster surface of her face, and age lines stretched over her brow and bloomed in the corners of eyes that were as familiar as his own.

Because they *were* his own. He'd gotten his face from his father, but his eyes?

Those belonged to the woman standing before him.

They belonged to his mother.

TWENTY-TWO

....

FOR WHAT FELT LIKE ETERNITY but was probably only seconds, neither of them spoke. Neither of them moved. The Red Queen remained standing and Jason remained sitting, motionless. He struggled silently; was it the truth she spoke or another trick, an illusion meant to draw him in? But she already had him where she wanted him and could kill him with a flick of her wrist, yet she did not. He opened his mouth to say something—anything—but in the end it was the Red Queen who broke the silence.

"I had to know," she said. "I had to know you weren't another of Carter's deceptions. That's why I challenged you on the Metro, to see if you were who you claimed. You could have exited the train at any point, but you were willing to lay your life down to save those mundanes without a second thought. No true Mage of the Invisible Hand would make such a sacrifice." "

"And if I hadn't played ball?" he asked. "Would you have killed me, like you killed Damon?"

"Carter told you I killed him, didn't he?"

"Well, he sure as shit didn't jump off a building!"

"Didn't he?

He stared at her, and in her gaze back he saw that this was no deception.

This was real. This was fact.

Damon *had* jumped. He had taken his own life. But why?

"My mother's dead. She died not long after I was born. That's what they told me."

"My child is dead. He died not long after he was born. That's what they told me."

Her hand fell to her side. He expected her to cry, which would've made everything worse than it already was. To her credit she didn't; like she knew tears, genuine or crocodile, would just widen the gulf already separating them.

"We were deceived," she said. "Victims of other peoples' lies."

"For thirty years?" His shout echoed through the chamber.

She didn't speak. She just stared.

Then she began to hum. The melody was lilting, high, then low, sad and joyful at the same time. It shuddered through Jason with a familiarity that pricked gooseflesh. He knew that melody.

That lullaby.

She sang, "Blow the wind, blow; swift and low. Blow the wind o'er the ocean. Breakers rolling to the coastline. Bringing ships to harbor . . ."

She trailed off. Her eyes gleamed. She'd tried to remain calm. Cold. Regal. A queen. But she remained, in her heart, a mother. She held out her hand. There was something in it: a weathered photograph of a woman holding a newborn child and smiling with a mixture of joy and sadness. It was creased, and its corners were frayed. It was an exact copy of the one Jason had lost years before.

"For years I believed you were dead," she said. "I grieved you, I carried on. I never had another child—I couldn't, after the complications, they also told me. All I had was this photo . . . the one I carried with me ever since they told me you were gone."

She held the photo out to him. He didn't take it. Something wasn't right.

"I knew Damon was hiding something from me somewhere in the Hudson Valley," she continued. "Two of my agents caught up with him on Storm King Mountain fifteen years ago, but it wasn't until later that I realized what he'd been hiding. By the time I found your town, your street, and your house, you were gone. They told me you were dead, Jason; all of them."

"*They.* You keep saying *they.* Who the hell are *they*?"

"Damon, and the Acolytes who delivered you. Jason, you were *born* in the Citadel."

If he'd been standing he would have fallen to the same patch of ground he was sitting on now. Born in the Citadel? His birth certificate said New York Presbyterian. Then he remembered the Acolytes who had tended to Vasilisa in her final days. Their dark robes, their matronly demeanor. Something *had* been familiar about them.

The Citadel. Its magic had unlocked that memory too.

"Why would he make it up?" Jason asked, finally. "Why would he lie?"

"That's a secret he took to his grave. There's a reason Mages are few and far between: because we can't breed other Mages. We don't know why. No attempt was ever successful . . . until you."

"So, what, I was just an experiment?!"

"*You were our child.* We were just kids ourselves, barely into our twenties. We trained together from the moment we both arrived in the Citadel. We advanced through the ranks to become Diabolists in perfect symmetry. We were inseparable, the best of friends, sharing everything: meals, music especially—we both loved David Bowie." She smiled. "After years of training, and dozens of missions with many close calls and many more near deaths, it just happened. Put two young people in deadly situations with enough frequency, they'll hold on to life at all costs. We grasped onto each other for comfort, for love. We kept it a secret, but it didn't stay secret for long. When I learned I was pregnant, I was terrified; no child born of two Mages survived, but I carried you to term anyway. As infinitesimal a chance as there was, I grasped onto it like Damon and I had grasped onto each other. When Damon told me you had died, I believed it. It wasn't until much later, when I had mourned and returned to the world of the living I realized I had never seen your body. Damon told me I was too fragile, that the sight of your tiny body would be too much. But you were so strong, Jason; I felt you kicking in my womb for months and when you uttered your first cry, it was the most joyful noise I had ever heard. How could someone born so strong die so suddenly? I thought it was just my grief whispering, but over time those whispers became screams, and I began to suspect something else."

She offered him her hand but he stood without her help. He didn't want that, not yet.

"Carter told me you were a defector, a double agent," he said. "That you wanted to lead the Invisible Hand, that there was a power struggle . . ."

She nodded, knowingly. "I'm sure he told you many things; lies, all of them."

"Really? Because in that library you seemed hell-bent on killing me."

"I was hell-bent on separating you from Abigail Cord. She's a very dangerous Mage."

"Abigail? Christ, she's just a kid!"

"She's Invisible Hand. She's the enemy."

"And Kel? Was he dangerous? Don't tell me you don't remember him because you killed him in Scotland three days ago."

"*This is war*, Jason. If he'd had the upper hand, he wouldn't have hesitated; I would know, after all. I was the one who trained him. . . ."

Sofia's face, which was already ashen, went two shades paler. That prickling sensation he'd felt trudging north from Place de la Concorde returned in a wave.

Someone else was in the catacombs. The one who'd been following him.

"Were you followed? From the Louvre . . . ?" she asked.

"I thought I lost them on the Metro. . . ." He trailed off as he realized what she was implying. "Wait—I thought they were one of yours."

The bundle containing the Sphere leapt off the ground and landed in her hand. Jason tensed, but she handed it back to him. This thing, this prize; she was just giving it back? He didn't have time to ask why when her cold hand clasped his wrist and once more it was the Red Queen's features that met his.

"You know how this works," she said.

There was a flash of light and an earsplitting bang and then silence—all-encompassing compared to the disquiet of the catacombs. All was dark; there was no source of light or sense of direction. The Red Queen's frigid hand was still around his wrist.

The Red Queen. He was still calling her that. But what else should he call her?

Sofia? Mother? *Who was she?*

She released her grip.

"Give it a moment. Your eyes will adjust," she whispered.

And after several moments, they did.

The chamber vaulted above them, and looked like it had been molded by human hands. It was cylindrical, and ridged with smooth walls rising to lace together in the middle like entwined fingers. Everything glistened wet in the dim light but when he touched a wall it felt cold, hard, and dry.

"This way," Sofia said.

She was standing at a small alcove hewn into the wall. Flickering light beckoned from within.

"Where are we?" he asked.

"Geographically, still in Paris," she said. "The catacombs the tourists see are just a fraction of the labyrinth running beneath the city, and Paris is built on ancient bones. This particular chamber is a safe house, one of many scattered across the globe. We call this one the Temple of Bones."

"Charming. Dare I ask why?"

The question was answered when he followed her through the alcove into a smooth tunnel. The walls, ceiling, and floor were plastered with bones embedded in every surface like it had been carved through a mass grave. Everywhere he looked, eyeless sockets gazed back. Carter's story of subterranean schools where practitioners of the dark arts studied for an infernal master passed through his memory.

"You may not know this, but when I met Damon he was a

studious sort," Sofia said. "Nose always buried in a book when he should have been focused on his training. I think in his previous life, his mundane one, he didn't have many books. He never talked about his parents, but I didn't need to be clairvoyant to know he had an unhappy childhood. But he was an avid reader, myths and legends being his favorite, Arthurian ones in particular. You know the story?"

"Which one?"

"*Le Morte d'Arthur*. Merlin prophesized a king would rise to unite the warring factions of England. He spirited the infant Arthur away to be raised far from those who wished him dead. A place where he could grow among the common people he would one day rule."

"You know, Allegra already sassed me over that Chosen One bullshit," Jason said. "Now you're telling me it's all real? Damon believed he was Merlin and I was Arthur?"

"I don't know what he believed or why he hid you—"

"But you found me anyway, right?"

She stopped and stared at him with confusion.

"What do you mean?" she asked.

"Come on! Winnie? *Your* Enchanter? She spied on me for more than a year!"

"This Enchanter you speak of, she wasn't one of ours."

"Then who was she?"

Sofia considered the question for a moment, and then motioned him to follow.

"Come on, there's someone I want you to meet."

The next chamber was even larger than the previous, as wide across as it was high, with entry points leading to other tunnels and chambers. Obsidian walls vaulted up around Jason and Sofia, the ceiling lost in the gloom. Hundreds of candles floated in the space above, casting light and warmth upon the wretched figures huddled beneath. Some hungrily devoured food and gulped water, some wrapped bandages around wounds, others just sat and stared a thousand yards into nothingness. As Jason followed his mother, he realized they were survivors of the battle in the Louvre. If he was worried any would recognize him, he didn't worry very long, as a tall African with arms like howitzers stood, spilling a plate of rice and beans across the floor.

"What is *he* doing here?" the man spat.

Around him, other Golden Dawn paused their eating, their medicating, and their staring. Those who could stand did. Those who couldn't set their eyes on him and glared with undeniable loathing.

"Shadow, *enough,*" Sofia said. "He isn't a threat."

"Isn't he? Because in the Louvre he did damage enough." The African man thrust his bare chest out, the slash marks on it still red and swollen from where Jason's cards had cut him. "You bring this Mage before us? To wave him in our face, to show us *again* how you were successful where we were not?"

His hands clenched. His tattoos shimmered. A spell was on his lips.

"Shadow, do not threaten my son," Sofia said, quietly.

The hairs on Jason's arms stood rigid, and by the reactions of the others, theirs had too. The Red Queen wasn't one to be trifled with. Shadow met her gaze with equal silence and sat back down.

Sofia scanned the chamber and stopped when she found what she was looking for.

"Whisper, come here please."

At the edge of the light's radius, a woman stood and approached. Jason was stunned by her beauty; she looked like a supermodel with sharp features and dark, probing eyes. She belonged on a catwalk, not skulking in the shadows, but through those shadows she approached, her hands folded neatly before her as she stood to face them.

"My Queen," she nodded. The look she gave Jason was far less cordial.

"Show him," Sofia said.

Whisper rolled up her sleeves, exposing spells tattooed delicately into well-sculpted arms. The markings shimmered as she spoke, glowing white, then translucent.

"*Annorum factus,*" she said.

A wave seemed to ripple over her, and in place of the supermodel stood a stooped old woman, her beauty long ago crushed by arthritic decay, her eyes riddled with cataracts, her slack-jawed mouth nearly toothless. Even her clothing had changed, from Whisper's fashionably grungy attire to a worn and patched dress. The transformation was so complete that Jason couldn't believe it; she even *smelled* ancient.

Whisper spoke again.

"*Qui factus est iuvenis.*"

And she shifted again, from the old woman to a coltish gamine seventy years younger, clad in a private-school uniform and just blossoming into womanhood. The young girl fixed Jason in her deep, impenetrable eyes as she spoke a third time.

"*Sicut et ego.*"

And the starkly beautiful woman who'd stepped out from the shadows returned. Whisper bowed smartly and stiffly, but her eyes never left Jason, as though she was waiting for her Queen to end this charade and exact vengeance on him for those the Invisible Hand had taken from them.

"Do you see?" Sofia asked Jason.

Jason met Sofia's gaze, and looked to Whisper with astonishment.

God help him, he *did*. . . .

Winnie had spoken no spells when she attacked him, not like Whisper. Not like the ones who'd attacked Damon on Storm King, or attacked in the Louvre. Winnie had silently harnessed those primordial forces she wielded.

Winnie was a Mage, not a Conjurer. She was Invisible Hand, not Golden Dawn.

He clenched his coat tight, squeezing it until it felt as if the Sphere would shatter like glass. But it wouldn't even give him *that* satisfaction; nothing would, not with that blunt-force comprehension screaming through the hollows of his memory.

Winnie *had* been an illusion from the moment they met. To maintain such a subterfuge took an Enchanter so skilled even their comrades couldn't entirely trust that they were who they claimed.

He knew only one capable of such deception. One who'd recently returned to the Citadel after a long, deep-cover mission. One whose presence had unsettled him from the moment he returned to his room and found her waiting.

Winifred Hobbes had never been Golden Dawn.

She'd been Katja Eis all along.

TWENTY-THREE

....

THE GIRL SAT CROSS-LEGGED, HER blank eyes fixed ahead. She was a Watcher, one who could cast spells that let her tune into wavelengths broadcast by the mundane mind, to piggyback on them and see the world through their eyes. Sofia crouched with two other agents and listened to the girl speak. One was the formidable Shadow, who still wanted to kill Jason and didn't need to broadcast it. The other, Hammer, looked even more imposing: immense, with a scarred head shaped like a bullet. What he thought of Jason was a mystery; his face seemed to wear the same look of disdain no matter whom he was speaking to, or who was speaking to him. The Watcher's words flowed in an endless babbling stream, but Jason didn't know or care what she was seeing. He was still reeling from the realization he'd been a pawn in this game from well before the Invisible Hand made their dramatic entrance into his life.

Winnie had been Katja. She'd always *been* Katja. That meant the Invisible Hand knew of Jason's existence a year before Damon's death. Had his father known? He tried to remember the last time he'd seen him. Had it been after he met Winnie?

"No, it was just before . . ." he muttered.

A nearby conjurer looked up from the baguette he was munching, and then returned to it. Jason's stomach growled. His mouth felt like hard, dry clay. He wanted food and would have settled for water, but knew if he asked he would receive neither. Sofia was the only thing keeping him alive at this point; without her, they'd fall on him like a pack of wolves. He was a prisoner of the Golden Dawn and of that moment more than a year ago when his life had changed without knowing.

The last time Jason saw Damon alive had been just before Jason's twenty-ninth birthday. Damon had swung by Traders— the Wall Street watering hole he'd been working at—to say hello and that he couldn't stay long as he was off to the Middle East for *another great opportunity*. Jason had taken it in stride; by then, "taking it in stride" had become the default anytime Damon darkened his door. By the time the Wall Street crowd had departed for their trains to Greenwich and New Jersey, Damon had vanished without so much as a goodbye, a typical visit from dear old dad.

Winnie had entered his life a week later.

It had been all orchestrated, right from the moment Carter made his grand appearance. And all of them—Kel, Abigail, Teo, Katja . . . and Allegra—had been in on it.

Jason had been betrayed many times before. He *knew* what betrayal felt like, and this felt a hundred times worse.

They'd played him for a fool, an easy mark, the dupe in the audience a stage magician always calls up onto the stage to humiliate to the roar of the crowd. They weren't his friends; they never were.

The Watcher was still muttering; Sofia and her conjurers were listening and talking quietly. At one point Shadow had looked past Hammer to Jason, a quick glance, but enough for him to know that somewhere in that flow of words his name had come up. Or maybe it was just the general hatred Shadow was broadcasting at him.

He wasn't the only one either. The other conjurers huddled and gnawed at their food like mangy dogs, but were all still fearsome. He was their enemy, and in his face they saw every Mage who'd taken a friend, a comrade, or a lover from them. Soon there would be sparks; he knew it, they knew it, and it would scorch everything—

Sparks. They'd lit the sky the night Winnie revealed herself, and he was rescued by Teo and Allegra.

If they hadn't been battling the Golden Dawn, who *had* they been fighting?

He nearly smacked his forehead with his palm. They'd been fighting other Invisible Hand; all of it an illusion to make him believe he was in danger. He'd seen what they wanted him to see. Every magic trick needed an audience and he'd been theirs. But why spend nearly a month training him in the art of magic? What was Carter trying to get him to do?

That question was answered as Sofia stood and crossed the chamber toward him.

Carter wanted me to kill her. My own mother.

"No sign of them," Sofia said. "No sign of the Invisible Hand anywhere in Paris."

"They wouldn't leave," he said. "Not without me or the Sphere."

"I know. They're not gone; we just can't see them, which is troubling for many reasons, not the least of which is in that bundle at your feet. May I?"

"You all outnumber me fifty to one," he said. "Be my guest."

She plucked the Sphere from the folds of Jason's coat and examined it closely. She turned it slowly, studying its every contour.

"What is it?" she asked.

"*The Sphere of Destiny?*" he said. "I thought you knew; you sent your people after it."

"I didn't send them to the Louvre for this; I sent them for you."

Jason's brow furrowed with confusion. What the hell was going on?

"According to Carter, this artifact, whatever it is, has the power to shatter the balance between our side and yours. It has the power to end this war you've been fighting."

He gave her a rundown of what Allegra had told him about the Sphere, but the longer he talked, the more confused Sofia looked.

"You referred to them as *your side*," she said. "After all I've told you, after all their lies, you *still* side with the Invisible Hand?"

"Yeah, they lied, but *you're* lying and don't tell me you aren't because *that* would be a lie, too."

"Tell me then: which faction would you choose?" she asked. "Forget all you know about the Invisible Hand and Golden Dawn. You have free will, Jason, so choose."

"Order," he said without hesitation. That was so easy he was surprised she asked at all.

"*Why?*"

"Have you seen the alternative? Turn on a TV once in a while! What the hell is the world we live in *but* chaotic? Christ, the stuff we've done to this planet alone, what we're still doing to it . . ."

"Chaos is the natural order of things," said Sofia. "It always *has* been. Out of chaos comes art and music, thought and ideas. The Invisible Hand represents order; they want to be mankind's masters. They will never allow for those things that make life both terrifying and beautiful and real. That's why they didn't share their knowledge with man. There's an old story, maybe they told you, about a farmer—"

"The chess game, I know," he said.

"Two sets of pieces, one board, both sides equally balanced. The game has been played for centuries, each trying to out move and outplay the other. But you *can't* win; balance *must* be maintained for them to remain at bay, just like they need to keep us at bay. If either side wins, mankind loses everything."

Jason couldn't believe what he was hearing.

"What the hell are you saying? *You don't want to win?*"

"The Golden Dawn's goal was never victory over the Invisible Hand. To achieve that would be disastrous. We're the bulwark, the opposing force keeping their plans at bay. If we win, chaos will be unleashed upon the world without order to counter it. If the Invisible Hand wins, mankind is brought under their whip. They will be man's master; they will control nations and wage war by proxy. They'll set man against one another, thin the herd, murder millions along the way. Don't you see? The game *must* continue; the war must never end. That's why I had to kill Kelvin; because we are so few, and the Invisible Hand are so many. They have become too powerful, too arrogant, and too dangerous. Balance has been tipped in their favor, and I don't know if we have the strength to counter them. What you see here is nearly all that remains of the Golden Dawn, and we're losing this war."

"Then who are they?" he asked. "Not the Invisible Hand . . ."

He gestured to the chamber. Sofia considered his question silently.

"Ask them yourself," she said. "Irons, come here . . ."

A conjurer set his plate down and approached. He was forty-something, short, fierce, built like a tank, with muscles rippling beneath a tight gray T-shirt and cargo pants. His heavily tattooed arms were a mash-up of spells mixed in with logos for various punk and hardcore bands, a few of which Jason even recognized. He looked at Jason with the same distaste as the others.

"Introduce yourself," she said.

"Name's Irons." He folded arms that were as thick as Jason's legs. "You want a CV?"

"Wouldn't hurt," Jason replied.

"CV is DC, NYC, then LA. Sang with some bands, did some spoken word. Nothing stuck. You know what it's like arriving to the nineties party a decade after it peaked?"

"I was born in eighty-seven, so no."

"Well, it's like the best years of your life were just waiting for you to arrive only you never got the invite. I drifted for years looking for something to fill that empty feeling—you know the one? The one keeps you up at night wondering 'If only I'd . . . *dot dot dot.*'"

A semblance of a smile crossed Irons's face, which just made him more unpleasant to look at.

"Yeah, you *know* that feeling. Same one I had until I found them, or more exact, they found me. She showed me my destiny and she's been more a mother to me than she'll ever be to—"

"Thank you, Irons," Sofia said curtly.

Irons trudged back to his plate and his solitude. Sofia pointed past him through the chamber to a South Asian man, tending to the wounded.

"Haath was a doctor in Calcutta, or he wanted to be but his caste kept him out of medical school. He learned ways of healing from us more effective and more powerful than he ever imagined. The woman he's tending, the one wearing the wool cap? That's Ice from Yellowknife, fighting stage-four breast cancer for . . . ten years now? Our magic is keeping her alive. Every one of them has a story, some tragic, some not, all brought to a point in life where they questioned everything, seeking the same thing you seek—"

"What *am* I seeking, Sofia? Because from where I'm sitting, you're still just a goddamn face in a photograph! You may be a biological mother but you're not my mother and the only woman who came close has been dead way too long!"

Sofia stared at Jason silently, and it took considerable effort for him to stare back. She studied him, and he studied her, and wondered how on earth he'd ended up here, in a cavern beneath Paris, facing the mother he thought was long dead, when a month ago he was slinging drinks in Inwood.

"You're looking for a purpose," she said. "You're looking for some sign that you're meant for greater things. In this chamber and in ones like it around the world, you'll find schoolteachers and runaways and addicts and musicians and laborers and secretaries. Young and old, rich and poor; they were all searching for something to fill that emptiness in their lives . . . and what they found was magic. But unlike the Invisible Hand, there's no limit to how high they're allowed to climb. There's no levels, no 'proper place.' Those levels are designed to keep you locked into a skill set, to be a piece on the chessboard, no weaker or more powerful than is absolutely necessary. The Invisible Hand refers to the one who moves those pieces, and through the centuries there's always been a master who wields them. Carter Block is the latest, and the most dangerous."

She looked at him like she hoped that would be enough, but it wasn't by far. She could have talked his ear off for a year and a day and he still wouldn't fully understand.

"Okay." He nodded. "Say you *are* telling the truth; why are you telling me this at all?"

"Because I want you to know who you've been fighting. We're a check on the Invisible Hand's power, the bulwark against their plans for domination. An army willing to lay down their lives to protect the ones they love—"

"And the Invisible Hand isn't?"

"I don't mean brothers- or sisters-in-arms; I mean mothers and fathers, husbands and wives, sons and daughters. They're fighting and sacrificing and dying for the people in the world they left behind. The Golden Dawn aren't born Mages like you and I; *they're mundanes* who've sacrificed everything to push back against the magical supremacy the Invisible Hand wishes to impose; and with the Golden Dawn eliminated, they *will* succeed."

He stared at her numbly. If Sofia was worried she wasn't reaching him, she should have worried about the opposite. His head, which had already been packed full, felt like it was splitting at its seams.

"I saw where Carter's machinations would lead; I needed to stop him," she continued. "To do that I needed an army; I needed the Golden Dawn, and they needed a leader with intimate knowledge of their enemy's dealings who could help them challenge the Invisible Hand. Before, they were scattered pockets—cells of resistance. I made them what you see now: a force to be reckoned with. But there've been too many casualties, too much loss. We're nearly spent, and Carter knows it. That's where you fit in. You've been his pawn, moved into position to draw me out and—"

Voices. They were rising in a wave rippling through the chamber.

Sofia sensed it. Jason sensed it, too. Something was coming.

He heard the footsteps before they arrived—two figures supporting a third—emerging from the same tunnel Jason and Sofia had entered through.

"We found him!" one shouted. "He's alive, my Queen, he's alive!"

Their words echoed, rousing those who could still stand. Sofia strode quickly to meet them, still clutching the Sphere. Jason followed to where the two new arrivals had laid the third on the floor. The others streamed over, forming a barrier that kept Jason at bay. Sofia had passed through them without impediment, but they were holding him back.

All he could hear were voices—

"We heard him scratching to get in."

"We thought it was them."

"He survived!"

"Who else?"

"My Queen . . . ?"

"Who else survived?"

"He was the only one."

The anger in the chamber rose to a boil. They were too focused on their wounded comrade to turn on Jason but something surged through him like it had when he'd navigated the tangled Parisian streets: that sense of approaching danger. But why would he feel danger here?

He pushed through. Closer to the voices. Closer to Sofia.

The crowd jostled him angrily, but he cleared the barrier of bodies and emerged to see a body sprawled on its back. Sofia was crouched over it, the Sphere still in her hand. Jason sucked in a stunned breath.

It was Mallet; the hulking Swede Jason had embedded in the corridor ceiling in the Louvre.

The man he'd killed.

There was something in his hand: a femur, its ragged, broken end sharpened to a serrated point. Something rippled over his face, but before Jason could shout a warning, Mallet lurched with the femur and rammed it into Sofia's chest. Black-and-red clotted blood gushed from the wound and Sofia lurched back. The Sphere fell from her hand to clatter against the hard floor and as it rolled, the true face of the Mage who'd delivered the killing blow was revealed, etched in cold triumph.

The face of Allegra Sand.

TWENTY-FOUR

....

FOR A MOMENT NOBODY MOVED, not the gathered conjurers, not Jason, not Allegra . . . and not Sofia even as thick blood pulsed from her wound like a lanced boil draining pus. It was like being back inside one of the paintings in the Louvre; Jason imagined someone frantically applying paint to canvas, trying to capture the moment before the spell broke. But for an impossibly long time it seemed like nothing would happen. Sofia's blood dripped down the femur slow enough to see it gleam in the candlelight. She didn't gasp or cry out in sudden pain, or clutch at her wound and fall. Sofia didn't do anything, which made the silence that had fallen so much worse. Then she smiled, and that smile was carved in ice.

"Oh, you'll have to do much better than that," she said.

Sofia's hands were around Allegra's wrists so quickly there wasn't even a blur of movement to register. But then the air in the chamber grew cold, an arctic chill that Jason could feel in his marrow. The crowd backed away but he stood rooted in place as the Sphere rolled lazily, awkwardly over the uneven ground to nudge against his foot. He could see the blood in Allegra's veins turn cold, and marked its frigid progress as it ran up her arms toward her chest and her heart. Her lips turned blue, and her eyes met Jason's for a final, panicked instant.

"Stop—STOP!" he shouted.

Sofia stared at him without warmth, and released Allegra to fall shuddering to the floor. For a moment Jason feared she'd shatter against it like the marble statuary of the Louvre had. But she didn't; she lay there, trembling, and defiant to the end.

"She—ki—killed Damon!" she gasped.

"You want to prove your loyalty?" Sofia asked Jason. She nodded to the shuddering form at her feet. "Then prove it. Kill her, in front of everyone. Then they'll trust you. Then *I'll* trust you."

Jason stared at Allegra, whose eyes were fixed on his.

"She's—lying—Jay—Jason—she's—the—ene—enemy—kill—her—before—it's—too—late!"

Liar, he thought. *You and all the others. You lied from the moment we met.*

Sofia grasped the bone protruding from her chest and pulled it out, exposing a jagged hole that spilled out a black, foul-smelling bile.

"Allegra Sand has murdered more people in her very young life than you could ever conceive," she said. "If you don't believe me, ask her; ask her what she did to her family."

Allegra's eyes were frozen on Jason. He felt himself falling into them and as he did there was

A flash—

Of a girl running. Of a stone being thrown. Of that same stone stained with blood.

He snapped back. His eyes narrowed.

On Sofia.

On Allegra.

They were both lying. And he'd been lied to long enough.

He grabbed Sofia's wrist. It was cold and hard, like one of the marble statues in the Louvre. No blood ran through its veins. No pulse pumped it.

His mother *was* dead. The Red Queen was all that remained.

He released the dead woman's wrist, crouched, and grasped Allegra's hand. It was so cold that it burned his palm, but he kept his grip and stared at the hook-shaped scar on her forehead as it grew larger and closer and—

Allegra Sand was running for her life, but she wasn't Allegra Sand.

Jason knew this, just as he knew her real name: Anush Hurik. He was tethered to her like he'd been tethered to Damon and Kel, only this time and in this moment he knew *everything* about this frightened thirteen-year-old girl scrambling through the tangled streets of the city of Bam in southeastern Iran. He knew this was the morning of December 26, 2003—a date burned into Allegra's memory.

Jagged rocks cut the soles of her bare feet and trailed blood marking her passage. Her flimsy nightshirt fluttered as she ran, through streets that had become unfamiliar even though she'd lived there more than half her life. After her mother disappeared she was brought to Bam to live with her father and his family, the aunts and uncles and cousins who never embraced her as their own. And now that family was among the mob howling for her blood.

She hadn't meant to do it.

Those were her frantic thoughts as she ran but she knew they wouldn't satisfy the mob. Her family wouldn't listen; they never listened, even when deep down she knew she was not like them.

She'd always known.

They began just after her twelfth birthday: headaches sharp and persistent, like a blade jammed into the soft gray meat of her brain. Then the voices—a woman's (it was always a woman's)—telling her everything would be okay and they'd be together again one day.

But that voice lied; they wouldn't be reunited, and it wouldn't be okay at all.

She stumbled and nearly fell but righted herself and kept running over precious ground lost to the encroaching mob. She could do such amazing things, but what she couldn't do was outrun those things; the mob was evidence of that.

After the voices came the magic. That was all she could describe it as.

There was the rain of cherry blossoms that fell in her bedroom one morning. Then the snowfall in her backyard at the height of summer, when waves of heat cracked the pavement. Then the wellspring that erupted from the playground behind school one day. At first they had happened without warning—errant thoughts that had briefly manifested in the physical world—but gradually she taught herself to control them. She found she had other skills, too: she could hide in shadows, letting them rise around her like she was submerged in dark water. She could make things lift off the ground: toys, her aunt's yowling cat, and once the entire living-room sofa. She even made a bully at school punch the wall repeatedly until his knuckles split and blood spread, radiating like the red trail she left through the streets of Bam. Still, she sensed she was capable of more, and that was when she'd made her first and likely fatal error.

It was supposed to be a secret.

She'd trusted Gulshan too much; she'd thought her cousin, so close to Anush's age, understood. Or maybe she'd wanted to be seen as more than an obligation and a responsibility. So, three days ago, after swearing her cousin to secrecy, she had made it rain rose petals in Gulshan's room. Gulshan gazed with wonder, but in those awestruck eyes Anush saw that first glimmer of surprise that slowly contorted into fear. Even as the petals flitted away, Anush feared Gulshan wouldn't keep her promise and she was proven right with a speed that surprised even her. Gulshan had told her brother, who told his father, who told Anush's father. Rumors spread like brushfire, and that fire now raged through Bam's streets, burning into a crescendo.

Something sailed past her ear, and a rock clattered across the ground ahead noisily, but the next found its mark. There was pain, and a jolt of surprise. Then the world turned upside down and she was hurtling to the ground, her forehead slamming the stones and leaving a fishhook-shaped gash above her left eye. She tasted copper and spat blood as throbbing pain coursed through her. Rough hands pulled her to her bloody feet and threatened to tear her limb from limb as she was dragged down the gentle incline to a square just ahead where more townsfolk gathered to carry out their sentence.

Jason watched helpless through Anush's eyes as the night sky swung into view, then the world upended and she was thrown to the ground again. Agony tore through them both, and the stunned cry that erupted from her mouth felt propelled by his lungs.

Anush cowered, pleading for mercy, and even though Jason didn't understand the language spilling from her mouth or the angry screams of the outraged mob, he knew exactly what they were saying, as though he'd been fluent in it. She was begging for her life, but her tears fell on unyielding ground. Rocks clutched tight in hands, waiting for the signal to unleash death.

Then her father stepped forward. His dark eyes were piggish in the yellowed electric light bathing the square, his shadow staining the ground like the Angel of Death's. He called her an apostate and while Anush didn't know what that word meant, by the crowd's roar she knew it was the very worst thing he could have called her. He said she was no child of his, that he took her from her mother because she was just as dangerous as this wretched child had become. He called her mother a witch and called Anush one, too, and what hurt her more than her battered, bleeding body was his words. There was no love in those eyes, only hate. He picked up a jagged stone the size of an egg and set his loveless eyes on her. But as she stared at her father and at the crowd who had gone silent, licking their chops at the blood they could almost taste, she felt a wellspring of hatred bubble up inside her. She loathed her father more than she'd detested anything. Despite the cold December air, she began to perspire, her body growing warm, and then hot, then screeching to a boil that should have poached her organs but only fueled every neuron firing through her. The crowd had awakened something in her straining to be set free.

And as her father reeled back and let the stone fly, she unleashed it.

Time shattered into fragments. Her father's jowls shuddered as he released the projectile. It tumbled end over end, electric light dancing across its surface. Anush stared into it, through tightly packed grains and molecules and deeper inside it to an atomic level and its many nuclei orbited by glittering protons and neutrons and electrons. Even without being told, she knew she was gazing into the heart of the universe itself.

Light. The stone was filled with light. And it was good.

As it reached her, she raised a defensive hand—

And *pushed*.

Something sounded like a gunshot. Her father reeled, his hand to his mouth, red pulsing through his stubby fingers. The stone he'd just thrown fell to his feet, stained with crimson, and his hand dropped away to reveal his ruin of a mouth as jagged flecks of shattered teeth pattered down his stained shirt. The crowd shrieked as stones scattered over the ground rose slowly into the air to glide around Anush. They held there, an ocean of them undulating as if they were being churned by an invisible current. Horror rooted the mob in place.

Then, Anush *pushed*.

The stones tore into the crowd, opening cheeks, piercing flesh, shattering teeth, and fracturing bone. Wave after wave followed, a maelstrom of rock swarming like a locust storm that just kept coming and coming and coming. Blood splattered the street and walls; gouts of crimson sprayed the air. The next howl to rise from the mob was of agony and the few who didn't flee the onslaught wished they had as they gazed upon Anush Hurik as she rose from her crouched, cowering position to her bloody feet . . . and then ascended off of the ground to drift above it. Her eyes rolled over white, her arms rigid, her back arched, and her hair rippled in the unseen current. There was a low throbbing rumble from deep underground, and the walls of the buildings lining the square cracked and crumbled, sending cement and masonry plummeting to crush those underneath. Screams rose and panic seized the remaining crowd, who ran, tumbling over each other, falling, trampling, and being trampled in kind. Then Anush

292 • Brad Abraham

pitched forward, her right hand outstretched, and slammed it into the earth.

The ground beneath Jason shuddered. Everything rumbled, like a freight train was barreling toward them. The candles that had been suspended flickered and fell, some extinguished and some still lit. Conjurers struggled to clear the falling debris. Some succeeded. More did not. Something was coming; some unimaginable power about to unleash itself upon them all.

Allegra met Jason's gaze. She raised her hand, fingers spread wide . . .

Like she had in Bam.

"No *DON'T!*" he shouted.

She brought her hand down.

Fissures exploded across the chamber floor with the force of an artillery strike. The entire hollow heaved violently, walls collapsing, and burying screaming bodies beneath an avalanche of debris. The fissures widened into fractures, which deepened into chasms, sending conjurers pitching over the edge and plunging into darkness. Slabs of stone and bone fell and pounded hapless others to a bloody ruin. There was a ripple of smoke and sound as the rest screamed spells and blinked out of the chamber.

Allegra stood slowly amidst this carnival of destruction, her face a cruel mask. The ground tore open beneath her but she floated up off it as a chasm opened underneath her. The Sphere jumped off the floor and settled in her hand and she looked past it to Jason.

There was a fleeting pause in the devastation.

The tremors ceased, the screams faded.

And for a moment the only people in the world were Jason Bishop and Allegra Sand.

Then Sofia's voice filled his ears. She was screaming.

"Jason, LOOK OUT!"

Something struck the crown of his skull, and an indescribable agony tore through him. He clutched his head and had just a stunned instant to cry out . . .

Then the chamber floor ripped open beneath him and he was plunging into the abyss.

TWENTY-FIVE

HIS FEET TROD A HARD road beneath a sky the color of an open wound. He didn't know how long he'd been walking, he didn't know his destination. He didn't even know his name but still he continued through the barren landscape. Nothing living flitted through the sky, nothing crashed through the wilting brush dying alongside the road. There were no cities, no mountains, nothing on the horizon. At one point he stopped and turned around but saw the same view there on a road winding through this desolate countryside.

He turned back and pressed on. For minutes, for hours, for what felt like days, even though there was no sunrise or sunset in the toxic sky to mark his progress. His shoes scraping gravel like a metronome lulling him to sleep. His eyes grew heavy, they closed—

They snapped back open.

There was something at the roadside up ahead, the first significant *thing* he'd seen since this journey began. It was an old, dying oak, its twisted branches grasping at the wounded sky.

A large flattop boulder sat beneath it, its surface polished to gleaming. He approached the tree and the boulder and as he did he saw a dark-and light-checkered pattern of interlocking squares etched into the smooth, flat surface: a chess board.

Two groupings of game pieces were arranged atop, carved from obsidian and ivory respectively, and someone sat on the opposite side, like she'd been waiting her entire life for him to arrive, even though he was certain she hadn't been there a moment before. She was ancient, her face swollen with age and creased like dry desert ground. Her dress was tattered, the nails of her knotted hands as yellow as the nonexistent sun. But her eyes were alert, like someone's he'd known in another life.

There was a carved stone slab on the ground opposite her seat at the chessboard. He sat, his body grateful for the rest. Was this his destination? There was something familiar about it, like a story he'd been once told, or something out of a dream.

The woman took a pawn in her gnarled hand and moved it forward.

He countered with one of his. She countered with one of hers; he counteracted.

The game had begun.

The first game ended in victory for her. The second ended when he toppled her king. She won the next, him the one after. Both scored equal victories, winning the battle, but not the war.

"How long do we play?" he asked, as she reset the board for what seemed the twentieth time.

"Until someone wins."

She nodded to the board. It was his turn to start.

He selected his pawn and slid it forward. Obsidian scratched the surface.

He stopped. He looked past the pieces and saw her glittering eyes watching him intently.

He slid the pawn back to its starting square and shook his head.

"But we can't win, can we?" he said. "Neither of us can, because this game can't end . . ."

The old woman was silent, and when she spoke again it was with another voice.

A younger voice. A boy's voice.

"So you *have* been listening."

The old woman pressed her hand to her visage, dragged it down, and revealed a face of a boy, twelve or thirteen, with olive skin and dark ringlet curls framing a narrow face capped by a proud Roman nose.

Jason stared as the boy smiled. The face had changed; the grin had not.

"Vasilisa . . . ?"

"In the flesh," the boy said. "This is who I was at the very beginning. Vasilisa was just the latest of many stops along the way."

"So you're still dead. Does that mean . . ."

He trailed off. He dreaded the answer, but the boy shook his head and laughed softly.

"No, you're not dead. You're not sleeping, either. You're somewhere between those two worlds, caught, as always, between two factions, two impulses . . . two parents."

Jason breathed slowly, in and out. So it was true.

"Sofia—the Red Queen. She is my mother?"

"She is," the boy said. "Though, like you, she is trapped between worlds also. The world of the living, the world of the dead . . . Sofia always had a flair for the theatrical; it's why she chose the catacombs to reveal herself to you."

"So she *is* dead."

"No. But she's not alive either."

"I don't understand . . ." Jason said.

"Do you know what happens when we die?" the boy asked. "Not violent death or sudden death; the one that comes at home, surrounded by your loved ones—the so-called 'peaceful death'? I remembered those more than any of the others. You know death is coming, you see; you can hear its footsteps approach. They're distant, but you can hear them, always walking, always moving forward. First, you sleep more in the daytime, you lose interest in food, eating just enough to remain functional, and then you only want water. By this point you can hear death closing in as soft as a whisper; that's when you move into what they call 'active' dying. This is where your arms and legs grow cold and mottled as blood concentrates in your trunk. By now the rhythm of your breathing is shattered by sudden, intermittent gasping. Your sight goes next, then your voice. The very last thing to go is your hearing. Do you know why that is?"

Jason shook his head slowly.

"So that up until the very end you can hear your loved ones telling you they love you. That's why everyone says they want to die in bed, surrounded by loved ones. Because deep down they know that's how the story ends. But death is not the end. Not of *this* story."

The boy pushed himself away from the board and stood.

"You're going?" Jason asked. "You can't leave—I just got here!"

"I'm not the one who summoned you, Jason. I'm still searching for a suitable host . . . but I wanted to tell you that this last death was different. This time, I could hear them."

"Hear who?"

The boy's smile was a mixture of sadness and joy.

"Voices, of children, of men and women, a multitude . . . I think they were my family."

"Which one?" he asked.

"All of them."

The boy drew his hood back up and when he lowered his hands, it was the old woman's face staring at him again.

"If you're successful, we'll meet again," she said. "If not . . . I enjoyed our games."

She turned and stepped onto the road and began to walk. Jason stood, hands grasping the cold hard stone. It was real. This was really happening. But where was he?

He sensed him before he saw him; he was behind him, leaning against the dead oak, as casual as always. He'd been watching and listening the entire time.

It was Damon, dressed as he always had; for business, never for pleasure. His dark suit was impeccably tailored and looked brand new; it wasn't caked with dust like Jason's had become on his very long walk. Damon looked to the chessboard, and smiled, before addressing his son.

"I owe you a hell of an explanation, don't I?"

"You owe me a lot more than just the one," Jason said.

"I know. That's why we're here."

Damon crossed over and sat opposite Jason.

For a very long time neither spoke.

Jason took the opening in that silence to study his father for the first time. He saw the sparkle in his eyes, the bravado cloaking him, the image Damon always projected of Teflon confidence.

But as Jason dug his fingers under the surface, he dredged up the fears, the worries, the choices his father had been forced to make. There were so many questions Jason wanted to ask, but now that he had Damon's full attention he didn't know where to start.

"I never told you about your great-grandmother," Damon said. "She was an amazing woman. She survived two world wars, broke her back in a car crash when she was a teenager; she'd survived pneumonia three times by the time I was born and twice after. But she was extraordinary in other ways. She could read tea leaves, you see; she was very good at it. As a child I'd visit her and see the locals arrive to take tea with her. She'd make the tea, letting the leaves steep and stain the water dark. They'd sit and drink and talk, like it was all just teatime. Then, when the tea was done and the leaves settled, she read them. Sometimes what she read was reassuring, sometimes . . . it wasn't. But she was *always* honest and that's what people liked about her; she didn't hide the truth or say it was murky or uncertain. When I watched her I could see in her eyes it was no joke, too; she believed it as much as anyone."

His hand drifted to the queen on his side of the chessboard. He stared at it, then at Jason.

"The one thing she never did, though, was read for family. That, she refused, because, as she said, 'If I read a bad fortune I won't be able to live with myself.' But one day, I tricked her. She had a customer drop in, and she made tea like she had hundreds of times before. As they talked, I made my own tea, the way she did. I drank it, like her guest did. And when they were waiting for the leaves to settle I caused a distraction, long enough to switch her customer's cup with mine. Then I watched. She studied the leaves for a long time, so long the client was getting worried.

Then my grandmother did something I'd never seen her do; she lied. It was as plain to me as if she screamed it, but she told the client what they wanted to hear. The client left, happy . . . but from that day forward my grandmother never read another leaf. She'd seen something in my cup that frightened her, and days later, when I couldn't stomach the guilt anymore, I confessed to her that it was my cup. And do you know what she told me?"

"She knew, didn't she?" Jason nodded. "She knew it was yours."

Damon stared at him with more force than he'd ever stared at his son.

"She knew the whole time, but she looked anyway; she said she couldn't help herself. She wouldn't tell me what she saw, but in that moment I knew. She *had* read the leaves of the other family members. She *had* known their triumphs, their tragedies; she'd known which grandchild would die in their crib—my baby cousin—and which would not live to see adulthood—my older sister. She never told them what she saw, and she carried that burden to the end of her days. You can have *too* much knowledge, Jason. That was what she was trying to tell me, because she knew that, like her, I was different. I was special. I could see things, too. That was her gift, and that gift passed to me. That's what made me such an effective agent; I always knew going in what the outcome would be. I knew how many guns they'd have; I knew the surprises they had in store. I knew who'd live, and who'd die. I knew everything, right up to the end. Do you understand?"

"Your last mission . . ." Jason stared in disbelief. "You knew going in it would be your last?"

"But I had to go," Damon nodded. "Because that was the only way I could save you."

He picked up the queen, and contemplated it.

"When I saw my death I ran every possible scenario, every step I could take to avoid it, but all roads led to my demise. I had to die for everything to happen; for us to meet here. Without this meeting, Carter would win. He still may."

"When did you see your death?" Jason asked.

Damon sighed. Never before had his father looked so tired, so old, so beaten.

"I saw it the night you were born. I saw it when I held you for the first time. That event set my death in motion, approaching slowly but steadily over the next thirty years, bringing me closer to that moment on the roof."

He flicked his queen against Jason's king, knocking it down.

"I had to die for everything to happen," he said. "You, them, the Invisible Hand, the Golden Dawn, the Sphere of Destiny . . ."

"The Sphere!" Jason was rising from his seat. In his confusion, in this place, he'd completely forgotten about it. "Carter has the Sphere, Allegra stole it, I was inside . . ."

Damon looked as unsurprised as if he'd seen rain fall from a storm cloud.

"Yeah, I know. That gift is hereditary. My grandmother had it, I had it. It skips a generation best as I can tell, but as the off-spring of two Mages, something of it latched onto you. You can see, Jason, just like I could see that while Carter Block is a powerful and a dangerous Mage, he never had a thought that wasn't secondhand. I didn't need to be clairvoyant to know what he was planning. He thought he was clever, finding you and maneu-vering Katja into place. She watched, and he waited, and when he had me out of the way, made his move. The paintings? The ones with the symbols you discovered? *He* put them on a flash drive and gave it to a broker named Bennett Fraim. He let Sofia know where and when I'd go after it. He set the trap because he *needed* me out of the way, so he could take you, mold you, and use you against her. He didn't know you could read the symbols there because he didn't know they were there . . . but I did. I knew, because I could see them, just like you could. Carter needed you because he knew when the cards were down, I couldn't kill someone whose life I had already destroyed. But you wouldn't hesitate to kill the one you believed murdered your father."

"If you knew, why didn't you stop him?"

Damon set the queen down on the board before one of Jason's pawns.

"He has the loyalty of the Invisible Hand, and Katja is his most steadfast soldier. He had her create the illusion of Winnie Hobbes, in case I paid you a visit before he'd had time to move all his pieces into position. She would have killed you before Carter's heart stopped beating. She was his ace, and still is. Do *not* underestimate her."

"But what does he *want*? To rule the world? Some diabolical supervillain bullshit? It can't be that—"

A word danced on his tongue, but he didn't speak it. He didn't need to.

"I believe the word you're looking for is *simplex*," Damon said. "At their heart, all magic tricks are simple misdirection, nothing more. Remember that, and you will survive this."

He pushed back from the table and board, stood, and made for the road.

"Wait—you can't go!" Jason scrambled to follow. "You have to help me get out of here!"

Damon stopped and glanced back at him.

"I can't go anywhere, kiddo. There's something you forgot. Until you remember what that was, I'll be trapped here."

He pulled a deck of cards from his pocket and tossed it to Jason, who caught it.

"Good luck," Damon said.

Jason clutched the deck tight. What did he mean by *trapped*?

The answer came quickly, not from Damon, but from the realization crashing through Jason.

"You can come back?!"

The wind whipped up into a gale. Jason scanned the horizon behind Damon and saw a wall of white stone that hadn't been there before, looming distant like an angry wave, undulating like . . .

It was water. A wall of it surging across the plain. Rising into the sky so high and so far it seemed to scrape its face. Panic seized Jason. But Damon just flashed that familiar grin.

"Come on, Jason . . . what kind of magician would I be if I didn't have an escape plan?"

"*How?!* Tell me how and I'll bring you back!"

The wave was upon them. Jason shoved the deck into his jacket pocket and braced for impact.

"I was always fond of Glenfiddich, wasn't I?" Damon asked.

The wave hit, knocking Jason off his feet. Water filled his mouth, the waters rising so fast he was carried up and away. The oak uprooted and swirled past, its branches scratching his face. He saw the chessboard pieces swirl around him. The current buffeted Jason, twisting him under and over, no way of knowing which way was up or down.

Like before. Like Murder Hill. When this journey began.

But not like before. This time, he was ready.

An unearthly calm took hold of him. He steadied himself, exhaled slowly, and watched the bubbles float away above him. He kicked hard and was swimming, lunging movements through water that was rising above him with the speed of a missile launch. Dull darkness gave way to more of the same; he was impossibly far from the surface. He kicked harder. Air escaped from his lungs. But the surface was still distant. He wasn't going to make it . . .

Tranquility took him. Like the day at Murder Hill. The day he first manifested magic of his own.

No, he wasn't going to die. He was a Mage.

He pictured the surface of the water. He imagined the sunlight glinting off its surface. He tasted that first breath of clean, crisp air on his tongue. He pictured all of it—and he was slicing through water that became brighter and lighter as he raced to the surface. As the last of his oxygen expelled reflexively from his lungs he broke through the water and gasped air. A dark hand gripped his wrist and pulled him to his feet. He landed on solid ground, gulping air with a ravenous hunger. He choked and gagged and vomited water, spilling it over the cobblestones and washing it against the boots of his rescuer.

"Back among the living, are we?" a gruff voice asked.

Jason strained his gaze against angry eyes now digging into his. Shadow's smile dripped menace.

"We gonna have our fun with you, *mon ami,* and then we send you back to the dead."

TWENTY-SIX

....

SHADOW COULDN'T WAIT TO PUT his hands around Jason's neck and squeeze. No magic, no sorcery, just the right amount of pounds per square inch. Jason knew the feeling; he'd once joked to Owen that you couldn't really call yourself a friend until you'd stifled the urge to throttle him. The anger radiating off the conjurer was like an open oven door blasting five hundred degrees, and it radiated off the others who had joined them—Whisper, Irons, and Hammer. Jason couldn't blame them though. Hell, *he* would have choked the living shit out of himself if he could, but that was no way to make a friend of an enemy and he needed all of them.

"You probably won't believe me when I say this, but I'm on your side!" he said.

"You're right; we don't!" Shadow spat.

"Whose side would this side be?" Whisper's voice dripped contempt. "*Yours?* You led your assassin to our camp to murder our Queen! That was your plan all along!"

"I swear I had nothing to do with that! I'm just as much a victim in this as you!"

"Bullshit!" Irons thundered. He strode forward, cracking his knuckles.

"Don't . . ." Jason said. He backed away

"Or what?" Hammer growled. "You'll kill what's left of us?"

Shadow flexed his muscular arms, and the tattoos on them shimmered with malignant power. Jason felt something take him, grasp him, and lift him off the stony ground, the City of Light falling away beneath him. He was floating high up the face of what looked like the Basilica of Sacré-Cœur, summiting its Byzantine domes in a brief and terrifying instant. There was no one other than the four far, far below him, nobody to hear his screams. But to his credit and considerable control, he didn't cry for help or mercy.

He had a job to do. He focused on the cobblestones behind the group. He felt their pull.

He blinked—

He broke Shadow's grip and landed behind the group of conjurers, at the edge of the stone promontory overlooking Paris. The summit they were on rose above a tightly packed tangle of streets. Music and laughter wafted up from cafés and restaurants, but on Sacré-Cœur there was just them.

"Listen to me!" Jason said. "They have the Sphere! We need to get it back!"

"We *will* get it back," said Irons. "Emphasis on *we*!"

They advanced on him. Whisper doffed her coat to expose her bare arms. The spells etched in her flesh began to shimmer.

"I'm not here to fight you," Jason said.

"Sucks to be you then," Irons replied.

He flexed his muscular arms, igniting the tattoos on them.

"There's just us versus you and we outnumber you four to one, *mon ami*," said Shadow.

"The Invisible Hand has a lot more than that," Jason said. "How many do you have?"

Something in their reaction snatched the remaining words away from him.

"How many . . . ?" he asked. "How many survived?"

"You're looking at it," Hammer said.

"Everyone else is dead?"

"Not everyone," said Whisper. "Some survived. Broken, but alive. The rest, scattered."

"If you've been hit that hard, you'll need me more than ever, if—"

"If what?" Whisper asked. *"They have the Sphere!"*

"How long have they had it?" he asked. *"How long?!"*

"A day, give or take," said Whisper.

Jason focused on the cobblestoned ground, on its cold, hard surface, and pushed. There was a crack and a buckle, and the impact tore through the earth. Stone chips rained down with a noisy clatter, bouncing off the ground and the conjurers.

"Enough! Somebody kill this *cochon* or I will!" Shadow shouted.

"Wait!" Jason shouted. "Just wait!"

"We waited long enough . . ." Shadow began.

The words died on his tongue.

An arctic wind blasted dead leaves over the ground, billowing her cloak as she descended. She set down on the basilica steps, her eyes black pools amidst her spectral face, her hands clutching the lifeless, bloodied body of the Watcher Jason had seen in the temple. Her conjurers avoided her gaze as she set the body down gently on the steps and approached.

"Wait for what?" Sofia asked.

Jason swallowed. He hoped he was right about this. He looked at the cobblestones . . .

And smiled, with the greatest relief he'd ever experienced.

The stones had repaired themselves. The balance between order and chaos had worked its strange alchemy, mending the damage and erasing every sign that magic had been wielded. It took a moment for their minds to comprehend what their eyes were showing them, but in the end they did see.

"The Sphere. Carter hasn't opened it yet," Jason said. "There's still time."

"Maybe he's waiting for the right moment," said Hammer.

"Carter? Wait?" Jason laughed. "Carter wouldn't wait; he's been desperate to get his hands on this thing. If he could open it, he would. The fact he hasn't—"

"Means he's unable to," Sofia said. "But just because he hasn't found a way to open it yet doesn't mean he isn't working on one. He'll figure something out, and when he does . . ."

"We can make a battle plan later," said Shadow. "What about this traitor?"

Sofia turned her cold gaze to Shadow.

"Shadow, what did I tell you about threatening my son?"

The markings on Shadow's flesh boiled, then simmered, then settled. He turned away from her, and from Jason, and stalked away to seethe in private.

"So what do we do?" Sofia asked Jason.

The idea formed with astonishing speed. There *was* a way. The signs were there, a storm surge of memory collated and collected over the past weeks. Scraps of words and visions bombarded him. It was there; he just needed time to piece it all to-gether. There was a solution, to all of it.

He just had to figure out what that was.

Despite the fact he'd just evaded the Golden Dawn's wrath by the skin of his teeth, Jason found the sight of another burial ground oddly reassuring. With so much of his recent journey through worlds mundane and magical shrouded in death, Mont-martre Cemetery felt like an old friend. The graveyard was a low-lying plot of land, partially concealed beneath a bridge con-necting the roadway into and out of the neighborhood. After blinking past the locked gates, he found himself standing on a cob-blestone path that wound its way through the burial grounds in the same haphazard way Montmartre's streets had. He trod the length of the cemetery, picking pieces of memory like scattered seeds off the ground and trying to make sense of them before hundreds of ravenous doubts descended to pick every idea that formed clean.

What he really needed was a drink. How long had it been since he'd had one?

That was easy. The Locksmith. Carter and his deck of . . .

He slowed and reached a hand into his pants pocket . . . and his fingers brushed the hard edge of the deck of cards Damon had given him in that lifeless purgatory. It hadn't been a dream; it had been real, just like his father's promise and the clue he left behind.

I was always fond of Glenfiddich, Damon had said.

He knew what they had to do. It was dangerous, probably doomed, but there was no choice.

What he was considering would be a betrayal of Teo, Abigail, and Allegra. Once the hard reality of their collusion had worn off he realized they'd all been Carter's pawns as much as he had and Carter would sacrifice them just as easily. But they were still his friends. . . .

Weren't they? That small voice in his mind began nattering at him, like "Winnie" had on the Metro-North. They weren't his friends; they were supporting players in The Jason Bishop Story, and they'd lied, too. But despite that, he didn't want them to die no matter who they fought for.

Something caught his eye and he stopped to note the familiar name on one of the graves. That was when he felt the air grow cold. A solitary figure materialized from the shadows ahead.

"Out for an evening stroll?" Sofia asked.

He nodded to the grave.

"I always *did* want to see where François Truffaut was buried."

"I would have thought you'd spent enough of your time in Paris among the dead."

His eyes glanced to the dark stain on the front of her shirt; the wound Allegra inflicted no longer pulsed black, but the wound remained, open and angry.

"What are you? What are you really?"

She stared at him silently, like she was contemplating how to answer, or maybe whether she could tell him at all. She put her fingers to her chest and pulled at the material covering it. The dark fabric tore, exposing bare skin and the deep puncture wound, and she kept tearing, digging her fingers into soft tissue. She pulled skin, tore muscle, broke bone, pulling it all away to reveal the hollow of her chest. It was lifeless, the organs shriveled and dry, the black lump of her lifeless heart hanging limp.

The dead woman stared at him, and it took everything he had in him not to run.

That was why he'd gotten no impression from her, like he had with Allegra.

Because there was no life in Sofia Aguirre.

"Carter told me you had survived, right before he killed me," she said. "I'd challenged him for control of the Invisible Hand, but he'd anticipated my move and countered it. We fought, and I lost, but it was his words that were the lethal blow. He told me, because he knew that knowledge would usher me screaming into the void. And I did scream, Jason. As the darkness took me and pulled me away from the light, I cried, not for help but for vengeance. I pledged myself then and there to whatever powers ruled that darkness so they would grant me the strength to return and find you. And in that darkness, something answered. It promised me retribution; all I had to do was promise it everything."

Her hands were trembling. If his hadn't been clenched they would have done the same. That story about schools of dark arts was no lie; it may have been the only thing Carter told Jason that hadn't been. For a very long moment, neither mother nor son spoke. A bitter autumn wind moaned through the cemetery, scattering leaves across the stony ground. They'd both come so far but had so much farther to go.

"I've had time to think," he said, finally. "About the Sphere. We have to get it back."

"It's too late, Jason. They may not have opened it yet, but they will soon enough," she said.

"We have to try," he replied. "We can't let them win."

"The Citadel is a fortress," Sofia said. "The impregnable kind. There's no way of getting in or getting the Sphere out without them knowing, and it's not like there's a back door or any-thing . . ."

Burned plastic and stale urine blasted Jason's memory.

"Wait—say that again?" he asked.

"The Citadel is a fortress?"

"No, the *other* thing."

"That there's no back door?"

Jason smiled slowly as that final puzzle piece settled into place.

There *was* a way.

"How many of your people *are* left? I'm talking everyone who can walk or crawl and still cast a spell?"

"Counting our wounded?" Sofia did the math. "A hundred, if that."

"Good. We're going to need all of them."

Sophia gaped, disbelieving, but he didn't care; his mind was accelerating.

This could work. It *would* work.

Still, that didn't stop his mother from being a cold splash of water to the face.

"Jason, they're scattered across the globe. Contacting them is one thing; assembling them for an assault is another. We don't have an Ingress to travel the world with."

"We don't need one," he said. "And we'll have help."

"Help? From whom?"

He reached into his pocket, and pulled out the deck of cards his father had given to him.

"From Damon," he said.

PART THREE

ASHES TO ASHES

TWENTY-SEVEN

....

THERE WERE FEW THINGS IN the world that brought Carter Block as much satisfaction as a flawlessly executed illusion, and as he strode the Ingress, he reveled in the mastery of his stratagem. His king, his queen, and his bishop had all served their purpose, snatching victory from the enemy and placing it in his hand. Everything that had transpired had unfolded precisely as he'd foreseen, as though it had been ordained by an all-powerful god. Only in this case, the almighty had been Carter Block, and his illusion was designed to undo God's creation itself: to shatter the Golden Dawn once and for all, to tighten his grip on the mundane world, to bring order to a world without it.

The mundanes *needed* the Invisible Hand; without it, mankind was doomed. They were careening toward their own destruction like a car steered toward a cliff. Toxic water, poisoned sky, nation-states led by thin-skinned demagogues rattling nuclear-tipped sabers; they were hurtling toward Armageddon and too busy fighting for possession of the wheel to see it.

But the Invisible Hand would take that wheel and guide them

to safety; it would be their god now, and Carter Block would sit on the throne. After years of planning, decades of struggle, and centuries of war, Carter had won.

Then why did such unease shudder through him?

After Allegra had returned victorious with the Sphere, he'd allowed himself a moment of triumph, but only a moment. Even then there'd been that very small, very quiet thought worrying at him. Too small to see, too seemingly insignificant to notice; a pinprick of doubt that had burrowed into his brain over the three days that had passed since the Golden Dawn fell. For an all-too-brief moment he'd entertained the thought that his victory over the Red Queen *had* been complete and there was no need for the Sphere. But a test of the waters—the reanimation of a cadre of terra-cotta warriors in Shaanxi before the visiting American president and a host of state media—had only proven that balance remained. No news broadcasts, no Internet leaks; nothing to indicate anything out of the ordinary had transpired. The Golden Dawn *were* still out there, hiding and waiting, and that knowledge festered like an infected wound. He cursed Allegra for not being more thorough; he cursed the Mages he'd dispatched to the mundane world who were unable to find any sign of the Golden Dawn. But most of all, he cursed himself for allowing pride to cloud his vision.

For the very first time, the Citadel felt like a prison, not a fortress. Everything had proceeded so perfectly he'd expected flaws and variables he hadn't allowed for, like Jason Bishop's hitherto undetected ability to identify the sigils hidden within the Louvre's paintings. The fact that it had all come together as the Oracle had foreseen screamed at him that he'd failed to account for *something*. The vision Vasilisa had shown him—Carter grasping the Sphere with triumph—*had* come to pass; he'd done it when Allegra handed him his prize. But that had been the limit of her vision; she hadn't told him what came after. All he'd known—what Vasilisa had told him—was that to find the Sphere of Destiny, they needed to find the son of Damon King.

They *needed* Jason Bishop.

But what Vasilisa, like Damon, hadn't known, was that Carter had found Jason well before that prophecy. The signs were there if you knew where to look: Damon's frequent but fleeting trips to an insignificant river town north of New York City, and his clash with agents of the Golden Dawn near that same town fifteen years prior, was proof that something of great value was hidden there. Carter's proficiency was patience, and he wielded it like a knife, peeling the skin away from the truth slowly and deliberately. He watched, he waited, and the real surprise wasn't that Damon's and Sofia's child had survived, it was that Carter hadn't been surprised at all. Once he pieced it all together, he set a watch, not on Jason, but on Damon, knowing that at some point he'd visit his son. And when Damon did see Jason at a bar on Wall Street the year before, his most loyal Enchanter was there to observe. She shadowed Jason, she waited, and when opportunity arrived, she worked her magic. Bringing Jason into the fold had been Carter's long game, and Katja's long con. To create Winnie Hobbes from scratch allowed Katja to be Katja when Jason *was* eventually brought in. The Winnie illusion had also diminished the possibility of Damon finding out his son was being watched, had their paths crossed after Katja had made contact. Jason had been the ace up Carter's sleeve, and after baiting Sofia with the flash drive and sending Damon to his death, Carter had played that card.

Jason responded as Carter knew he would: with skepticism. But Carter had predicted that, too; even before he arrived at The

Locksmith, he'd set the performance in motion. Katja had her orders; Allegra, Teo, and the rest had theirs; and when Jason returned to the girlfriend whose love he'd thought was true, the performance began. He believed *everything* he saw, and everything Carter told him. Vasilisa had said Carter needed Jason, and she had been right; Jason *had* seen the symbols no one else had. He deciphered them. He followed them. He found the Sphere.

But still, something was wrong. He just didn't know what that *something* was.

A clatter of footsteps mingled with his and he looked up to see Allegra approaching, followed a few steps behind by Teo. Despite his troubled thoughts, Carter smiled.

That had been the piece of the performance he'd been most pleased with. He'd ordered Teo to sneak Jason out of the Citadel, to make him think they were defying Carter's orders, because the best way to convince a prisoner they were anything *but* that was to grant them the illusion of freedom. But he'd expected the two of them to abscond to some tavern or nightclub, not get into scrapes with mundanes in Peckham. Teo hadn't told Carter why they were in his old stomping ground even after Carter cast the *Incuratus* spell on him, opening a wound that wouldn't heal. But when Jason endured twenty-four hours of paralysis rather than betray his friend, Carter knew Jason would do all he asked.

The plan had been carried out without error, and *that* was the problem.

Because plans *never* went the way you expected them to.

"Our team in Rio has reported in," Allegra said.

"And . . . ?"

She shook her head.

"No sign of them anywhere?"

"Oh, the *signs* are there. They're watching, but not engaging. Waiting, but not moving."

"That's unlike them," said Carter. "They must know they're outnumbered. We have the Sphere; they should be trying to even the numbers as much as possible before we open it."

"And *have* we opened it?" she challenged.

Under normal circumstances he would have reprimanded her but these circumstances were anything but normal. Allegra was reliable but she was dangerous; the fact she'd been powerful enough at age twelve to shatter balance, destroy an entire city and thousands of lives, was proof. But she was also the only Mage strong enough to challenge him. She'd been Damon's protégé, not his, and if the truth behind Damon's death was ever made known . . .

"We haven't," said Carter. "The power the Sphere holds, if accurate, is something you only want unleashed once you understand it."

"And *do* we understand it?"

Did they? He looked to Teo, who was looking everywhere but at Carter.

There was only one way to find out.

The walls were awash with images of the Sphere, taken with such detail it was like gazing at the landscape of an alien planet. Varying spectrums of ultraviolet, visible, and infrared light blasted its surface, X-rays scanned its interior, and still the Sphere sat on its pedestal as cloaked in mystery as it had been when Carter first discovered the journals pertaining to it. It was a literal and figurative Pandora's box, and to open it without understanding it could unleash untold misery without the faint promise of hope.

"Anything?" Carter asked, after entering with Allegra and Teo.

The Acolyte he'd assigned to run the tests had been a brilliant young ingénue poached from MIT years before with the promise the mysteries of the universe would be unveiled to her. Of all the mundane minds Carter had encountered, hers possessed knowledge of the universe that Einstein and Hawking couldn't have imagined in their wildest dreams. But by her expression, the Sphere had perplexed even her, and Carter's heart sank into an abyss.

"Nothing," she said. "I've run every test in the spectrum, but there's no way to open it, and no way of knowing what's inside. It could be nothing, it could be anything. . . ."

"Give me something," Carter said. "There *has* to be a way to open it!"

"Were you listening?" Allegra asked. "There's no way of knowing what's inside. For all we know it *can't* be opened—"

"Everything can be opened," he said. "There isn't a lock invented . . ."

He trailed off. There was a way. It was so obvious. In the moment of silence that followed, Allegra saw the same thing.

"No," she said. "Absolutely not."

"I know what you did to the Temple of Bones, what you did to Bam. If anyone can open it—"

"I lost control in Bam! I was a child, I was untrained—*I was frightened!*"

"You were magnificent . . ."

And she had been. An earthquake registering six point six on the Richter scale had leveled the Iranian city of Bam on

December 26, 2003. Seismologists blamed plate tectonics, but Carter had known that kind of destruction could only be caused by magical means and he'd been right. Damon had found her wandering the wilderness in the aftermath: the girl who'd killed twenty-five thousand and injured twice that number. Hers was a magic so powerful it hadn't just shattered Bam; it had shattered balance itself. She had undone reality, all by the age of twelve, and that was over a decade ago. She was much more powerful now. She could open it.

She *would* open it, if Carter had to force her.

"I did find one thing on my scans," the Acolyte said, almost as a meek afterthought.

She tapped keys, and on the screens the high-resolution image of the Sphere enhanced, blurred, and clicked into focus. There was a thin line of symbols etched in the wood around the Sphere's equator. The camera tracked them, like a satellite in low-earth orbit taking photographs and beaming them back to mission control.

"What do they say?" Carter asked. "They look like a jumble."

Allegra squinted at the screen displaying the symbols. Her eyes widened.

"They're no jumble. Pull up the *Sigillum*!"

The Acolyte clattered keys, and the *Sigillum Dei Aemaeth* appeared on another screen.

"See?" Allegra pointed. "The letters."

Carter followed her gaze, and he saw it; the letters on the *Sigillum* were identical to those on the Sphere. Teo stepped forward, his eyes transfixed.

"It's a message . . ." he said.

"A message from John Dee." Carter looked to the Acolyte. "Extract them."

Within moments the sigils—twenty-two of them—were extracted and positioned on a third screen. The markings on the Sphere joined them there.

"We have a problem," the Acolyte said, after studying the symbols for a moment.

"More good news . . ." Carter sighed.

"It's a twenty-two character code, not twenty-six. It's not going to translate directly into English; some symbols must have double meaning. It'll take time to translate."

Allegra studied the symbols silently. "How many letters are in the Latin alphabet?"

The Acolyte stared at the screens. "Twenty-two."

"Will that work?" Allegra asked.

The Acolyte crunched keys. The letters rearranged themselves, finding matches in the Latin alphabet. Symbols became letters, which became words, which became a message.

Sors reserata ab eo qui infra sphaeram invenit.

"In English," Carter said. His voice was calm, but his pulse was racing.

The Acolyte tapped keys. The letters transitioned to English.

The destiny within this sphere will be unlocked by the one who discovers it.

Carter felt something seize him and tighten its grip. He felt warm, despite the cooling CPU fans roaring dully through the room. *That was it*. The nattering thing burrowing into his mind.

The one who discovers it.

Jason discovered it. He was the key. The Sphere had waited centuries to be opened . . . by him.

Carter squeezed his hands into fists until his fingernails bit flesh and drew blood.

They still needed Jason Bishop.

. . .

Carter stormed the Ingress and Allegra followed, casually wondering how easy it would be to break his neck. Would he sense her hands on him and know their purpose? Would she be quick enough to finish him? It was an idle thought, but the fact that it escaped his detection told her Carter wasn't as all-knowing as he claimed. She'd had these thoughts for some time now, since well before Jason had entered the Citadel, and well before Damon fell. But could she act on them?

They'd marshaled every resource at their disposal; they'd strung Jason along for almost a month and wielded him like the pawn he was. If she'd felt guilt at her role in the deception it was buried deep. Her loyalty had always been to Damon, and with him gone, she'd been adrift. She'd focused her grief, her anger, on defeating the Red Queen, and Jason was the means to that. For her, that was the finest way to gain her vengeance, even though it made Jason expendable. But a very small part of her *had* regretted the deception, and over the past weeks that lament had deepened. Damon would have never forgiven her for using his son; thankfully, in the end her killing move had failed. As she'd escaped the collapsing Temple of Bones, she'd seen the floor give way, she'd seen Jason plunge into the abyss, and seen the Red Queen leap through the destruction to snatch him safely away. They had escaped, and now they were hiding, plotting, and planning. That was why Carter had ordered Teo to remain with the Sphere: to guard it. From what, he wouldn't say, but she already sensed what Carter wouldn't reveal.

They were coming. The Golden Dawn *would* attempt to breach the Citadel.

As they rounded the next bend in the Ingress they found

Katja waiting. Allegra's back stiffened. She didn't like Katja; none of them did. And it wasn't just good old-fashioned Enchanter mistrust; Katja Eis was distasteful at the best of times, and this was far from the best of anything. Between Carter's dithering and Katja's smirk, the day was shaping up to be a long one.

"Yes, Katja . . . ?" Carter asked with no small amount of exasperation.

"I was wondering whether the Sphere had been opened yet," she asked.

A lesser Mage would have shrunk back under Carter's furious gaze, but Katja was hardly lesser, and after Carter updated her, the contemptuous smile on Katja's scarred mouth widened.

"You find this amusing?" Carter growled.

"In a manner of speaking," Katja said.

There was a gleam in Katja's eye, like some seemingly inconsequential detail she'd filed away before had just proven to be useful. Allegra didn't like it one bit.

"You need Jason; you must force him come to you," Katja said. "You bait him, you draw him into the open, and you give him no choice but to do your bidding."

"Bait him with what? He has nothing in this world or the mundane one he cares about—"

"That's not entirely true . . ." Katja began, but she trailed off as footsteps clattered down the Ingress toward them and a familiar figure entered into view.

"No sign o' them in Ottawa."

"Teo, what are you doing here?" Allegra asked.

Teo slipped his bulky winter coat off and dropped it to the floor.

"Tellin' you there's no sign of any Golden Dawn in O-town."

"I ordered you to guard the Sphere!" Carter said.

"Must've been while I was freezin' me arse off . . ."

Carter was about to reply, when he focused his eyes on Teo and frowned.

Allegra followed his gaze, not seeing what he did.

Then she did. Teo's forearm was still bandaged, the wound the Incuratus spell Carter had cast on him as punishment still tender.

There'd been no bandage on Teo's arm when they left him . . .

With the Sphere.

Panic seized her as she thundered back down the Ingress, clearing hundreds of feet in seconds. She slammed her hand against the computer room's door, blasting it apart. She lunged through the opening to find the Acolyte lying unconscious on the floor by her console. The imposter's dark hand clutched the Sphere, lightening as his true form broke the surface of the illusion he'd wielded the moment he'd entered the Ingress. He clutched the Sphere to his chest and a thunderclap shattered the computer screens, spitting the images they held into a thousand pieces before extinguishing them in a wave. There was smoke and the aftereffect of the blast rang in her ears.

By the time both had cleared, Jason Bishop was gone.

TWENTY-EIGHT

TEO STONE HAD FIGURATIVELY SHIT the bed enough times to know when he was on Carter's bad side; in fact, he'd done it so frequently he was convinced Carter only *had* a bad side. He'd just frozen his ass off scouring the world's least interesting country's least interesting city trying to roust what Golden Dawn *might* be there and come up empty-handed. And here was Carter glowering at him like *he'd* done something wrong when he thought he'd done everything right.

Bloody typical . . .

Katja the Eis Queen was no help either, but that was expected given her dislike of Teo was as strong as his loathing of her. He almost wished he had done something to piss Carter off because the way he was glowering at him, Teo might as bloody well have earned his indignation.

"So, either of you mind tellin' me what the 'ell's goin' on?" Teo asked.

Neither of them did. That was typical, too.

He hated this, just like he'd hated lying to Jason. He'd kept quiet about Teo's back way out of the Citadel and that was *after* Carter put the whammy on both of them. That kind of loyalty was bloody golden, and here he was, Carter's little foot soldier, goose-stepping around the globe to hunt down a person who'd treated Teo square in the brief time he'd known him. He was about to tell Carter where, exactly, he could get off, when a barrage of sound tore through the Ingress and Allegra erupted from the smoke, her eyes wild with panic.

"It was Jason! He has the Sphere!"

The enormity of what she was saying swelled through the corridor.

"*Where?!*" Carter asked.

"He blinked away! I don't know where!"

"Sound the alarm!" Carter barked. "Lock down the Citadel! *Find him!*"

A wave of lights washed through the Ingress, from cold white to angry red, bathing the corridor crimson. A deep thrum coursed through the expanse, echoing through countless chambers beyond.

"*How the hell did he teleport?*" Carter spat. "He's just an Archmage!"

"Tell him that," Allegra said. "He was making for the Necropolis—"

Teo frowned. Something wasn't right.

"'Ang on, you said he blinked . . . ?"

"That's what he did!"

"You *never* call it blinking. I do, an' he does . . . because that's what I told him I called it . . ."

Something was tucked under her arm. Something small. Something spherical.

Thunder tore the air again and disgorged Allegra—the real

one—who took a moment to orient herself, then thrust an accusing finger at her doppelgänger.

"He has the Sphere!" she screamed.

Allegra's shroud slipped off Jason in a heartbeat and as it did he *pushed*. The impact struck Teo with force, sending him careening backward into Carter, sending the two of them into Katja, and sending all three to the floor. Jason pushed again and Allegra flew backward into the Ingress wall, striking it with a painful snap. Jason blinked over them, blinked past them, and blinked down the Ingress around the corner and out of sight.

Teo was on his feet before Carter could order a pursuit, blinking rapid-fire down the corridor after Jason. Doors raced past, hundreds of meters covered in each windblown footstep. He saw Jason draw near, his skill not as refined, and his knowledge of the Ingress not as second nature. Teo closed the gap, reached a hand out, and as he grasped the back of Jason's jacket, Jason threw himself into a door, spilling them both into brilliant sunshine and scorching heat.

Minutes before Teo had been freezing his arse off in Canada; now he was broiling on the Indian subcontinent. The air was thick with curry and noise, scooters belching stinking diesel, and stunned faces gaping at the new arrivals. It was a marketplace; Teo could smell the spice and hear the din of haggling ripple through the space. Jason wrenched free of his grip, knocking Teo into a stall filled with bootleg CDs and DVDs and sending them all clattering noisily to the ground. Jason blinked deeper into the marketplace, surging between stalls, knocking mundanes aside, sending them crashing into each other. Teo recovered, sighted Jason, focused, and pushed—

The shock wave blasted the market, upending tables, scattering customers, sending a cloud of merchandise billowing after Jason, who turned just in time to see the wave. It knocked him off his feet before Teo sent a second blast his way, throwing Jason end over end to land hard on the sunbaked ground. The Sphere slipped his grasp and rolled but Teo didn't wait for it to stop. He blinked through the settling cloud, caught a face full of cardamom, and blinked back ahead of Jason, scooping up the Sphere. When Jason blinked and collided with Teo, the shock was sudden as air blasted from his lungs. The Sphere flew, arcing into the air, then snapped back, stinging Teo's ear and landing back in Jason's hand with a loud slap.

Teo pivoted, ready for anything . . .

Except the look on Jason's face. Anger he could swallow. He'd have drunk fear like fine ale.

But disappointment was a flavor he couldn't drink so easily.

"You lied to me, Teo," Jason said. "I kept your secret, and you still lied."

Teo narrowed his gaze. Jason was with *them* now. He was the enemy.

"I was just following orders," he said. "Weren't personal. Weren't nothing. Just orders."

"I trusted you!" Jason shouted. "You were my friend and I protected you!"

Jason was right; he *had* trusted Jason with a secret. Jason had kept it.

And Teo still betrayed him.

"This isn't your fight, Teo. Just walk away."

"Can't do that," Teo said. "They're my family; I can't betray them."

"They aren't your family. Your family's in Peckham where you belong. You still have someone who cares about you. You really want to waste what time she has left fighting me?"

Jason backed away toward a rusting door, the Sphere held tight as Teo stepped forward—

"*Et non praeteribit*," a deep voice bellowed.

Teo felt something seize him in a grip like steel.

"*Volant per manum meam*," the voice boomed.

That same something lifted him. Fingers closed around him, their grip squeezing tighter and tighter. He looked for the source, through clouds of spice, past the running, screaming mundanes . . . and saw him: a *massive* coal-skinned man in a waistcoat and trousers, his bare chest etched with tattoos, his face caked in skull-like war paint moving through the cloud, his arm outstretched.

Shadow. Teo knew Shadow. He'd fought the conjurer many times before.

"Get movin', *mon ami*," Shadow said. "Me an' your 'friend,' we gonna have *beaucoup* fun."

"Remember your promise, Shadow," Jason said. "He's still a friend. You know the deal."

Teo blinked out of Shadow's hold and dropped to the ground into a crouch. By the time he rebounded, Jason had disappeared through the rusted metal door at the far end of the marketplace.

Shadow flexed his muscular arms, igniting the spells on them. The sky above grew dark as a storm-front moved in unnaturally quick and against the wind. Despite it, Teo took a moment to wonder just how Jason had gained entry to the Citadel without any of them knowing.

Then he realized. The secret way. The way Teo had sworn his friend to keep secret.

In Peckham.

Despite the clash about to begin, Teo smiled.

Then, he *pushed*.

Before everything went pear-shaped it had gone mostly according to plan. Jason ran. He blinked. He ran again. He blinked again. Down the Ingress. Through doors. Through cities, through nations, across continents. But he didn't traverse them alone. At every turn he encountered Mages. Some familiar. Most not. All after him. After the Sphere.

He ran. He blinked. He ran again.

Carter's call had gone out and they'd come running, and he led them across the world. To icy Malmö and desiccated Pisa, to polluted Caracas and muggy Santo Domingo, to energetic Havana and neon Miami, to vigorous Montreal and neon Tokyo, to dreary Moscow and parched Marrakesh, to filthy Pretoria and sun-kissed Melbourne, to rainy Wellington and crowded Guangzhou, to desolate Pyongyang and snowbound Juneau, to midday Malibu and sunset Boston. Everywhere he broke into the mundane world there were Invisible Hand following and Golden Dawn waiting. They knew the entry points; they watched, they waited, and when Jason emerged with the Sphere, they struck, as Sofia promised.

But they wouldn't kill. That was his condition.

The Invisible Hand? They wouldn't hesitate. That's why when the tide turned, when offense became defense, the Golden Dawn were to retreat; by then the next stage of the plan would be well underway. This was his task: keep them busy and keep their eyes off the back door. That part of the plan had worked brilliantly . . . until it didn't.

His feet skidded to a halt. He clutched the Sphere tight and struggled to gain his bearings as the ground plunged away before him. Stairways crisscrossed the span between the top of the chamber and its bottom far below. Or was that up? Everywhere he looked it felt like he was on the ceiling, the floor dropping an impossible distance away. The room seemed to sway and spin everywhere he looked. He felt gravity tug him in one direction, then yank him in another, dragging him into a chasm. Even when he clenched his eyes shut, he felt those forces loosen his foothold. Down was up, up was down, and everywhere his eyes settled he felt gravity wrench him away.

He was on the Spire; the Invisible Hand's main training facility.

And he'd never done the Spire.

Everywhere he looked and focused he felt gravity's pull, like it was waiting for him to decide where safe ground was. He felt his feet drag, felt his equilibrium curdle, and felt that fright take him.

He steadied himself. He focused on a point midway down and midway forward, and on the person standing there, waiting for him all this time.

Allegra. She'd done this. She'd drawn him in and he'd appeared right where she wanted. She thrust her hand out, spread her fingers wide, and he felt them slip over the Sphere. She grasped it and pulled, and he held it steady but his feet were slipping.

She was too strong. If she wanted it there was no way she couldn't take it from him . . .

So he let her.

He stopped resisting.

The Sphere snapped toward Allegra and Jason kept his grip, releasing his hold on the Spire, sending him falling along with the prize. She had a brief moment to realize what he'd done when he collided with her in a bone-jarring jolt. Both fell, bouncing off the walls and sliding down away from each other. The Sphere rebounded off the floor and up a set of stairs to the ceiling above. Allegra recovered and blinked to Jason, grasped him and threw him, sending him reeling backward, flailing to find purchase. He looked to the staircase to his right, focused, blinked, and landed hard atop it. He gripped the edge and crouched, keeping his center of gravity low. The nausea and vertigo passed. Flesh-to-surface contact: that was the key to keeping grounded. He spied the Sphere rolling down the ceiling away from him. He reached for it; his mind brushed its surface and took hold. He pulled it toward him, and it closed the gap. Ten feet. Five.

It bounced—

It stopped. Something else held it.

Allegra. Perched on the other side farther up. Hands outstretched and straining.

She pulled. He pulled. The Sphere held.

Allegra blinked and her hands were around his throat before he realized she was atop him. She tightened her grip, leaning in close enough for him to feel her breath on his face.

"You're siding with the bitch who murdered your father?" she hissed.

"She didn't kill him!" he choked.

"That's a lie! I was there!"

"Did you see him jump?"

"He didn't jump, she KILLED HIM!"

She was cutting off his air. He was light-headed. Passing out.

"He's not—dead—there's a—way—"

"Another of her LIES!"

"She didn't tell me—Damon did—"

Allegra's grip slackened just enough for blood to flow to his brain.

He took a rasping breath. Air roared down his raw throat.

"*DON'T!*" another voice shouted.

Jason looked past Allegra eighty feet down to the Spire floor, where Carter stood.

"We need him alive!" he shouted.

In the beat of that moment, Allegra stopped squeezing, from confusion, from uncertainty.

Above her, Jason glimpsed the Sphere, rolling along the floor gently, and forgotten.

"Alive, huh?" He grinned. "That complicates things, doesn't it?"

He blinked to the ceiling, yanked the Sphere toward him, caught it, and then blinked again. He landed at the top of the Spire, threw himself into the door, and tumbled through it.

The atrium vaulted above Jason as he raced through and in the moment he was glad to have an open space to cross without *some-one* trying to finish him off. Where the hell was Sofia? She was supposed to be there by now with reinforcements but something had delayed her. He'd been running for what seemed like hours, and probably had, at that. He was so goddamn tired. He needed a moment to rest, to recharge, but by the looks of it that wasn't going to be in the—

The cards! He patted his jacket pocket for reassurance. The deck was still there.

But could he use it?

Carter needed him alive to open the Sphere, however he was supposed to do that. In his hands it was just a piece of wood, warm and pulsating, its heartbeat tremoring through him. But would Allegra hold back? No, she'd break his legs and his back and throw in two broken arms for good measure. She destroyed a city; she could cripple him with a flick of her wrist. That meant he'd have to take her out before she took him down. Even as he pictured wielding his deck, throwing the cards at her, guiding them to cut arteries and bleed her out, he knew he couldn't do it.

He wasn't a killer but she was. They *all* were.

The fountain's water splashed and churned, spilling twin streams into the air to twist and coil around each other. They reached their apex and kept climbing, swaying and growing to a height he hadn't seen before. The plume whipped to one side of the atrium, then to the other . . . then plunged, holding form as it flowed at him. He dodged as it hammered the floor, sending water cascading, dislodging chairs and tables and sending them awash. The water churned froth, and drew itself back into the column to slam down again. This time, it found him, bludgeoning him like a rogue wave. The Sphere was wrenched away and for a moment he was floating suspended in the neck of the waterspout, kicking, flailing, and trying to break its hold. Then it retracted and he fell to the floor. He sucked in water mixed with air and coughed both back up. Through stinging eyes, he sighted the Sphere rolling across the floor as a shoe planted atop it and halted it, then it leapt into the air and settled gently into Abigail Cord's hand.

"Carter says he wants you alive," she said. "But he didn't say I couldn't have fun, and darlin' . . . I'm gonna have myself a barrel full."

TWENTY-NINE

"**YOU ARE A FORCE UNPARALLELED** in all of history. You possess skills that make you gods among men. You have the resources at hand, and power within each and every one of you to render you all but unstoppable, so tell me . . . how impossible is it for this army of Mages *TO STOP ONE FUCKING PERSON*?!"

The question thundered up the rows of seats into the darkness beyond and found no answer by the time those words echoed back down to Carter Block.

Standing forgotten—or perhaps ignored—at the edge of the Necropolis stage, Katja allowed a small, secret smile to cross her scarred lips. It was all coming undone, unravelling like a thread tugged from a blanket, a surprise to everyone but her. She *knew* this would happen, not from clairvoyance, but from a lifetime of proximity to powerful men. Carter was raging, assigning blame to everyone and anyone within earshot for his failures, like all powerful men did when confronted with theirs. Men— they were *always* men—so used to hearing yes that a no sent them into paroxysms of confusion, their perceived power inadequate in the face of their own failures. The current victims of Carter's ire were few and far between; he'd sent the majority of their Mages to the farthest corners of the Citadel and into the mundane world beyond to hunt their quarry. Rather than concentrate their power like Katja would have, they were now scattered about all of creation searching for a man who could be captured with the greatest of ease, if only they'd listen to the one person they all did their best to ignore.

This was going to be easier than she'd anticipated.

In the past month Carter had proven far too weak to continue leading the Invisible Hand. He'd placed all his chips on the table but another player was holding the winning hand, and that wasn't Carter Block. It wasn't even Jason Bishop, though in his own way he had surprised Katja, who made it a point of pride never to be surprised. When she met him, Jason had been a lost, lonely child looking for someone to say "I love you" and mean it. Katja had said those words to Jason many times and demonstrated it with her body. But they were just words, it was just a body; it was just a performance. At Damon's funeral she saw Jason was too mired in the past to ever be truly happy; too busy looking at what could have been rather than at what was possible. He would never amount to anything as long as he remained obsessed by memory and by loss. At least that was what she'd thought; it turned out Jason Bishop was full of surprises. He'd been a War Seer all along and none of them had known. But deep down she'd always suspected there was more to him than met the eye.

If anybody had been paying attention to her they would have seen the small smile on her face widen. But they didn't pay attention; they didn't like Katja any more than she liked them, so they at least had that in common. She'd spent enough time with Jason to know him better than he knew himself, just like she knew Carter was living on borrowed time. When this current crisis was ended, she would deal with him. The beauty of that plan was nobody would know. She'd spent a lifetime studying Carter and when it came down to it she'd be a better Carter than he ever was. The winning hand was hers, and when the time was right, she'd play it.

Carter barked a command. The Mages dispersed, some walking, some teleporting, all grateful to be out of their leader's increasingly erratic gaze. But that just left his gaze to settle on Katja, and it did as he stomped toward her like a petulant child.

"Did you hear my order?" he asked.

She nodded.

"And you're still here because . . . ?"

"I'm here because someone needs to tell you that you're going about this all wrong. It might as well be the one with the solution."

Carter couldn't have looked more surprised.

"Then please, enlighten me," he said.

"You don't chase a target; you lead them. You dangle something before them they can't resist. Something so important he'll do whatever you ask."

"Get to the point!" he snapped.

Poor, petulant Carter. Your stubbornness will be your undoing. I'll see to that.

"In his heart Jason is still a mundane," she said. "He will always belong to their world, and there *is* one thing mundanes care about more than anything. It's not money, it's not power; it's the ones they love. The ones they'd die for."

Carter stared silently, the machinery of his brain turning slowly. She doubted *love* was in his lexicon, but it was in Jason's, and that love would be his downfall.

"Everyone he loves in the mundane world is dead . . ." Carter said slowly.

"Not everyone." Katja smiled.

Abigail's face was a joyless mask. If this was her definition of fun she needed to get out more. This was her job and she was doing it with the air of a stone-cold professional: not trying to kill Jason but only trying to keep him from escaping. Every time he had a chance to blink away the water serpent slammed him into the floor. The scared girl he'd seen in the library was gone, replaced by a thing of pure malice. He coughed saltwater and struggled to stand but his legs had gone to jelly. He could only scurry back to the edge of the fountain and watch as she tossed the Sphere above her head and it held there, floating above her.

"Y'know, for all your dumb questions, you never did ask about the names," she said.

The serpent was rising from the floor, swirling and swaying like a cobra lured out of its basket. Gathering size, gathering mass, gathering itself to strike.

"When we say goodbye to the mundane world we choose a new surname. Something to indicate we've truly left our old selves behind. I chose *Cord* because of my family. They were evangelicals, Jason, the very worst kind, the born-again kind. The kind who sinned Monday through Saturday just so they'd be forgiven on Sunday. They were leaders of the community, and their church. They were, as the locals called 'em, a Good Christian Family."

The waters rose above the fountain's edge and climbed higher, past the first level of the atrium, then the second, then the third.

"To me, they were a daddy who came to my room late at night, tellin' me God would punish me if I told anyone about what he did. They were a mama who buried herself in her bottle and her Bible and pretended not to hear my cries from the next room over. But she knew what he was doing because he'd done the same thing to Andie."

The spout swirled like a tornado, tendrils of water brushing against the edges of the atrium. He stared through it to Abigail, bathed in the light mounted on one of the columns behind her.

"That last time I saw my sister, she was content. She'd found a way out, she said; a place where our mama and papa couldn't hurt us anymore. That was the last thing she told me; the last thing she *did* was hang herself from the live oak in our backyard. I didn't see her at first because the branches and the moss covered her from view until I was right under her. Then I saw her and I screamed. But that wasn't the worst part; do you know what the worst part was? The worst part was what my Good Christian Family and their church called her. They called *her* a sinner."

He focused on the light. He felt his mind take it. He felt his hand grow warm, then hot.

"But what about my parents' sins, Jason? What about their punishment?"

His hand was blistering. He couldn't hold anymore, he had to—

PUSH.

The light above Abigail burst, peppering her with jagged shards of glass. She cried out. The Sphere dropped and the waters collapsed, washing across the atrium knee-deep and sending her pitching to the floor and the Sphere bouncing away. Jason found his strength and leapt to the fountain's edge and dry ground, then pulled the Sphere back into his hand. Sparks spat from the shattered light, showering Abigail and the sodden ground, extinguishing themselves in wet puffs of smoke. Jason reached another hand out, felt it grasp the exposed wiring, and yanked it, sending the cable slicing through the air like a snake spewing electric venom.

"I don't know if that's enough juice to kill you, but it'll sting like a mother," he said.

Abigail looked to the electrical cord swaying above. If she saw the irony she didn't indicate. He heard the fountain's waters behind him gather strength and rise.

"Not bad," she said. "But are you going to go all the way, like I did to my parents? I didn't choose *Cord* for nothing; it's what I used to strangle them in their sleep. By then my abilities had manifest and I could've used those, but killin' them with my own hands was *much* more satisfyin'."

She stood slowly, water dripping from her saturated clothing.

"Abigail . . . please don't."

She glared. She wouldn't back down. She wouldn't stop. She had her orders and she'd follow them to the end as long as there was still breath in her lungs.

Forgive me, he thought.

He clasped the wiring, twisted it down . . . and stopped as a low rumble filled the air. The water pooled on the atrium floor churned with the vibration, like everything lay on a guitar string that had just been plucked. The ground trembled and the walls fractured, sending hunks of plaster to splash into the water and break apart on the ground. Then there was the sound of hundreds of windows shattering, and the doors of seemingly every suite above burst off their hinges, unleashing a deluge into the atrium, like the ocean waters that swirled about it had found a way inside. The ceiling dome shattered, and Jason stood rigid as white death fell upon them both, but as it did, the waters parted like a curtain, striking the ground harmlessly around him, but smashing into Abigail and knocking her into the support column. She fell facedown and sank beneath the churning water. Jason lunged into the surf, pushing through it and searching for her, but the water level dropped as quickly as it had risen. It flowed back into the fountain then back up the center of the atrium like a geyser, through the shattered ceiling and outside. The retreating waters revealed Abigail, gasping for air and trying to stand. Then she fell back to the ground, coughing and collapsing unconscious.

For a moment, all was silent. Then there was a sound of fabric rippling in a sudden breeze.

Sofia descended through the ruined skylight above, her cloak billowing, to alight on the ground behind Jason. He wiped water from his face and stared at her for a moment.

"Took you long enough . . ." he said.

"You're welcome," said Sophia.

The air around her shimmered and split silent as a sigh as the rest emerged. He saw Hammer, Whisper, and Irons, who was carrying something in his beefy hand.

"Took time to red-eye from CDG to JFK and back to London but it was where you said it would be, tucked behind a bottle of Glenfiddich," he said. "But when you said we needed your old man I thought we were getting *him*, not a jar of ashes. You gonna add water, make him grow?"

"A good magician never reveals his secrets," Jason said.

Irons handed the urn to Jason with a scowl. Jason took it . . . and handed the Sphere to Sofia.

"I can't carry both," he said. "And I need to get these ashes to Cold Spring."

"That's a lot of trust you're giving me," she said, clutching the Sphere with surprise.

"Well, apparently I'm the only one who can open it, so it's not *much* trust."

"The only doorway still open is the one we used in Peckham," said Whisper. "I assume that's nowhere near Cold Spring?"

"They aren't all locked down," said Sofia. "The Athenaeum will be open. You can't enter the Citadel through it, but you can exit to anywhere on earth, assuming you know which door to take."

"I know which door," Jason said. And he did; Carter had shown it to him after all.

"Then what are we waiting for?" Sofia asked.

All up the atrium they emerged, from doorways torn open by the wave. Jason lost count of them by the eighth floor. They weren't nearly enough to match the Invisible Hand for numbers, but they'd sure as hell cause some chaos.

Sofia nodded to Abigail, still unconscious on the floor. "What about her?"

Jason stared at Abigail. She looked so helpless, so small. He knew she was anything but that, but she was as much a victim of this war as they all had been.

"Leave her. She's suffered enough," he said.

Sofia gave the order. The conjurers descended and followed them as they streamed out of the atrium and into the Ingress. Jason fired a parting glance back at Abigail, still lying where the wave had deposited her. But had he lingered a moment longer, he would have seen her eyes open, and realized she'd been listening all along.

• • •

When she pictured the path her married life would take, Carla Rickert never envisioned it would end in cardboard. The bungalow was filled with them: corrugated cardboard boxes holding the remnants of her life in Cold Spring. Owen's things had been packed and taken to the Goodwill: clothes mostly; she couldn't stand having them around when they still smelled so much like him. The books went, too, though she kept some for Noah: old paperbacks his father had read as a teen—highlighted and underlined Vonneguts and Bradburys and Salingers. When he was older maybe Noah would read them and happen upon some note scribbled by Owen in the margins and for a moment know something of the father who was now a distant memory.

Carla was leaving; there were too many memories in the small bungalow, too many ghosts walking the streets of this small town. Everywhere she looked she sensed him—his smile, his voice—and she could sometimes feel him in the empty spot of the bed they'd once shared. Carla Petrozzi had been a religious person once, but Carla Rickert had given up on the idea of a God who'd take a father away before his child would ever know him. It wasn't just the house; the entire town was haunted by memory. There was too much of Owen in Cold Spring and his ghost needed rest just as she needed to move on, for Noah, but especially for herself.

Noah was sleeping in his crib: the one piece of furniture that hadn't been disassembled and packed up. That would happen when her parents arrived with the U-Haul from Greensboro in the morning. She stared at her son, watching his chest rise and fall, hearing his soft breaths.

It wasn't supposed to be like this, Owen. We were supposed to watch him grow up, together. . . .

The doorbell rang, its sharp jangle piercing the quiet of the near-empty house. Noah flinched, whimpered, almost woke, then settled back down. Carla double-timed it to the front door before whoever it was rang the bell again. God, it was after ten on a Saturday night. Who could it be?

It was a woman, dressed in a fashionable dark-blue pantsuit, like she'd just materialized on her doorstep directly from Midtown Manhattan. The fact Carla noticed her clothing the moment she opened the door told her this wasn't a social call or a solicitation. Carla looked to the street expecting to see the woman's car, but there was just Carla's battered old Kia rusting in the driveway.

"Carla . . . ?" the woman asked. "Carla Rickert?"

Something, or someone, walked over Carla's grave, and she shivered. The woman was familiar, but from where? She nodded slowly, unsure whether she should speak to this stranger at all.

"My name's Winnie Hobbes," the woman said. "I need your help."

THIRTY

....

WHAT WOULD ONE DAY BE known as the Battle of the Citadel unfolded in Jason's peripheral vision as he ushered his father's remains through collapsing corridors, through flashes of light and flame, from end to end of its crumbling reality. As he followed Sofia's path through the labyrinthine fortress, he glimpsed snatches of battle, brief bursts of action, a clash of gods unfolding in glances. Clutching the urn tight, he wondered if this was how it was for everyone who witnessed battles from the middle of them, so consumed by your own survival that you were only a piece of a much larger canvas being painted in broad strokes. Only after survival did you realize you'd lived through a moment in history that would be spoken of long after you were dead.

That was assuming you survived at all . . .

The Golden Dawn met heavy resistance at every bend in the Ingress and in every chamber they passed through. The Invisible Hand, caught off guard by the invasion of what they'd thought was an impregnable fortress, rallied quickly, using their familiarity with the environs to press back the vanguard of the assault. At every juncture the invaders were met by an opposing force, and that force stripped conjurers away from the larger group, pulling them into skirmishes, into brawls, into one-on-one duels. They met the heaviest resistance in the games room; Sofia's force had numbered roughly a hundred when they started but as they fought through it, the strength of their charge was peeled away like the layers of an onion. By the time Jason, Sofia, Irons, Hammer, Whisper, and the rest reached the Spire and their penultimate destination, their force had been depleted by half. When they stormed the Spire the full force of the Invisible Hand met them like an anvil meeting another anvil. Cinder blocks hurtled into bodies. Barriers were erected to block their way. Columns of flame formed serpentine shapes that spat fire and roasted men and women alive. Piles of scrap twisted into hands and fists that plunged into the fray, battering Golden Dawn and Invisible Hand alike, crushing bones and spraying blood through the air in a wet mist. There was a choked gasp to Jason's right and he glanced there long enough to see Irons take a storm of blades to his neck and chest, dropping him dead to the ground before he had a chance to realize it.

"Keep moving!" Sophia shouted in Jason's ear.

Somehow, he focused on the windowed bunker looking down on the Spire and its warring factions. That was their goal: the entrance to the Athenaeum and to Cold Spring.

Someone else screamed close behind him—its pitch so high he couldn't be sure if it was Hammer or Whisper—but he felt the remaining conjurers fall back and fall away until it was just him and Sofia. He clutched the urn tighter. He'd bet everything on this one hand, and if he was wrong, every death rattling through the Citadel would be on his head. He focused on the bunker: the cold feel of the walls, the buzz of its fluorescent lights. He pictured the view out its window when he first gazed on the Spire. Then it had seemed truly magical; racing through it now, there was only death and horror.

He blinked . . . and he was inside the room, looking out the window over the Spire. Battles were raging on every wall, in every corner, *everywhere*. He did it. He was inside.

"Come on, we need to keep moving," Sofia said, arriving a heartbeat after him and beelining for the heavy steel door at the bunker's rear, the Sphere in hand.

"Where are the others?" Jason asked.

"There are no others."

She pushed. The door swung open with a jarring screech. As Jason followed her through he wondered why, in their race for the Athenaeum, he hadn't seen Carter or Allegra. But when he entered the massive chamber, he found his answer.

Allegra was standing in the central passageway, flanked by rows of doors vaulting into the unseen heights above, a coiled weapon waiting to strike. For a moment the entire Athenaeum seemed to hold its breath as Sofia and Jason faced her.

"Do you see it?" Sofia whispered to Jason.

He looked down the rows and up them. There were so many he didn't know where to begin. Then he reached out with his thoughts, with his memories. The countless times he'd grasped that cool brass door handle, coming home from school and work. How, no matter his mood—joyful, heartbroken, proud—opening that door always felt like he was safe and loved. He reached out with everything he had, and in the cavernous expanse of the Athenaeum, it answered. He set his gaze forward and then he spotted it; a tiny postage stamp of white, fifteen levels above them and three rows down, its curved handle as familiar as it had been when he lived on Cedar Street. He felt a slight tug as his memory grasped onto it.

"*Do you see it?*" Sofia asked, anxiousness in her voice.

"I see it," he nodded.

"Then buckle up!"

Sofia threw her free hand forward and pushed. The brunt of the blast took Jason from behind, but rather than being pulverized by it, he was launched upward into the air, soaring high, soaring long. As he flew, a hurricane howled through the Athenaeum below him and above him, ripping a multitude of doors from their brackets and flinging them into even more. The impact tore those from their mountings, sending them tearing through the cavern and each other. They shattered passageways, amputated chambers, and sent the debris of everything funneling at Allegra.

Allegra pushed back.

Doors behind her ripped from their mounts and whistled past to deflect Sofia's assault. The waves collided, shattering doorways, crashing into the shelves to splinter more. The ground heaved and pitched, like the destruction of the gateways was inflicting mortal wounds on a great lumbering beast.

Jason clutched the urn and blinked. He saw the door lurch closer to him. His fingers brushed the cool brass handle—

The door launched upward, soaring high into the cavern. Jason sailed past, fell, blinked, and skidded to a halt on the floor of the shelf. The door halted its ascent a hundred feet above.

The door seemed to jolt, like the wires supporting it had snapped.

Then it was falling. It was going to smash to pieces on the hard ground.

He blinked reflexively, the cavern fell away beneath him, and he was on top of the door, grasping the handle as it fell. He struggled to pull it open. The ground raced to meet them. They were both going to shatter on it. Then the door slowed, stopped, and launched itself up. The wind howled, forcing him against the hard surface as he was carried aloft to the topmost level of the Athenaeum.

What the hell was happening?

Then he knew. Gazing upward, Jason could see the Diabolist's smile: a sharp crescent moon in the darkness, drawing him in like he was a fish pierced by a hook.

Carter.

She'd failed before but this time she wouldn't miss; she'd grind the Red Queen's body into a paste of bone and meat. Allegra let fly with doors torn from their hinges. The Red Queen redirected them into shelves and rows. Wood shattered, metal tore, and dozens of doors tumbled to fall, to break, to be redirected, to fill the air with shrapnel that buzzed like rabid hornets. They were tearing the Athenaeum and the Citadel apart piece by piece but she didn't stop; adrenaline was raging through her like fire, and she couldn't have stopped it if she'd wanted to. And she didn't want to; she wanted everything to burn. Flames shot from her fingertips, licking the wood that soared past her, igniting it and blasting flaming debris through the chamber, setting all it touched ablaze.

Before, Damon would have stopped her. He would have brought her back, like he had after Bam and many times following, showing her how to harness that anger, to control it.

But Damon was gone.

And despite whatever Jason thought, he wasn't coming back. Her hatred flowed atop flaming wreckage and she intensified her assault. The Red Queen leapt to a walkway thirty stories above, broke the railing, and loosened a row of doors to send them crashing down. Allegra dodged away from the impact, grasped the railing on the row opposite, and leapt onto the metal walkway. The Red Queen leapfrogged floor to floor, level to level, bursting in and out of smoke, and Allegra matched her, clenching her hand into a fist, summoning more flame and hurtling it against the door rows beside her. As they caught fire, she yanked them from their mounts and sent them at the Red Queen. Flames raced up the rows, blistering and charring and igniting ancient wood that erupted in a white-hot flare of heat. They were spreading, raging uncontrolled, and she didn't care. She would have her vengeance.

She saw Jason far below, leaping from falling door to falling door, landing on top of one, and blinking to the next, then the next, then the next, leapfrogging toward the door someone else had sent plummeting. She saw him latch onto it and grasp it as it fell, riding it like he was riding a skateboard. He grasped the handle for balance, and the door lifted, climbing higher and higher.

But it wasn't Jason who was lifting it. It was Carter. He was perched on the topmost level of the Athenaeum, lifting the doorway and Jason to him.

The Sphere is the objective, not the Queen, Carter's voice hammered through her skull.

Go to hell, she thought.

But the mention of the Sphere took root in her brain, and as the Red Queen raced away from the flame, Allegra reached out, felt fingers grasp the Sphere, and she pulled. It yanked from the Red Queen's grasp and arced across the chamber, landing in Allegra's palm with a satisfying sound. The Red Queen slid to a stop. She looked at Jason, rising above, and at Allegra and the Sphere below.

"Come on, come on, make your choice . . ." Allegra whispered.

She brandished the Sphere triumphantly.

"COME ON!" she shouted.

Carter stared across the chasm at Jason, perched atop the door. It was so close, the thing tucked under Jason's coat; all Carter needed to do was take it. But forcing Jason to hand it to him would be the sweeter victory. Sour, noxious smoke rose around them. The levels below were burning, the flames climbing. The Citadel was dying, but Carter didn't need the Citadel or the Mages battling within it and across the world. The conduits between the mundane and the magical realms were being severed to wither and die, and still he didn't care.

All he needed was the Sphere.

"Of all the things I expected of you, Jason, sentimentality was never one of them."

"Then you don't know me very well," said Jason. "This was your aim all along, wasn't it? Use me as bait, draw her in, force me to choose?"

"The key to any successful stratagem is to explore every option, and every possible move, especially the ones that don't unfold as predicted. You almost beat me, Jason, but only almost."

"It's not over yet," Jason said.

"Isn't it?"

354 • Brad Abraham

"You lied to me! From the moment we met, you lied about everything!"

"I saved you!" Carter shouted. "You spent your entire wasted life seeking a purpose I provided! You should be thanking me, not fighting me! You should be by my side, not your bitch of a mother's! I gave you more than she or your father ever did! *I made you a Mage!*"

Carter stretched his hand out. He felt for the object hidden in the folds of Jason's jacket.

The jacket opened and the object concealed within lurched out—

Jason clasped his hand on it.

It wasn't the Sphere. It was an urn; a simple pewter urn.

Carter stared, confused. What was Jason playing at . . . ?

Then he saw. He recognized the urn. He knew whose remains it held.

Damon.

If she had a pulse to speak of, Sofia's would have quickened at the sight of the Sphere in Allegra's grasp. So many of her people lay dead by Allegra Sand's actions, and the desire to see the Mage choke out her last dying breath was overwhelming. But Allegra wasn't their mission.

Sofia looked to Jason high above, perched atop the door facing Carter.

That was the mission. They'd come this far. This was their moment. What they'd fought for. What so many had died for. Their destination wasn't just in reach: Jason was literally standing on it.

She hadn't forgotten what Jason told her when they hatched their plan. It was a desperate gambit. The nuclear card. The one to use only when all other options had been exhausted.

And for that gambit to work, they needed Allegra Sand.

Don't kill her, Jason had said. *She's a weapon. She destroyed a city and can destroy the Citadel.*

So use her.

And she did. Allegra had triggered the calamity raging through the Citadel and the chamber. Now it was Sofia's task to finish what she'd started.

She glanced at Jason once more, hoping it wouldn't be the last time she saw him.

Then she pushed.

The blast shook the foundations of the Citadel. The walkway pitched, Carter slammed into the railing, and Jason felt the door plunge beneath him. He fell to his knees and grasped the handle, steadying himself on it as it fell. His gaze was drawn down into the chasm of fire and debris ripping open beneath him. He saw Sofia hurling doors at Allegra. He saw Allegra strike them, splinter them, shatter them, tearing through them and reality itself in a frenzied movement, losing her senses, losing control. The shock wave blasted through the Athenaeum, shattering every shelf. The air shrieked violently through the chamber as every last door pitched from their moorings, falling like dead leaves from a burning tree. The railing Carter was leaning against buckled and broke and he was plummeting into space, plunging in tandem with Jason. Their eyes locked for a brief moment, then Carter tucked his arms into his side and dove through the air, slicing through the chamber in a guided free fall toward Sofia, diving for the Sphere, which had slipped Allegra's grip and was dropping to the flame-blanketed floor.

Jason pulled the urn close and tried again to pull his door open, but it wouldn't budge. He threw a desperate shoulder into it. It buckled inward.

He was on the other side! It didn't open into the house, it opened *outside*!

He grasped the handle, turned it, and it swung into the view out the front door of the house on Cedar Street. He glanced back into the Citadel one last time to see Allegra floating rigid amidst the destruction raining down around her. He saw Carter dive for the Sphere. He saw Sofia leap for it. As their hands grasped it simultaneously, a blinding flash obliterated everything.

Then he pitched himself through the doorway and was gone.

THIRTY-ONE

JASON'S FEET STRUCK SOLID GROUND, and the unexpected inertia sent him staggering forward, legs twisting as his heels hit the hard edge of the front porch. He tripped and then toppled down the steps, the world canting wildly above as his back slammed painfully into hard cement. A jarring agony tore through him, and he uttered a sudden, gasping scream. The urn slipped from his hand, soared up into the air, and then hurtled down to smash open on the ground—

The urn froze midair, inches from the hard paving stones of the front walk.

Jason held his hand forward, and the urn held in the air. He took a breath in; he pushed it out, and tugged the urn back to him with a gentle smack of pewter to palm. He tightened his grip, rolled onto his side, then to his knees, and slowly sat up. A knife's blade seemed to dig between his vertebrae with every movement, and he choked back a startled cry. He waited for the pain to subside, but it flared again as he grasped the front porch railing and pulled himself up. The dagger struck again, white hot with each step he took down the driveway, past a parked Range Rover with Jersey plates, and then he turned and looked back at the house. Its powder-blue front had been repainted the color of a headstone. Cathryn's beloved garden was barren, Aaron's prized front lawn fallow, with crabgrass punctuating the areas that hadn't died. The house lights were off, but as he took a pained step backward, a motion sensor clicked on and a hard spotlight bathed the front, washing unexpected familiarity over it. He saw Cathryn on the porch, a fierce wisp who would die to protect the child she had raised as her own. He saw Aaron cutting the grass, eyeing Jason as he shirked chores to hang out with Owen but letting him go anyway because childhood was too brief a gift.

Then the light clicked off, snatching those ghosts of memory with it.

A burst of fresh pain tore through him, like it was reminding him he'd lingered long enough. He unlocked the Range Rover with a press of the hand, and deactivated the alarm before it could sound. He climbed in awkwardly and set Damon's urn on the passenger seat. The car was a standard shift, thankfully, and after popping the clutch, he rolled it back down the driveway, threw it into gear, and steered it down Cedar to the stop sign at Mountain Avenue. He pressed a hand to the steering column, tumblers turned and mechanisms clicked, and the engine rumbled to life.

By the time he skirted Foundry Cove and pulled to a stop alongside the Metro-North tracks, the ache in his back had become a piercing shriek. Climbing out with the urn, his spine felt like it was comprised of broken china plates grinding into each other.

The sky above Storm King flashed incandescence, though no

thunder followed. The urn was an iron weight pulling him down, compressing his spine, making his every step torture.

Then lightning illuminated the rusted iron hulk of Murder Hill perched at the Hudson's edge like some prehistoric beast. The chain-link fence was peeled back like the skin of a rotten apple, like it had been waiting for him to return. Clenching his jaw against the persistent stabs of pain grating through him, he cleared the edge of the fence and trudged to the water's edge, pausing midway to gather his strength. More silent lightning flashed, casting electric light through Murder Hill's bones.

The iron monster had seen better days. It was barely standing, and the wind that whistled through its skeletal structure sounded like it was deliberately trying to tear it down. The sheet metal that had once covered it had been stripped away by decay and theft, and the ladder the three boys had climbed that blistering summer day a lifetime ago had fallen into a twisted heap at its foundation. The chute still stood, still pockmarked, still diseased, the end rusted to a jagged, cleft lip.

Lightning blasted the sky, and his back seized with each step he took, until he reached the dark waters at the river's edge. This was where he'd gone in, where he'd first worked his magic. That had been his baptism, the moment his life changed, though it would be almost twenty years before that dormant power would be unleashed. There was no more fitting place on earth to fulfil his father's final wish. He popped the lid off the urn and tossed it to clatter against a heap of twisted metal and splintered wood at the site's perimeter. Under normal circumstances he would have said some words, but these circumstances were far from normal. There'd be time to say a lot more later.

Assuming it worked.

He tilted the urn. The ashes spilled out, streaming into the water with a soft hiss, blanketing the surface and sinking slowly beneath it. Fresh agony spasmed through him, and he dropped the urn to clatter against the concrete ground. A final flash of lightning turned night briefly into day . . . then it was gone. The storm broke as suddenly as it had swept down the mountainside. A bright crescent moon emerged from behind the parting clouds, casting its cold light over Murder Hill and over him.

Everything had gone quiet.

He watched. Waited.

Nothing happened.

No magic.

No Damon.

Nothing.

There was a distant, plaintive cry somewhere above, but Jason barely heard it. Pain tugged at his nerve endings, but now it was as severe as a skinned knee compared to the guilt howling through his battered body. He'd failed, and all those lives lost in the Citadel were on his head.

The cry sounded again, closer this time.

Ice ran up his throbbing spine. It wasn't a bird's cry. It was a human's.

A child's.

He looked into the sky and what he saw shredded every last ounce of strength he had left.

A car was hanging high above the Hudson, floating like it was a balloon, its headlights slicing the night sky as it slowly descended toward the water. It was battered, rusted, dented . . . and too familiar. He saw Carla inside, gripping the steering wheel, rigid with fright. He couldn't see Noah but he could hear the baby yowling. When Carla saw Jason she screamed his name, but neither

her cry nor the terror in her voice was what horrified him the most; that was reserved for the person perched atop the car's roof and staring down at him with a cold, cruel smile.

"Hello, lover," Winnie said.

Katja. He'd forgotten about her. She'd been Carter's agent when they met, and she remained his loyalist even now. She'd known about Carla and Noah, but how . . . ?

Because of him.

Carla had come to Damon's funeral to offer condolences and say goodbye . . . and Katja had been watching. This was *his* doing; Carla and Noah were going to die because of him. Before, he'd doubted whether he had it in him to kill, but seeing Katja those doubts faded. He felt the weight of the deck of cards tucked inside his jacket pocket. If he could maneuver it out of there and into his hand . . .

Katja released the car. It plunged out from under her, hurtling for the river before lurching back with a jolt. Carla's forehead smacked the wheel hard, and her cry made Noah's howls rise in pitch to the point they threatened to shatter the car's windows.

"*STOP!*" he shouted.

Katja set down to the car's roof with a ballerina's grace, and her glamour faded, Winnie's façade slipping away to reveal the hateful Enchanter beneath it.

"I know what you're thinking," she said. "If you push, you can knock me off the car. But then the car falls, it sinks, and they drown . . ."

She tapped her heel against the roof. It echoed metallically across the water.

"You hear that, Carla? That's the chink in Jason's armor. He cares for you, you know? He cares for you both so much. That's not just concern for the widow of his dead friend. No, he's carried a torch for you a good long time. Even before I put your face to the name, I knew it was yours he saw when we fucked. Your face he saw reaching climax, not mine faking it. Poor Jason Bishop, the little orphan boy who couldn't let go of the past."

He glanced to the pile of scrap metal alongside the riverbank. Projectiles he could use against her: lift, push, direct. Maybe he'd get lucky, maybe he'd sever an artery, maybe she'd be bleed out before she hit the water . . .

But that was a hell of a lot of maybes, and even if they *did* come to pass, the car would still fall.

He needed more time. To formulate a plan. To wait for help.

But there was no time. He had to act.

He raised his hands, slow and steady. He focused his thoughts on the deck. He felt its hard edges, he felt its weight. And then, he felt it slowly lift out of his pocket.

"You have me, you don't need them," he said.

"You know something, Jason? You're right."

She released the car. Carla screamed and Jason cried out. It lurched to a halt again. Katja settled back down on it as gentle as a falling leaf as Noah's wails pierced the night.

"I don't need them, but you do, so keep your hands where I can see them and your eyes on me, not on that heap of scrap metal. We're going to wait for the others to arrive, and then this ends."

Others? What the hell was she talking about?

There were no "others." . . .

She was outside the Citadel when it happened. She wasn't there when the Citadel fell.

"You don't know . . ." he said.

Katja frowned. "Know what?"

He lowered his hands so she could see them, and as he did, slowly moved the deck down the inside of his jacket.

"The Citadel's gone. Carter's gone, and the Sphere with him."

Even at this distance he could see surprise cross Katja's face.

"That's impossible!"

"I barely made it out myself. It's gone—all of it."

"How?" Katja spat.

"Allegra," Jason answered.

She stared at Jason with a slow dawning realization that blossomed into acceptance. She knew just as well as Jason that when pushed, Allegra would push back hard.

Then a smile spread across the Enchanter's face.

He felt the presence before he turned, and when he did his last shred of hope died.

Carter Block was standing between Jason and Murder Hill. Something was clutched in his hand.

The Sphere.

THIRTY-TWO

THE RIGHT LEG OF CARTER'S trousers were shredded and stained with blood pulsing from the raw wound visible through the mangled fabric. His suit jacket was gone, his shirt charred and torn. His face was caked in gore, the hair and skin on the side of his temple burned and blistered. Even from the distance between them Jason could smell the odor of burning wood and flesh radiate off him, and hear Carter's every wet, rasping breath. If Katja had doubted Jason's account of the Citadel's annihilation, Carter was the proof. However long he had battled Sofia in the inferno of the Athenaeum for possession of the Sphere, she hadn't let him take it without exacting a terrible price. If Jason felt any grief at the loss of his mother for the second time in his life, it didn't register between the pain rattling through him and his fear for Carla and Noah. Wherever Sofia Aguirre was now, he hoped she was at finally at peace.

"She put up a fierce fight," Carter said. "I'm sure that's cold comfort, but it confirms I shouldn't have entrusted you to do a job you didn't have the iron for."

Fury sent heat blasting through Jason's pain-wracked body. The healing wave washed over him, his spasms subsiding, the throb of his tortured back fading. Two parents dead by Carter Block's hand. He'd taken everything from Jason, and he was going to take Carla and Noah, too . . .

The card deck held its descent, resting at the bottom edge of his jacket above his right hand. An inch more and it would be in his palm.

Carter thrust his hand out. The Sphere lifted off his palm and rose slowly.

"That leaves us, and your destiny," said Carter. "With order ruling chaos, we needn't hide in the shadows anymore. We'll be gods, as we were meant to be, once you do what you were meant to."

"I won't open it," Jason said. "You'll have to kill me."

Carter looked to Katja. There was a jolt, and the car fell, snapping back more violently this time. The driver's side air bag exploded, knocking Carla into the headrest with a brutal snap. She slumped against the wheel, and Noah's sobs rose to compensate for the loss of hers. The car was ten feet above the river's surface. One more jolt and it would be in the water. Katja settled back on top, crossed her arms, and waited for the order.

"Jason, it's over," Carter said. "You lost the game, but you're still a Mage. There's still a place in our new order for you and those you love. All you have to do is open the Sphere."

Check and mate. Carter had him. He couldn't sacrifice Carla and Noah, and the elder Mage knew it. But it couldn't end like this, not with Carter victorious. There had to be a way. . . .

Carter pushed gently with his hand, and the Sphere floated toward Jason, crossing the gulf between them silently and coming to a slow stop an arm's length away.

All he had to do was take it and open it, and it would be over.

For a moment all was silent but for Noah's distant cries.

That . . . and a voice inside Jason's mind.

Not his voice: Damon's.

At their heart, all magic tricks are simple misdirection, nothing more.

Jason reached his hand out and took the Sphere.

Remember that, and you will survive this.

He held the Sphere, felt its smooth surface, and traced its topography with his fingers. He reached his thoughts into it, searching for a way in, searching for some indication of what would happen when he *did* open it. But there was nothing there; it was just an old, hollow piece of wood . . .

No, it can't be that simple, he thought. *It can't be . . .*

Simplexity. Jason side-eyed the scrap pile in his peripheral. He felt the weight of the deck against his waist.

There was a way.

"It doesn't have to be difficult!" Carter shouted. "You have a choice, so choose!"

Jason's pulse, which had raced ever since the arrival at Murder Hill, settled into a quiet calm.

"Are you watching closely?" he asked.

He held the Sphere out to Carter, drawing his and Katja's eyes to it . . .

Right where he wanted them.

"Abracadabra," Jason said.

He threw the Sphere up into the air. It rocketed upward, slowed its climb, held for a brief moment, then fell, hurtling to the ground. As it dropped within Jason's proximity he leapt up, propelling himself higher off the ground than he ever had.

Then, as the Sphere plunged past him, he reared back, and he pushed—

The Sphere struck the concrete with the speed of a bullet fired from a gun and shattered against it, breaking apart with an audible snap. The imprint of Jason's hand caved the ground at the point of impact forcing the remnants of the Sphere into it even further so it was trapped in the bowl-shaped depression. The pieces clattered and settled, and were finally still, lying there as hollow and empty as they'd always been.

Both Carter and Katja stared in stunned disbelief at the broken, useless pieces of Sphere. When their attention was on it to the exclusion of all else, Jason pivoted to the scrap pile and pushed again.

The pile exploded into a deadly cloud of shrapnel. Carter had a brief moment to register surprise when the first jagged piece of metal struck his shoulder, yanking him around, jagged iron jutting from soft meat. Another shard pierced his thigh, and his legs collapsed from under him, sending him to the ground. As Carter fell, the deck dropped into Jason's palm and he spun around to blast a storm of cards at Katja. They engulfed her, ripping her jacket, opening a cheek, separating an ear at its base, and tearing a wet strip of scalp away. As sudden agony seized her, Katja's features dissolved to reveal a horribly mutilated face. Her nose was a fleshy nub, her cheek a mass of tangled scar tissue, like her true appearance to everyone had been an illusion all along. Katja clasped her hands over her disfigured features and toppled backward into the water. The car held in the air for a delayed moment, then her enchantment slipped away and it was falling.

Jason thrust his hands out, felt the cool metal of the car brush his fingertips, and grasped on tight.

The car lurched. Listed. The front wheels brushed the water.

He slid across the concrete ground, his muscles spasming violently. He screamed, but held on.

The car shuddered, dropped . . . then held there.

He had them. He was doing it—

Terror worried its fingers into his brain, digging into its soft gray pulp to seize his amygdalae and squeeze. He collapsed to the ground and tried to cry out but couldn't make a noise or move a muscle as pain exploded through his paralyzed body. His grip slipped off the car. He heard it fall and splash, and heard Carla's waking cries join Noah's, but his gaze was frozen on Carter, who gripped the jagged spear in his shoulder and pulled it through, ripping meat, and spilling blood. A femur jutted from Carter's thigh, glistening wet in the moonlight. He clenched his hands into fists, the bone snapped back into place with a noise that sent sympathy pain rippling through Jason. Carter lurched to his feet, and then rose off the ground, his legs dangling limp beneath him, his eyes blazing hateful fire.

"What did you do?!" he screamed.

"It was . . . an illusion . . ." Jason said. "It was a lie . . . just like yours."

Jason looked to the car, the waters now just below its windows. Then it began to sink, not from gravity, but from the force of Carter's hand pressing down like a child sinking a toy in the tub.

"You'll watch them die, then you'll join them in the hell I sent your father and your BITCH OF A MOTHER!" Carter snarled.

Carla screamed. Noah shrieked.

You crazy son of a bitch, don't let them die!

A voice. In his head. *Owen's voice.*

But it wasn't a ghost or a whisper or some enchantment; it was the piece of his friend that had imprinted on him, like Murder Hill had. It was an extension of himself, his life, his experiences. Like the line that had tethered him to Cold Spring all those years had stretched out from that rusted, monstrous hulk. The memory of that day, this place, and that moment seeped into his marrow, blasted his nerve endings, and sent adrenaline roaring through him. It made him the person he was, and in the end it was that memory that released Carter's grip on him. He'd faced down death before and survived; he could handle Carter Block.

Murder Hill *was* his home. As much a parent as Damon. As much a teacher as Carter.

He was The Boy Who Broke Murder Hill.

The rusting, decrepit hulk shuddered, bent, and contorted. Metal groaned and shrieked as Jason manipulated the hulking iron and steel like it was his own appendage. It had waited years for his return and he didn't disappoint. On that day on Murder Hill eighteen years earlier he'd been, for a moment, a god, and that god returned one final time to work his magic. He harnessed those memories with white-hot intensity, working them into Murder Hill's teetering structure like he was manipulating wet clay with his hands. The chute bent and buckled inward, its jagged edges becoming serrated teeth. The tower collapsed into a primitive brow, creasing itself into a contorted face. Heavy support pillars twisted and bent and tore out of the earth, shattered supports clattering and twisting into clawed talons.

Then it attacked.

Carter turned just in time to see it lunge, then jagged steel speared his chest, shattering bone, tearing organs, and showering the ground beneath him in gleaming crimson. The beast carried

Carter aloft like a prize, the ground shuddering beneath it as heavy quadrupedal footsteps punched holes in the earth. The great beast charged to the water's edge and then plunged into the Hudson with an explosion of displaced water, sinking with each lumbering step. Waves slammed the shore as it descended beneath the surface, the twisted metal of its jaws holding Carter aloft. There was a final moment as Carter's dying gaze met Jason's, then the beast went under, carrying the Mage with it. There was a final churning eruption of flotsam, and then they were both gone.

Jason pulled himself into a sitting position as back pain shuddered through him again. A brief image flashed before his eyes, of that iron monstrosity descending into darkness and touching the river's bed, Carter's body lolling lifeless in the current—

"JASON!"

Carla's cry brought him back in time to catch a final glimpse of her face against the window as the compact slipped beneath the river's surface, and then they were gone. He was on his feet a heartbeat later, adrenaline powering his torn muscles. He charged into the bracing waters and, after taking a lungful of air, dove underneath them.

Frigid water bludgeoned his senses but he forced the cold away, sighted the compact's headlights stabbing the darkness, and swam toward it. He slammed against the door and grasped the handle. The car listed, headlights pointing to the surface five, now six feet above. Water streamed inside, soaking Carla and Noah, who was wailing his throat raw. Carla's terrified eyes met Jason's through stinging waters and as they did he pushed his thoughts at her.

Can you hear me? Nod if you can hear me.

Carla stared numbly . . . and nodded.

Get Noah out of his seat and hold him tight.

He clenched the car door handle and began to lift. He'd turned Murder Hill into a rampaging beast; he could do this. Inside the car, Carla twisted around and slid from the front seat into the back as water flowed inside. She worked at the straps holding Noah, her struggles frantic. The car shifted onto its side, putting Jason on top of it. Water crashed against Carla and Noah, knocking her back against the door. She recovered and fought the straps but they weren't going to give. Jason considered shattering the window and flowing in with the water that would fill the car and drag it deeper. He could get Carla out but Noah . . . ?

The hopeless expression on Carla's face pierced his heart.

She grasped Noah's hand and squeezed her eyes shut as the water rose to her neck.

They were going to die.

But not alone. He fought every instinct telling him to surface and tightened his grip on the car. Maybe it was better this way. There was nothing to fear, not from what Vasilisa told him. If she had heard the voices of her loved ones, then death wasn't the end, just a transition. That meant Owen would be waiting for Carla and Noah. Jason forced his eyes to meet theirs so that they would be the last thing he saw as—

Something splashed into the water and he felt the car right itself. He stared through the windows to the face on the other side of it, the current whipping her rat's-nest hair like seaweed.

Allegra. She stared forcefully through the car window at him.

He met her gaze and nodded.

She pressed her hands against the car and he did the same.

He felt it become lighter. The car lifted to the surface. He kept his hands pressed to it, his gaze on Carla, who focused on Jason with amazement as the car broke the river's surface. He choked back cool, crisp air as water spilled out of the car, the level dropping beneath Carla's chin, neck, and chest. They cleared the embankment and drifted with the car several feet into safe harbor before settling it on the ground.

Jason collapsed, panting. He lay there, staring up at a sky blanketed with stars, the crescent moon punching a hole in it front and center. He took a calming breath in and let it out slow . . . and felt his throat constrict, as if someone was squeezing it tight.

He clawed at his throat and writhed. And in his periphery he glimpsed a nightmare.

Katja was standing on dry ground, water and blood dripping from her clothing. Her glamour had returned, but she was still a mess. A strip of her scalp was peeled back and exposing raw and angry meat beneath. Her left ear had been shaved away clean. Her cheek had been cut at the corner of her mouth, making her hateful scowl seem to stretch across her face. Her hand was out and closing into a fist and he felt his windpipe collapse—

Something sliced through the air and embedded itself in Katja's chest. It was long and narrow, and Jason recognized it as a piece of Murder Hill—one of its steel reinforcements. He felt Katja's hand slip from his throat and he took in a hard swallow of air. Katja staggered back, clutching the reinforcement, her face twisted in a horrible grimace.

But she didn't scream. She wouldn't give anyone that satisfaction. She staggered backward into the shadows, and as they slipped over her there was a cloudburst, and the reinforcement fell to the ground with a noisy clatter. By the time it settled and was silent, she was gone.

There was a scrape of bootheels against concrete. Allegra crouched over him, her hair dripping.

"Before you get all choked up, that was for me, not for you," she said.

"How'd . . . you know where I'd be?"

"Did anybody ever tell you that you ask too many questions?"

"Yeah . . . a lot . . ."

"I followed Carter through a doorway into a funeral home, and followed him here. I was tired, weak, it . . . took me longer to put myself back together . . . but I got here in time to hear his confession. He killed Damon, didn't he? He set it in motion."

Jason nodded.

Something dark passed over Allegra's face. He could sense the turmoil boiling inside her. The knowledge of what she'd done would have cracked a lesser being, but not Allegra Sand.

"Just tell me one thing," Jason said. "Was I Mozart . . . or was I Salieri?"

Allegra stared at him, and then a glimmer of a smile crossed her face.

"One of these days that mouth of yours is going to get you into trouble."

"If this all *hasn't* been trouble I can't wait for the genuine article."

"Did you know your father was the one who found me?" Allegra asked. "The one who brought me into the Citadel? He found me wandering the desert outside Bam. I was frightened; I blamed myself for what happened. But he told me it wasn't my fault.

That I wasn't a monster. And when he told me there were others like me, it was the greatest thing I'd ever been told. Then he took my hand and told me a story. I think you know which one."

He did.

Once, long ago, there was a modest man who owned a modest farm . . .

Allegra stood. The fire was gone from her eyes. She was at peace, or at least some momentary semblance of it.

"Look," he said. "If you're going to kill me, just promise you'll let Carla and Noah—"

"Oh, Jason, grow up! Damon saved my life, and I betrayed the trust of his son because those were my orders. That's why we're even. But the next time we meet, things will be different. That's the only warning you'll get."

She stepped over him and walked away. He pulled himself into a painful sitting position.

"Hey, Allegra . . ."

She turned back, her green-gold eyes settling on him.

"You're not a bad person, you know that?"

She stared at him . . . then smiled wryly.

"Keep telling yourself that, Jason, and one of these days you won't be so lucky."

The air tore. Smoke erupted. Then it faded just as quickly and when it did, Allegra was gone.

A spasm rippled through Jason and he fell back to the ground. He lay there as he heard the car door open and heard water splash concrete. When Noah's whimpering cry followed, it was the most wonderful sound he had *ever* heard.

Carla crouched over him, runoff from her hair spattering his face. Noah's head was buried in her shoulder, muffling his confused sobs.

"She said she was your girlfriend and that you were in trouble," Carla said. "She said to take Noah with us and I did everything she asked even as she got out and the car lifted off the ground and she changed into someone else and Jason, *what's going on*?!"

He reached a tentative hand up to her. To his relief, she took it.

"Carla . . . it's been a *really* weird month."

EPILOGUE

A BITTER WIND PROWLED the cemetery, raking its skeletal tree branches across a lifeless sky. For a moment he was back in Paris, in the Jardin des Tuileries. The next, he was moving through the Empire of the Dead, listening to the scrape of bone against limestone. He was trudging through that lifeless, barren landscape next, wandering aimlessly until he found the chessboard beneath an ancient, withered oak. Then the memories dissipated, and he was back in Cold Spring. The real world, the mundane world, had intruded on his solitude once again, to sever the last thread tying this life to the one he'd lived a lifetime before. He tugged at the collar of his mourning suit, chafing his neck as always; at least some things *didn't* change. As he gazed over the familiar sight of Cold Spring Cemetery, he likewise felt that familiar wave of sorrow. He'd trod this ground twice before, first for Cathryn, the second for Owen. Now Jason Bishop had come home, one last time, to say goodbye.

. . .

Even as a child it had struck him as unbelievable that every time the hero in the movie was grazed by a bullet, how quickly they bounced back with a wink and a quip. His back injury took the better part of fall to recover from, healing in the weeks following Murder Hill, only to flare up again when he strained his muscles the wrong way. It had taken months, but he had those to spare; he'd spent the remainder of autumn, the entirety of winter, and the first weeks of spring in hiding, making his way up the Hudson Valley and through the Adirondacks as far as the Canadian border. Upstate New York in winter was far from a holiday spot; that was why he chose it—it was literally the last place on earth anyone would think to look for him.

He'd managed to get Carla and Noah back to their bungalow after Murder Hill fell and dragged Carter Block down with it. Her car was, in a word, fucked, but Carla had a million questions, none of which pertained to a beater halfway to the scrap yard before it went into the drink. After a freshly bathed, changed, and comforted Noah fell asleep in his mother's arms, Jason told her everything, not because he knew Carla would forget all of it once balance was restored but because he *needed* to tell someone. By the time he'd finished his tale, the first rays of dawn had arced the sky, leaving Carla with tired eyes and a million more questions. But by then it was too late; her parents were arriving in a matter of hours, and she was still leaving Cold Spring. She'd taken Noah to his crib and collapsed onto her bed with the promise that Jason be there when she woke up. He agreed without hesitation, and stood watch until dawn's light reflected off the kitchen floor. He sat there, trying to guess where on that scratched and faded linoleum Owen had died. When he heard Noah stir in the bedroom he knew it was time to go.

After raiding the still-to-be-packed bathroom of its over-the-counter pain killers, he was gone, like he'd never been there to begin with. Carla would wake to discover the bungalow empty of all but her and Noah and the memories of a once happy home, but she wouldn't remember he was ever there. Balance would repair her car and deposit it back in her driveway. He walked, painfully, back to retrieve the Range Rover, considered returning it, then decided a set of wheels and a full tank of gas would put enough distance between himself and Cold Spring. He'd almost driven away when he stopped, gingerly picked his way back to the site, and, after searching, recovered all the pieces of the thing he'd almost forgotten amidst all of it: the Sphere. Something compelled him to take it with him; some small voice in his mind telling him it had a purpose yet to be revealed.

Then he drove.

In the end it was the YouTube video that drove him out of exile.

He'd spent the winter in a small town nestled amidst the Thousand Islands called Garrison Creek. It was a summer town and a tourist town, which made it the ideal place to lay low. He'd gone into hiding, honing his skills as an Adept, an Archmage, an Enchanter, a War Seer . . . and Diabolist. He'd crossed *that* bridge on Murder Hill when he manipulated its iron and steel hulk. In the moment he hadn't realized it, but when he did months after, he knew he'd reached the summit. He practiced, he trained, and he slept when he could, but his dreams gave him little comfort. They replayed the events of that night over and over again, like he was a spectator, not a participant. Like it was trying to tell him something he'd forgotten. Sometimes he succeeded; other times he failed and had to watch Carla and Noah drown. Every time he awoke in a cold sweat. On sleepless nights, which were frequent, he would sit with the pieces of the Sphere spread out across the kitchen table of whatever house he was squatting in, its owners wintering in warmer climes. It had been prophesised to shatter balance and put the advantage in its owner's grasp. Instead, it was just an empty shell with a coded message carved into its skin, a message he already knew the meaning of. That the Sphere would be opened by the one who discovered it.

And then . . . ?

The suspicion that somehow the Sphere had one more secret to reveal kept him company all winter, and in the end it was the Sphere that brought him out of hiding. He'd been about to discard its remains when his fingers brushed the smooth, concave hollow of its interior . . . and felt something small and raised inside it. He'd found a magnifying glass—this particular homeowner had been a model-ship enthusiast—and examined the markings closely. They traced the interior of the Sphere at its equator, and once he got a close enough look, recognized them as symbols from John Dee's *Sigillum Dei Aemaeth*. He transcribed the symbols onto paper and paid a visit to the Garrison Creek Public Library the next morning. Finding a computer in the back corner of the squat redbrick building, he opened a browser, searched, and found a diagram of the *Sigillum Dei Aemaeth,* and with it, began the painstaking process of translating the sigils into Latin, and from there into English. It took him the better part of the day, and when he had it translated, he felt that unease return to him. That, more than anything else, was what had prompted him to make another search just before the library closed; after wading through seemingly endless Internet links to stage magic and obvious fakes, he found what he was looking for.

"Peckham Superhero???" the video was titled. It was shot on a phone, grainy and jittery. The location was familiar: that sickly plot of land leading to Elysian Fields that in daylight looked even worse than it had the night he stood upon it. The video caught a brawl about to erupt, two groups of young, dumb toughs facing off, chests thrust almost comically forward. The video was shaky, mostly screams and yelps and shouts, then steadied in time to see one of the young dumbasses pull something metallic and gleaming from the folds of his heavy coat—a gun. The camera held on the gunman just long enough to record the loud fracture of air being split and the burst of smoke that followed. A fist drove the man's skull into the hard earth with a violent crack, and the gun clattered away in a shower of springs and metal and bullets. The hooded figure stood, reached a hand out, and yanked the camera out of its owner's hand, sending it rocketing into *his* hand and framing his face into an extreme close-up.

"Elysian Field's off-limits, boys," he said.

The camera dropped with a jolt, framing the unconscious gang member in the foreground as the attacker walked away. There was a blast of smoke, and he was gone. Then the video ended. The comments below were filled with barely coherent babblings of "OMG SO FAKE" and "NICE FX—LOOKED REEL." Jason played the video a good twenty times before he realized he was attracting too much attention from staffers waiting to close up for the night. He left the library, blood roaring in his ears. It had taken him months to cross the distance between Mumbai and London, but in the end, Teo Stone had finally come home.

The implications of that video hit Jason with the force of a hurricane. What its existence implied was that the world had changed, irreparably. The barriers between order and chaos had somehow fallen. Magic was finding its way back into the world. That, along with the message he'd found inside the Sphere, was what told him that it was time for his solitude to end. It was time to go home.

But by the time he did, death had come again, to sever that final link to his old life.

Jason's uncle had once told him that the truest measure of a man's life was how many came to his funeral, so by that reckoning Aaron Baile had been a king. The hillside service was packed with mourners, faces familiar and unfamiliar, people who'd worked at the store, people who'd spent their entire lives in Cold Spring—even Rita, Aaron's caregiver—and some, like Jason, who had returned to pay their respects. Only Jason hadn't returned in the mundane sense; the glamour he wore was one he'd lifted on the Metro-North at Poughkeepsie: some man Aaron's age who could have been an old school acquaintance. He hadn't felt comfortable showing his true face and appearance there; the last thing he wanted was to be found.

The pastor droned on about the resurrection with the enthusiasm of someone who'd committed the service to memory. Then the service ended and the mourners departed. Jason waited for everyone to leave before approaching the closed casket resting on the lift. He stood there and stared at it. He wished he'd been there at the end, to hold Aaron's hand in the way he had been too afraid to hold Cathryn's. He wished for a lot of things, but mostly he wished Aaron knew that he and Cathryn mattered to Jason more than anyone ever would. He wanted to tell Aaron so many things, but it was too late for that.

"He was a heck of a guy," a voice said.

Jason felt ice run up his spine. Not because of a detected threat, but because that voice was familiar. When he turned to the speaker and saw who it was, he almost blurted out the man's name.

"How'd you know Aaron?" asked Buck McCain.

The acid-wash and ripped denim were gone, as was the long hair and bad metal-head mustache. Buick McLame had become respectable, his hair now short, gray, and thin at the top. But those eyes were the same and that gravelly voice, which had dropped a couple octaves in the intervening decade, was too. Jason wondered if Buck still listened to T. Rex, but Buck was still waiting for an answer.

"Went to school together," Jason said. "You?"

"I worked for him, once," Buck said. "Not long; just a summer and a bit, till I got back on my feet. I was in a rough place then, drinkin' too much, thinkin' too little. But Aaron saw through all that, and he gave me a chance when nobody else would. That was a long time ago, but when I heard he'd passed, well, I had to come pay my respects."

"I'm sure he'd appreciate that," Jason said.

"I appreciated him, and I never forgot him," said Buck. "Kinda surprised his stepson did."

"Oh?" Jason asked.

Buck shrugged. "Never can tell. Families, y'know? They grow up together, and they grow apart. Aaron loved him like a son though. Always said he'd go places. I guess he did."

Buck thrust out a hand.

"Buck McCain."

Jason took it in his. "King. Jason King."

Buck gawked at him with surprise and with confusion. Then he grinned.

"Well, don't that beat all? That was his name—Aaron's stepson! Jason. That's weird, huh?"

"Like the song said, 'Life Is Strange.'"

Jason gave Buck's hand a firm shake and released it.

"Nice to meet you, Buck," he said. Then he pushed a thought at him.

Forget this conversation. Go home to your family. Cherish every day you have with them.

Buck stared, slack-jawed, then turned and trudged back down the hill. As Jason watched him go, he saw the air shift against the trunk of a large oak at the foot of the incline. She stepped out of its shadows as Jason descended to meet her. He noticed her limp, just as he noted the scar creasing her face from her ear to her jaw, and then running along it. It was a ghostly slash against even paler skin. However much damage she'd inflicted on Carter, he'd given her some back.

"My condolences on your loss," Sofia said.

He slipped his glamour off. There was no reason to maintain the illusion anymore.

"How are you, Sofia?"

She hobbled forward, favoring her left leg over her right. The dark attire was appropriate for the occasion, he granted her that. But she hadn't come to mourn; she'd come for him.

"I've been better. It took some time to put myself back—"

"That's close enough," he interrupted. "Just . . . stand there, let me look at you."

She stopped. He approached slowly. A breeze clattered the oak's branches like bones, and for an instant they were back in the catacombs, under the watchful eyes of the dead. When he reached her he held out his hand. She placed hers in it. He squeezed it tight. It was cold, lifeless, a dead battery. Anything other than that, he'd know it was a trap. He released her.

"I had to be sure," he said. "I thought you were . . . you know . . ."

"I was, but I'm back. Again."

He felt cold, though the warm spring sun was radiating its warmth directly above them. He wondered what price she'd paid to return. Then he realized he didn't want to know.

Some mysteries were best left unsolved.

"Has there been any sign of them?"

She shook her head, with resignation and maybe a little bit of relief.

"Nothing. But they're still out there; you can sense them, can't you?"

Jason sighed. He *could* sense them, like a distant storm threatening rain. They were down, not out. In time they'd be a force to be reckoned with again, and then the storm would come.

But until then . . .

"So where does this leave us?" she asked.

"You tell me," he said. He folded his hands in front of him and waited.

"The Invisible Hand may be sidelined but they're not finished. The Golden Dawn is weak, our numbers diminished. We need to rebuild and recruit and train a new generation. . . ."

"And you want me to join you." Jason sighed.

"You know the Invisible Hand; you know their secrets. With the Citadel destroyed they'll be vulnerable. We'll never have an opportunity like this again to—"

He was walking, away from Aaron's grave, away from her. He was down to the path and on the concrete when she emerged from behind a marble mausoleum ahead.

"Jason, we need you. Without you . . ."

"Without me, the war can't be won?"

"*Yes!*"

The sun was already slipping behind a bank of clouds. The chill was returning to the cemetery.

"That's the way it has to be," he said. "That's why you have to let me go—"

"Jason, please, I—"

"You have to promise. You won't come looking for me, you won't send agents to shadow me, and you won't assign some Enchanter to tell me she loves me. If I mean *anything* to you other than the means to an end, you *have* to promise."

She wasn't going to, he thought. Just looking at her he knew; she'd climbed so far out of that pit she couldn't accept defeat. She would *never* accept it.

The next word his mouth formed felt blunt, alien. But that was because he'd never spoken it aloud to her before.

"Mom . . . please. If you love me, you have let me go."

She didn't reel, not physically. But she seemed to sink into herself. Her glamour shimmered, and for a moment a much older woman's face stared at his. Then she nodded sadly, stepping off the path and clearing the way for him. But he didn't pass her; he approached slowly, met her eyes, leaned in, and kissed the cold, dead flesh of her forehead. When he stepped back she was in her glamour again, as much a shield as it was an enchantment. She'd passed through life and death and rebirth to find him, and he was walking away. As he continued down the path he swore he wouldn't look back, but when he heard her call after him, he stopped.

"The Sphere. You opened it, didn't you? What was inside?"

He considered telling her the truth. But he chose the lie instead.

"Nothing," he said. "It was empty . . ."

He turned back to Sofia but she was gone. He took in the space where she had been moments before and looked back through the cemetery up the hill where workers had arrived to begin lowering Aaron's casket into the ground to join Cathryn's.

It was over. There was just one final bit of business to tend to.

It was a single slab of polished marble sunk into the cold, hard ground. He crouched over it, removed some twigs and dirt that had gathered over the winter, and stood over it. For a while he didn't speak, not because he didn't have a million things to say, but because he didn't know where to begin.

"They'll be okay," he said. He heard someone approach, shoes crushing twigs that sounded like brittle bones.

"What took you so long?" he asked as he turned.

The face and body might have changed, but that smile and those eyes were as bright and alert as ever. She was Chinese now, and her voice carried a slight Valley Girl twang. She was wearing a red overcoat, either for fashion or to grab his attention; she certainly had it.

"Like your mother, I was a little delayed," she said.

"You're looking well," he said. "But I'm guessing it's not Vasilisa anymore?"

She did a graceful pirouette, her black hair flashing in the brief sunlight.

"Say hello to Pandora Chang, from Sherman Oaks, California. Nice girl, full of dreams of Hollywood, only in Pandora's case, she actually had 'it'—that X factor that separates the good from the spectacular. She even had the name; Pandora Chang would look dynamite on any marquee, right? That must have been what she was thinking when it happened, because she forgot the one thing Mama and Papa Chang always told her: look both ways before crossing the street."

"Ouch," Jason winced.

"An SUV clipped her crossing Ventura after an audition—an audition she aced, by the way. Doctor told Mama and Papa Chang she was brain-dead. Zero hope for recovery. Her folks were making ready to pull the plug when the most amazing thing happened. . . ."

"Let me guess," Jason said. "The Miracle of Sherman Oaks?"

"That's *just* what the producers wanted to call her life story. Hollywood came knocking, as they always do in the wake of an inspirational true-life story. Only Pandora had changed; she wasn't interested in Hollywood anymore. She had *greater* concerns."

Jason folded his arms. "So this isn't a social visit?"

She grinned. "Still a quick study, I see."

"My claim to fame," he said. "So what *is* happening?"

"What do you mean?"

"You know what I mean, *Oracle*. I saw the video from Peckham."

"The world has changed," she said. "There's been a split, with multiple factions each vying for control of what remains of the Invisible Hand. You can probably guess the primary culprits . . . ?"

Culprits? He had a pretty good idea: Allegra, obviously, but he realized with increasing dread that her kill shot had missed the mark, and Katja had survived. That was a mistake that would come back to haunt them both and he didn't need to be clairvoyant to know it, either.

Did she know? About Carter, about Katja? About all of it?

Pandora smiled. "After all you've done, after all you've accomplished . . . does it even matter?"

"Not in the grand scheme. And we're all just pieces on the board, right?"

"The grand scheme . . ." Pandora nodded. "The Invisible Hand was stronger than the Golden Dawn for decades. Order held chaos at bay. But with them warring amongst themselves, and with neither faction dominant, magic is escaping into the world again, and ancient powers long hidden will soon emerge to stake their claim. It's starting slowly, but it will accelerate and where it ends not even I can foresee. My powers are as limited now as they were when Carter set the pieces on the board and plotted his stratagem. But my time with the Invisible Hand is done. I'm like you . . . looking for purpose in this new world."

She offered a sympathetic smile.

"But that's a worry for another day. Where will you go now?"

"I wish I knew," he said. "You don't have any advice, do you?"

There was a melancholy in her eyes that hadn't been there before and he knew why: he'd just asked the question she'd been asking herself.

"I used to believe that all roads, in the end, lead home," she said. "But that was the old world; in this new one . . . I'm just as lost as you."

The moment the train neared the bend and he saw Murder Hill was gone was when he realized how much the world *had* changed. The structure hadn't returned, it hadn't reformed, it hadn't reset; it was *gone*. Right now it lay somewhere beneath the Hudson, Carter Block's remains possibly still held in its tangled wreckage, swaying gently with the current. Or maybe the body had loosened from it to be carried down the river, past the Tappan Zee and the GWB, cast adrift to wash out to sea. Jason wasn't surprised; it just confirmed that this wasn't same world he'd glimpsed out the window the previous year. The last time he'd taken this train, the valley had been in autumn's grasp; now spring was breathing renewed life into the land. Trees were beginning to bud, birds were flying north; a fresh start for everyone after the cold, dark winter. Once he got to NYC, though, who knew where his path would take him? He was a Mage now, and even without the easy navigation of the Citadel he could march up to the first-class counter of any airline and get a ticket anywhere he wanted just by asking. There was no place on earth he couldn't go.

Except home. He'd left Cold Spring for good. He wasn't Jason Bishop anymore; he was someone else. He'd passed through fire and death and emerged reborn. As the train reached the bend below Murder Hill, he craned his neck back and glimpsed Storm King Mountain one last time. Then the train rounded the bend, and it was gone.

He settled back in his seat and closed his eyes. As he did, the image of those sigils on the paper, the Latin translation of them, and the English translation of that filled his vision. The final piece of the puzzle, etched within the Sphere that hinted at a larger puzzle still to be assembled.

The power to change the world lies within us all, and none more so than in you, Jason Bishop.

It was when he opened his eyes that he saw the playing cards.

It was a deck of them, sitting on the seat beside him. They hadn't been there when they departed Cold Spring and hadn't been there when he closed his eyes. But they were there now . . . as was the person who had appeared in the seat facing his. Jason met the passenger's gaze and settled slowly back into his chair.

"You owe me a hell of an explanation, you know that?" Jason asked.

"A good magician never reveals his secrets," the passenger replied. "But I should probably make an exception in your case."

Jason stared a moment more, to make sure his eyes *weren't* playing tricks on him, that this *wasn't* another illusion. When he was satisfied, he nodded.

"We're an hour from New York," he said. "Will that be enough time?"

"Should be," the passenger said. "Though to be fair, I'm dying for a drink."

"I know a place near Fort Tryon."

"Time enough for me to answer some of those questions of yours?"

"Time enough for you to answer *all* of them," Jason said.

Damon King reclined in his seat and flashed that grin his son thought he'd never see again. But just like everything that had happened over the last six months, Jason accepted it. This was a new world now, and in it, *everything* was possible.

"So where would you like to start?" Damon asked.

Jason considered the card deck and smiled back.

"How about a magic trick?"

ACKNOWLEDGMENTS

While the name on the cover may be mine, this book would not be possible without the considerable efforts of many individuals of rare talent. To be an author is to stand on the shoulders of giants and I am fortunate to have had so many supporting me.

First among them is editorial wizard Brendan Deneen, who saw something in my original concept and provided that missing piece to take it to the next level. His focus on details I'd missed, his availability to bounce fresh ideas off of, and his dedication to making this book a reality will never be forgotten. I'd also like to thank Thomas Dunne, who was intrigued by this book the moment he glanced at the title, and gave his blessing, and Nicole Sohl, who gave support just as it was taking flight.

I'd also like to thank Michael Neff, who developed some of the early concepts in the novel.

The design team at St. Martin's Press deserves high praise, especially after I drove them nuts with constant requests to tweak the final cover design. Thanks also to copy editor MaryAnn Johanson for her genuinely magical attention to detail, production editor Megan Kiddoo, production manager Jason Reigal, interior designer Michelle McMillian, editor Cameron Jones, marketer Joseph Brosnan-Black, and publicist Justin Velella.

Thanks also to my agent, Jodi Reamer, of Writers House, who helped a novice writer navigate this strange new world of publishing with a steady hand. You'd think two decades in the film and TV biz would prepare you for the literary world. You would be wrong. I would also like to thank Jodi's assistant, Alec Shane, for his help throughout the entire journey.

Many of the locations in *Magicians Impossible* are real. Though you won't find The Locksmith on Broadway just below Dyckman, you will find, in the shadow of Fort Tryon Park, the Tryon Public House, which helped inspire it. Likewise the Metropolitan Museum of Art and the Cloisters provided a great wealth of information through many repeat visits to get the details of the Langon Chapel just right.

I would also like to acknowledge and thank the village of Cold Spring, New York, and the nearby Storm King Art Center; the Vasa Museum in Stockholm, Sweden; and in Paris, the Louvre Sacré-Cœur basilica, the catacombs, and Montmartre Cemetery, where you can indeed see where François Truffaut is buried.

I consider myself grateful to the many people who were there to offer moral support, advice, and selfless assistance during the long writing of this book. In particular I'd like to thank Don Coscarelli for taking time out of a very busy schedule to bestow upon the book the highest praise possible. Thanks also to my former colleagues at *Rue Morgue* magazine for their unwavering support over the years. I'd also like to thank Ally Malinenko, David Buceta, Kris Booth, Bryce Mitchell, Clair Hibbert (for supplying me with valuable background information on Peckham), Kristen Falso-Capaldi, Richard P. Clark, Mark Fraser, Libby Cudmore,

LeeAnn McNabb, Ben Mazzotta, and Maria Kennedy Mazzotta. Thanks to Erika Lewis, Lisa Maxwell, April Snellings, Harriet Seltzer, Bob Josen, James Frachon (for his help mapping the Paris Catacombs), and my parents and sister, for their encouragement during what has been the greatest challenge of my professional life.

And lastly, none of this book would have been possible without the unwavering support of my wife, long my greatest champion, who has always believed in me especially when I didn't believe in myself.